NOT THOMAS

NOT THOMAS

by
Sara Gethin

HONNO MODERN FICTION

First published in 2017 by Honno Press, 'Ailsa Craig', Heol y Cawl,
Dinas Powys, South Glamorgan, Wales, CF64 4AH
2 3 4 5 6 7 8 9 10
Copyright: Wendy White writing as Sara Gethin © 2017

A catalogue record for this book is available from the British Library.

Published with the financial support of the Welsh Books Council.

ISBN 978-1-909983-62-5 (paperback)
ISBN 978-1-909983-63-2 (ebook)

Cover design: Ruth Rowland
Cover image: © Shutterstock, Inc
Text design: Elaine Sharples
Printed by Bell & Bain

For Simon, Rebecca and Jonathan

Acknowledgements

I began writing about Tomos several years ago, when I studied creative writing with the Department of Adult Continuing Education based at Swansea University. I am indebted to my tutors there, particularly Peter Thabit Jones and the late Kate D'Lima, for the enthusiasm they showed for my work and the encouragement they gave me.

I belong to a wonderful writing group, full of talented people who have listened to snippets of my novel as a work in progress. Over the years they have given me insightful feedback and I've thoroughly appreciated their advice and friendship.

In 2016, under my real name Wendy White, I submitted a short story based on this novel to the Colm Tóibín International Award, organised by Wexford Literature Festival. I was very encouraged when it was shortlisted, and this gave me the incentive to finish the novel and approach a publisher.

I am hugely thankful to Caroline Oakley, my editor at Honno Press, for taking a chance on the simplistic writing style of this book. It was important to me that Tomos's experiences should come to the reader first hand. It was his voice I wanted to portray, and I am so grateful that Caroline never once suggested I change the viewpoint. Thank you, also, to Helena, the committee and the whole team at Honno.

Lastly, thank you to my wonderful friends and family – especially my husband, Simon, children, Rebecca and Jonathan, and my mum and dad. Without their love and support *Not Thomas* would still be just another file on my laptop.

Waiting for the Christmas Concert

The lady's here. The lady with the big bag. She's knocking on the front door. She's knocking and knocking. And knocking and knocking. I'm not opening the door. I'm not letting her in. I'm behind the black chair. I'm very quiet. I'm very very quiet. I'm waiting for her to go away.

I've been waiting a long time.

'Thomas, Thomas.' She's saying it through the letter box. 'Thomas, Thomas.'

I'm not listening to her. I'm not listening at all. She's been knocking on the door for a long long time. I'm peeping round the black chair. I'm peeping with one of my eyes. She's not by the front door now. She's by the long window. I can see her shoes. They're very dirty. If Dat saw those shoes he'd say, 'There's a job for my polishing brush'.

She's stopped knocking. She's stopped saying 'Thomas'. She's very quiet. The lady can't see me. I'm behind the big black chair. And I've pulled my feet in tight.

'Thomas?' she says. 'Thomas?' I'm not answering. 'I know you're in there. Just come to the window, sweetheart. So I can see you properly.'

I'm staying still. I'm not going to the window. I'm waiting for her to go back to her car. It's a green car. With a big dent in it. If I hide for a long time she'll go. She'll get back in her car and drive away. She's knocking. And knocking again. She's saying 'Thomas.' And knocking and knocking again. 'Thomas.'

That is not my name.

'Thomas.'

I'm trying to think about something nice. I'm trying to

1

remember Cwtchy. I'm trying and trying. I'm remembering his purple fur. And his chewy ears. I want him to be here. I want to hug him. I don't want to be on my own. Behind the big black chair.

'Thomas, Thomas. Thomas, Thomas.'

If Cwtchy was here he would whisper 'Don't be sad'. And I would whisper 'I'm not sad anymore, Cwtchy'. And I wouldn't be lonely. Behind the big black chair. Until the lady goes away.

Knock knock. 'Thomas, Thomas.' Knock knock. 'Thomas, Thomas.'

I'm waiting for the lady to go away. And I'm thinking and thinking about Cwtchy. I'm wishing Dat was here too.

She has stopped knocking. She's stopped calling me Thomas. I'm listening. I can hear her shoes on the path. The shoes I saw through the window. There are no noises now. My ears are full of quiet. I'm listening through it. I can hear an engine starting. The engine of her car. It's very rattly. I can hear her car going down the road. Rattle rattle. Rattle rattle. I can hear it turning the corner. Rattle rattle. Rattle rattle. I'm listening hard. I can hear it going away. I'm listening harder. Rattle. And harder. Rattle. I'm listening and listening.

I can hear it gone.

I'm staying behind the chair and I am remembering Dat and Cwtchy. I'm staying here until the yellow light comes on. The yellow light across the road. And then I'm going to go to the cupboard and get some crisps.

* * *

I am up in my high sleeper bed. It's the bed the lady next door gave me on the day we moved here. She said it was her Jason's bed. Jason is her grandson. She said he can't come to stay anymore because he hasn't got a bed to sleep in now. She said he is rude and he eats too much. Brick borrowed the lady next door's screwdriver and he turned the bed into bits in the lady's house. Then he made it into a bed again in my room. There's a wooden ladder that I climb up. It goes quite high and it has hooks on it. The ladder hooks on the bottom of my bed and it hooks off as well. The bed rattles a lot when I climb up the ladder and it rattles when I climb down. It shakes a lot too. The bed has a sticker on it that says 'For seven years and up'. I am not seven yet. I am nearly six.

My train table fits under my bed. Dat made the train table for me. Mammy got into Nanno and Dat's house with her key when Dat was out. Then Mammy and Brick brought my train table here in Brick's car. A bit of it stuck out of Brick's boot. That bit of table got wet in the rain. Mammy got all her clothes too and she brought my trains. But I haven't got them anymore.

I wish I still had my trains. There's a blue one and a green one and a red one too. I like the red one best of all. It's a tippy train. It tips logs. I like tippy trains that tip logs but I haven't got the red one now. Or the blue one or the green one. Because Mammy sold them to a man called Leper.

I'm looking at one of Dat's train magazines. Dat gave them to me when I moved to this house. I keep them under my train table. I'm not looking at all the sentences just some words. I'm looking at the pictures too and I am trying to find the words Dat showed me. They are locomotive and turntable and pistons. I'm pulling the clothes all round me. I'm putting Mammy's jumper on my legs and I'm pulling her tee shirt up to my chin. I am trying to make myself warm.

This is my favourite magazine. It has a picture of a blue engine on the cover. It's a steam engine and its name is Mallard. I keep it right on top of my pile of magazines. Then I can see it every time I come into my bedroom.

The front door has banged. Mammy is home. She says, 'Put the kettle on. I'm goin' for a pee.' Brick has come back with her. He won't put the kettle on. She has forgotten that. She's coming up the stairs.

'Hello, Mammy.'

She says, 'You still awake?' Her words don't sound right. They are all slidey. Brick is banging in the kitchen. He's opening and closing the cupboards.

'The lady with the big bag came,' I say.

Mammy is saying a lot of rude words.

Brick is shouting, 'There's nothin' to eat.'

Mammy says, 'There's crisps in the cupboard by the sink.' Then she says to me, 'You didn' eat all the crisps, did you?'

'I left the pink packet for you.'

'Brick don' like prawn cocktail,' she says. She's shouting downstairs again. 'Blurry social woman's been roun' today, so I'll go to Tesco tomorrow.'

Brick is shouting, 'Goin' down the chippy.'

Mammy's shouting, 'Bring me somethin'.' Brick has slammed the front door.

I say, 'Will you get my big box, please, when you go to Tesco? And my red shiny paper?'

Mammy says, 'Wha' you on about?'

'For me to be a present in the Christmas concert that you're coming to see. I need it for Thursday. Miss is going to cut holes for our heads and holes for our arms.' Mammy's moving the ladder from the bottom of my bed. She's putting it on the floor. 'Are you going out again?'

She says, 'Don' think so.'

'Please can you put my ladder back then?'

'Please can you put my ladder back?' she says. She's copying me. But her words have come out all messy. They are slipping over each other. She's hooking my ladder back on my bed.

'Thanks, Mammy.'

'Thanks, Mammy,' she says in her slippy slidey way. She's putting off my light. 'Get in the bath tomorrow, 'fore school.'

'Okay,' I say. 'Will you get them?'

'Get wha'?'

'My box and my red shiny paper, please, from Tesco.'

Mammy's going out of my room. 'Yeah,' she says. 'I will.' And she's closing my door tight.

* * *

We are in the big hall in school. We are sitting on the floor and it's very hard and cold. We have been singing 'Away in a manger'. Sir has been showing us the words and Miss has been playing the piano. We have been singing for a very long time.

Nearly everyone is quiet now because Sir is talking. 'What we need is someone with a good voice,' he says. 'Someone to sing the first verse on their own. Someone to sing the solo.'

I like the word solo. I'm saying it again and again in my mind. Lots of people want to sing the solo. Sir is pointing to a big girl. She's waving her hand. 'Stand up, Alisha, and have a go,' he says. Alisha is standing up and singing. She has a loud voice. It's scratchy too. 'Well done, Alisha,' Sir says. 'Who else wants to try?'

He's pointing to the boy next to me. It's Eddie. Eddie is standing up. He's starting to sing. He's singing 'Away in a manger, no…' He's stopped. 'I don't know the rest,' he says. Some people are laughing.

Sir says, 'Good try anyway, Eddie.' Lots of other children are trying. Some of them make the song sound nice. 'Would anyone else like to try?' Sir says. No one puts their hand up.

Miss says, 'What about you, Tomos?' She's sitting by the piano. I'm looking at Miss because she said 'Tomos' but I know she is talking to a Tomos in another class. He's a Tomos I don't know. Miss is smiling at me and I am smiling at her.

'Who is Tomos?' Sir says. He's looking at everyone in the hall. All the children are looking round. We're looking to see the other Tomos that Miss is talking to. We're waiting for the other Tomos to put his hand up. He's taking a long time.

Miss says, 'Tomos Morris. He's in my class, Mr Griffiths.' Miss is still smiling at me and I'm still smiling back. She's waving her hand. I'm looking and looking at her. She's waving it again. 'Get up, Tomos,' she says.

'Me, Miss?'

'Yes, Tomos,' Miss says. She's still smiling. 'You.'

I'm getting up. I'm getting up slowly.

'Oh bless,' Mrs Caulfield says. She's Carrie-Anne's helper. She helps Carrie-Anne push her wheely chair. 'Leave the poor kid alone.'

I'm standing up now. Everyone in the hall is looking at me. The children are looking at me and the teachers are looking at me too. Miss is starting to play the piano. I'm taking a big breath and I'm filling myself up. I'm making myself big with a big breath. I'm singing 'Away in a manger, no crib for a bed, the little Lord…' all the way to the end.

I've stopped singing and Miss has stopped playing the piano. She's pushing a bit of her brown hair behind her ear. 'Well done, Tomos,' she says in a quiet voice. She's still smiling at me. Her smile is very big. I'm sitting down again.

'Well, well,' Sir says. He's looking at me through his big glasses. 'Well, well.' He's shaking his head and smiling. He's smiling and smiling at me. 'Who'd have thought it?'

* * *

I'm running to Kaylee and her mammy. They're standing outside school. 'So you're singing the solo?' Kaylee's mammy says. 'In the Christmas concert?'

'Yes,' I say. 'I'm singing the solo.' I've been saying the word solo all day in my mind. Solosolosolosolo.

Kaylee's mammy is rubbing my shoulder. 'You take after your mother, you do. She's got a great voice too.'

'Has she?' I say. We're walking now. Kaylee and her mammy are walking to their house and I'm walking with them.

'Oh yeah,' Kaylee's mammy says. 'Haven't you heard your mother singing? She used to sing a lot in school. She got to sing all the solos too.'

I'm trying to remember if I've heard Mammy singing. I've heard Nanno singing. She used to sing to me every night when I went to bed. When I lived in her and Dat's house. She used to sing lots of songs but I don't remember Mammy singing at all. 'I haven't heard her,' I say.

'Oh well,' Kaylee's mammy says.

We're still walking. I've remembered a song Nanno used to sing to me. It's her favourite song and it's my favourite too. I'm singing '*Calon lân yn llawn daioni…*' I'm singing it all the way to the end.

'That's lovely, that song is,' Kaylee's mammy says. 'I don' know what some of those Welsh words mean though.'

'Nanno showed me how to sing it another way.' I'm singing 'A pure heart that's full of goodness, is fairer than the…'

I've stopped singing because we've come to our gate and I can see Mammy in the front room. I can see her pretty yellow hair. 'Mammy's home. My mammy's home!' I'm shouting it and I'm running up the path.

'See you tomorrow,' Kaylee says.

8

'See you tomorrow,' I say.

Kaylee and her mammy are going down the road and I'm running up the path fast to Mammy. I'm going into the kitchen. 'Hello, Mammy,' I say. 'Hello, hello, hello.' I'm hugging her legs.

'Eat this.' She's giving me a plate. It has three fish fingers and some chips on it.

'Thank you, Mammy.'

I'm sitting on the settee with Mammy and I'm eating my fish fingers and chips and they're hot and yummy and we're watching people trying to win money on the telly and Mammy's texting on her phone too.

'You 'ad fish fingers for tea yesterday.' She's saying it to me but she's still texting.

I'm trying to remember yesterday. 'I had crisps for tea yesterday,' I say. 'After the lady with the big bag went away.'

'You 'ad fish fingers, okay?'

'I had crisps,' I say. 'A blue packet and a green packet. I left the pink one for you.' I've got the last bit of chip in my mouth and I'm trying not to chew it because I want to make it last a long long time.

'Just say you 'ad fish fingers.' She's saying it slowly.

'I had fish fingers.' I'm saying it slowly too.

'Yeah,' Mammy says. 'Tha's right.' Her phone is buzzing. She's looking at it. 'Remember to say tha' when the social woman comes.'

'The lady with the big bag?' I'm chewing my last bit of chip. I'm chewing it fast now and I'm swallowing it. 'Is she coming again today?'

9

Mammy's texting. 'Yeah,' she says.

'Are we waiting for her? Is she coming now?'

'Wha' do you blurry think? Did you 'ave a bath this mornin'?' I'm nodding. Mammy's putting her face next to my jumper. 'Don' smell like it.'

'I washed my hair too,' I say. I'm remembering this morning. I'm remembering the bath. The water was very cold and I was shaky shaky shaky. I tried to make a bubbly hat with shampoo like Nanno used to make. It was very hard and the bubbles went down my face. They went in my eyes and it was hard to make the prickly go away. But I tried to wash my legs like Nanno showed me and my arms and my bottom. And my front and my neck and my face but my eyes were still prickly. They were still prickly when I was watching for Kaylee and her mammy. And they were still prickly when we were walking to school. Kaylee's mammy said, 'Your hair's all wet.' And I said, 'I've had a bath.' And Kaylee's mammy said, 'Your eyes look sore.' And I said, 'I got bubbles in them.' And they were still prickly when we got to school. And Kaylee's mammy told me to go to the toilets and put water on my eyes. After I did that they didn't hurt so bad.

There's knocking on the front door. I'm running behind the big chair.

'Come back yerr,' Mammy says. She sounds cross. I think it's because my jumper is smelly. I'm running to Mammy and she's opening the door. There are two ladies outside. One of the ladies is the lady with the big bag.

'Hello, you two,' the lady with the big bag says. She's smiling a bit. 'This is Gwawr.' Her mouth is making a very big circle when she says 'Gwawr'. She's pointing to the other lady. 'Gwawr's my supervisor. Do you mind if she comes in too?'

The other lady who is Gwawr is saying something to Mammy. She's talking like Nanno and Dat do sometimes.

'I don' speak Welsh,' Mammy says.

Gwawr is looking at her piece of paper. 'It says here you do.' She's smiling a big smile at Mammy.

'Norr anymore,' Mammy says.

'Oh, that's a shame,' Gwawr says. 'And Rachel here's just started going to Welsh classes.'

The lady with the big bag is nodding. 'Trying my best to learn,' she says. 'But it's not easy when you come from Kent.'

Mammy is shaking her head. 'Nah, I don' speak Welsh.'

'Oh well,' Gwawr says. She's still smiling a bit. 'English it is then.'

* * *

We are in the front room. The ladies are sitting on the settee and Mammy is sitting on the big black chair. I'm on Mammy's lap. It's nice on Mammy's lap. The ladies are asking her lots of questions and they're writing things down on their pieces of paper. They're smiling at Mammy sometimes and sometimes they're smiling at me. They're nodding their heads a lot.

'Well, Tomos,' Gwawr says. 'Have you had your tea yet?'

'Yes,' I say.

She's nodding. 'What did you have?'

11

'Three fish fingers and chips.'

'And what did you have for tea yesterday?' the lady with the big bag says.

'Crisps,' I say. 'A blue packet and a…'

Mammy is looking at me. Her eyes are big. She is making them bigger. 'An' wharr else?' she says.

'A green packet.' I am saying it slowly. I'm not sure if I'm allowed to tell the ladies.

Mammy's eyes are very big now. I say, 'Oh,' because Mammy is pinching my arm. The one that the ladies can't see.

'Remember what you 'ad yesterday?' she says.

I'm remembering now. 'I had fish fingers,' I say.

'Good,' Gwawr says.

The lady with the big bag says, 'Well, let's have a look in the kitchen then.'

We are going into the kitchen. Mammy has put all the rubbish in the bin. The kitchen is very big now. The ladies are looking in the cupboards and they're looking in the fridge. Mammy has been to Tesco like she told Brick and she's bought lots of food. There are chips and fish fingers and chicken nuggets and milk and bananas and bread and a big bag of crisps.

'Wow!' I am doing a dance. 'Did you get my box and my shiny paper?'

Mammy hasn't heard me. She's looking at the ladies looking in the cupboards.

'What will you have for breakfast tomorrow, Tomos?' Gwawr says.

'Chicken nuggets,' I say.

The ladies are smiling.

'Toast an' jam,' Mammy says.

I say, 'We've got jam!' I'm doing the dance again.

Then the lady with the big bag says, 'Thomas, can you show us your bedroom, please?'

* * *

The ladies like my bedroom. They are asking lots of questions about my train set. I'm telling them all about Dat and his train noises.

'Has your dat been here,' Gwawr says.

'No,' I say.

She's looking at my bed. Mammy has taken the quilt off her bed and she's put it on my bed. I can see it peeping over the top. I can see a bit of her pillow too.

'When did you last see your dat?' Gwawr says. She's going up my ladder now. The bed is wobbling.

I am thinking about the last time I saw Dat. I'm feeling sad. 'A long time ago.'

'In this house?' the lady with the big bag says.

'No. In Nanno and Dat's house.' I'm remembering Dat giving me his train magazines. I'm remembering him saying 'Bye, Tomos, see you soon.' I'm remembering him squeezing me. And waving and waving. I say, 'I'm not allowed to see Dat anymore.'

Gwawr is half way up my ladder. She's looking down at me. 'That's right,' she says. She's coming all the way down now.

We're going out of my bedroom and we're going past the bathroom. The door is open. Mammy has moved all the things I must NOT touch. She's put them away. We're going downstairs.

'Well, Rhiannon.' Gwawr makes Mammy's name sound nice. She says Rhiannon like Nanno and Dat say it. 'There are some things we need to talk about.' The ladies are only smiling a little bit now. They are sitting on the settee again and they're looking at their pieces of paper.

'About the bed,' the lady with the big bag says. 'I said it was dangerous the last time I was here. Do you remember me saying that?'

Mammy's lifting her shoulders and she's picking up her phone.

The lady with the big bag says, 'Your next door neighbour gave you the bed, didn't she? That was very kind of her, but it's meant for older children.'

'Yeah well,' Mammy says. 'Beggars can't be choosers.'

The lady with the big bag is looking at Gwawr. 'Could we get another bed sorted?'

'Not before Christmas,' Gwawr says. She's looking through her pieces of paper and she's writing something down.

'The side rail is high enough, I suppose,' the lady with the big bag says. 'But it's the ladder that's the problem. You must be with him every time he goes up and down it, Rhiannon.' The ladies are looking at Mammy.

Mammy's looking at her phone. She's putting it down now. She's looking at the ladies again and her face is cross. 'It's not Rhiannon,' Mammy says. 'It's Ree.'

14

The ladies are not smiling. 'This is important,' the lady with the big bag says. 'We're trusting you with this until we can get another bed. And the screws need tightening up. The whole bed seems to be wobbling.'

'Maybe you could put the mattress on the floor, Ree,' Gwawr says. 'If you can make enough room. Just for the time being.' They've stopped looking at Mammy and they're looking at their papers again.

I'm getting back onto Mammy's lap but she's put one of her legs over the other one. It's not comfy like it was just now.

'So other furniture,' Gwawr says. She's looking round the front room. 'You have this sofa and chair. And the TV. Would you like a table and a couple of dining chairs, Ree?'

'What for?' Mammy says.

'Somewhere for you to have your meals. And you could use it as a desk when you're a bit older, Tomos.' Gwawr is smiling at me.

'No room,' Mammy says.

'You could put it there.' Gwawr is waving her pen. 'In that corner, near the kitchen door. I've got the number of a charity that'll give you free second hand furniture. You could get a wardrobe or chest of drawers for Tomos's room too.'

Mammy's lifting her shoulders.

'And they might give you curtains for this room and for Tomos's bedroom. Help cosy things up a bit. And they'll decorate for free too.' Gwawr's looking at the walls now. And the floor. Mammy has picked up all the big bits of wallpaper. The bits she pulled off the walls a long time ago. They were all over the carpet. They're in a big black bag by the back door. She didn't pick up the little bits. There are still lots of them on the carpet. 'You're not a fan of flowery wallpaper, then Ree?'

'Nah,' Mammy says. 'It's 'orrible.'

'Well, you've already made a good start stripping it. It wouldn't take them long to finish off and redecorate.'

'It would brighten up the place,' the lady with the big bag says. She's looking round and round the front room. 'And make it more homely.'

'Think about it.' Gwawr is giving Mammy a little card. 'Here's the number. A bit more furniture and some new wallpaper would make all the difference. How long have you lived here now, Ree?'

'Don' know, like five months?' Mammy's putting the little card down the side of the chair.

'Since September,' the lady with the big bag says. 'So three and a half months, more or less.'

'And how's it going?' Gwawr says. 'How are the neighbours?'

Mammy's lifting her shoulders. 'Okay s'pose. There's a nosy ol' bag across the road, always in the window.' Mammy's putting her leg down and it's nice on her lap again.

'She's probably just lonely,' Gwawr says. 'And the neighbours either side? You had a problem at your last place, didn't you, Ree?'

'Had a right cow in the flat next door. Always knockin' on the walls, 'cusing me of stuff.' Mammy's lap has gone hard again.

'And when you first moved in, your next door neighbour rang the police,' the lady with the big bag says, 'didn't she?'

'Tha' bitch,' Mammy says. 'I hadn't drunk nothin'. The cow.'

'But you were making a lot of noise,' the lady with the big bag says. 'And you share a wall. The police came round and spoke to you.'

Gwawr says, 'But there wasn't an arrest, not even a caution. So we don't need to worry too much.'

'She's gone now anyway,' Mammy says. 'Said she was movin' in with her son.'

'So she was the side that's joined onto your house?' Gwawr is waving her pen. 'And the new neighbours, what are they like?'

'Don' know,' Mammy says. 'Never seen 'em. Never heard 'em.'

'So you get on with all the neighbours then,' Gwawr says. 'And one of them gave you a bed for Tomos. She must be friendly enough.'

'The one on tha' side.' Mammy's pointing to where the lady next door lives.

'So no complaints about the neighbours.' Gwawr is smiling at us.

The lady with the big bag says, 'And so far, only one complaint *from* them.' She's writing something down.

'Would you say you're coping on your own?' Gwawr says.

'Yeah,' Mammy says.

'Because you did have a lot of support until recently from your foster parents.' Gwawr is looking at her papers. 'The Ifans. They're very well thought of.'

Mammy has made a funny noise. 'Yeah right.'

'We know you fell out with them, Ree,' the lady with the big bag says. 'But they did an awful lot for you.' She's looking at Mammy with a bit of a cross face. 'They were very involved with Thomas's care, and you can't deny you were away a lot.'

Mammy's legs have gone very hard. I am wriggling a bit. I'm trying to get comfy.

Gwawr says, 'But all that's in the past now.' She's holding out her hand to the lady with the big bag. I'm wondering if she wants to take her pen but she isn't taking it. She's putting her hand back on her papers now. 'You're here and you're taking care of Tomos yourself.' Gwawr's mouth is nearly smiling. 'And you feel you're coping all right, Ree?'

Mammy's moving her legs. She's sitting up straight. 'I didn' "fall out" with them.' She's saying it in a loud voice. 'That man...' She's moving her legs again. I'm trying not to slip off her lap. 'My foster father was violent to my boy.' She's putting her arms round me and squeezing me tight. 'Did you forget that?' She's squeezing me more. She's looking at the lady with the big bag. 'Dafydd hit 'im.'

'No, we haven't forgotten,' Gwawr says. 'We're looking into it.'

Mammy's still squeezing me tight. 'You don' need to look into it. 'Less you don' believe me.'

I'm wriggling a bit because I want Mammy to stop squeezing me. And I want to get down off her lap.

'These things have to be properly investigated,' the lady with the big bag says. 'Or people could say whatever they wanted. About anyone.'

'Anyway.' Gwawr is saying it fast. She's saying it in quite a loud voice. 'You say you're coping, Ree. That's good.' She's nodding at Mammy and she's writing something on her paper.

'Bed wetting's still a problem though,' the lady with the big bag says.

'Yeah well,' Mammy's not squeezing me anymore. I'm getting off her lap and I'm sitting on the floor by her feet.

'Thomas needs clean clothes,' the lady with the big bag says. 'And a sheet on his bed.'

'He'll have a new mattress,' Gwawr says. 'With the new bed. Until then, air Tomos's room and use the mattress covers Rachel brought last time. And you'll have a little help at Christmas, Rhianno... Sorry, I mean Ree,' she says. 'If you want it.'

Mammy's lifting up her shoulders. 'Like wha'?'

'A food hamper and something for the little one,' Gwawr says. She's winking at me like Dat does. 'Something from Santa.'

Something from Santa? I'm looking forward to having something from Santa. Last year at Nanno and Dat's he brought me the new red train for my train set. The one that tips logs out. And he brought me chocolates in my stocking. And a blue torch that has a light that changes colour. And a box of paints and a colouring book. And Santa is the same as Father Christmas. And Father Christmas is the same as Siôn Corn. That's what Nanno and Dat call him.

'Something from Siôn Corn?' I say. 'Yes, please!'

'Siôn Corn,' Gwawr says. '*O cariad, da iawn!*' She is smiling and smiling but Mammy's face is cross.

19

'Yeah, I'll have wharrever,' she says.

'Good,' the lady with the big bag says. 'They'll be dropped off in a couple of days.' She's writing something on her papers.

'Okay,' Gwawr says. 'We're done for now.' The ladies are standing up and Mammy is too. We're all going into the hall and Gwawr's opening the front door.

'It was nice to meet you, Ree,' she says. 'And you too, Tomos.' The ladies are going out. They're smiling at us.

'You have my number, Ree,' the lady with the big bag says. 'Ring if there are any problems. Bye, Thomas.'

'See you in the new year,' Gwawr says. They are going down the path.

'See you in the new year,' I say.

They are going to a car. It isn't the lady with the big bag's car because it isn't green and it hasn't got a big dent in it. It is shiny and red. The ladies are getting in. Gwawr is driving it. I'm waving to the ladies. They're driving away and I'm still waving to them. I'm waving and waving and waving.

Mammy's pulling my arm. The arm that's waving. She's closing the door. She's making it bang. She's going into the front room. She's shouting and shouting and shouting. 'Think they can blurry tell me wha' to do.' She's shouting. And shouting it. She's picking up her mug. She's throwing it at the wall. Her tea is flying out. It's splashed onto the telly. A big chunk of mug has broken off. Mammy is shouting. And shouting. And shouting. Lots of rude words.

I'm going out into the hall. I'm going quietly. I don't want Mammy to see me. I'm going up the stairs. I'm going into my bedroom. And I'm closing my door tight.

* * *

The man is here. The man with the web tattoo. He's knocking. On the front door. He's knocking. And knocking. And knocking. And knocking. I thought it was the ladies. I thought they'd come back. I nearly opened the door. I nearly forgot. But I must not open the door. I must not open it. When Mammy is out.

He's been knocking a long time. I'm behind the black chair. I'm waiting for him to go away. His knocks are very hard. I can see the door shaking. I can see it with my one eye. The eye that's peeping round the chair. I'm waiting. And waiting. For him to go away.

The man's friend is here too. The friend with spiky hair. He's round the back. He's looking through the window. The one in the kitchen. He can't see me. I'm behind the chair. He's by the back door now. He's shaking the handle. He's shaking. And shaking it. But he can't make it open. I locked it tight. After Mammy went out. And the key is in my pocket.

The man with spiky hair has gone. He's not by the back door anymore. I can hear him walking. He's going past the long window. And the front room window. He's by the front door now. He's talking to the other man. The one with the web tattoo. 'No one in there, Fly,' he's saying. 'Just the kid.'

The letter box is opening. I can see fingers. They're pushing through the hole. I can see them with my one eye. 'Hey, kid.' It's the man with the web tattoo. He's shouting it. Through the letter box. I can see a corner of his tattoo.

21

The corner by his mouth. Now I can see his eyes. I can see them through the letter box. They're brown eyes like my eyes. 'I know you're in there.' He has a very loud voice. 'I can see your feet.' I'm pulling my feet in. Tight. 'Tell Brick I want my money. Don't forget.'

The letter box has closed. I can hear the men walking. Down the path. I can hear them getting into their car. I can hear doors closing. I can hear them starting the engine. I can hear them driving away.

I'm going to stay behind the chair. I'm going to stay here. And wait for Mammy. I'm going to keep my feet pulled in tight. So no one can see me. I will wait here.

Until Mammy comes home.

* * *

I can hear Mammy coming up the path. I'm running out from behind the chair and I'm running to the back door. I'm putting the key in the lock and I'm opening the door. She has come home at last. Brick is with her. He's coming in fast through the door.

'Move yourself,' he says. 'Shift.' He's pushing me out of the way. 'I need a dump.'

Mammy's behind him. 'I keep tellin' you.' She's saying it to me. 'Don' lock the blurry door.' Brick is going up the stairs fast. Mammy's all wobbly. She's holding onto the worktop.

'The men came,' I say. 'The man with the web tattoo and the man with spiky hair.'

'Blurry Fly,' Mammy says. She's lifting up her head. She's trying to shout to Brick. 'Fly's been round 'ere and blurry Psycho.'

'They want their money,' I say.

Mammy is shaking her head. 'You said you paid 'em.' She's trying to shout it to Brick but her words are slippy. 'I don' want them coming round my 'ouse. I told you.'

'Shurr up,' Brick says. He's shutting the bathroom door. He has banged it.

I say, 'I don't like it, Mammy. I don't like it when the men come.'

I'm helping her to the settee. 'Blurry Fly,' she's saying. 'Blurry Psycho.'

'I don't like it, Mammy. I don't like them coming when you're not here.'

'I don' wanna think abou' them,' she says. Her hand is looking for something. It's looking and looking on the settee. 'Where's the blurry remo?' I'm finding the remote and I'm giving it to her. She's trying and trying to press a button. I'm helping her. I'm putting the telly on and I'm finding her favourite programme.

'I don't like hiding behind the chair, Mammy. I don't like the men.'

'Shurr up,' she says. She's lifting her hand. She's trying to put it over my mouth. 'Don' talk abou' them. My programme'zzzon.'

I'm being quiet. I am trying not to remember the men. I'm watching telly with Mammy and I'm curled up by her side. She's not cross with the ladies anymore. She's not cross with the men anymore. I don't think she's cross with me anymore. She's a little bit sleepy. Her head is all floppy. It's rolling to one side. Now it's rolling to the other side.

A man is shouting on the telly. He's in a café and he's shouting at a lady. Mammy is trying to lift her head. She wants to look at the telly. I am kneeling up on the settee. I'm putting my hands under her chin and I'm helping Mammy to lift up her head.

'Gerr off,' she says. Her voice is all muddy. I'm letting go of Mammy's chin. I'm letting go very slowly. I am putting her chin back down on her shoulder. I'm trying to be very careful because her head is very heavy. She's opening her eye a little bit again and she's looking at the telly with it.

'Mammy,' I say. 'I forgot to tell you.' She's still looking at the telly but her eye is closing again. 'Mammy.' I'm tapping her arm. 'I'm singing the solo. In the Christmas concert on Friday. Sir said I was good enough.' She's moving her arm a little bit. 'Are you coming to see me?' I say. 'Are you coming to see me singing the solo?'

Mammy is making a funny sound. I'm putting my ear right next to her mouth. 'Yeah,' she says. She's saying it very quietly.

'Thank you, Mammy. Thank you.'

Brick's coming down the stairs. 'No blurry bog roll.' He's rubbing his hands on his trousers.

'Whaah?' Mammy's moving her head. One of her eyes is open a tiny bit.

'Used the kid's crappy comic.' Brick is lifting me off the settee. He's putting me on the floor. He's sitting down next

24

to Mammy. She's putting her head on his shoulder but he's pushing her away. He's finding another programme to watch.

'Fly,' Mammy says. It is hard to hear her. 'Hee waants.' She's taking a big breath. 'Hhhiss maanee.'

'I'm seeing 'im tomorrow,' Brick says. He's still trying to find a programme to watch. Mammy's head has flopped onto the settee again.

I'm going upstairs. The bathroom door is shut. I am opening it a tiny bit. There's a stinky smell in the bathroom. There are two bits of paper on the floor. I can see some letters on them. I'm running in. I am picking up the first one. The letters on it are R and D. I'm picking up the next one. It has a M and a A. And two Ls on it. There's a tiny bit of the colour blue on it too. I know that blue. My eyes are starting to be prickly. I'm putting the bits of paper safe in my pocket. I am running out of the bathroom. I'm going into my bedroom. My pile of magazines has been knocked over. I'm picking them up and I'm looking for my favourite one. It's hard to look when my eyes are prickly. I keep my favourite magazine on the top of the pile so I can see it when I come into my bedroom. It has a blue train on the front. The train is called Mallard. It's my favourite train. My favourite train in all the world. On my favourite magazine. And I am looking and looking for my favourite magazine.

* * *

I'm peeping through my window. I am pushing my cheek

25

flat against it. The window is cold on my face. My face is very hot and my eyes are very bulgy. When I press my cheek flat I can see Kaylee's house. It's across the road and it's six front doors down. Sometimes I can see Kaylee playing by her gate. I can't see her playing today but I can see twinkly lights. They're on a Christmas tree in her window. I can see a tiny bit of the tree and it looks very pretty. There's a light out in the road too. It's a yellow light and it shines into my bedroom a bit. It helps me see my books when the lectric has run out. It's run out tonight. Mammy says she's going to take the lectric key to the shop tomorrow. She's going to put more money on it.

I've been playing with my train table and I've been looking at my book. It's my library book from school. It's by someone called Roll. I can't say the name the right way. Miss can say it. I'm trying to learn it but it's hard to say. The book is called *James and the Giant Peach*.

I am going up into my bed now. I'm climbing my ladder. I am pulling some tee shirts over me and some towels and jumpers too. I'm trying to get warm. I am thinking about the pictures in the book. I'm thinking about other pictures too like the ones in *Charlie and the Chocolate Factory*. That is my favourite book. I had it last week from the library in school. It's my favourite because of the film me and Dat used to watch. We love the film. We used to sit on the settee and watch it in Nanno and Dat's house. Dat used to call me Charlie and I used to call him Grandpa. And Nanno used to bring us tea and biscuits. I like Nanno's tea and biscuits. I wish I had some now.

I'm looking at my new favourite magazine. It has a green engine on the front. The light from outside is shining on it. The engine is called The Flying Scotsman. Dat showed me lots of good pictures and words in this magazine. He showed me water tower and signalman and points. I've found the pictures but it's hard to find the words. I am trying and trying to find them. I've put the ripped magazine at the bottom of the pile. It's the one that had the picture of Mallard on it. The picture that Brick used for toilet paper. And my nose has nearly stopped running. But my breath is still bumpy.

The lights have gone off on Kaylee's Christmas tree. But the yellow light is still on in the road. I am looking through my magazine again. There are pictures of stations and mountains and cities. I am turning the pages slowly. I am looking for good words but my eyes are still watery. Something is in the magazine. It's a bit of paper folded up. I am opening it. It's a letter and it says *Dear Tomos* at the start and it says *Lots of love* at the end and there are kisses too. I know who this letter is from. It's a letter from Nanno!

I like Nanno's letters because they are always good and she liked writing letters to me when I lived in her and Dat's house and she put her letters in books or under the settee cushions or in my coat pocket and then she said, 'Can you find your letter, Tomos?' and I'd look in the cupboard and she'd say, 'Cold,' and I'd look in the fridge and she'd say, 'Warm,' and I'd look under the rug and she'd say, 'Freezing cold,' and sometimes when I looked in my pile of DVDs she'd say, 'Boiling hot!' and there it was in the middle of the pile and sometimes Nanno forgot where she put the letters and Dat and me hunted and hunted and sometimes we found them but sometimes we didn't.

Nanno always puts *Dear Tomos* to start and she always puts *Lots of love from Nanno* at the end and a P.S. too. A P.S. is an important thing you forgot to put after *Dear* and before *Love from*. That's what Nanno told me.

I'm looking at Nanno's letter up in my high sleeper bed and I'm making the light from outside shine on it. I'm looking at the words Nanno taught me. I can see the word dinner. Nanno likes telling me about her dinners in her letters and I can see the words rice and pudding. Nanno taught me those words. She makes rice pudding every Sunday and it's very nice. Nice rice pudding. That's what she calls it and I can see the word chicken. I like that word. Nanno says it's clever because it has a baby in it and a baby chicken is a chick.

I'm reading the letter now. I'm reading it from the start and I'm pointing to the words the way Nanno taught me. It says *Dear Tomos, How are you?* Nanno's letters always start like that. I like questions and I like question marks too because they are curly and I can nearly do them myself now when I'm writing sentences in school. I'm reading some more of the letter. *I am well. I am going to make chicken pie for dinner.* I like Nanno's chicken pie because it has mash potato on the top and I like it with peas and carrots because the peas and carrots stick to the mash potato and they don't fall off your fork and it's my favourite dinner ever. *I am going to make nice rice pudding too. I hope you will like it.* I will like

28

it because Nanno's nice rice pudding is yummy yummy yummy and I am licking my lips. *Lots of love, Nanno xxx P.S. I like Nanno's P.S.s best of all because they are always very good. P.S. I love you. I love you. I love you.*

I am reading the letter again. I'm reading the P.S. again and again and again. I'm smiling and smiling. And my cheeks are all wet.

If I had some paper I would write a letter to Nanno and it would say *Dear Nanno, How are you? I am well thank you. I am glad you are well too. Thank you for your letter. Yes I did enjoy reading it. I have a lot of news. Sir says I can sing the solo in the Christmas concert on Friday so I will be singing the solo and being a present and before my solo I must say, 'I have come from the North Pole. This is my gift for you.' I must not say it after my solo. I must not say it in the middle of my solo. I must say it at the start. It is hard to remember sometimes and on Thursday we are taking a box to school and red or green shiny paper and I am having red shiny paper. Mammy's getting it from Tesco and she's getting a box too. We are wrapping our boxes and Miss is cutting holes for our arms and holes for our heads and when we are presents we will sing and dance round the Christmas tree who is Eddie because Miss says Eddie will make a good tree. Miss says he will stand in one place and shake his branches and he won't have to worry about dancing and you can't crash into people if you are a tree and you can't turn the wrong way if you are a tree and you can't fall off the stage if you are a tree. That's what Miss says. I'm glad I'm not a tree. I like being a present. Miss says that some of us will have bows and some of us will have labels and the labels will be sparkly and they will say 'To' someone and 'Love from' someone. A bow is nice but I would like a sparkly label and I would like my label to say 'To Mammy Love from Tomos' because Mammy is coming to see me being a present and she is coming to see me singing my solo and I hope you enjoy the chicken pie and nice rice pudding lots of love, Tomos xxx P.S. I hope you like it in Heaven x*

* * *

It's dinner playtime. Wes is by the fence and I am running over to him. I want to tell him about Nanno's letter.

Wes is making circles in the dirt with his shoe. He likes making circles in the dirt. 'Wotcha.'

'Wotcha,' I say. It's our new word.

'What was for dinner?'

'Meat,' I say. 'And carrots.'

'And mashed potato then, with lumps in. Pukey.' He's trying to put faces in the dirt circles. He's making big mouths. 'What was for pudding?'

'Yogurt.'

'*Deee*sgusting,' he says. 'Did you eat it?'

'Yes,' I say.

'Then you're disgusting too.'

'What did you have?' Wes sits on a special table for children with lunch boxes. His lunch box has monsters on it.

'Usual,' he says. 'Something not disgusting. And crisps. And a chocolate bar. And cola.'

'Sir says people can't have cola.' I'm trying to draw circles with my shoe too. I'm trying but Wes is using most of the dirt. 'Sir says cola's not allowed. And chocolate's not allowed too.'

Wes is rubbing out my circles with his shoe. 'How would you know?' he says. 'You're on free meals.' He's rubbing out his own circles now. 'You should tell your mam to make you packed lunch.'

'Maybe.' I want to tell him about Nanno's letter. 'Last night—'

Wes isn't listening. 'Nah, she won't anyway. Your mam's a lazy cow. Uncle Vic told me.' He's starting to run down the playground. I'm watching him. He's turning round and he's trying to run backwards. 'Come on, thicko.'

I'm running after him. I want to tell him about Nanno's letter from Heaven. It's hard to catch up with him because he's very fast. He's running round the corner. I'm running round the corner too. He's stopped. He's waiting for me by the pipe.

'Last night, Nanno sent—'

He's still not listening. He says, 'Uncle Vic knows your dad.'

I am looking at Wes. He's staring at me. He's not laughing. 'I haven't got a dad.'

'Everyone's got a dad,' he says. 'That's how everyone's made. Everyone's got a dad.'

'I haven't,' I say. 'Mammy told me.'

'Mammy told me.' He's trying to copy me. He's making his voice sound silly. And he's laughing now. 'Your mam had to do sex with your dad, like the people do it in Uncle Vic's DVDs. That's how babies are made so you've got to have a dad.' He's picking up tiny stones. He getting them from round the pipe. He's putting them in his pockets. 'Uncle Vic says your dad had your mam behind the leisure centre when she was fourteen.' He's putting more stones in his pockets. 'Everybody knows your dad. He's that man with the web ta…'

Some girls have come round the corner. 'Go away,' Wes says to them. The girls have stopped to look at us. They're laughing a bit. 'Go away!' He's shouting it. He's putting his hands into his pockets. He's running at the girls. He's throwing the tiny stones at them. The stones are falling in their hair like rain. The girls are screaming. They're running away.

Wes is rubbing his hands. Some tiny stones are falling onto the floor. He's wiping his hands on his jumper. He's looking at me. He's looking at me from the sides of his eyes. 'Your dad's a pervert,' he says. 'That's why you're weird. Uncle Vic told me.' He's bending down to get more stones. He's putting them in his pockets. He's running again. He's running back round the corner. I'm trying to catch up with him. He's shouting over his shoulder to me. 'That's why no one will play with you.'

He's running very fast. It's hard to catch up with him. The bell is ringing now too. And I haven't told Wes about Nanno's letter yet. He's shouting. 'They won't play with you cos you're weird.' He's very loud now. His shouting is very very loud. 'You're weird,' he says. 'And you smell.'

* * *

I'm all on my own. I'm all on my own in the house. I'm trying to hide from all the knocking. I'm running round and round the front room. Round and round trying to hide. But the front room is empty. The big black chair has gone. The settee has gone too. There are people knocking on the doors. And on the windows. They are knocking and knocking. And knocking and knocking. The lady with the big bag is here. And the lady with the Gwa name. The men are here too. Their knocking is very loud. They are all knocking on the windows. And there's nowhere to hide. Nowhere to hide at all.

Nanno and Dat are here now. I'm very happy because I can see Nanno's grey hair and I can see Dat's smiley eyes through the window and they have come for me at last. Dat is trying to open the door and he's trying and trying. But it won't open. I'm trying to open the door now too. But I can't find the key. I've lost it. I'm pulling and pulling on the handle. But it still won't open. And the men have nearly broken the windows. They are nearly coming inside the front room. The ladies are nearly coming in too. The ladies and the men are going to try to grab me.

'Dat,' I say. 'Dat, help me, help me!' I am crying and crying. There's a lot of shouting. Lots and lots of shouting and knocking. 'Dat, come quick, come quick!' The knocking and shouting is very loud now. The men and the ladies are going to get me.

I am sitting up. I'm sitting up with a fright. I'm in my

33

high sleeper bed. And it's very dark. I can still hear the knocking. It's downstairs. It's very loud. There's a lot of shouting too. It's Mammy shouting. I think she's by the back door and she's shouting and shouting. I'm getting up and I'm running downstairs. I'm running into the kitchen. Mammy is outside. I can see her through the glass. She's forgotten her key again and she's knocking on the door. 'Why did you blurry lock it?' She's shouting it through the glass.

I'm running back upstairs to my bedroom. I'm running to get the key from the pocket in my trousers. Mammy is still knocking. Her knocking is very very loud. I'm running back to the kitchen and I'm letting her in.

'Stupid kid.' She's pushing past me. 'I've told you and told you – don' keep locking the door.'

'But what about the men? What if they come round again?'

She's going into the front room now. 'I don' like standing out in the cold, do I? I don' like waiting for you to let me in.' She's going up the stairs. 'Stop locking it.' She's going into the bathroom. She's getting all her things out of the cupboard. All the things I must NOT touch. 'Stupid kid,' she says. 'Don' do it again.' And she's banging the bathroom door.

* * *

I'm watching for Kaylee and her mammy through the window. I've been watching a long long time. I'm waving to

34

the lady across the road too but she's not waving back. She's just moving her white curtains.

Kaylee and her mammy are here and they're stopping by the gate. Kaylee's mammy is holding a big box. I'm running to the door and I'm running down the path. 'Is it Thursday?'

'Yes,' Kaylee says. 'Have you got your box?'

'I'll go and get it. I'll be fast.' I'm running back up the path. I'm going round the back and I'm opening the door. I'm looking in the kitchen. I'm looking in the cupboards. I'm looking in the front room. I'm looking behind the big black chair. I'm looking behind the settee. I'm running up the stairs and I'm creeping into Mammy's bedroom. I'm trying not to wake her. I'm looking for my box and my red shiny paper. I'm looking under the pile of clothes. I'm looking under the bed. I'm looking and looking and looking and looking. I can't find them anywhere. 'Mammy,' I say. I'm trying to be very quiet. 'Mammy, it's Thursday. Where's my box and my shiny paper?'

Mammy's opening one eye a tiny bit. She's looking at me through her yellow hair. 'Uh?'

'My box from Tesco. It's Thursday. I need it.'

Her eye is closing again. She's making snorey noises.

'Please, Mammy.' I'm tapping her arm a bit.

'Wharr?' she says.

'I need my box for school so I can be a present.'

She's not moving. She's making snorey noises again.

'Mammy,' I say. 'Mammy, I need my box today.' I'm running to the window and I'm looking out. Kaylee and her mammy are waiting for me by the gate. I'm running back to the bed. I'm tapping her arm again. 'Please, Mammy. Please. I need the box.'

She's opening her other eye and she's moving her head a bit. 'The wharr?'

'The box. For me to be a present. In the concert that you are coming to see tomorrow.'

She's moving. She's moving a bit. She's turning over onto her tummy. Her hand has flopped onto the floor.

'Mammy.' I am tapping her shoulder. I'm tapping and tapping. 'I need my box.'

She's moving her hand a little bit. She's moving it on the floor. Her hand is trying to find something. It's trying and trying. She's picking up Brick's cigarettes and she's turning the box upside down. The cigarettes are falling out onto the floor. She's lifting her hand. She's holding the empty cigarette box. She's holding it out to me.

'Yerr,' she says. 'Take this.'

* * *

'Right, Tomos,' Miss says. She's smiling at me and her eyes are very kind. 'That's all sorted. Give your nose another good blow.' I'm blowing my nose on the tissues Miss gave me. The tissues are very squidgy now. 'Drop those in the bin,' she says.

I'm dropping them in the bin. I'm dropping them next to the cigarette box. 'Have some clean ones.' Miss is holding the tissue box out to me. I'm taking two. She is shaking the box. I'm taking two more.

'Right.' She's still smiling. 'In a minute you can go to the toilets and put lots of water on your face.' She's looking at Seren. 'You'll look after him, won't you?' Seren is nodding. Miss is looking at me again. 'Seren will go with you and wait outside the toilets. And then…' Miss is getting some things out of the cupboard. She's giving us a black bag each. 'It's our class's turn for litter picking, so you and Seren can do that for me this morning. It'll give you a chance to get some cold air on your face, Tomos.'

'Can we use the pinchy things?' I say. My voice is all bumpy. I'm wiping my nose again on the tissues Miss gave me. 'I like the pinchy things.'

'Yes.' Miss is getting them down from on top of the cupboard. 'Don't use your fingers, just these.' She's showing us how to make them pinch. She's giving them to Seren. 'Right, off you go, both of you.'

We are going down the corridor. I'm going into the toilets and Seren is waiting for me outside the door. She's holding my black bag and my pinchy thing. She's singing a song about cherry Chapstick.

I have filled up the sink where we wash our hands. I've filled it with cold water. I'm splashing the water on my face. It feels nice on my eyes. I'm thinking of Nanno. She showed me how to wash my face. Nanno would say, 'Have a good swill.' And I would splash and splash my face.

Seren is still singing. I can hear her outside the door. I can hear her shoes squeaking and squeaking on the floor. She's singing about kissing a girl. She's singing 'And I liked it.' I'm wiping my face on the tissues Miss gave me. They're turning into lots of tiny bits and they're falling all over the floor.

Seren has stopped singing. 'Are you ready?' She's saying it from outside the door.

'Yes,' I say. I'm trying to pick up the little bits of tissue. There are lots and lots of them and they're hard to pick up. I'm putting them in the bin. I'm running out of the toilet. Seren is giving me my black bag. 'Can I have my pinchy thing?'

'When we get outside,' she says.

We're going along the corridor and past lots of classrooms. We're going through the doors to the playground. 'Here.' Seren's giving me the pinchy thing. I'm making it pinch pinch pinch pinch. 'You stay up here,' she says. 'I'm going down to the bottom of the playground.' She's running off.

I'm looking for something to get with my pinchy thing. I'm looking and looking. I'm going over to the drains. There are lots of bits round the drains. I've found a brown leaf but it's quite hard to pick up. It keeps jumping away when I pinch it. I'm pinching and pinching and the leaf is jumping and jumping. There are some more things in the drain. I'm trying to pinch them. It's quite hard. It's taking me a long time to pinch them with the pinchy thing.

'Tomos, isn't it?' a big voice says.

I'm turning round fast. Sir is standing behind me. 'Yes, Sir,' I say.

'Tomos Morris with the wonderful voice. You're doing a good job there. What have you got?'

I'm opening my big black bag. We are looking in. We're

looking at the brown leaf and the sweet paper. 'Yes,' he says. 'Well done.' I'm smiling up at him. He's smiling down at me then he's squashing his eyebrows together. 'Has something upset you, Tomos?'

I'm taking a big breath. It sounds all jumpy. 'Yes, Sir.'

'Want to tell me about it?'

'Yes, Sir,' I say. 'I didn't have a box.'

'You didn't have a box?'

'I did have a box, but it was too small.'

'Too small? What was it too small for?'

'For me to fit in,' I say. 'It was a cigarette box.'

'I see,' he says.

'And I didn't have shiny paper.' Sir is looking at me through his big glasses. 'Mammy said she was getting them from Tesco,' I say. 'But she forgot.'

'Oh.' Sir's big glasses are slipping down his nose.

'But Miss had a spare box and spare shiny paper. She has green shiny paper,' I say. 'Green is almost as good as red.'

'It is,' Sir says.

Seren is running up the playground. She's carrying her black bag and it's quite bulgy. Sir says, 'You've got a lot there, Seren.'

'Yes, Mr Griffiths.' Seren's looking at my bag. My bag that has a leaf in it and a sweet paper. Seren's opening her bag and we're all looking into it. It's full of crisp packets and cola bottles.

'Well done, Seren.' Sir's taking her black bag. He's taking mine too. Now he's taking our pinchy things. 'Come to the office, you two,' he says. 'I've got another important job for you.'

* * *

We have got another very important job. We must go to all the classes and show the teachers a piece of paper with Sir's writing on it. They must read the paper and put their name on it. Seren is holding the paper and I'm holding the pen. It's Sir's special pen. I must take it back to him when we've finished our job.

We must start with Year Six. We're going into their classroom slowly because it's very scary. Seren is going first. She's holding out the paper. The children are very big in Year Six. They have big chairs and big tables and a big Christmas tree. It's silver and red and sparkly like the one in our class. It's quite noisy in the classroom. The children have got shiny paper on their tables. And scissors and glue sticks and pots of glitter. Mrs Gregory is their teacher. She has red lips and bouncy hair.

'Mr Griffiths wants you to read this,' Seren says. She's giving the paper to Mrs Gregory.

Mrs Gregory's reading it. 'Yet another meeting about the Christmas concert. Well, there goes my break time.' She's trying to give the paper back to Seren.

Seren is keeping her hands behind her back. She's knocking me with her shoulder. 'Pen,' she says. She's saying it with the side of her mouth. I'm holding out Sir's pen to Mrs Gregory. 'You have to write your name,' Seren says.

Mrs Gregory is taking the pen. She's smiling at Seren and me. 'Mr Griffiths has found two excellent helpers.' She's writing on the paper and she's smiling at me with her red lips. 'You're the boy with the lovely voice, aren't you?' I'm looking at her. I don't know what to say. 'You're the one singing the solo in the concert,' she says. I'm nodding. It's gone very quiet in the class now. Everyone's looking at us. They've stopped making their glittery things. 'Well, you sing it beautifully,' Mrs Gregory says. 'I think we've found quite a little star.' She's giving the paper back to Seren.

'Thank you, Mrs Gregory,' Seren says.

Mrs Gregory's giving the pen back to me and I'm taking it. Seren is knocking me again. She's whispering the words 'thank' and 'you'.

'Oh! Thank you,' I say to Mrs Gregory.

We are going out of Year Six. We're going into Year Five. It's quite scary in Year Five. The children are still very big. I'm holding the pen tight tight.

* * *

We have been to Year Six and Year Five and Year Four and Year Three. We are standing outside Mrs Pugh Year Two's class. We are waiting for her to tell us to come in. She's waving her hand at us and we're starting to go into her classroom. She's sitting at her big desk. There's a Christmas tree on it in a blue pot. It's a very small tree. It's not sparkly like Mrs Gregory's tree. It's very quiet in Mrs Pugh Year Two's class. The children are all doing their work. They're all writing. I can see the back of Wes's head. He's sitting by the big cupboard. In the corner.

I'm going into the classroom with Seren.

'Stop there, Tomos Morris,' Mrs Pugh Year Two says. She's holding out her hand like a policeman stopping cars. She's getting a little bottle out of her bag. She's spraying it on her clothes. She's spraying it into the classroom now. It smells like pink. It smells like Nanno's bathroom. 'What are you two bothering me with?'

'Mr Griffiths sent us,' Seren says. She's giving the paper to Mrs Pugh Year Two. I'm trying to give her the pen. I'm trying and trying. But I'm too far away because I had to stop by the door. I'm stretching out my arm. I'm standing on my toes. I'm holding the pen out as far as I can. I am stretching and stretching. But I'm a long way away from Mrs Pugh Year Two. My arm isn't long enough to give her the pen.

'So Mr Griffiths wants us all in the staffroom at break time,' Mrs Pugh Year Two says. 'To talk about the rehearsal.'

'Yes, Mrs Pugh,' Seren says.

'I'll have to write down that I'm on playground duty.'

Seren is taking the pen from me. She's giving it to Mrs Pugh Year Two.

'Did you remember a box today, Tomos Morris?' Mrs Pugh Year Two says. She's writing a long letter on the paper. She's looking at me now. She's stretching her neck so she can see round Seren. She's tapping Sir's pen on her desk. I'm looking at my shoes. There's a lot of black fluff stuck to my Velcro.

Seren says, 'I remembered a box, Mrs Pugh.' She's taking back the piece of paper.

'I know *you* will have remembered,' Mrs Pugh Year Two says. 'We can depend on *you*. But what about Tomos

42

Morris?' She's shaking Sir's pen at me. She's tapping it on her desk again. She's scratching her head with it. She's putting it in her pencil pot.

Seren says, 'Tomos *has* got a box, haven't you, Tomos?' She's saying it in a loud voice. Wes has turned round and he's looking at me.

I'm nodding. 'I have.' I'm saying it to Mrs Pugh Year Two. My voice is still a bit bumpy and my nose is still a bit runny. 'I have got a box.'

Wes is jumping up. He's pointing to me. 'Look at his eyes!' He's laughing. All the children are looking at me. 'He's been crying,' Wes says. He's very loud. Now he's singing 'You've been crying. You've been crying.'

'Wesley Weston-Rees! How dare you shout out in my classroom. Sit down at once.'

Wes is sitting down again. He's making faces at me. Seren is pulling my arm. She's pulling me towards the door.

'The pen.' I'm saying it to Seren. I'm saying it quietly because I don't want Mrs Pugh Year Two to hear me.

'What?' Seren says.

'She kept Sir's pen. It's in her pencil pot.'

Seren is looking at Mrs Pugh Year Two's desk. She's walking back to it like a soldier. Mrs Pugh Year Two is looking up. Her mouth is making a little circle. Seren is putting her hand over the pencil pot and she's taking the pen out. She's taking it very fast. 'This is Mr Griffiths' pen,' she says. She's saying it to Mrs Pugh Year Two. Seren is turning round. She's walking back to me. She's walking very fast. She's holding out the pen. She says, 'Here you are,

Tomos.' I'm taking the pen and I'm holding it tight. Seren is opening the door and she's going out. She's got the paper ready for Miss in our class.

I'm looking at Mrs Pugh Year Two. She's sitting at her desk. Her mouth is still like a circle and her eyebrows are up high. They're like two furry brown caterpillars on top of her glasses. I'm walking through the door. I'm walking backwards. I am bending my head and my shoulders. I'm bending them like a king. I am like a king in front of baby Jesus. And I'm walking backwards through the door.

'Thank you, Mrs Pugh Year Two,' I say. I am bending and bending like a king. 'Thank you, thank you. Goodbye.' And I'm closing the door tight.

* * *

It's a very important day today because it's the day of the Christmas concert and it's the day I am being a present and singing the solo and I'm waiting for Kaylee and her mammy. I'm waiting for them to stop by our gate. I've been waiting a very long time and I've been waving to the lady across the road too. I've been waving and waving but she isn't waving back.

There's a van going past our gate. It's going very slowly. It's a big red van and a man is looking out of it. It's stopping near next door's gate and the man is getting out. I'm watching him. The lady across the road is watching him too. He's looking at me through the window and he's waving to me. I'm bending down fast fast. And I'm peeping through

44

the bottom of the window. The man is coming up our path. Now he's knocking on our door.

I'm running to the door and I'm hiding behind it. His knocking is very loud. I don't want him to wake up Mammy. The letter box is opening. I can see his mouth through it. There's a lot of white hair round his mouth.

'Hello,' his mouth says through the letter box. 'Is this Rhiannon Morris's house?' His mouth and the hair have gone. I can see his eyes instead. They are quite smiley eyes. They're looking through the letter box at my eyes. 'Hello there,' his eyes say. 'Is your mummy in?'

I'm not allowed to say Mammy's in bed. She told me a long time ago. I have to say Mammy's somewhere else. 'She's in the bath,' I say. 'She can't come to the door.'

'Oh dear,' his eyes say. 'I've got some things for her.' His eyes are opening and shutting a lot but they're still smiley. 'Is her name Rhiannon? Rhiannon Morris?'

'Yes,' I say. 'Rhiannon Morris. She's in the bath.'

'Oh well then,' his eyes say. 'I'll leave them with you. Can you open the door?'

'I'm not allowed to open the door,' I say. 'When she's in the bath.'

'I haven't got time to come back later.' I can see all his face through the letter box hole now. I like his face. It's nice like Dat's. It has a white beard and a red nose but Dat doesn't have a white beard and he doesn't have a red nose. 'Tell you what.' His eyes have come back again. 'I'll put them round by the back door for her.'

The letter box has closed. I'm running to the window.

He's going down the path to his red van. He's opening the big door in his van and he's getting some things out. He's coming back up the path again and he's wearing a red hat now. It has fluffy white stuff on it. He's carrying a big box with gold paper all round it. There's something on top of the box. It's a white bag. It has pictures of Father Christmas on it and it has writing on it too.

He's going round the back of our house. I'm running out of the front room into the kitchen and I'm looking through the glass door. He's putting the box down outside. The bag is still on top of it and I can see the writing on the bag now. I can read the words too. They say 'Santa Sack'.

'Is it Christmas?'

'What's that?' He's putting his head near the glass in the door.

'Is it Christmas?'

'Soon. Enjoy the presents.' He's waving to me through the glass. He's smiling too. 'Ho, ho, ho!' he says. His white beard is moving up and down. 'Merry Christmas one and all!' He's still smiling at me. He's waving now. 'Ho, ho, ho!' His round tummy is jumping up and down under his jumper. I'm watching him turn round. I'm watching the fluffy white bit of his hat swing swinging. He's going round the corner.

I know who he is. It's him. The lady with the big bag and the other lady with the Gwa name said he would come. They said he'd come before Christmas. I'm running from the kitchen. I'm running to the window in the front room. I'm watching him going down the path. He's getting into his red van. I'm waving and waving and waving. He's looking and waving too. He's smiling.

'Thank you.' I'm saying it quietly. I don't want to wake up Mammy. I'm saying it through the glass. 'Thank you, Siôn Corn.' The window is getting misty. I'm rubbing the mist with my sleeve. The van is moving away and I am waving and waving and smiling and smiling. He's nearly gone. His red van is nearly round the corner. I'm watching it and I'm watching it until it's gone and I'm still waving.

'Thank you, Father Christmas,' I say. 'Thank you, thank you, thank you.'

* * *

I have stopped watching for Kaylee and her mammy and I'm watching the gold box outside the back door instead and I'm watching the bag that says 'Santa Sack' on it. I'm watching them through the glass and the bag is blowing a bit in the wind and some drops of rain have landed on the gold box but I don't want lots of rain to land on it because lots of rain would spoil the gold paper.

I can hear banging upstairs. Mammy has got up. She's in the bathroom. I'm still watching the box and the bag and I'm watching the wind and the drops of rain and I can hear Mammy coming out of the bathroom and I'm running to the stairs. I can hear her saying, 'Blurry knocking on the door.'

'Mammy, Mammy. Come quick! Father Christmas has been. He's left something outside for us.' Mammy's coming

47

down the stairs. I'm running back to the door and I'm checking the box and the bag are still there. Mammy's coming into the kitchen. 'Happy Christmas, Mammy!' I'm pointing to the things outside the door but Mammy's eyes are not very open. She can't see my finger pointing. 'Father Christmas came,' I say.

'Who?' She's putting water in the kettle.

'Father Christmas. He came this morning. He brought us presents.' She's picking up a mug from the sink and she's tipping out the dirty water. 'He was wearing a red hat. He said, "Ho, ho, ho".'

She's putting a tea bag in the mug. 'Yeah right.'

'Look,' I say. 'Look!' I'm pointing to the presents outside the back door. 'He left those.' She's going to the back door now and she's looking out and I'm jumping and jumping. 'Happy Christmas. Happy Christmas.'

'Fetch 'em in.' She's going back to her mug.

'I can't,' I say. 'I don't know where the key is.'

'Go ou' the front then.'

I'm running to the front door and I'm opening it and I'm running out and round the corner to the back of our house. I've come to the box and the Santa Sack and the wind is blowing the Santa Sack a little bit open. I can see inside it. I can see a black wheel with a silver shiny middle and I can see a bit of cardboard and I can see some letters. They are S U P E R T R U C. I'm lifting the Santa Sack off the gold box and I'm running round the front of our house with it and I'm running into the kitchen and I'm putting it on the floor. I'm running back to the front door and round the back of our house again and I'm putting my hands under the gold box. It's very heavy. It's full of tins and boxes and there are some sweets in it too. It's very hard to pick it up. I'm trying and trying to pick it up but it's too heavy. I'm putting it down again.

I'm looking through the glass in the door. I can't see Mammy. She isn't in the kitchen anymore. I'm opening the back door. 'Mammy.' I'm saying it loud. 'Mammy!' I can hear some music. She's put the telly on in the front room. 'Mammy, it's too heavy.'

I'm going back to the box and I'm bending down. I'm trying and trying to pick it up and trying and trying and trying. I'm making myself very strong. I have very strong arms and very strong legs. I am the strongest boy in the world. I am the strongest boy ever. The box is moving. I'm picking it up. I'm turning round very slowly and I'm taking one step. I'm taking two steps. I am going through the back door into the kitchen. I am very strong. I'm very very strong. Mammy is coming back into the kitchen. She's got the key. She's holding it up. 'Was down the side o' the sofa,' she says.

She can see me carrying the box. She can see how strong I am. I'm bending my knees and I'm putting the box down on the floor. 'Oomph,' I say. All my breath has whooshed out of me. I feel floaty and my arms and legs are wobbly. I'm sitting down on the floor next to the box. 'These are our presents from Father Christmas.' My words are wobbly too. 'Happy Christmas, Mammy.'

Mammy is looking at the box and the Santa Sack. She's looking at the back door. 'Stupid kid,' she says. She's throwing the key at me. She's turning round. She's going back into the front room. I'm still sitting on the floor. I'm sitting next to the box. And the key.

'Stupid kid,' she says again. She's saying it over her shoulder. She's saying it over the noise on the telly. She's saying it to me. 'Makin' me look for the blurry key. Back door wasn' even locked.'

* * *

I am waiting for Kaylee and her Mammy again. I'm waiting for them to stop by our gate. The box and the Santa Sack are in the kitchen. Mammy is on the settee. She's nearly asleep.

'Mammy, the concert is today,' I say. 'Miss says it starts at half past three.' I'm trying to look at Mammy and I'm trying to look out of the window too. 'I'm singing the solo.' She's not saying anything. 'Mammy, Mammy. I'm singing the solo today.' Mammy's nodding her head a bit but her eyes are still shut.

Kaylee and her mammy are here and they've stopped by our gate. I'm running to the front door. 'See you at the concert, Mammy. At half past three.' I'm shutting the front door behind me and I'm running down the path to Kaylee and her mammy. 'Father Christmas came,' I say. 'He brought us a gold box and a Santa Sack.'

'That's nice,' Kaylee's mammy says. We've started walking to school.

'It's not Christmas yet,' Kaylee says. 'It's not Christmas 'til next week.'

50

'I know,' I say. 'We're keeping our presents for Christmas Day.'

'Did you tell your mother about the concert this afternoon?' Kaylee's mammy says.

'Yes. I told her it starts at half past three.'

'Good.'

'Mrs Pugh said we're practising all day today,' Kaylee says.

Her mammy is starting to walk fast. 'We better hurry up then. You know what Mrs Pugh's like. She'll go spare if we're late for her practice.'

* * *

We are waiting at the back of the stage. We're waiting behind the big curtains. It's very dark. Mrs Pugh Year Two is guarding us. She's checking we don't talk or fight. Or peep through the curtains to wave to the people. The people in the hall. We're waiting for it to be our turn to sing. It's a long wait. We've been practising all day. I'm very tired. And we're waiting a long long time.

I am a present. I'm wearing the big box that Miss gave me. My head is sticking out of the top and my arms are sticking out of the sides. It's hard to move your arms and legs when you are a present. I'm standing next to Eddie. He's the Christmas tree. He's waving his branches and he's knocking my shiny green paper. His tinsel is falling off. Mrs Pugh Year Two is shaking her head and putting his tinsel back on him. She's making a cross face.

Miss is starting to play our song. Mrs Pugh Year Two is

listening by the curtains. She's giving Eddie a push. Eddie's branches are trying to find a way in between the curtains and now we are all going onto the stage.

It's scary on the stage. Some of us are standing round Eddie because we are the Christmas presents. Some children are standing behind us because they are the elves. Miss is playing the piano. And now we're all singing 'Oh Christmas tree, oh Christmas tree…' and Eddie is waving his branches slowly. We're singing and doing our dance. And there are lots of people in the hall. They are all looking at us. They are looking and looking. It is very scary on the stage.

Eddie's waving his branches faster. He's starting to move his feet too. His feet are his roots. Miss said he's not allowed to move them. He must only move his branches. He must stand still and wave his branches. But he's not standing still. He's turning round and round. He's starting to dance too. Eddie's not allowed to dance. He is a tree.

Seren says, 'No, Eddie. Stand still.' Seren is an elf. She's talking in quite a loud voice. She's stamping her foot too. Miss is looking up from the piano. Mrs Pugh Year Two's looking cross at the side of the stage. 'Stand still, Eddie,' Seren says. 'You can't move. You're the tree.' She's shouting it now.

Eddie's not standing still. He's dancing round and round. He's knocking into presents and knocking into elves. Nadia's starting to cry. She's a blue elf and she's wearing big rabbit slippers. Seren's trying to make Eddie stand still. She's grabbing his arms. His tinsel has fallen off and we've all forgotten the words to our song. We've forgotten to keep dancing too.

Mrs Pugh Year Two is on the stage. She's putting her hand on Eddie's back and she's moving him off the stage. There's a big noise in the hall. All the people are talking and lots of them are laughing. I'm looking out. I'm looking out at the people. I'm looking at all the faces. I'm looking for Mammy but it's hard to find her. It's a bit dark because Sir closed the blinds. There are lots of faces. There are lots and lots of people. I'm looking and looking. And looking and looking. There she is. I've found her. I can see her pretty yellow hair and she's near the back and I'm waving to her and I'm waving and smiling and waving and waving and waving.

Miss is starting to play the piano again. We're doing our dance and singing our song. We're singing 'Oh Christmas tree, oh Christmas tree…' but we don't have a Christmas tree anymore. We're dancing round the tinsel that fell off Eddie.

I'm looking out at Mammy. I'm trying to look at her and dance too. It's quite hard because I'm turning and dancing. I can't see her anymore. I'm looking and looking for her. And dancing and singing too. I've found her again. She's looking at the stage but she isn't watching me singing and dancing. She's watching someone else. I'm trying to wave a little bit more. We're not allowed to wave when we're singing and dancing. Mrs Pugh Year Two told us in a very long assembly.

We've finished our song and dance and everyone is clapping. Everyone's smiling too. I'm looking and looking at Mammy and I'm smiling and smiling and waving at her and now I see. I see the lady that wasn't watching me isn't Mammy. It isn't Mammy I was waving too. It's another lady with pretty yellow hair. It isn't my mammy at all. Because it's Seren's mammy.

* * *

We're standing at the back of the stage. We're watching Mary and Joseph. They are at the front of the stage. They've found somewhere to stay. The shepherds have brought Mary and Joseph baby Jesus. And a lamb. The kings have brought them some shiny boxes. There are lots of fairies at the front of the stage too. They're dancing and singing a song about angels. I'm waiting and listening for Emma Louise to say, 'Now sleep, baby Jesus, sleep.' Then I will go to the front of the stage. With the fairies. And I will sing my solo. I'm waiting. And waiting.

And I'm looking for Mammy in the hall. I'm looking in between Mary and Joseph and the shepherds and the kings. And all the fairies. I'm looking and looking. And looking and looking and looking. But I can't see her. I think she might be watching *Murder, She Wrote*. And she might have fallen asleep on the settee. I'm looking and looking. And looking and looking. And I'm waiting to sing my solo.

'Tomos.' Mrs Pugh Year Two is whispering in a loud voice. 'Tomos, go. Go!' She's flapping her hand at me.

I'm going to the front of the stage and I'm squeezing through the fairies. It's quite hard to squeeze through because I am a present. I'm checking my label is round the right way. I want Mammy to read the words. They say 'To Mammy, Love from Tomos'. I'm standing right at the front of the stage now. I have to say my words first. I must not say them halfway through my solo. And I must not say them at the end. Mrs Pugh Year Two has told me.

'I have come from the North Pole,' I say. 'This is my gift for you.'

Then Miss is starting to play the piano and I'm taking a big breath. I'm starting to sing 'Away in a manger, no crib…' and then I see. I see him.

I see Dat.

He's at the back of the hall. He's standing near the door. He's looking at me. He's smiling and smiling and smiling. And he's lifting up his hand to wave. And I am singing my solo and I'm waving to Dat. And I'm smiling and waving and waving and waving.

* * *

The concert has finished now and the people are going. I'm on the stage with Wes and someone else. The someone else is a boy with black hair. I don't know his name. Wes is coming to stand next to me. He's got a towel on his head. 'Wotcha,' he says. I'm not saying 'wotcha' back. I'm trying not to look at Wes because I want to keep looking at Dat. He's still at the back of the hall and he's talking to Miss. Wes is trying to grab my sparkly label and he's trying to rip my shiny paper. It's hard to move my arms to stop him because I am a present.

'Stop that, Wesley Weston-Rees,' Mrs Pugh Year Two looks very cross. 'Where's your mother?'

'In work,' Wes says.

'Who's collecting you then?' she says.

'Rockie. She's my sister.'

Mrs Pugh Year Two says, 'Your sister's called Rockie? Good gracious, what is the world coming to?'

I can still see Dat. He's by the big doors now.

'Well, I wish she'd hurry up,' she says. 'And who's collecting you, Tomos Morris?'

'I think it's Dat,' I say.

'What? Speak properly, child. Who's collecting you?'

I'm pointing to Dat with my finger. 'Dat,' I say.

'Dat?' Mrs Pugh Year Two says. 'Dat? The word is "that" and when you're referring to a person you say "him" or "her", not "that".' She's shaking her head. 'What on earth is happening to children these days?'

'He's my dat,' I say. 'My *dat*. I'm not allowed to see him anymore.' I'm still pointing. 'I did something, I think, and now I'm not allowed to see him.'

Mrs Pugh Year Two isn't listening. She's talking to the boy with black hair. She's saying, 'And who's collecting you, Malachi Morgan?'

'My name ain't Malachi, Miss. It's Malky.'

'Oh dear lord,' Mrs Pugh Year Two says. 'A good, biblical name ruined.'

The boy called Malky is talking about his aunty. He's saying she's collecting him. Miss is still talking to Dat. They're still by the doors. Miss is rubbing Dat's arm. I'm waving to them. I'm waving and waving. But they're not looking at me. A girl has come in through the doors. She's a big girl. She's walking to the stage. She's nodding at Wes. He's showing her his tongue.

'Are you Wesley's sister?' Mrs Pugh Year Two says. 'Are you this person called Rockie?'

The girl's nodding. 'Yeah, that's me.'

'Well, kindly tell your mother that every other shepherd brought their own tea towel,' Mrs Pugh Year Two says. 'I sent out letters weeks ago. Wesley had to borrow one from the school canteen.' She's pulling the towel off Wes's head. 'Some shepherds even brought their own stuffed lambs. Some parents make an effort.'

'Okay,' the girl called Rockie says. 'I'll tell her. Wes, come on let's go.'

Wes is jumping down off the stage. 'See you, thicko.' He's saying it to me.

'Bye, Wes. See you.'

The girl called Rockie is looking at me. She's shaking her head. 'Don't let him talk to you like that. Don't let him bully you.' She's going away now. She's going out of the hall with Wes.

There are only two of us left on the stage. There's me and the boy called Malky. We're waiting to be collected. I'm wondering if I'm waiting to be collected by Dat. I am hoping and hoping I am. Miss is still talking to him. She's nodding and putting her hand on his arm again. She's giving him a hug. She's saying, 'Bye, Dafydd. Take care.' She's turned round now and she's coming back to the stage.

Dat has opened the hall door. He's smiling at me. He's waving to me too. He's waving and waving and I am waving and waving. Dat's mouth looks all wobbly. And I'm waving and waving and waving. He's going through the door.

He's gone.

Miss is talking to Kaylee and her mammy. They're coming over to the stage. 'It's awful,' Kaylee's mammy's saying. 'After everything Dafydd and Nannette did for Ree.'

'I know, Karen,' Miss says. 'I know.'

'And it's just so she can be with that waster Nick Brickland.'

'I don't think it's about her boyfriend really,' Miss says. 'I think she's had a shock, you know, with Nannette dying so suddenly…'

Kaylee's mammy's shaking her head. 'Well, it was a bigger shock for Dafydd. And then Ree goes an' accuses him of stuff. I knew she was nasty, but this is just really horrible.'

'I know,' Miss says. 'But I think she's finding it difficult to—'

Kaylee's mammy hasn't heard her. 'She only cares 'bout herself,' she says. 'She don't say a word to me no more, and we used to be best friends.'

They're next to the stage now. Malky has gone. I didn't see him going. I am the only one on the stage. I'm the only one waiting to be collected. Miss is looking at me and she's smiling and smiling. 'Well done, Tomos. Your solo was lovely.'

'Yeah.' Kaylee's mammy's smiling at me now too. 'It was really good.'

'But spoilt by all that waving,' Mrs Pugh Year Two says. Her face is cross.

58

Miss is still smiling at me. 'Your dat wanted me to tell you that he's very proud of you.'

I am smiling. I'm smiling and my head is hurting and there's a funny lump in my tummy. 'I'm still waiting to be collected,' I say. 'Am I waiting to be collected by Dat?' I'm hoping and hoping and hoping I am.

Miss looks sad. Her eyes are watery. 'Not tonight.' She's smiling a little bit again now. 'But Kaylee's mum says you can walk home with them.'

Kaylee's mammy is holding out her hand. 'Come on, then.'

Miss says, 'Thanks for seeing him home, Karen.'

'No problem,' Kaylee's mammy says. 'I do it all the time. Don't think she even notices.' She's helping me down off the stage. It's hard to get down when you're a present. And when there's a big lump of sad in your tummy.

'You'd better hurry,' Miss says, 'before it starts raining.'

We are hurrying to the hall door. Miss is shouting, 'Have a good Christmas.'

'An' you, Lowri,' Kaylee's mammy's shouting.

Miss is shouting, 'You too, Tomos.'

And I'm shouting, 'You too, Miss.' I'm looking back. Miss is waving but she's not smiling now. Her mouth looks sad and her eyes look sad too.

I am hurrying as fast as I can. I'm hurrying down the corridor with Kaylee and her mammy. I don't want the rain to start. It will spoil my green shiny paper and my sparkly label. I want to get home before it starts raining and I want to get home looking nice. I want to get home with nice shiny paper and my nice sparkly label. I want to get home to show Mammy.

* * *

We have stopped by our gate that doesn't shut. Kaylee's mammy says, 'You okay from here?'

'Yes, thank you. Is my label the right way round?'

Kaylee's mammy is turning my label. She's turning it round so Mammy can read the words. I'm looking over her shoulder. I can see the lady across the road. She's moving her curtains. I'm waving to her. I want her to see my shiny box and my sparkly label but she's not waving back. 'There you go,' Kaylee's mammy says. 'Can you squeeze through the gate?'

I'm nodding. 'Thank you. Bye bye.' I'm waving. Kaylee and her mammy are waving too. I'm squeezing through the gate and I'm squeezing down the side path. The lady next door's hedge is catching my shiny paper. I can hear my sides ripping a bit. I'm opening the back door and I'm squeezing inside.

I can see Mammy in the front room. She's on the settee with Brick. They are watching telly. I'm squeezing myself through the front room door. Mammy is looking up. She's seen me. 'Wha' the…' she says.

My shiny paper is stuck on the handle on the door. I'm trying to make it not stuck. I'm pulling it. Quite a big bit is ripping. I'm trying to smooth the ripped bit but it's hard to reach. It's hard to move your arms when you're a present.

I'm trying to smooth and smooth my shiny paper. I am going to stand by the telly and I'm trying to tap my label. I want Mammy to read the words that say 'To Mammy, Love from Tomos'. My fingers can nearly reach the label. I'm taking a big breath.

And now I'm singing my solo. I'm singing 'Away in a manger, no crib for a bed, the little Lord…' I'm singing it loud. I am trying to sing it louder than the song on the telly. But it's hard to sing it louder. I'm singing 'cattle are lowing, the baby…' all the way to the end.

I've finished my solo. Brick is turning the telly to another programme.

'This!' Mammy says. She's pointing to the telly. 'I wanna watch this.' Brick hasn't heard her. He's turning it to a different programme. Mammy is looking up at me. I'm trying to make my fingers very long. I'm pointing to my label again.

'I have come from the North Pole,' I say. I forgot to say it before my solo. 'This is my gift for you.'

I think Mammy's smiling a bit. 'Yeah good,' she says. 'Go to bed now.'

* * *

I am up in my high sleeper bed. I've been to the toilet one last time. Mammy has put my ladder on the floor. She's in the kitchen. She's with Brick. They're shouting. They're saying a lot of rude words. I am looking at my magazines. I'm trying to find some nice words. I'm looking at the

61

pictures. Miss says if you can't read a word the pictures might help you. The pictures are good but the words are hard.

I am listening now. Mammy and Brick aren't shouting anymore. I'm listening for the other sound. The sound I don't like. I'm listening for the click. It's a big click. A very very big click. I'm listening. And listening.

CLICK.

Mammy has closed the front door. She's gone out. I can hear her and Brick getting into the car. Brick has started the engine. It sounds like he's going for a race. I can hear him driving Mammy away. The racing sound is getting quieter. And quieter. I'm listening. And listening. It's gone. I wish I had Cwtchy. If I had Cwtchy I could cuddle him. And I could chew his purple ears. And I wouldn't feel all on my own. Up on my high sleeper bed. Until Mammy comes home.

I'm looking for Nanno's letter. It's under the pile of clothes on my bed. I've found it and I'm reading it again. And again and again. I like the P.S. It says *I love you. I love you. I love you.* That's what Nanno has written. I like that word. L. O. V. E. It's one of my favourite words. I'm reading the sentence again. *Lots of love, Nanno xxx P.S. I love you. I love you. I love you.* I like reading it over and over and over.

If I had some paper I would write *Dear Nanno, How are you? I am well. I sang my solo for Mammy. She said it was good. She saw my sparkly label too. My box is downstairs. It's in the front room. It's very hard to go upstairs when you are a present. It took me a long time to get to my bedroom and then I couldn't get the box off. I tried and tried but it was stuck and I had to*

62

go back downstairs and ask Mammy to help me. It took a long long time to go back downstairs. You can't see your feet when you are a present. Mammy was very cross because I was spoiling her programme. She pulled and pulled and some of my paper ripped. I don't want my paper to be ripped. And I don't want my box to be downstairs. I tried to bring it upstairs again but Mammy said no and she put her mug on it. A bit of tea went on my green paper. I don't want tea on my shiny paper. And I saw Dat at the Christmas concert. But I am not allowed to see Dat. And I waved to him and he waved to me. I am allowed to wave to him I think. Lots of love, Tomos xxx P.S. I miss Dat xxx And I miss you too xxx

Christmas Holidays

I am waiting for Kaylee and her Mammy. I've been waiting a long long time. I'm standing by the window in the front room. And I'm waiting for them to stop by the gate and wave. I'm waiting to walk to school with them. But I can't see them anywhere.

I'm looking for Nadia and Eddie and Lisa. They go past our house in the morning. Nadia goes past with an old man and a black dog. The black dog has three legs and it runs up and down the road. Up and down. Up and down. Eddie and Lisa go past with their mammies. Their mammies are always talking and talking and talking. Lisa holds her mammy's hand but Eddie runs away when his mammy calls him.

I can't see them today. I've been waiting a long long time but I can't see them. I can see a lady. She's got a big bag with wheels. She's shouting to a man in a garden. She's shouting, 'Hello, Gareth. Lovely frosty day, isn't it?'

I'm remembering a lady shouting at me and Dat when we used to walk to school. Not to the school I go to now. To the one I went to when I lived at Nanno and Dat's house. The shouty lady was Poor Sandra and she used to shout the word thief. Me and Dat didn't listen because Poor Sandra was ill and she couldn't help her shouting. That's what Dat said. But the lady outside now isn't Poor Sandra. Poor Sandra isn't the lady with the wheely bag.

I can see the lady that lives across the road too. She's moving her white curtains. I'm waving to her but she's not waving back.

I'm thinking and thinking about it being Monday. It's Monday today because yesterday the lady across the road had her blue coat on and the little van with windows came. It stopped outside her house and toot tooted and she came out of her house. And she had her black book under her arm. She got into the white van with the windows and then it went off. And it is always the day before Monday when the van full of ladies comes.

My Santa Sack is behind the big black chair. I can see a corner of it. And the box that Father Christmas left is on the floor. Mammy opened it on the day he brought it. She has eaten the cakes and the biscuits. And she's eaten the sweets that were in the big plastic tub. I've eaten some sweets too. I had a shiny gold penny sweet and a long thin toffee one. I've eaten the ones in brown paper too. They were the coffee ones. Mammy doesn't like coffee sweets. I think they are quite nice. They are nice if you try and taste the chocolate and you don't taste the coffee. I have eaten a cake too. It had brown icing all over it. On the box it had the word logs. But the cake wasn't made of wood like a log. It was nice like Nanno's cakes.

Mammy has come downstairs. 'Wha' you wearing tha' for?' she says.

'Wearing what?'

'Your school jumper.'

'For school.'

Mammy is shaking her head. 'Stupid kid. There's no school.' She's going into the kitchen.

I am going into the kitchen too. 'Where's it gone?'

'Wha'?'

'School,' I say. 'Where's it gone?' I don't want school to

be gone. If there's no school there's no Miss. Or dinosaur chickens and chips.

'It's Christmas,' Mammy says. 'It's 'olidays.' She's making a mug of tea and she's talking to herself. She's saying, 'Stupid kid.'

'So there's no school because it's Christmas.' I'm saying it carefully. I don't want her to say stupid kid again.

'Stupid kid,' she says. 'Course there's no school.' She's taking her mug of tea into the front room.

'Is it Christmas Day today?' I'm going into the front room too.

She's got the remote. She's looking for something to watch on telly. 'Wha' now?'

'Is it Christmas Day today?'

'No.' She's found a programme to watch. It has a lot of people shouting at each other on it.

'When is it Christmas Day?' I say.

'Why?'

'I can look in my Santa Sack when it's Christmas Day.'

'Jus' look in it now.'

'You can't open Christmas presents until Christmas Day,' I say.

'Go 'way.' She's putting her mug down on my box. Some tea is splashing onto the green paper. She's turning the telly up. The people shouting are very loud now. They're pointing to each other and their faces are red.

'Go up to yorr room,' Mammy says. 'And gimme some peace.'

I am going out of the door. 'Will you tell me, please?'

'Wha'?' She's looking cross now. I don't like making her look cross. But I want to know.

'When it's Christmas Day,' I say.

She's looking back at the people shouting on the telly. 'Yeah, I'll tell you. Now go away.'

* * *

I have stopped waiting for Kaylee and her mammy and I'm waiting for Christmas Day instead. I've brought the Santa Sack up to my bedroom. It's under my high sleeper bed. The sack has got something quite big in it. It's a bit heavy if I hold it with one hand. I saw a tiny bit of what's in it when I carried it into the house. I haven't peeped inside it again because that would spoil Christmas Day. I'm going to open it then. Christmas Day is taking a long time to come but Mammy's going to tell me when it's here.

I like Christmas. I like Kaylee's Christmas tree. I like squashing my face on my bedroom window so one of my eyes can see Kaylee's window down the road. And her Christmas tree.

Nanno and Dat have got a Christmas tree like that. Their tree is very tall. It has lots of lights on it. They are red and blue and green and yellow and it's got lots of decorations too. There are snowmen and Santas and candles and robins and there is a train decoration. Dat bought it specially for me. It is red and white and it's made of wood. I wish I could see their tree instead of Kaylee's when I squash my face on the window. I wish I could see Nanno and Dat's house again.

And my bedroom. And Nanno and Dat. I wish I wish I could.

* * *

I have been looking at my pile of train magazines. I've found some more letters. They are letters I wrote to Nanno at her and Dat's house. I'm reading one of them now. Dat helped me write it and it says *Dear Nanno, I am very well thank you. How are you? Yes I did like having Rhys round to play. He liked my train set. He liked the tea you made. Lots of love, Tomos xxx P.S. Thank you for mending Cwtchy's ear.* That is the letter I wrote. A long time ago.

I miss Cwtchy. I miss his purple fur and his chewy ears. I miss Rhys too. He was in the school near Nanno and Dat's house. The one I used to go to. Rhys is my friend there. Wes is my friend now. He's a good friend to have but I like Rhys more. Rhys doesn't run away from me. And he doesn't call me smelly.

I'm reading another letter Dat helped me to write. It says *Dear Nanno, Thank you for the book. Yes I do like the trains in it. It has good words too. Dat is helping me to read them. Lots of love, Tomos xxx P.S. I like the cake you made.*

I'm thinking of Nanno's cakes now. They are lovely. Sometimes they are chocolatey and sometimes they are strawberry jammy and sometimes they have white icing on them and sometimes they have cherries in them and sometimes they are lemony and I don't like lemons but Nanno's lemony cakes are lovely and I wish I had some lemony cake now and my train book.

And Cwtchy.
And Nanno.
And Dat.

* * *

I have been asking Mammy about Christmas Day for a long time. I am not allowed to ask her about it anymore. I'm hoping Mammy will remember to tell me when Christmas Day is here. I'm hoping and hoping but Mammy is not very good at remembering. She forgets things when she's watching telly. She forgets things after she's been out with Brick. I am hoping and hoping and hoping she'll remember to tell me. When Brick comes round I'll ask him about Christmas Day.

* * *

I am not allowed to ask Brick about Christmas Day. I'm not allowed to say the word Christmas. I cannot say 'Happy Christmas'. Or 'Shall we sing a Christmas song?' or 'Merry Christmas one and all'. It's hard not to say 'Christmas' when it's Christmas time.

And I am not allowed to say 'Day'.

* * *

Mammy has told me to open my Santa Sack. She said it doesn't matter if it's Christmas Day or not. She said I should just open it anyway. I don't want to open it until Christmas

72

Day so I said, 'I don't want to open it until...' And then I had to think for a long time because I'm not allowed to say 'Christmas Day'. I said, 'that special time' instead. Then Mammy told me to go to bed.

* * *

I am in my bedroom. I've been in my bedroom a long time. Mammy and Brick have gone out. And there isn't any food left in the kitchen. I think Mammy and Brick have gone to get chips. But they are taking a long time. My tummy is rumbly. I hope they'll bring some chips for me.

I'm trying to look into Kaylee's front room. I'm trying to see under her tree. Her house is a long way away from here. It's hard to see under her tree from my bedroom window. I'm looking to see if there are presents under it. If the presents have gone it is Christmas Day and Kaylee has opened them. That means I can open my Santa Sack from Father Christmas. I'm trying and trying to see. I'm pushing my cheek right against the window. The window's very cold. It's got sparkly bits on it. Sparkly frosty bits. I'm rubbing the frost with my sleeve. I can see the twinkly lights now. The lights on Kaylee's tree. They are very pretty and Christmassy. But I can't see if there are any presents under the tree.

Someone is near the pavement outside our house. It's the lady who lives in the house next door to us. The lady that gave me my high sleeper bed. She's very old and she has a climbing frame with wheels. She pushes it round in front of her. She's putting a black bag by her gate.

I'm running downstairs and I'm running out of the front door. I'm running to our hedge. The lady has turned round. She's pushing her climbing frame back up her path. She's pushing it slowly.

'Hello!' I am saying it through the hedge. I'm saying it where there's a big hole in the leaves.

She's still coming up her path. She's very near the hole in the leaves now.

'Hello!' I say again.

'Yessee *mawr*!' She's turned her head quite fast. 'Oh it's you, *bach*.' She's making a big cloud with her breath. 'You gave me a fright.'

'Happy Christmas,' I say. I'm not allowed to say 'Happy' or 'Christmas' but Mammy and Brick can't hear me. They went out a long time ago. 'Is it Christmas Day?' I'm not allowed to say 'Day' either.

The lady has stopped. She's looking at me through the hole in the hedge. 'What did you say, *cariad*?' She's got plastic things in her hair and she's got a hat on made out of a net.

'Is it Christmas Day today?'

'Oh gracious,' she says. She's rubbing her face. 'Christmas Day? Now let me think.' Her mouth makes a shape when she's thinking. It makes a small pinchy circle. 'What day is it today?' She's thinking again. I can tell by her mouth.

'Christmas Day?' I am trying to help her think because she's taking a long time.

'Oh no. No. No,' she says. 'Today is Monday.' She's still thinking. 'Christmas Day…' She's doing more thinking now.

'Is tomorrow?' I say.

74

She's looking at me through her glasses and her eyes are opening and closing a lot. 'No, no. Not tomorrow. I went to Moira's Friday. Clive's yesterday. So Thursday.' She's thinking again. 'Have I got that right?' She's looking at me.

I'm lifting up my shoulders. 'I don't know.'

'Yes, I have.' She's nodding a lot. 'I'm right. Christmas Day was last Thursday.'

'Last Thursday?'

'Yes,' she says. 'It'll be time to go back to school soon. Next Tuesday I think Moira said. That's when our Jason is starting back.' She's turning her climbing frame towards the hedge now. 'Did Father Christmas come to your house?'

'Yes.' I want to run back to my bedroom. I want to open my Santa Sack. I'm taking a step back.

'What did he bring you?' the lady says. 'Something nice, I expect.'

'Something in a Santa Sack.' I'm saying it fast and I'm taking another step back.

'Oh goodness. SomethinginaSantaSack. These new-fangled toys. I can't keep up with them.' She's putting her hand into her pocket. 'Here, for you. *Calennig* for a happy new year. It's a bit early, but it'll still bring you luck.' She's holding a silver coin. It's like the ones we have in school. The ones that have a number fifty on them. She's holding it through the hedge. 'Come on, take it. It's yours.'

I am stepping towards the hedge again. I'm taking the coin. It's not like the ones in school. They aren't heavy. 'Thank you.' I'm taking a step back again now. I want to know what's inside my Santa Sack.

'Wait a minute,' the lady says. 'I've got something else for you. Stay there.' She's going up her path. She's pushing her climbing frame and she's going very slowly.

I'm waiting and I am trying not to take another step back. I am waiting and waiting and waiting and waiting. And the path is making my toes very cold.

The lady next door is coming back. She's holding something. It's a long yellow triangle box. 'Here, lovely chocolate for you.' She's poking the box through the hole in the hedge. 'I won it at bingo.' She's shaking the box at me now. 'But I can't eat it, too hard for me. Too chunky. All those corners. You'll enjoy it, though. You've got your own teeth.'

I'm taking the box. It's quite heavy and there's something slip sliding about inside it. 'Thank you,' I say. 'Thank you very much.'

'Haven't you got nice manners?' The lady is smiling at me.

I am saying, 'Thank you' again. I'm taking a step backwards.

'That's what our Jason needs. Manners. I keep telling Moira.'

I am taking another step backwards.

'Well, I'll be off,' the lady says. 'It's cold out here.' She's turning her climbing frame. 'Nice to chat.'

I'm taking a lot of steps backwards. 'Merry Christmas,' I say. 'Merry Christmas, one and all!'

And I am running to the front door. I'm holding the box and the coin tight and I am closing the front door behind me. I'm running past the front room and up the stairs to my bedroom. I'm running and running and running and running. All the way to my Santa Sack.

* * *

I have been playing with my truck for a long time. The truck that was in the Santa Sack. It's a tipper truck. It has a tippy bit on the back and it is red with black wheels. The black wheels have shiny silver bits in the middle. On the box it says SUPER TRUCK and it is a super truck. It is the best truck I have ever seen. The best one that isn't real. I'm pushing it in its box because I can't get it out. The wheels are stuck tight to the cardboard. I'm pushing my truck in the box round and round my bedroom and I'm pushing it under my train table and on my train table and up my ladder and over my bed and down my ladder and over the floor.

'Why you still up?'

Mammy is by my door. I didn't hear her come in.

'Look,' I say. 'This was in my Santa Sack.'

Mammy is looking a bit. 'Yeah good.' She's holding her shoes. Her toes are very dirty.

'Mammy can you help me? I can't get my truck out of—'

'Ge' to bed,' she says.

I can hear Brick downstairs in the kitchen. He's opening the drawers. 'All the forks are dirty.' He's shouting it from the kitchen. They've brought a takeaway home with them. I can smell it. It smells like the silver trays on the kitchen

77

floor. The ones that have yellow and orange puddles in them.

My tummy is making a big rumbly noise. 'Did you get chips?'

'No,' Mammy says. 'I'll be there now!' She's shouting that to Brick.

I'm standing up. I'm going to my ladder. 'My truck is stuck in the box.'

'Ge' to bed,' she says. 'I'm starvin'.'

I'm at the bottom of my ladder and I'm holding my truck so Mammy can see. 'It's these.' I am pointing to the back of the box. 'I can't get them off.'

'Ge' to bed,' she says. 'Now.'

I am going up my ladder fast. I'm taking my Super Truck with me. Mammy is putting my light out. She's closing my door.

I am looking for the box the lady next door gave me. It's under the clothes on my bed. I have had two bits of the chocolate inside it already. They were big chocolate triangles and they were lovely. I am breaking off another triangle. It is quite hard to break. I'm putting it in my mouth. It's very chocolatey. I'm putting my truck next to me in bed and I am finding the silver coin the lady next door gave me. It's under my pile of clothes on the bed. I'm putting the coin in the back of my truck. It's special cargo. I like the word cargo. It's one of Dat's special words. Cargo. I'm putting the silver paper from the chocolate into the tipper bit of my truck too.

I am pulling my pile of clothes all round me. The

chocolate is getting soft in my mouth. Mammy is home and I am very sleepy and I have a lovely new red truck.

* * *

I am in the front room. I have been watching telly with Mammy. We are on the settee. We've been watching *Murder, She Wrote*. Mammy is starting to wake up.

'It was the lady,' I say. 'The one with the hat.'

'You wharr?' Mammy is having a big yawn. She's stretching her arms now.

'The lady put something in the man's drink. Jessica said.'

Brick has come down from the bathroom. He's picking me up and putting me on the floor. He's sitting down next to Mammy. 'When's the kid back in school?' he says.

I'm getting my truck. It's behind the chair.

'Don' know,' Mammy says.

'Tuesday,' I say. 'The lady next door told me.' I'm pushing my truck round the carpet. I'm picking up all the little bits of wallpaper and I'm putting them in the tipper part. 'When is it Tuesday?'

Mammy and Brick haven't heard me. I'm pushing my truck over to the settee. I am pushing it up onto my green box that I was a present in. I'm pushing it past my shiny label. I am reading the words 'To Mammy, Love from Tomos' and I'm pushing it to the top of my box. I'm pushing it round the tins Mammy and Brick have left on top of it.

There's a lot of knocking on the front door. I'm running behind the big black chair. I'm taking my truck with me.

There's more knocking. I am peeping out with one eye. Brick is looking out of the window.

'Saint!' Brick is shouting it. He's opening the front door. A man is coming in. He's got a bag on his back. He's holding a lot of tins. He has some in one hand. He has some in his other hand. He's holding them up. He's waving them. He's doing a sort of dance.

'Saint, man,' Brick says. He's doing a sort of dance too. 'Look, Ree. Saint's yerr!'

I'm watching Mammy with my one eye. She's looking at the man called Saint. 'I can see that.' She's not smiling. She says. 'Righ' Dewi?' She's watching telly again now.

'Happy new year to you, too, Ree,' Saint says. He's giving the tins to Brick.

'Wha's all this?'

'We're celebrating,' Saint says. 'I made it big.' He's laughing. He's taking a tin from Brick and he's opening it. Brick's laughing now. He's putting the tins down in a pile on the floor. He's opening one too. They're banging their tins together. Yellow stuff is sloshing out. They're laughing and laughing. Mammy is turning up the telly.

'Tell me 'bout it, man,' Brick says.

'Okay,' Saint says. 'But I'm starving. Make me a bacon butty, Ree.' He's putting his bag on the carpet and he's sitting down next to Mammy.

'No bread. No bacon,' she says. She's still watching telly.

Saint is getting something out of his pocket. It is a little plastic bag. It's got a bit of white stuff in it. He's waving the bag at Mammy. She's stopped watching telly. She's watching the bag instead. She's lifting up her hand. Saint is moving the bag fast. He's putting it back in his pocket.

'See, Ree. You be nice to me and I'll be nice to you.' He's getting something else out of his pocket. It's a big lump of money. He's opening it up. He's giving Mammy some purple money. 'Nip to Spar, *cariad*. Bread and bacon. Get brown sauce too. And rum and Coke for yourself. You can keep the change. Then I'll give you what you really want.' He's smiling at Mammy.

Mammy's looking at Saint. She's looking at the money. She's taking it fast. She's putting her boots on and she's tucking her pyjamas into them. She's putting on Brick's jumper.

'Ge' me some vodka,' Brick says. 'And some fags.'

'No chance,' Mammy says. She's going out of the door.

I'm running out from behind the chair. 'Get me some…' I say. But I don't know what I want her to get me. Mammy has shut the door. I'm too late.

'Is that Ree's kid?' Saint says. He's looking and looking at me.

Brick is nodding.

'He's a funny little thing, in't he?' Saint says. 'Got brown eyes like his father.'

'Who's tha' then?' Brick says. He's looking at me too now.

Saint's laughing. 'Who do you know with eyes like that, man?'

'Don' know,' Brick says. 'Loads o' people.'

Saint's calling me with his hand. '*Dere 'ma, bach.*' He's still looking and looking at me. I'm running back behind the chair. I'm running fast. I am running back to my truck. Saint is laughing a lot now. 'Hasn't Ree told you who his father is?'

'Yeah,' Brick says. 'Some boy back in 'er foster place. Buggered off when she got pregnant.'

'Some boy?' Saint's laughing.

'Yeah,' Brick says. 'Norr really interested anyway.'

Saint's still laughing. I'm peeping out from behind the chair. 'You would be if you knew.' He's taking a big drink from his tin.

'So tell me wha's been 'appening, man,' Brick says. 'Where you been?'

'Scotland,' Saint says. 'Got a contact in Glasgow now. Can't believe my luck. There's loads of stuff there, just waiting to be picked up. You should try it.' Saint is tipping his tin right up. He's squashing it in his hand and he's throwing it onto the carpet. Brick is doing the same. They're opening more tins.

'Hell of a long way to go,' Brick says. He's taking a drink from his tin.

'No, I mean it,' Saint says. 'It got a bit dodgy when I was there. I had to come home fast, like. Can't go back myself for a while. But I can give you my contact, cut you in. You should do it.' He's taking something out of his bag. 'Do me a favour, Brick.' He's holding up a block. It's got plastic all round it. Like the plastic Nanno uses when she puts things in the fridge. 'Keep this for me, just for a while, 'til things calm down a bit.' He's giving the block to Brick. 'And you'll get paid.' He's laughing. 'So long as you don't let Ree find it.'

Brick is holding the block. He's looking and looking at it. He's turning it round and round. He's saying a rude word. He's saying it very quietly. 'Saint, man, is this the stuff from Glasgow?'

'Only some of it,' Saint says. 'See what I mean? I can give you the contacts. You can make the money if you want, and cut me in.' He's tapping the block. 'You keep that safe for me for a bit, and I'll see what I can do. But find somewhere to hide it before Ree comes back.'

'I gorr a place I 'ide stuff,' Brick says. 'Righ' under her nose.' He's laughing.

'That's good,' Saint says. He's laughing too. 'Cos if she does find it. Or if you lose it or someone nicks it. Or if you decide to sell it to those…' He's saying a lot of rude words '… suppliers of yours, I'll break your legs.' He's smiling and smiling at Brick. 'Or worse.'

Brick is holding up his hands. 'Saint, you know me. You can trust me. I swear.'

'Course I can,' Saint says. He's laughing again. 'Only kidding.' He's hitting Brick's tummy a bit. Tap tap tap. 'Better go hide it quick 'fore she comes back.'

Brick is taking the block and he's going out of the front room. He's running up the stairs.

I'm peeping out from behind the chair.

Saint is looking at me. 'Hello, little Fly.' He is saying it quietly. He's smiling. 'Come on out. Let's see you properly.'

I am not going out. I'm not looking at him anymore. I'm playing with my truck.

Brick is running back downstairs. 'She'll never find it

there. She don' know you can pull up the floorboard by the window in 'er bedroom.'

'So what do you think, Brick?' Saint says. 'You interested in doing a job for me? It won't be for a few months. Needs to calm down a bit first.'

'Yeah,' Brick says. He's nodding his head. 'But I'd have to be careful, like, cos of Fly. He won' like me getting my stuff from someone else.'

'That English tosser don't need to know,' Saint says. 'And it'd be good money for you.'

'Yeah,' Brick says. 'Yeah, why not? I could do with the money.'

Saint's laughing. 'You could always do with the money, Brick.' He's squashing his tin and he's laughing again. 'You could always do with the money.'

* * *

Saint is talking and talking. Brick is saying, 'Yeah, I could. Yeah, yeah' all the time. They're drinking lots and lots of the tins.

Mammy's coming in and she's got a carrier bag.

''bout time,' Brick says.

I'm coming out from behind the chair. I'm going to see what's in the bag. Mammy's pushing me away and she's going into the kitchen.

'I'll have my bacon crispy,' Saint says. He's shouting it to Mammy in the kitchen. 'And loads of brown sauce.'

'An' me,' Brick's shouting.

'And me,' I say.

I'm watching Mammy. She's taking things out of the bag. She's got bread and bacon and some bottles. She's tipping the bacon into the frying pan. It's making a lot of noise. It's making a lovely smell too. I am smelling and smelling it. It's like the smell in Nanno and Dat's kitchen sometimes. I am dancing to the smell of the bacon.

'Ou' the way,' Mammy says. She's pushing me away from the cooker. 'Stupid kid.'

I'm going to the other side of the kitchen but I'm still dancing. The smell is making my tummy hungry and it's making my tongue lick my lips. Mammy's wiping three plates with the sleeve on her pyjamas. She's putting bread onto the plates. She's putting bacon on the bread now and she's putting more bread on top. My tummy is making a loud noise.

'Brown sauce,' I say.

Mammy is looking at me. 'Wha'?'

'We want brown sauce, please.'

Mammy's putting brown sauce in the sandwiches. She's picking up the plates. She has one in one hand and she has two in the other hand. She's going into the front room. I am going too and I'm sitting down fast fast on the floor and I'm holding up my hands and I'm waiting for my plate.

She's giving a plate to Saint and she's giving a plate to Brick. I'm waiting for my plate. She's sitting down and she's putting the last plate on her lap. It's not a plate for me. It's a plate for her.

Mammy is taking a bite of her sandwich. It's a big bite. Brick and Saint are taking bites of their sandwiches too.

'Mammy,' I say. 'Have I got a sandwich?'

Saint is looking at me. 'Didn't you make one for the kid?' He's saying it through the sandwich in his mouth.

'He's 'ad 'is dinner,' Mammy says. She's taking another big bite.

I am thinking about the dinner I had. I am thinking and thinking. I think it was a blue packet of crisps.

'Make him one,' Saint says. 'He looks half starved. Are you hungry, *bach*?'

I'm nodding. I am looking at the sandwich on his plate. It looks very yummy. My tummy is making loud noises.

'I used all the bacon,' Mammy says. She's picking up a bottle and she's tipping something into her mug.

'Give him some bread then, and some sauce,' Saint says. 'And some of your Coke.'

'In a minute.' She's finishing her sandwich.

'*Duw*, you're a heartless cow, mind Ree,' Saint says. He's looking at me now. '*Dere, bach*. Come to Dewi.' He's calling me with his hand.

I'm going over to him slowly. He's pulling a bit of bread off his sandwich and he's giving it to me. I'm putting it in my mouth. I can taste a bit of the brown sauce on the bread. And a bit of the bacon. It's a lovely taste. My mouth is all watery. Saint's picking up a mug. He's picking it up off the floor. He's tipping some cola into it and he's holding it out to me.

'There,' he says. 'Dewi will look after you, see?'

I'm taking the mug but I'm not drinking the cola.

'The kid's got brown eyes like his father.' Saint's saying it to Mammy.

'How would you know?' Her face is very cross. 'You never even seen 'is father.'

'Course I have,' Saint says. He's laughing. 'Everyone knows who his father is.'

I'm holding the mug but I'm not drinking the cola. I'm not drinking it yet. I am trying to keep the bacon taste. I am trying to keep it in my mouth for a long time.

'Shurr up, Dewi,' she says. 'You're talking crap as usual.' She's finding another programme to watch on the telly.

'Don't you want your drink?' Saint says. He's looking at me again now. 'Don't you like Coke? You're not like your mother then. She loves her coke.' He's laughing and his laugh is very loud.

Brick's laughing too. 'Good one, Saint.'

'Ha blurry ha,' Mammy says. 'Tha' reminds me.' She's holding out her hand to Saint.

Saint is getting something out of his pocket. It's the little bag with a bit of white stuff in it. He's throwing it at Mammy. 'Enjoy,' he says. 'There's plenty more where that came from. At a price.'

Mammy's taking the bag and she's getting up. She's going to the door.

Saint's shouting after her. 'I've just been telling Brick – loads in Scotland. Could make you both a tidy bit. You could do with it, looking at the state of this place.'

Mammy's turning round. She's holding up her finger and she's showing it to Saint. She says, 'You're full of sh—' She's banged the door. I can hear her going upstairs.

Saint is shouting after her. 'That's it, be a right cow now

you've had what you want.' He's looking at me again. 'Stick to the Coke that comes in bottles, *bach*,' he says. 'Then you won't turn out like your mother.'

* * *

Brick and Saint are watching telly. They are watching men fighting. They're shouting a lot and standing up and waving their arms. They're saying lots of rude words. Mammy's sitting on the settee. She's nearly asleep. I am behind the chair and I'm playing with my truck.

Saint is putting his head round the chair. He's saying something to me. I'm looking up. 'I said, why are you behind the chair?' I'm lifting my shoulders. 'Come out,' he says. 'Come and have a drop more of this.' He's showing me the bottle of cola and he's smiling at me. I think he's friendly after all.

I'm coming out from behind the chair. I'm coming out with my truck.

He's tipping some cola into a mug and he's giving it to me. 'Nice truck. Did Siôn Corn bring you that?' I am nodding. I'm drinking all the cola. 'When're you going back to school?'

'On Tuesday,' I say. 'The lady next door told me.' I'm putting down the mug and I'm playing with my truck again. I'm pushing it on the floor. 'When's Tuesday?'

Saint's looking at me and my truck. 'Why's he playing with it like that?' He's saying it to Brick.

'Like what?' Brick says. He's opening another tin.

Saint is still looking at me. 'Like that. With it in the box.'

I have stopped pushing my truck now. I'm lifting it up for Saint to see. 'I can't get it out. I need something from Dat's tool box to take these out.' I'm showing Saint the back of the box. I'm pointing to the two plastic bits. They are black and they have silver circles in them. The silver circles have criss-crosses in the middle.

'A Phillips screwdriver,' Saint says.

'Yes!' I say. 'Like Dat's got in his shed.' I'm tapping Mammy's knee. I am tapping it a bit. 'Mammy, can we borrow Dat's screwdriver? I like playing with my truck in the box but it would be better out of the box and I could make the wheels go round on the floor and I could tip the tippy bit all the way up and I could make the things fall out. Can we borrow his screwdriver? Can we? Can we?'

'Shush,' Mammy says.

'*Duw*, Brick man, can't you help the kid get it out of the box?' Saint says. Brick is looking at my truck. Saint's getting up. He says, 'Need a dump.'

'Bog's top of the stairs,' Brick says.

Saint is going out to the hall. Brick's holding out his hand and he's taking my truck. He's looking at the back of the box.

'Don' need a screwdriver,' he says.

He's taking his car keys out of his pocket. He's pushing one key into a silver bit. He's pushing and pushing and turning and turning. The key is slipping. It's making holes in the box. I don't want holes in the box.

'Thank you, Brick. I don't mind playing with it in the

box.' I'm trying to take the box away from him. I'm trying but he is holding on to it. He's holding on tight.

'Blurry thing,' he says. He's made a lot of holes in the box.

Mammy has woken up a bit more. 'Give it yerr.' She's taking the box off Brick and she's pulling at it. She's ripping its sides and she's ripping its back.

'It's okay, Mammy,' I say. 'I like it in the box.'

I am trying to take it off her. But she keeps moving it away from me. The box is messy now. Bits of it are all over the settee. And all over the carpet. But the truck still won't come out.

'Please,' I say. 'I like it in the box.'

Mammy's pulling at the plastic bits. She's pulling at the bits keeping the truck in. She's pulling and pulling.

'Please,' I say.

She's getting something out of her boot. Something silver and shiny. She's pushing a button on it. It's opening up quick quick. It's a little knife. She's putting her knife under the plastic bits. And she's trying to cut them.

'Please, Mammy.' I'm holding the box. I'm trying to pull it away from her. She's cutting and cutting and I'm pulling and pulling. The knife is slipping on the plastic.

'Ow!' I say. I'm moving my hand fast and I'm putting my finger in my mouth. There's a funny taste. I think it's blood.

'Wha'?' Mammy says. I'm showing her my finger. She's looking at the cut. 'Tha's nothin',' she says. She's closing the knife. She's putting it back in her boot. Back in the little pocket on the side of it. And she's throwing my truck. She's throwing it over my head to Brick. He's pulling at the plastic

90

bits now. He's pulling and pulling and pulling and pulling. The plastic bits won't come off.

I'm looking at my finger and the little cut. A bit of blood is coming out of it. I'm looking at my truck again. 'It's okay,' I say. I am starting to feel very sleepy. 'I like it in the box. Please, Brick, please can I have it back?'

He hasn't heard me. He's not giving it back. He's pulling at the truck now. He's trying to pull it out of the box. He's pulling and pulling and pulling and pulling.

'Please,' I say. 'Please, Brick.'

I want to grab my truck. I want to run upstairs with it. I want to hide it in my bedroom. I want to hide it from Mammy and Brick.

But I'm not grabbing it. I'm not running away. I'm not hiding it. I am sitting on the floor. And I am putting my hands over my eyes.

There's a cracky sound. I forgot to hide my ears.

''bout time,' Brick says. 'There you go.'

Something has knocked my knee. I am opening my fingers. I'm peeping through them at the floor. I can see my truck. It's on its side. It's not in the box anymore. I am putting my hand out. I'm picking up my truck. I can see the box. It's all ripped. The words SUPER and TRUCK are in little bits. All over the carpet. I can see two black wheels with two shiny middles. They are still stuck to a bit of the box.

I'm grabbing my truck. The other wheels are falling off it. I'm grabbing them. I'm grabbing them off the floor. I'm grabbing the bit of box too. The bit of box with the two wheels stuck to it. I'm running out of the front room. I'm running up the stairs. And my cheeks are all wet.

Saint is coming out of the bathroom. 'What's wrong, *bach*?'

I am trying to say, 'My truck is broken.' I'm trying. But the words are stuck. They are stuck tight like the wheels. I'm running into my bedroom and I'm closing the door.

'Tuesday's the day after tomorrow.' Saint is saying it through the door. 'That's when school starts again.'

I am standing in my bedroom. I'm holding my truck and I'm listening. Saint isn't talking now. I can only hear his breaths through the door. I am listening and listening.

'Okay?' He's saying it quietly. He's saying it on the other side of the door. 'Day after tomorrow. Two more sleeps.'

'Okay.' My okay is all wobbly. 'Thank you, Saint.'

'*Croeso, bach*,' he says. His voice is very quiet through the door. 'You're welcome.'

Back to School

I am waiting for Kaylee and her mammy. I'm watching for them through the window. It's hard to watch for them because of the rain. But it's not very dark outside now. I can see the lady across the road moving her white curtains. I'm waving to her but she's not waving back.

I've parked my truck under the pile of clothes. I've put my coin in the tipper bit with the bit of box and the wheels. I've put Nanno's letter in it too. If I had Cwtchy he could sit in the tipper bit. He could sit on top of my coin and my letter and the wheels. He would be a bit squashed but he wouldn't mind. He could look after my truck and my coin and my letter. He would keep them safe when I'm in school.

A big pink umbrella has stopped by our gate and I can see Kaylee's mammy's face under it and I am running out of the front door and I'm closing it behind me and I'm running down the path. It's nice to see Kaylee and her mammy again.

'Is it Tuesday today?' I say.

'Yes,' Kaylee says. She's smiling at me. She's got a small umbrella. It's pink like her mammy's.

Kaylee's mammy isn't smiling. She's looking and looking at me. 'Have you got a coat?' she says.

I'm thinking. 'Yes, but I haven't got it here. It's at Nanno and Dat's house.'

'Well, come under my umbrella then,' she says, 'or you'll get soaked.'

I'm walking under Kaylee's mammy's umbrella. My jumper is only getting a little bit wet.

'Have you had some breakfast?' she says. I'm shaking my head. She's putting her hand in her pocket. 'Here.' She's giving me a little bag. There are three sweets in it. They are toffees. I like toffees. Nanno likes toffees too.

'Can I have one?' Kaylee says.

'No,' her mammy says. 'You had a big breakfast this morning.'

I'm chewing one of the toffees. It's yummy and sweet. My tummy is making lots of rumbly noises.

'I like your Christmas tree,' I say.

'We've got to take it down,' Kaylee says, 'in a couple of days.'

I'm sad about that. I like looking at it from my window and I like the twinkly lights. 'Were there presents under it? I couldn't see from my window.'

'Yes,' Kaylee says. 'This umbrella and a scooter and—'

'We've got some chocolate for you, Tomos,' her mammy says.

'Have we?' Kaylee says. She's walking backwards in front of us. She's making her new umbrella spin round and round. All the rain is flying off it.

'I'll bring it at home time,' Kaylee's mammy says.

'Thank you. I like chocolate.'

We've got to school. Kaylee's mammy's giving her a kiss.

'Thank you for letting me walk under your umbrella,' I say. 'I'm only a little bit wet.'

Kaylee's mammy is rubbing her hand on my arm. 'See you both later,' she says. 'And I'll have that chocolate for you, Tomos.' She's waving.

And Kaylee and me are running to our classroom and we're running and running because we're going to see Miss.

* * *

It's morning playtime. It has stopped raining. Miss says we can go outside but we must not step in the puddles. And we must all put on our coats.

'Tomos, wait a minute.' Miss is standing by the door to our classroom. 'Before you go out to play, could you help me with something?'

She's getting a plastic box out of her bag. She's putting it on her desk. 'My husband made some sandwiches for me today, and I can't eat them all.'

The other children have gone now. She's opening the box. There's an eggy smell. There are a lot of sandwiches in the box and a yogurt and a chocolate biscuit. My tummy is making a rumbly noise.

'Do you like egg sandwiches?'

I am nodding. I like egg sandwiches a lot. Nanno used to make them for tea on Sundays with crisps and cold rice pudding for afters.

'Do you think you can help me eat them?' I am nodding again. Miss is giving me the plastic box. 'You can eat everything if you want,' she says. 'It's a long time 'til dinner. You'll be hungry again by then.' She's pulling out one of the big cushions. 'You can eat them there.'

We are not allowed to eat in class. Sir told us in a long assembly. Eating in class makes crumbs. Rats like crumbs. We don't want rats eating our crumbs in our classrooms. 'What about the rats?'

'Don't worry.' Miss is smiling. 'I'll clear up afterwards.'

I'm sitting down on the cushion and I'm eating the sandwiches. I'm eating them all and I'm eating them fast. I'm opening the chocolate biscuit and I'm putting it near my mouth. I am looking at the plastic box. It's nearly empty. I'm putting the biscuit back in the box. 'Miss,' I say. 'What are you having for dinner?'

Miss is looking up. She's tapping her pen on her chin. 'Did you say something, Tomos?'

'I've eaten all the sandwiches. Shall I save the biscuit for you?'

Miss is smiling. 'It's okay, Tomos. I'll get some dinner from the canteen. But thank you for asking. You go ahead and eat everything.'

'Thank you, Miss.' I am picking up the biscuit again and I'm taking a big bite. I'm opening the yogurt. Miss's husband has put a little spoon in the box. I'm eating the yogurt with the little spoon. 'Oh,' I say. 'This yogurt is rice pudding.'

Miss has stopped marking our work. She's looking up. 'Don't you like it?'

'Oh yes. I love rice pudding. I like it cold like this best of all.'

Seren is coming into class. She's looking at me. She's seeing me on the cushion and she's seeing me eating the rice pudding. 'Eddie has fallen in a puddle, Mrs Davies.' She's talking to Miss but her eyes are looking at me. 'His trousers are all wet.'

Miss is looking up. She's pushing her brown hair behind her ear. 'Poor Eddie. Go and tell the teacher on playground duty, Seren.'

'It's Mrs Pugh.' Seren is still looking at me eating the rice pudding.

'Oh.' Miss is standing up. 'You'd better send Eddie in to me then. I'll find him some dry clothes.' Seren is running off and Miss is looking at me now. 'Wait here until I come back, Tomos. I'll just be a minute.'

'Okay,' I say. I have nearly finished the rice pudding. I'm getting all the bits from the sides of the pot. Eddie is coming into class. He has big wet splodges on his trousers.

Miss has come back. 'I found these in lost property.' She's holding up some trousers. 'Try them on, Eddie.' Eddie's taking off his wet trousers. 'And I wondered if these might fit you, Tomos.' Miss is holding up some black trousers. They're like the ones I'm wearing. 'Your trousers are a bit wet too, after the rain this morning.'

I am feeling my trousers. 'I think they're dry now.'

'Well, try these on anyway.'

I'm taking off my trousers. Eddie's putting on his dry trousers and I am putting on mine. My new trousers feel snuggly.

'And I found this in lost property too.' Miss is holding a blue coat. She's showing it to me.

'It's not my coat,' I say. 'I didn't lose my coat at school. My coat's at Nanno and Dat's.'

'It doesn't matter. You can borrow it. It'll keep you warm at playtimes.' She's helping me to put my arms into it. It's snuggly like the trousers. 'Right,' Miss says. 'You can both go out to play. There's five minutes left before the bell goes.'

I'm giving Miss the plastic box back. 'I think I made some crumbs for the rats.'

'Don't worry,' she says. 'I'll take care of them.'

I am wondering about Miss taking care of the rats. I am wondering if Sir knows Miss takes care of them. Sir doesn't want rats in his school. He told us in a long assembly.

Miss is smiling at us. 'Go on, or the bell will ring soon.'

Eddie and I are going outside. It's still not raining.

'Wotcha,' a big voice shouts. It's Wes's voice. He has shouted it in my ear. He has run up behind me. He's holding my shoulders. 'Where you been?' he says.

'Helping Miss.'

He's making little splashes in the puddles with his shoe. 'For Christmas I got ten Xbox games. And a tablet and an iPhone with a contract. And loads of other stuff. What did you get?'

I'm not putting my shoes in the puddle. Miss said we must keep our shoes dry. 'A Super Truck.'

'Why's it called that?'

'Because it's a super truck.'

'How big is it?'

I am thinking. I'm making a shape with my hands.

'That's small,' he says.

'It's not small.' I'm looking round for something that is as big as my truck. 'It's that big.' I'm pointing to the rubbish bin.

'That's massive,' Wes says.

I am wondering if my truck is as big as the rubbish bin. 'I think it's a bit smaller than that,' I say.

The bell is ringing. Everyone is running up to Mrs Pugh Year Two. She's standing at the top of the playground.

'Bring it tomorrow,' Wes says. 'So I can see.'

We are running to Mrs Pugh Year Two. I am not running in the puddles. Wes is making big splashes. 'I don't think we're allowed,' I say. 'Sir says toys are only for Toy Day.'

'I want to see it,' Wes says. 'Bring it.' He's holding my shoulders again. His fingers are catching my hair.

'Okay,' I say. 'I will then.'

We've got to the top of the playground now. Wes is letting go of my shoulders. We're standing with our classes.

'I'll bring my Super Truck tomorrow.' I'm shouting it a bit. I am shouting it over to Wes. 'I'll bring it in so you can see it.'

Seren is telling me to be quiet. She's holding her finger in front of her mouth.

'Okay, thicko.' Wes is shouting it. 'It's a deal.'

'Okay, Wes,' I say. I'm being quieter now. Everyone else is being quiet too. 'It's a deal.'

* * *

I am waiting for Kaylee and her mammy. I've been waiting a long time. It's raining again today like it was yesterday. I'm waiting for the pink umbrellas to stop by the gate and I'm waiting and waiting. I'm holding my truck with one hand and I'm waving with the other hand. I'm waving to the lady across the road because she's moving her white curtains. And I'm showing her my truck. But she's not waving back. And I am waiting and waiting and my truck is getting very heavy.

They are here. The pink umbrellas have stopped. Kaylee

and her mammy are waiting for me by the gate and I'm running out of the front door. I'm closing it tight behind me and I'm running down the path. I'm being careful because I don't want to slip. I don't want to drop my truck.

'What's that?' Kaylee says. Her and her mammy are looking at me from under their umbrellas.

'It's my Super Truck. Father Christmas brought it for me.'

It's raining a lot. Kaylee's mammy has pulled me under her umbrella and Kaylee has come up close. The umbrellas are making a pink tent over us. Kaylee and her mammy are looking at my truck.

'Why's it like that?' Kaylee says.

'Like what?' I say.

We are not walking. We are just standing by the gate and looking at my truck.

'Like that,' Kaylee says. 'With the wheels in the back of it.'

They're looking at the bit of box with the wheels stuck to it. They're looking at the other wheels too. The two wheels that fell off. They're all in the tippy bit. I have taken Nanno's letter out of it and I've taken my coin out too. I don't want to lose them in school. My fifty pence might get mixed up with the plastic ones. Someone might rip up Nanno's letter and put it in the bin. I don't want Nanno's letter to go in the bin. And I don't want my coin to get lost. I've left them under Mammy's pink tee shirt on my bed.

'Brick broke the wheels,' I say, 'when he was getting my truck out of the box. Because we didn't have a screwdriver.'

'Are you taking it to school?' Kaylee says.

'Yes. Wes wants to see it.'

'You're not allowed,' Kaylee says.

'I know,' I say.

Kaylee's mammy is putting her hand on my arm. She's squeezing it a bit. 'Take your truck back home,' she says. 'You don't want Mr Griffiths telling you off.'

She's right. I don't want Sir to tell me off. 'Will you wait for me?'

'Yeah, don't worry,' Kaylee's mammy says. 'Be quick, though.'

I am running up the path. I'm going round the back. Mammy has forgotten to lock the door again and I'm running inside. I'm running up the stairs. I'm trying to be quick and I'm trying to be quiet. I don't want to wake Mammy. I'm going up my ladder and I'm finding my coin and my letter. I'm putting them in the tippy bit with the wheels and I'm parking my truck under my pile of clothes. I'm going back down my ladder and I'm going back down the stairs and I'm going out of the front door. I am closing it tight behind me and I'm running down the path.

Kaylee and her mammy are still waiting for me. Kaylee's mammy is looking up at our house. Her face is cross. I think she's cross because of the rain. She's looking at the windows upstairs. I think she might have seen Mammy. I'm looking at the windows too. I want to see Mammy because I want to wave goodbye to her. But I can't see her. I can't see her through any of the windows.

Kaylee's mammy's looking at me now. Her face isn't cross anymore. 'Okay?' she says.

'Yes, thank you,' I say. 'Did you see Mammy?'

'Where?' Kaylee's mammy is looking at our house again.

'At the window just now.'

'No. Is she up?'

'I don't think so,' I say.

Kaylee's mammy is putting her arm round my shoulders. 'We better get a move on,' she says. 'Or we'll be late.' She's pulling me tight to her under the pink umbrella. 'Did you like the chocolate?' she says.

I'm remembering the bar of chocolate she gave me yesterday after school. It's very big. It's too big to fit in the tippy bit of my truck. 'Oh yes, thank you. It's very nice.' It's raining a lot now.

'Have you eaten it all?'

'Oh no,' I say. 'Only a little bit. I'm keeping it safe with my truck and my letter and my coin.' I'm still under her umbrella and her arm is still round me. She's holding me tight.

'Here you go,' she says. She's giving me three biscuits. They have a creamy bit in the middle.

'Thank you,' I say. 'Thank you very much.' I am eating the biscuits fast.

Kaylee's mammy is saying something. She's saying it very quietly. And she's holding me tight tight. It's raining and raining and raining and raining like it was yesterday. But I'm not getting wet.

I'm not getting wet at all today.

* * *

It's morning playtime but we're not allowed to play outside because it's still raining. We have got to stay in class. Miss has given us scrap paper and pencils and crayons. We are allowed to draw. We're allowed to write too.

I'm drawing round the sides of my scrap paper. I'm drawing my truck. I'm drawing it like it was in the box. With black wheels. I'm trying to give the wheels shiny middles. It's hard to make them look shiny. I'm drawing my coin now and the bar of chocolate the lady next door gave me and the bar of chocolate Kaylee's mammy gave me. I am not drawing in the middle of the paper. I'm leaving a big space for my writing.

I've finished my drawings and I'm writing now. I'm writing *Dear Nanno, How are you? I am well. Here are my things. My Super Truck is the best thing. It was in my Santa Sack.* It's taking me a long time to write. Miss is telling us to tidy up. I'm writing *Lots of love from Tomos.* She's asking Seren and Eddie to collect the crayons and the pencils. I haven't written my P.S. yet. I am trying to write it fast. I'm writing *P.S. Did you have* but Seren is taking my pencil.

'Can I finish my sentence, please?'

'No,' Seren says. 'It's time to tidy up.'

'I've only got…' I am counting the words. Seren is going away with my pencil. 'Five words left,' I say. I'm running after Seren and I'm pulling her jumper. I'm trying to make her turn round.

'Don't!' Seren's saying it loud.

Miss is looking up. 'What's wrong, Seren?'

'Tomos pulled my jumper, Miss.'

'Did you, Tomos?' I am nodding. 'Why?' Miss says. 'Is something wrong?' I'm nodding again. 'What's wrong, Tomos?'

'I need to do five words and Seren's taken my pencil.' I'm holding up my letter.

'Bring it over here,' Miss says. 'You can finish it on my desk.'

I am taking my letter over to Miss's desk. She's giving me a pencil and I'm finishing my P.S. I'm writing *a Santa Sack in*. I have stopped. 'How do you write Heaven, Miss?'

'Heaven?' Her eyebrows are lifting up. 'Like this.' She's writing it on a bit of paper.

I am copying her word. *Heaven*. Miss is watching me. She's pointing to my sentence. 'And that's a question, isn't it, Tomos? So you put one of these at the end.' She's drawing something.

'That's a question mark,' I say. I'm putting one at the end of my sentence. 'Nanno used to put lots of those in her letters.' I'm reading my letter again. I've forgotten to put kisses after *Tomos*. I'm putting them after the question mark instead.

'Is that a letter?' Miss says.

'Yes,' I say. 'To Nanno.' I'm showing Miss.

Miss is reading my letter. Her face looks kind and it looks a bit sad too. She's looking at my drawings now. 'That's really lovely. Did you have this truck for Christmas?' She's pointing to my drawing.

'Yes. Father Christmas brought it for me in a Santa Sack.'

'Good.' She's smiling a big smile. 'That's really good. And what are these?' She's pointing to the chocolate bars.

106

'Chocolate. The lady next door gave me this one.' I'm pointing to the triangle one. 'And Kaylee's mammy gave me this one.' I'm pointing to the flat one.

'And is this a fifty pence piece?'

'Yes, that's my coin. The lady next door gave me that too.'

'That was kind of her.' Miss is smiling. 'And did Father Christmas leave this under your tree?' She's pointing to the drawing of my truck again.

'No. We didn't have a tree. He left it outside the back door.'

Seren is putting the pencil box on Miss's desk. She's looking at my letter. Eddie is still collecting the crayons. He's dropping a lot of them on the floor.

'Oh,' Miss says. 'Father Christmas left your present outside the back door?'

'Yes, I saw him. He said, "Merry Christmas. Ho, ho, ho."'

There's a big crash. Eddie has dropped the box of crayons. Everyone's laughing. There's a lot of noise in class. Seren is rushing over to Eddie. He's picked up the box and Seren is picking up the crayons. She's picking them up fast.

'Quiet, everyone,' Miss says. 'Settle down. Don't worry, Eddie, accidents happen to everybody. Thank you for helping him, Seren.' Miss is looking at me again. 'What are you going to do with this letter?' She's holding it out to me.

'I'm taking it home. I'm going to put it in one of my magazines.' I'm taking the letter from Miss. 'For Nanno to find.'

Miss's eyes have gone all twinkly and her face is a bit sad. I'm folding the letter up. Miss is rubbing her eye with her finger and she's smiling at me now. I'm putting the letter in my pocket. Seren's putting the crayon box back on Miss's desk. Everything is tidy and nearly everyone is quiet.

'I'm sure Nanno would like your letter.' Miss is saying it quietly. She's squeezing my arm a tiny bit. 'In fact, I know she would,' she says. And her eyes are all twinkly again.

* * *

It's dinner playtime and it's stopped raining. I'm running outside. I'm wearing the coat Miss gave me from the lost property box and it's nice and warm. My tummy is very full.

'Wotcha,' Wes says. He's standing by the corner and he's looking at some stones in his hand.

'Wotcha.'

He's throwing his stones in the air and he's trying to catch them. 'What was for lunch?'

'Dinosaur chickens and chips,' I say. 'We had seconds.'

'What's that?' Wes says.

'What's seconds?' I'm trying to find some stones but I can only find little ones.

'No, thicko. What's the dinosaur things?'

I've found a bigger stone and I'm picking it up. 'They're like chicken nuggets but they're dinosaurs really. They're nice.'

'What was for afters?' Wes is taking the big stone from my hand and he's putting it with his stones.

'Milkshake and a biscuit. I had seconds of that too.'

'Pukey,' Wes says. 'I'm glad I'm packed lunch. I had cola and crisps.'

We are looking for more stones. We're going near the field. There are some bigger ones there.

'Did you bring it?'

'Bring what?' I say.

'Your truck thing?'

I am remembering now. I'm remembering our deal. 'No. I wasn't allowed.'

'Bring it tomorrow. I want to see it.'

'Maybe.' I'm not saying it's a deal because I don't think I'm allowed to bring it tomorrow.

We're still looking for stones. I've found some big ones and I'm putting them in the pockets in my trousers. They're the trousers Miss gave me from the lost property box. I'm trying to put the stones in fast before Wes takes them.

'What's that?' Wes is pointing to the floor.

I'm looking at where his finger's pointing. It's pointing to a piece of paper. A bit of the paper is in a puddle. 'It's my letter.' I'm picking it up fast. I don't want it to get wet.

'What letter?'

I'm opening the paper. My drawings are a little bit wet. 'It's my letter to Nanno. I did it in wet play this morning.'

'Who's Nanno?' Wes is looking over my shoulder. He's looking at the letter.

'My nanno.'

'Your nan?' Wes says. 'Like a gran?'

I'm thinking. 'I think she's like a gran.'

'Is that your truck?' He's pointing to my drawing.

'Yes.'

'It's red.' He's rubbing his finger over my drawing.

I'm nodding.

'What does it say?' He's rubbing his finger over the words now.

'It says, *Dear Nanno, How are you? I am well. Here are my things. My Super Truck is the best thing. It was in my Santa Sack. Lots of love, from Tomos. P.S. Did you have a Santa Sack in Heaven?*'

'Why'd you say that?' Wes says.

'What?'

'Heaven.'

'Because that's where Nanno is.'

'Heaven?' Wes says. 'Is she dead?'

I'm folding up the letter.

'Is she? Is she dead?'

I'm nodding. I'm putting the letter back in my pocket.

'How did she die?'

'I don't know.'

'Was she stabbed?' He's putting his face next to my face. 'With a big knife?'

I'm shaking my head.

'Was she cut in half?' Wes says. 'With a chain saw?' His face is very close to my face now. His nose is by my eye. 'Did she have her head cut off with a sword, like those women me and Uncle Vic saw on the internet?'

'No.' I'm trying to move my face away from him. 'She was ill. She went to hospital.'

'Oh,' Wes says. '*Booo*ring.' He's taken his face away from

my face. He's looking for stones again. He's found a little white one and he's picking it up. He's showing it to me. 'No such place as heaven anyway.'

I'm looking at him. 'There is.'

He's shaking his head. 'Uncle Vic told me. When you're dead, you're dead.'

'No,' I say. 'There is Heaven. That's where Nanno is. She sent me a letter from there.'

'She can't do that,' Wes says. 'She can't send letters. She's dead.'

He's throwing the white stone into the air. He's trying to hit it with his hand. It's falling down by his feet. He's picking it up and he's throwing it into the air again. 'When you're dead they put you in the ground, then the worms eat your insides.'

'They don't.' I don't want to think about Nanno and worms.

'They do,' he says. 'They make you all empty like a boat. 'A boat?' I say.

'Yeah, like a big, pink canoe. Uncle Vic said.'

I don't want to think about Nanno like that. I don't want her to be a big pink canoe.

'Nanno's in Heaven,' I say. 'I know she is. She said pure hearts go to Heaven. Like in the song '*Calon Lân*'. And Nanno had a pure heart.' I don't want to look for stones with Wes. I don't want to look anymore.

'What's a pure heart?' he says.

'It's clean because you're good and you do nice things for people and you go to Heaven.'

'That's stupid,' Wes says. 'There's no such thing as a clean heart. That's stupid.' He's throwing his stones at me. He's throwing them one at a time. 'Everybody's got dirty hearts. Like all those men in Uncle Vic's DVDs.' He's throwing his stones hard at me now. 'Dirty, dirty, dirty.'

The bell is going and I'm turning my back to Wes. I'm starting to run up the playground. I'm leaving him by the field because I don't want to hear about Uncle Vic and his DVDs. I don't want to hear about dirty hearts. I'm running and running and I'm getting a long way away from Wes.

I am getting a long long long way away from him.

* * *

We're tidying up our desks. The bell is ringing. It's telling us it's the end of school for today. Miss is standing by the door. She's saying goodbye to everyone.

'Goodbye, Miss.' I'm going out of the door.

'Oh, Tomos,' she says. 'Just wait a minute.'

I'm waiting. The other children are going past me. They're going home.

Miss is calling Kaylee over. 'Can you ask your mum to come in please, Kaylee? I'd like to have a word with her.'

Kaylee's going to get her mammy. All the other children have gone now and Miss is looking in her bag.

'You didn't get a chance to help me with these today because it was wet play this morning.' She's holding out the plastic box. I can see a little pot of rice pudding inside it and a chocolate biscuit.

'Is it your packed lunch? Did your husband make too many sandwiches again, like yesterday?'

'Yes, he did. You can sit down there and eat them.' She's pointing to the cushions in the Quiet Corner. 'They can be your tea – your first tea – and then you can have another one at home.'

I'm sitting down on a cushion in the Quiet Corner and I'm getting a sandwich out of the plastic box. I'm going to eat it to help Miss. I like helping Miss.

Kaylee and her mammy have come into class.

'Hi, Karen,' Miss says. 'Sorry to drag you in.' She's going over to stand near them. 'I just wanted to tell you that Tomos is staying here for a bit. He's going to have something to eat, then I'll make sure he gets home.'

'Okay.' Kaylee's mammy is making her okay very long. 'You sure you don't want us to wait? You sure you wanna go round there yourself?'

'I won't go too near the house,' Miss says. 'I'll just see he gets back all right.'

I'm looking at the sandwiches Miss's husband has made. They've got pinky browny slushy stuff in them. And little yellow beans. The sandwiches smell funny.

'Sorry, Karen, can you wait a minute?' Miss is looking at me. She's coming over to the Quiet Corner. Kaylee is coming with her. Miss says, 'Shall we put the television on, Tomos?' She's switching on the telly.

Fireman Sam is on. Kaylee's sitting down next to me and Miss is turning the sound up. She's going back to talk to Kaylee's mammy again.

113

I'm not eating yet. I'm wondering why Miss's husband has made her smelly sandwiches today.

'I won't let her see me,' Miss says.

'Well, if you're sure,' Kaylee's mammy says. 'Cos if she does see you, she'll go mental.'

Miss says, 'I'll stop before the gate.'

I'm looking at the smelly sandwiches. I don't know if I want to help Miss with them. I had five dinosaur chickens for lunch. Three for firsts and two for seconds. And I had beans and chips too. I'm only a little bit hungry now.

'That boy is funny,' Kaylee says. She's pointing to the boy on the telly. His name is Norman and he's in a go-cart. He's going very very fast.

'And I'll do the same tomorrow and Friday,' Miss is saying. 'I want to make sure he's had plenty to eat before the weekend.'

'Yeah,' Kaylee's mammy says. 'That's good.'

Norman has fallen out of the go-cart. He's fallen into the sea. Kaylee is laughing and laughing. I'm laughing too. And I'm listening to Miss talking.

'I had a shock when I saw him after the Christmas holidays,' she says. She's very quiet now. It's hard to hear her because of the telly. And because of Kaylee laughing.

'Yeah.' Kaylee's mammy is very quiet too. 'I know. Looked like he hadn't been fed for the whole two weeks. And his clothes were so dirty. He smelt terrible.'

'I've found him some clean trousers in lost property,' Miss says. 'They're just like his own, so hopefully she won't notice I've swapped them.'

Fireman Sam is driving his truck now. He's going to help Norman. He's going fast fast. Fireman Sam's truck is red like my truck. I like Fireman Sam and his truck.

'She'll never notice,' Kaylee's mammy says. 'He could go out butt naked and she wouldn't have a clue.'

'Well, I'll keep his clothes clean.' Miss is talking very quietly. 'I'll get him a school jumper, too. And some underwear.'

'You shouldn't have to do that.'

'I know. But I can't just look the other way. I told the Head I was worried. He's ringing social services today. We're all going to have to keep an eye.' Miss is shutting a drawer in her desk. I'm wondering if she's keeping an eye in there.

'Yeah,' Kaylee's mammy says. 'Yeah.'

Fireman Sam has stopped his truck. He's going to help Norman get out of the water. Kaylee's clapping and jumping up and down on the cushions.

'It's such a shame how things have turned out,' Miss says. It is very very hard to hear her. 'She's being so difficult.'

'She always was trouble,' Kaylee's mammy says. 'But I still used to like her.'

'I know. Me too. She had attitude, that's all. And you couldn't really blame her after the kind of childhood she had.'

Kaylee's mammy's nodding. 'She used to be okay 'til she got into drugs and then she didn't wanna know me no more.' She's shaking her head now. 'We were fourteen with a baby each…and still she didn't wanna know me.'

'You could have supported each other so much,' Miss says.

'Could have been good…sharing stuff, doing things together. But she couldn't care less about me by then.' She's nodding her head at Kaylee and me. 'Or 'im.'

'Well, I appreciate what you're doing now, Karen, even if she doesn't,' Miss says. 'And thanks for coming in. Like I say, I'll make sure he's fed and gets home safely for the rest of the week.'

Miss is calling Kaylee. She's running to her mammy. 'Bye, Tomos,' Kaylee and her mammy are saying. They're waving to me and I'm waving to them. I'm waving with the sandwich I'm not eating. They're going out of the door.

Miss is coming over to the Quiet Corner again. She's looking at the plastic tub and she's looking at all the sandwiches in it. 'Don't you like them?' She's biting her lip and she looks sad.

I don't want Miss to look sad. I don't want her to look sad at all. I'm taking a big bite from one of the smelly sandwiches and I am chewing it a bit. 'Oh.' I am saying it because the sandwich doesn't taste smelly. It tastes lovely. I've got a lot of sandwich in my mouth and it's hard to talk. I'm chewing and chewing and I'm swallowing the bit of sandwich. I'm smiling at Miss. 'I thought it smelt funny, but it's lovely.' I'm taking another big bite.

Miss doesn't look sad now. 'They're tuna, mayo and sweetcorn. I'm glad you like them.'

'Oh yes.' I'm chewing and chewing. 'I liked the egg sandwiches your husband made yesterday by mistake,' I say. 'But I like these better.' I'm taking another big bite and the little yellow beans are popping in my mouth and they're sweet and lovely.

'Enjoy them.' Miss is smiling.

She's going back to her desk and she's picking up her pen and I'm watching Fireman Sam getting back into his red truck like my red truck and I'm taking another big bite of Miss's sandwiches and I am chewing and chewing and chewing and chewing.

* * *

I'm up in my high sleeper bed. I am waiting to go to sleep. I have been waiting a long time. Mammy has taken my ladder away. She's put it on the floor. I'm waiting to go to sleep. But I need the toilet. It's not nice when I need the toilet. And my ladder is on the floor.

I'm thinking about things that are nice. I'm thinking about the sandwiches Miss's husband made by mistake today. I'm thinking about the yellow beans. And the way they popped in my mouth. I've had two chunks of chocolate tonight from the bar Kaylee's mammy gave me. The chocolate was lovely but the sandwiches were nicer. And I'm thinking about the little pot of rice pudding.

I'm thinking about Miss too. I'm thinking about us walking home from school and I'm remembering us walking down the road. Me and Miss. I'm remembering us stopping at next door's gate and Miss saying I could run to our gate and she said, 'See you tomorrow, Tomos,' and I'm remembering her waving and smiling and I was waving and smiling too.

I'm nearly smiling now. But it's hard to smile when you

need the toilet. I'm trying to listen for Brick's car outside. And I'm trying to listen for Mammy opening the front door. I'm trying and trying. But I can't hear them. And I want the toilet. I want it a lot.

I'm trying to think about something else. About something that is nice. Something that is not the toilet. I'm trying to think about my truck. I'm trying to think that I am very small. I'm so small I can sit in my truck and I can drive it round and round and round and I can drive it down the path to the gate and I can show Kaylee and her mammy under their umbrellas and I can drive it all the way to school and I can show Miss and Seren and Eddie and Wes.

Not Wes. I don't want to think about Wes. I don't want to think about Wes at all. I don't want to think about the things he says. The horrible horrible things he says.

And I don't want to think about his Uncle Vic. I don't want to think about him at all.

* * *

I'm running. I'm running down the road and it's very dark and cold. I'm trying to get across to the other side. Because I need the toilet. And there's a toilet on the other side of the road. But I can't cross the road. The road won't let me. It keeps tipping me back. And I need to get across.

The road is changing. It's getting blacker and blacker and wetter and wetter. It's not a road now. It's a river. And I need to cross it. I need to get to the toilet.

There's something on it. It's floating down the river that

118

was a road. It is big and pink. It's stopping by me. I'm getting into it. It's a big pink boat. It's taking me across the river. It's taking me across to the toilet.

There's something in the bottom of the boat. Something squidgy. It's rice pudding. The boat is full of rice pudding. I'm grabbing it with my hands. I'm eating and eating the rice. And there is something else in the boat too. A big lump in the middle of the rice. And the lump is moving very slowly.

And now Dat is here. I'm shouting, 'Dat, Dat!' He's standing in the river and I am floating to him. I'm floating to him in the big pink boat. And I'm waving and waving to him. But he's not waving back. He's holding something. It's a big shiny saw. It's the one he keeps in his shed.

And the lump in the bottom of the boat is still moving. It's turning and turning until it's looking up at me. The lump has silver hair and pink cheeks. And it's smiling up at me. It's smiling from the bottom of the boat that is full of rice. Fat wriggly rice that is not rice at all. It is worms. Wriggly wriggly worms. The lump is smiling. It has pink cheeks and pink lips and silver hair and silver glasses. And the lump has worms coming out of its nose. Fat fat wriggly worms. They're wriggling and wriggling over the lump. And now I see the lump has got Nanno's face. The lump is Nanno's head.

I'm holding out my arms to Dat. I want him to pick me up. I want him to take me out of the boat. I want him to get me away from the worms. And Nanno's head. And I need to go to the toilet.

'Quick, quick, Dat. Help me, help me.' But Dat looks cross. And then I remember. I'm not allowed to see him anymore.

He's waving his saw at me. He's bending into the boat with the big saw. And my tummy is hurting. It's hurting a lot. It's hurting and hurting and hurting. And the tops of my legs are hot and wet. Something wet is running all over my legs. Because Dat's big saw has cut me in two and I'm sitting up fast in the dark. And my legs and my bed are all wet wet wet. They're all wet wet wet with wee.

* * *

I'm helping Miss. I'm helping her again. I've been helping her for a long time. For days and days and days and days. And days and days and days.

I'm sitting in the Quiet Corner and I am eating her sandwiches. They're ham sandwiches. Miss's husband makes a lot of sandwiches by mistake but I don't mind. I like helping Miss.

Mrs Jones has come into class. She's pulling a long hosepipe. It's like the one Fireman Sam has got. There's a funny box on the end of Mrs Jones's hosepipe. It's very noisy.

I'm holding a sandwich. It's the last one. I'm hiding it behind my back because we are not allowed to eat in class. Because of the rats.

'It's all right, Tomos *bach*,' Mrs Jones says. She's winking at me like Dat does sometimes. 'You eat your sandwich and I'll vacuum up the crumbs in a minute. We'll keep those rats away.'

'Thank you, Mrs Jones.' It's hard to say it with a lot of sandwich in my mouth. I'm watching a programme on telly. There's a lady dancing. She's singing too. Miss is standing on a chair. She's putting pictures on the wall.

'He's a funny little thing, isn't he?' Mrs Jones is saying it quietly. It's hard to hear her over the noise of her hosepipe.

Miss is looking down at Mrs Jones from her chair. 'A little old fashioned, maybe. I suppose it's because he was brought up by an older couple.'

Mrs Jones is nodding. 'And he's a credit to them, he's so polite. His foster mother would turn in her grave if she knew what was happening now.' She's pushing her hosepipe round the chair that Miss is standing on. The hosepipe is cleaning up all the little bits on the carpet like Nanno's vacuum cleaner does. 'After all her and her husband did for that girl.'

It's hard to hear her over the singing on the telly. It's hard to hear her over the noise from the box she's pulling along. She's looking up at the wall. 'Down a bit on the left.'

'Thanks,' Miss says. She's moving the picture down a bit.

'And that little child, that poor dab,' Mrs Jones is saying, 'he's stuck in the middle. The girl is using him, that's all. Using him to get a house.' She's pushing her hosepipe under the table. 'Oh, you're all sorted if you've been in and out of care like her. Go straight to the top of the queue. And there's my Nia and her Richard having to go to Llanelli because the rent's cheaper, and been on the waiting list for two years in Carmarthen with no sniff of a council house.' She's pushing and pulling her hosepipe. 'And that girl snaps her fingers and gets one the next day. I brought our Nia up too well. If I was a druggie or an alky, she'd have had a house by now.'

Miss is trying to make the picture stick onto the wall. 'I'm sure Nia wouldn't swap her happy childhood for a council house,' she says.

Mrs Jones is looking up at Miss. 'Oh, no. I'm sorry, Lowri…of course she wouldn't. I didn't mean to offend. When I said "alky" I wasn't thinking of your—'

'I know,' Miss says. 'Don't worry, Vi. It's fine.'

A man is dancing with the lady on telly now. He's not very good at dancing. The lady is trying to teach him but he's not very good at learning. I'm getting the chocolate biscuit out of the plastic box. I'm saving the little pot of rice pudding for last.

'And poor Nannette,' Mrs Jones is saying. 'Such a lovely woman. Such a shame about the cancer. It took her so quickly. And there's Dafydd, left on his own. They gave up the fostering so that girl could stay there with her child. And fostering was their life.'

'I know.' Miss is getting down off the chair. 'It's a terrible shame.'

I'm looking over at Mrs Jones fast fast. I'm looking over because I have heard her say two names I know. They are the names Nanno and Dat call each other. Nannette and Dafydd.

I can only see Mrs Jones's back but Miss is looking at me. 'Are you okay there, Tomos?'

'Yes, thank you.' I'm saying it over the music on the telly. I'm saying it over the noise Mrs Jones's hosepipe's making.

122

'Good,' Miss says.

Mrs Jones has turned round and she's looking at me now. She's smiling too.

'We'd better be careful what we say.' Miss is saying it to Mrs Jones. She's saying it quietly. It's very hard to hear her over the noises. 'Better not use names.'

I'm still looking at them and they're still looking at me. They're still smiling at me too. Miss is moving her chair to another bit of wall. 'Have you eaten the rice pudding?'

'Not yet. I'm saving it for last. It's my favourite.'

'Good,' Miss says. 'Enjoy it.'

She's getting back up on the chair. She's holding another picture up against the wall. She's looking at Mrs Jones. 'To be honest, I think…' She's looking at me again. I can see her out of the side of my eye. 'I'll use initials,' she says. 'I think N's death threw R.' She's saying it very quietly. 'She was doing okay until then. A bit unreliable, maybe, but not totally off the rails.'

'I think you're being far too kind to her,' Mrs Jones says. 'I wouldn't be.'

'Well anyway.' Miss is moving her chair again. 'Did you know she'd planned her own funeral? N, I mean.' Miss is still very quiet. I'm having to listen very hard. 'You-know-who was supposed to sing.'

The lady on telly has stopped teaching the man to dance. They're getting into a funny car. The car is blue with pink flowers on it.

'Her favourite hymn,' Miss says. '"*Calon Lân*". Not at the chapel, back at home afterwards.'

The man can't start the car. The lady's having to push it. She's getting very hot and cross.

'That boy singing "*Calon Lân*",' Mrs Jones says. 'Wouldn't be a dry eye in the place.'

Miss is climbing onto another chair. 'She just wanted everyone to hear him. She was so proud of him.'

'And to think that ungrateful girl wouldn't let her see him,' Mrs Jones is saying. 'Not even at the end. Makes my blood boil.'

I'm looking at Mrs Jones. I'm trying to see her blood boiling. I'm looking at her ears and her nose. I'm looking for smoke coming out of them. Like it comes out of the kettle when it's boiling. Her face is quite red but I can't see any smoke.

'It's just as well you're here,' Mrs Jones says. 'It's a real godsend you turning up. When is that Mrs Wright coming back?'

'I'm not sure,' Miss says. 'She was supposed to be back after Christmas, but she's got a doctor's paper for another month now.'

'It doesn't surprise me. She was in a terrible state before she went off sick.' Mrs Jones is pushing and pulling her hosepipe again. 'Perhaps she'll take early retirement. I shouldn't say it, but she's a bit long in the tooth for kids now-a-days. '

I'm thinking about someone called Mrs Wright. She was my teacher when I came to this school. Before Miss came. Mrs Wright had grey hair like Nanno but she didn't smile like her. She cried quite a lot. And she said Eddie was a horrible horrible child. I'm trying to remember Mrs Wright's teeth. I'm trying to remember if they were long like Mrs Jones said.

'Well, this supply work is perfect for you,' she's saying. 'Funny you and him turning up here about the same time. Some would say it was meant to be. Nannette would have.'

'Careful,' Miss says. 'No names.'

'Sorry.' Mrs Jones is putting her hand on her mouth. 'It just slipped out.'

I'm taking the little pot of rice pudding out of the box and I'm taking the top off it. I'm licking it.

Mrs Jones is switching off her hosepipe. She's standing up straight. 'But she would have been proud of you, Lowri. Proud of what you're doing.' She's rubbing her back. 'He was a scrap of a thing after Christmas, and just look at him now – rosy cheeks and he's filled out a good bit. God love you, girl.' She's taking the black bag out of the bin. 'It's a blessing, you turning up here.' She's saying it loud. 'It was meant to be, and it's a real blessing.' She's taking the bin bag out of the classroom and she's closing the door behind her.

I'm eating a big spoonful of rice. It's yummy.

Miss is shaking her head. 'It doesn't feel like a blessing.' She's saying it very quietly. It's hard to hear her. She's shaking her head again. She hasn't seen Mrs Jones take the bag away. She hasn't seen her go out of the door. She doesn't know she's talking to herself.

'This last month,' she says. She's still shaking her head. 'This last month, I'd say it's been more like a curse.'

* * *

I am up in my high sleeper bed. I have been looking at my book from the library in school. It has pictures of flowers in it. And pictures of trees. It's like Dat's Big Book of Plants and the words are very hard. I've been singing some songs too. I've been singing 'Away in a manger, no crib for a bed'. And 'Catch a falling star and put it in your pocket'. Nanno taught me that song. I like singing it because it makes me think about Nanno.

If I had some paper I could write a letter to Nanno. I could say *Dear Nanno, How are you? I am well. I have been to school today and I had a gold star from Miss. A star like catch a falling star. Because I did very good work. The very good work I did was hard sums. I did some writing too. I didn't cross out very much. Just three words. And I did a drawing of Dat. He was playing trains with me. And do you know where Cwtchy is? I am missing him a lot. I am missing Dat too. Do you know where he is? And I am missing you. But I know where you are. You are in Heaven and I don't care what Wes says. Love, Tomos xxx P.S. Do you know where Mammy is? She has been out a long time and I need the toilet.*

* * *

The bell is ringing. It's home time.

'Have a lovely half term, everyone,' Miss says.

Some children are saying, 'You too, Miss.'

All the children are going. I'm still in the classroom

126

because I'm eating Miss's sandwiches. I helped her with her sandwiches at playtime too. I help Miss with her sandwiches every day.

I had egg sandwiches at playtime. They were yummy. These sandwiches are tuna mayo and sweetcorn. Miss's husband has made them by mistake again. Sometimes her husband makes cheese sandwiches. They're nice. Sometimes he makes ham sandwiches. They're nice too. But my favourite ones are tuna mayo and sweetcorn. He makes them quite a lot and my second favourite is egg and he always puts a pot of rice pudding in the box and a little spoon and he always puts a chocolate biscuit in too and a banana or an apple and one day he put a little orange in but I don't like oranges and he doesn't put oranges in anymore and sometimes he puts a strawberry milkshake in the lunch box and I drink it with a straw and I like straws. I like milkshakes too.

He's put a milkshake in Miss's packed lunch today and I'm sucking on the straw. There's no milkshake left but I'm still sucking. I'm waiting for Miss to finish her marking. She says it won't take long. She says all the teachers are leaving early because it's the last day before half term. I'm sucking on the straw and holding the chocolate biscuit.

I'm giving Miss the lunch box because it's empty and she's putting it back in her bag. I'm still holding the chocolate biscuit. I'm going to eat it when I'm walking home with Miss.

'Have you got a library book for the holiday, Tomos?'

'Yes.' I'm showing her.

'*The Twits*,' Miss says. 'You like Roald Dahl's books, don't you?'

I'm nodding. 'I like the pictures.' I'm putting my library book under my arm.

'Next time you should look on the shelf that's for our class. There are lots of books on there that you can read.' We're going out of the classroom. We're going past the staffroom. Mrs Gregory from Year Six is in there. Miss is shouting, 'Have a good week, Fran.'

'You too, Lowri,' Mrs Gregory says. 'Are you definitely back after half term?'

'Yes,' Miss says. 'For at least a month.'

I've found a yellow bean on the front of my jumper. A yellow bean from one of my sandwiches. I'm putting it in my mouth and I'm popping it. It's lovely and sweet.

'Great,' Mrs Gregory says. 'Enjoy your week away from the madhouse.'

Miss is laughing and we're going out of the school door. Me and Miss. And out of the school gate. I'm still holding the chocolate biscuit. I'm looking forward to opening it.

'Aren't you eating that?' Miss says.

'I'm saving it 'til we turn the corner.' I'm waiting and waiting until we turn the corner.

We're turning it and I'm opening my chocolate biscuit fast fast. Miss is looking in her bag. She's taking out a box and she's showing it to me. 'Do you like these, Tomos? They're cereal bars. They've got chocolate chips in them.' I'm looking at the box. There's a picture of some biscuits on it. They look nice. I'm nodding. 'Good,' Miss says. 'Perhaps you can keep them in your bedroom and eat them in the holiday. There are nine biscuits in the box. One for each day of half term.' She's giving me the box. 'Tuck it up your jumper to keep it safe.'

I'm putting the box up my jumper. 'Thank you.' It's hard to say it because my mouth is full of chocolate biscuit.

We're nearly by our house now. I can see our gate that doesn't shut. We are at next door's gate. It's where Miss always stops when we walk home together but she's not stopping today. Miss is going a bit near our gate. 'Right,' she says. 'I wonder if your mum is home. Is she usually there when you get in?' Her voice sounds wobbly. She's looking round our hedge a bit.

I'm thinking. 'Sometimes she's there.'

Miss is biting her lip. 'If I stay here, can you run up the path to see if she's home? Just hold up your thumb to let me know you can see her.' Her voice is still wobbly. 'Because it's half term next week.'

'Okay. I'll see if she's in the front room.'

I'm running through our gate. I'm going to look through our window to see if Mammy's home. I'm starting to run up our path but someone is coming down it.

'Mammy!' I say. 'You're home.'

Mammy's not looking at me. She's pushing me out of the way. My library book has fallen onto the path. Mammy's face is scrunched up. It's very pink. 'Cow,' she says. She's shouting it. 'Blurry bitch.' I'm going after her. I'm standing by the gate. I'm watching her. She's waving her arms. And she's shouting at Miss. 'Don' you come round interferin',' she's shouting. 'Blurry bitch.'

Miss is holding her hands out. She's holding onto Mammy's arms. 'Calm down, Ree. I'm not interfering. I just want to help.'

Mammy's pulling Miss's hands off her arms. She's saying a lot of rude words. 'Dafydd told you to come an' spy on me, didn'ee?' She's walking away from Miss. She's walking backwards. 'Don' think I don' know wha' yorr both up to.'

'No,' Miss says. 'This isn't anything to do with him. Look, I know you're upset about Nannette—'

'Shurr up,' Mammy says. She's still shouting. 'You don' know nothing. You don't know nothing 'bout me now.'

'Don't be like this in front of Tomos,' Miss says. 'You're scaring him.' She's looking at me. I'm peeping round the hedge. I'm peeping at Miss and Mammy. 'It's okay.' Miss is saying it to me. Her face looks very kind. 'Everything's okay, Tomos.'

'Leave 'im alone,' Mammy says. She's shouting it at Miss. 'He's not your kid.'

'Okay,' Miss says. 'I'll go.' She's walking away a bit.

Mammy's shouting rude things. She's looking at me now. She's looking at my coat. It's the one Miss gave me. From the lost property box. 'This ain't yours.' Mammy's pulling it off me. The box of biscuits is nearly falling out from under my jumper. She's pulling my coat off one arm. She's pulling it off the other arm now. She's throwing the coat at Miss. It's fallen on the pavement.

Miss is picking it up. She's walking backwards. She's walking away from Mammy and me. She's hugging and hugging the coat. She's waving a tiny bit. 'Bye, Tomos.' She's turning round. And she's walking down the pavement.

'Tha's right,' Mammy says. 'Run away, bitch. You're good at that. Run away again.' Mammy's pulling me onto the pavement. I'm picking up my library book. I'm picking it up fast. I'm holding it under my arm. And I'm putting my hand on the box of biscuits. I'm stopping the box falling out from under my jumper. Mammy's putting her arm round my shoulders. She's squeezing me tight. I'm watching Miss walking down the road. She's walking very fast.

Mammy's poking me with her finger. She's poking me on my front. She's shouting at Miss. 'Ee's not your kid. Okay?' Her other arm is still round my shoulders. She's squeezing me very hard. She's holding my head now. She's squashing it. She's squashing it to her tummy. Mammy's shouting again. 'Oi, bitch.' She's shouting it even louder. 'OI, BITCH.'

Miss is not turning round. She's still walking away. I can see her with my eye that isn't squashed. I'm still holding tight to my jumper. My heart is banging on my box of biscuits. Bang bang. Bang bang.

Mammy's waving her finger. She's waving it at the house across the road. 'An' you can stop nosing out your window.' She's shouting it to the lady moving her curtains. Mammy's looking at Miss again. 'This is good.' She's saying it to me and she's laughing. 'This is real good.' Mammy's shouting at Miss again now. 'If you wanted a kid, bitch…' She is shouting and laughing and laughing. 'If you wanted a kid…' She is very very loud. 'You should have KEPT YOUR OWN.'

* * *

I'm waiting for Mammy to come home. I've been waiting a long time. I've been playing and playing with my truck. I've been driving it on my train table. I've been driving it round the hedges and on the train tracks and over the level crossings and on the little roads. I've been driving it past all the little people and past all the little animals. They've been talking to my truck. They've been saying they want to go for a ride in it. They want to but they can't. They're stuck down. They're stuck down tight with Dat's special glue.

I'm driving my truck up my ladder now. And I'm parking it with my letter and my coin. I'm pulling all the clothes round me. And round my truck. I'm trying to make us warm. And I'm trying to look at my library book. I'm tipping it to the window. It's very dark outside. It's very rainy too. The light outside is shining on my book. But it's hard to see the pictures.

I'm waiting to tell Mammy about the lights inside our house. I want to tell her they went off again. I was hoping she was taking the lectric key to the shop. I was hoping and hoping she was putting more money on it. But my fingers found the key down the side of the settee. That's where Mammy keeps it. And I want to tell her to take it to the shop. The light outside is shining in a bit. But I don't like it when the lights go off inside the house. I don't like it when the lights won't work. I don't like it at all. Mammy needs to put more money on the lectric key. And I am waiting and waiting to tell her.

I'm putting my hand under the jumpers on my bed. I'm looking for something with my fingers. My fingers have found my truck and they've found my fifty pence. And Nanno's letter. They've found the triangle box the lady next door gave me. It was full of chocolate. Lovely lovely chocolate. My tummy is making a grumbly noise. It's wishing the box was full of chocolate again. My fingers are moving past the box the lady next door gave me. They're looking for something else. They're looking for the box Miss gave me. The box of biscuits.

My fingers have found it and they're looking in the box. They're counting the biscuits. One. Two. Three. They're pulling one of the biscuits out.

These are nice biscuits. They're big and crunchy and they have bits of chocolate in them. I've been eating one every day of the holiday like Miss told me to. Every day so far. I think it will be time to go back to school soon. When the biscuits are all gone.

I'm eating my biscuit and I'm thinking about Miss. I'm thinking about the sandwiches she brings to school. The egg sandwiches and the tuna mayo and sweetcorn ones. I'm thinking about the little pots of rice pudding and the milkshakes.

I'm remembering the packet of crisps I had for tea. It was a blue packet. I don't like the blue packets very much. There are just pink packets left now. I'm saving them for Mammy. For when she comes home. I don't think Miss likes crisps. Her husband doesn't give her any for lunch. But he does make her tuna mayo and sweetcorn sandwiches. And egg sandwiches. And little pots of rice pudding. And milkshakes.

I think I have heard a noise. My ears are listening and

listening. They're listening to see if Mammy has come home. They're listening and listening and listening. They can hear the rain. It's tapping my window. They can hear lots and lots of tapping. But they can't hear Brick's car. And they can't hear Mammy. They can't hear her coming home. But my ears are still listening and listening.

I'm thinking about Cwtchy. I'm thinking about him and I'm missing him. I wish he was with me in the dark. Waiting for Mammy to come home. If he was here now I could hold him. And he would say, 'Don't worry, Tomos. Mammy will come home.' And he would say, 'The lights will work again soon.' And he would say, 'Mammy will get more crisps tomorrow.' And he would say, 'Don't worry about Nanno, Tomos. She really is in Heaven.'

And I would say, 'I know she is, Cwtchy. I know she is.'

* * *

I've eaten all the biscuits. I had the last one last night and Miss is right. It's school again. It's school again now the box is empty because Kaylee and her mammy have stopped by the gate and I'm walking to school with them and I've got my library book under my arm. It's very nice to see them.

'Be good,' Kaylee's mammy says. She has stopped by the door to school. Me and Kaylee are running in to see Miss.

'Did you all remember your library books?' Miss says. She's standing by the door to our classroom. She's talking to the children going into class. 'We're not allowed to keep

134

library books, are we? We take them home, read them and bring them back. We just borrow them.'

Some children are taking their library books out of their bags. Some children are saying they forgot them. Eddie is shaking his book at Miss. 'Well done for remembering, Eddie,' she says. 'Take it to the library and change it for another one.' Eddie is running off fast. 'Hello, Kaylee,' Miss says. She's seen us in the corridor. 'Did you enjoy your holiday?'

Kaylee's nodding. 'We went to soft play two times.'

'Lovely.' Miss is smiling at me now and I'm smiling and smiling at Miss. 'Tomos, don't you look happy? How was your holiday?'

'Nice,' I say. I think it was nice. And it's nice to be back. It's very nice to be back in school.

'Good.' Miss is smiling and smiling at me. 'Have you got your library book?'

'Yes.' I'm holding it up. 'I didn't read it. I just looked at the pictures. They're good.' The pictures have sticky people in them with arms and legs like sticks and hair that sticks out too.

'You can take it to the library now, and change it for another book if you like,' Miss says. 'You too, Kaylee.'

Kaylee and me are taking our books and we're going to the library. Eddie is running back to class. He's shouting 'Miss, Miss, I found this one.' I can hear Miss talking. She's quite far away now. She's saying 'Well done, Eddie. That looks interesting.'

Wes is in the library. He's pulling books off the shelves

and he's making a tower of books on the floor. Seren is in the library too. 'Don't do that, Wes,' she says. 'I'm telling. You're not supposed to be in here anyway. It's our class's turn today.' Wes is not listening. He's making his tower bigger and he's pulling his leg back. He's giving the tower a big kick. 'Right,' Seren says. 'I'm telling Mrs Pugh.' She's going out of the library.

Wes is going out of the library too. He's running. 'See ya later,' he says. I think he's saying it to me.

'See ya later,' I say. I don't think he has heard me because he's running very fast.

I'm trying to find a special book. It's my favourite. It's *Charlie and the Chocolate Factory*. But I can't find it. It's not where I put it back before the holidays. I'm taking another book. It's called *The BFG*. It has sticky drawings too like the book I brought back and like *Charlie and the Chocolate Factory*. I like sticky drawings and I'm going to draw some for Nanno on a letter if it's wet play.

* * *

It has not been wet play. It's been windy play and we've been playing outside. We've lined up but we haven't gone back into class. We've come to sit in the hall. Mrs Pugh Year Two's class is in the hall too. We have had to sit on the floor and we're all quiet now. Because Mrs Pugh Year Two has been shouting.

We're having to listen to her talking. She's been telling us about a trip. And about waterproof trousers. And behaviour.

And sensible shoes. She's been talking about them for a long long time.

'Who thinks they would like to come on my trip?' she says.

Lots of people are putting their hands up. I'm looking round at all the hands. Miss is putting her hand up. She's sitting at the front of the hall. I'm putting my hand up too.

Mrs Pugh Year Two is showing us her teeth. They are small and pointy. 'Good. You'll all have a letter to take home at the end of today.' She's holding up a piece of paper. There's a lot of writing on it. 'It might seem like next month is a long way away, but you must bring the permission slip back as soon as possible.' She's giving lots of the papers to Miss. 'Any questions?' Mrs Pugh Year Two is looking at us all. Everyone is very quiet. She's pointing now. 'Yes, Louisa?' She's still showing us her teeth.

'How much is it?' a girl says.

Mrs Pugh Year Two has stopped showing us her teeth. 'I've told you already. It costs twelve pounds fifty. That covers the bus too. You weren't listening, were you Louisa?' She's looking very cross. 'Were you?'

'No, Mrs Pugh.' Louisa's voice is quiet.

Mrs Pugh Year Two is showing us her pointy teeth again. 'Any other questions?' Everyone is very quiet. No one is putting up their hands. 'Well then, that's all I have to say.' Everyone is starting to move. There's a bit of a busy sound in the hall. 'I haven't finished yet.' Mrs Pugh Year Two is saying it in a loud voice. We are all staying still again. 'That is all I have to say, except for one last thing.' She is walking up and down at the front of the hall. She's looking at all of us. She's looking at us very carefully. 'I've been planning this trip for a long time. I've had to make a lot of phone calls. I've sent a lot of emails. I've had to write a lot of lists. Is anyone here going to spoil this trip for me?' She's looking and looking and looking at us. She's waiting for someone to say they will spoil her trip. Eddie's putting his hand up. 'Well, I know you'll spoil my trip, Eddie Edwards,' she says. 'I'm expecting that. You can put your hand down. Anyone else? Think hard.'

I am thinking hard. I don't know if I'm going to spoil Mrs Pugh Year Two's trip. I don't want to spoil it. But I think I might. I don't know if I should put my hand up. I'm putting it up just a bit. Mrs Pugh Year Two hasn't seen it. I'm putting it up a bit more. I'm looking at Miss. She's shaking her head at me. She's shaking it a lot. I'm putting my hand down. I'm putting it down fast.

'Right,' Mrs Pugh Year Two says. 'Apart from Eddie, not one of you is going to spoil my trip. Well, we'll see, won't we?'

* * *

It's dinner playtime. I'm running out of the school doors. The playground is very busy and it's very noisy and lots of people are shouting. Lots of people are running and running. I am running down the playground too. The wind is blowing on my face and I'm running with all the other children and I'm trying not to run in the puddles but there are too many of them. My shoes are getting wet and my feet are getting wet too but I'm still running and running and the wind is still blowing and blowing.

I'm putting my hands in the pockets in my coat. It's the coat Miss found in the lost property box. The one Mammy threw on the pavement before the holiday. Miss kept it safe for me so I can be warm at playtime. I'm holding my arms out. My hands are still in the pockets and the coat is making big wings. They are like an aeroplane's wings and I am running and running and flying and flying.

'Wotcha,' a voice says. It's Wes's voice. He's running next to me.

'Wotcha,' I say. 'Are you going on Mrs Pugh Year Two's trip?'

'Don't know. Sounds crap.'

'I'm going,' I say. 'I like zoos and I like animals.' I'm still running and flying.

'I like fish, 'specially sharks. They can bite you in half,' Wes says. 'Can I have a go of that?'

'Of what?'

'Of what you're doing with your coat.'

'Okay,' I say. We've stopped running now. 'You just put your...' Wes is pulling at the coat Miss gave me. He's pulling it round my neck and it's hurting my skin. I'm moving away from his hand and I'm looking at him. He hasn't got a coat on. He's grabbing my coat again. 'Go and get your coat,' I say.

'Can't. Haven't got one. Give me yours.' I'm shaking my head. 'Give it to me,' he says. 'Give me your coat.' He's still grabbing it. It's hard to stop his fingers. It's hard to stop them pinching me.

'I can't.' I'm twisting a bit. I am trying to get away from him. 'Miss gave it to me. I'm not allowed to lose it.' I'm remembering Miss saying I had to zip up the coat to keep warm. I'm zipping it up now. I'm zipping it up as fast as I can.

'Why did your teacher give you a coat? Did she buy it for you?'

'No. It's from the lost property box.'

Wes is laughing. 'Lost property? Your coat's from the lost property box? So that's why it smells.' He's pushing his face near the coat. 'It's *deee*sgusting. It smells as bad as you.'

He's starting to run again. 'Come on, thicko. I'm going to get some stones.' I'm not running. I'm standing still. I don't want to look for stones and I don't want to go with Wes. I don't want him to talk to me. I don't want to hear the things he says. He's stopped running. 'Come on, thicko,' he says. 'Come on.'

The playground is full of people shouting. It's full of people laughing. 'Come on.' He's calling me with his hand. 'Come on, thicko.' There are people running and running everywhere. And I am running too. I'm running and running towards Wes. I'm running and running and running towards him.

And he's running away from me.

* * *

140

I'm in our classroom and I've been helping Miss with her sandwiches. I'm waiting for Miss to finish writing then she's going to walk me home. She's going to walk to just past the corner and then I'll run the rest of the way on my own. She says she'll watch me from the corner to see I get home safe. I'm glad Miss is staying by the corner. I don't want Mammy to see her again. I don't like it when Mammy shouts at Miss.

'Right.' She's putting down her pen and she's picking up a piece of paper. 'This is your letter about the trip.' Miss is folding up the letter. She's giving it to me. 'Put it in your pocket and keep it safe 'til you get home. Ask your mum to sign it then try to bring it back as soon as you can.' She's smiling at me. 'Try your best to remember.'

I'm nodding. 'I will.' I'm going to try my best to remember to bring it back. 'I will.'

'A school trip will be fun, won't it?' Miss says. She's putting things into her bag. She's putting in the lunch box and her pencil case.

I'm nodding again. 'I'm looking forward to it a lot, lot, lot. I like zoos.'

'It's a farm really.' Miss is still smiling. 'But it'll be fun anyway. And don't worry about the list of things you need to bring, just as long as your mum signs the slip.'

I'm remembering Mrs Pugh Year Two talking in the hall. I'm remembering the things she said we needed. 'I haven't got wellingtons.'

'It's okay, you won't need them. Or waterproof trousers.'

We're going out of class now. 'I don't think we've got any sun cream,' I say.

Miss is laughing. 'You definitely won't need that. And you don't need to bring the money.'

'The twelve pounds fifty?'

'That's what some people will pay,' Miss says. 'But not everyone has to pay for the trip.'

I'm thinking about the money for the trip. I'm thinking about my coin in my tippy truck. 'I've got a fifty pence. The one the lady next door gave me. I can bring that.'

We've started walking out of school and I'm looking up at Miss. She's smiling at me but her eyes look a bit sad. 'That's very good of you, Tomos. But you keep that safe. School will pay for you. Just ask your mum to sign the letter. That's all you need to do.'

'Okay,' I say.

'And bring it back tomorrow.'

'Okay,' I say again. 'I will.'

* * *

The lady with the big bag is here. She's talking to Mammy. She's talking and talking. She's saying the house needs cleaning. She's saying the kitchen is very dirty.

'I would 'ave cleaned it,' Mammy says. 'But I forgot 'bout you coming.'

I'm behind the big black chair. I'm playing with my truck. And I'm hiding from Mammy. She's very very cross with me. Because I opened the door to the lady. The lady with the big bag.

'Do you mean you only clean up when you're expecting

a visit from me?' the lady says. She's sitting on the settee. Her face is very cross.

Mammy says, 'Oh, for fu—'

'Please. You're running out of chances, Rhiannon. I'm doing my best to keep you and Thomas together, but you're not making it easy. And we had a call from Thomas's school after the Christmas holidays…'

'That cow. Blurry Lowri interfering.'

'The school's only doing its job, Rhiannon. And that's what I'm doing too. I need to check things.' She's looking at her papers. 'Ah yes, the bed.'

'It didn't come,' Mammy says. 'You promised us a new one, but we haven't 'ad it.'

The lady is writing something on her papers. 'I'll have to chase that up. It should arrive soon.' She's tapping her pen. 'But you have put the mattress on the floor, haven't you, like we talked about last time? That ladder's dangerous.' Mammy's not saying anything. 'Well, I'll check his room before I go,' the lady says. She's writing something again. She's looking round the front room. 'You haven't taken up the offer of more furniture then, or had the house redecorated? It's all free, you know, Rhiannon. You only need to contact the charity.'

'I can do decorating myself,' Mammy says.

The lady's letting out a big breath. 'Stripping off wallpaper's easy,' she says, 'but putting it up is another thing altogether.' She's looking at me now. I'm trying to hide a bit more. I'm trying to be very small behind the chair. I don't want her to go to my room. I don't want her to see my high

143

sleeper bed. I don't want her to see my ladder. 'Show me that toy, Thomas,' she says. 'Come out and show me what you're playing with.'

I am staying still. I don't want to come out from behind the chair.

'Don't 'ave to and you can't make 'im,' Mammy says. 'Stay where you are, boy.'

The lady's shaking her head. 'You know, Rhiannon, I'm trying my best, but you're making it so difficult for me.' There's a buzzy noise. It's coming from the lady's bag. 'I'd like to have a little chat with Thomas,' she says, 'because a dirty house is one thing, neglect is quite another. And I have to check that he's being well looked after. You know that, so please encourage Thomas to come out and talk to me.' She's putting her hand in her bag. She's found her phone. She's looking at it a bit.

I'm wondering if I should come out. I'm peeping round the side of the chair. I'm peeping at Mammy. She's calling me with her hand. Her face is still cross. I'm coming out from behind the chair. I'm coming out slowly. On my knees and on my hands. I'm bringing my truck.

'What a shame the wheels have broken off,' the lady says. She's putting her phone down on her papers.

'I don't mind. It's still a super truck.' I'm showing her the tippy part. All the bits from the carpet are falling out. All the wheels are falling out too. I'm picking them up again. I'm putting them back in the tippy part.

'Need a pee.' Mammy is running up to the bathroom.

The lady's looking and looking at me. She's looking at my

144

trousers and at my jumper. They are the ones Miss brought to school for me. They smell very nice. They smell like cakes and flowers. They smell like Nanno and Dat's house.

'Have you had your tea yet?' the lady says.

I'm thinking about my first tea. The one I had in school after all the other children went home. 'Yes.'

'What did you have?'

'Egg sandwiches. And a strawberry milkshake. And a rice pudding. And a chocolate biscuit. And a banana.' I can hear Mammy in the bathroom. She's opening the cupboard. I think she's tidying up all the things I must NOT touch. I'm thinking about my second tea. The one I had at home. 'And a blue packet of crisps.'

The lady's smiling. 'And did you eat your lunch in school?' I'm nodding. 'What did you have for lunch today?'

'Cawl and bread and cheese. I had seconds. And pink custard and cake for afters. I had seconds of that too.'

'You've got a good appetite,' the lady says. 'Well, you look like you're getting big and strong.'

Mammy has come back from the bathroom. She's sitting on the chair again. I'm showing the lady my arms like Dat when he's being a strong man. 'I'm big and strong like Dat.' I'm making my arms really strong.

'Good boy,' the lady says. 'Have you seen Dat? Has he been here?' Her phone is buzzing again.

I'm putting my arms down and I'm shaking my head. 'I'm not allowed.' I'm picking up my truck. 'Can I see Dat? Can I show him my truck from Father Christmas? I'd like to show him my truck.'

Mammy is making a blowy noise with her mouth.

'Not at the moment,' the lady says. 'Sometime, maybe.'

Mammy is making the noise again. 'Never. Tha' man ain't coming near us.'

'Situations change, Rhiannon,' the lady says. Her phone is playing music now. 'Thomas is obviously attached to your foster father and it would be a shame—'

'Never!' Mammy says. 'An' stop calling me that. My name's Ree.'

The lady's shaking her head. 'Yes, of course. Sorry, Ree.' She's looking at her phone. She's standing up. 'I'll have to answer this.' She's walking to the window. She's holding her phone to her head. She's saying 'Oh no,' a lot.

I'm putting my hand in my pocket. There's something crinkly inside. I'm taking it out. It's the letter Miss gave me about the zoo. I'm showing it to Mammy. 'We're going on a trip to the zoo. In three weeks' time.' Mammy's taking the letter. She's putting it on top of the box I was a present in.

The lady is still talking on her phone. She says, 'I only went there yesterday. He seemed fine. Everything seemed okay. The father was a bit…you know, but…' She's shaking and shaking her head.

'It's to the zoo,' I say. I'm picking up the letter off the box. 'Can I go, Mammy? Please.' I'm showing it to her again. Mammy's lifting her shoulders. She's taking the letter. She's putting it on the arm of the chair. 'You need to sign it, to say I can go.'

'I'll meet you at the hospital,' the lady is saying to her phone. 'I'll get there as soon as I can.' She's putting her phone in her pocket. She's turning round. Her cheeks are very red. 'Right,' she says. 'Despite the mess in the house, Thomas is well fed, his clothes are clean and he seems happy and healthy.' She's saying it very fast. 'So I'll recommend we carry on as we are for now. There'll be another visit in a month or so.' The lady's picking up her bag. She's picking it up fast. 'And, of course, we'll carry on looking into your allegations about your foster father. But you must realise others speak very highly of Mr Evans.'

'Ifans,' Mammy says. 'Not Evans.'

'Of course,' the lady says. 'Mr *Eee*vans.'

She's going to the door. She's going fast. I'm going with her. The lady is opening the door and she's going outside. She has forgotten to look at my bedroom. She's forgotten to check my bed and my ladder.

'Bye,' I say.

'Bye. See you soon, Thomas.'

I'm smiling at the lady. 'My name's not Thomas,' I say.

The lady is squashing her eyebrows together. 'Not Thomas?' She's getting her keys out of her big bag.

'No.' I'm still smiling at her. 'It's Tomos.'

'Oh,' the lady says. Her eyebrows are going high. 'I see.' She's only smiling a little bit now. 'Okay. Tom*moss* it is, then.' She's making my name sound funny.

She's turning round and she's going down the path. She's going very fast. She's saying something. She's saying it to herself. I think she's saying 'Like mother, like child.'

* * *

147

I am up in my high sleeper bed. The bed I'm not allowed to have. I'm playing with my truck and I'm thinking about a letter I could write to Nanno if I had some paper and a pencil. My letter would say *Dear Nanno, How are you? I am well. Tomorrow is a very special day. It is the day we are going to the zoo. It has taken a long time to come. I have been waiting and waiting for it. I have given Mammy a letter about it. Miss asked me if I still had the letter and I said yes because I gave the letter to Mammy a long time ago. Mammy must sign it. Mrs Pugh Year Two said. And I must take it back tomorrow. Then I will see lions and tigers and monkeys like there are in Dat's Big Book of Animals and I will see giraffes and turtles and zebras and polar bears too and I am waiting and waiting to go and it is hard to sleep when I am waiting to go to the zoo and Wes says the zoo will be crap but I don't think it will be because I think it will be very good. Very very good. And I will tell you all about it. Lots of love, Tomos xxx*

I'm playing with my truck again. I'm driving it over my bed. I'm making big hills out of jumpers and towels and Mammy and Brick's tee shirts. I'm driving my truck over them and I'm making sound effects. I'm thinking about Dat's sound effects. They are very good. I'm trying to make my sound effects good too.

I have parked my truck now. I've parked it in the corner of my bed next to my head. And I'm looking at my library book from school that is *Charlie and the Chocolate Factory* and it's my favourite. A girl from a big class took it from the library. She kept it for a long long time. And then a big boy took it. And he had it for a long time too. Then he put it back in the library and now I've got it and it's my favourite favourite and it makes me think about the film. The one I used to watch with Dat. The words in the book are very hard and they are too hard for me to read but I still like the book lots and lots and lots.

I'm looking at the sticky drawings of Charlie and Grandpa. I can see them in the yellow light from the road and Charlie and Grandpa are smiling. They're laughing and smiling and they're making me think about Dat. They're making me think about Dat a lot. They're making me happy. And they're making me sad. I'm remembering something. I'm remembering something I forgot. I forgot a P.S. at the end of my letter to Nanno. I am doing it now. I'm thinking about the P.S. I would write if I had a pencil and some paper. I'm saying *P.S. I miss you and Dat. I miss you and Dat a lot.*

* * *

Today is the special day. The very very special day. It's the day we are going to the zoo. I've put on my school jumper and my school trousers and I've put my fifty pence in my pocket and I'm keeping it safe. I've been to the bathroom and I've climbed on the side of the bath so I can get to the tap and I've splashed some water on my face and I've brushed my hair with Mammy's hair brush. It's very hard to use her hair brush because it keeps getting stuck.

I'm going downstairs now. I'm going to wait for Kaylee and her mammy but I'm going to find my letter first. My letter for the zoo. I am hoping and hoping Mammy has signed it.

I'm looking in the front room. I'm looking under the settee. I'm looking behind the chair. I'm looking under the box I was a present in. I can't find it in the front room. I'm looking in the kitchen. I'm picking things up off the worktop. I'm looking underneath things. I can't find my letter in the kitchen. I'm going back up the stairs.

I'm going past the bathroom. The door is closed. I'm listening by it. I think I can hear Mammy in the bathroom. She must have come home in the night. I'm very happy that she's back but I'm not going to call to her through the door. She doesn't like me to talk to her in the morning. I'm going past the bathroom door that is closed and I'm going past my bedroom. I'm opening the door to Mammy's room quick quick.

I'm going in. 'Oh!' I am saying it because Mammy's in the bed. She's not in the bathroom after all. It must be Brick in the bathroom. I'm going into Mammy's room very quietly. I don't want to wake her. I'm looking for my letter. I'm looking under her bed. There are a lot of clothes under there. I'm trying to move them a bit. I'm trying to see my letter. It's dark under the bed. It's too dark to see. I'm going round the other side. I'm remembering the letter on the other side of the bed. On the floor. Mammy put it there after I showed it to her again yesterday. But it's not there now. I think Brick might have taken it. I think he might have taken it into the bathroom.

I'm standing up. I can see through the hole in Mammy's curtain. I can see Kaylee and her mammy. They're waiting by our gate.

I'm running out of Mammy's room. I'm running quietly. Brick is opening the bathroom door. He's coming out. A stinky smell is coming out with him. He's pushing past me. He's going back to Mammy's room. I'm putting my head into the bathroom. I'm trying not to take a breath. I don't want the stinky smell in my mouth. I'm looking and looking for my letter. I can't see it. I'm running downstairs and out of the front door. I'm closing the door very carefully. I'm running down the path.

'It's the trip to the zoo today, isn't it?' My words have come out fast. I'm taking a big big breath.

'Yes,' Kaylee says.

'We'd better get a move on,' Kaylee's mammy says. 'Or we'll be late.' We're walking to school together. We are walking quite fast. It's hard to walk as fast as Kaylee's mammy. I'm having to run. Kaylee is too. 'Come on,' Kaylee's mammy keeps saying. She's saying it over her shoulder to us. She's saying it over the click click of her boots. 'Or you'll miss the bus.'

* * *

We are not allowed to go to our classroom. Mrs Pugh Year Two is standing by the school door. She's telling everyone to go to the hall.

'Permission slip and twelve pounds fifty.' She's saying it to the children in front of us. She's holding out her hand. She's taking Kaylee's slip and she's writing on a piece of paper. Someone is making a noise. It's Eddie. He's shouting at Junior. Mrs Pugh Year Two is turning round. 'No shouting!' She is very loud.

She has forgotten to ask for my letter. I'm going into the hall with Kaylee.

We're all sitting on the floor. We have to keep our coats on. We have to keep our backpacks with us. I haven't got a coat and I haven't got a backpack. I've got a brown paper bag. There's an apple and a chocolate biscuit in it and sandwiches and some juice. I think it's orange juice. I don't like orange juice. Mrs Jenkins from the school kitchen gave me the bag. She's given one to Carrie-Anne and one to Kaylee. She's given one to Paul and one to Junior. She's given some brown bags to children in Mrs Pugh Year Two's class too. I don't know their names.

Mrs Pugh Year Two has come back into the hall. She's holding a big piece of paper. She's reading things from it with a cross mouth. 'I hope no one forgot wellingtons. Or waterproof trousers.' She's looking over the top of her paper. 'Yes, Louisa?'

A girl is talking from the back of the hall. 'I haven't got waterproof trousers,' the girl's voice says. Everyone's turning round to look. We are looking at the girl who hasn't got waterproof trousers.

'Well, your legs will get wet then,' Mrs Pugh Year Two says, 'when it rains.' She's looking at the piece of paper again. 'And I hope no one has forgotten sun hats or sun lotion.' She's looking at us over the paper. 'You don't want to get sunburnt.'

The hall door is opening. Miss is putting her head through the gap. 'The bus is here, Mrs Pugh.'

'Thank you, Mrs Davies.' Miss's head has gone again. There's a big noise in the hall. All the children are talking. 'Quiet!' Mrs Pugh Year Two is stamping her foot. The noise is going away. 'Now, before we can get on the bus, I just need to check…' She's looking at her paper. 'I need Eddie's permission slip and someone else's.' She's turning the paper over. 'Tomos Morris,' she says. 'I haven't had your permission slip either.'

Eddie is getting up. He's waving a piece of paper. He's running up to Mrs Pugh Year Two. He's shaking it at her. 'Eddie Edwards, don't think you can behave like that on my school trip. Mrs Davies might put up with your nonsense, but I certainly won't.' She is grabbing the paper from him. 'Where's the twelve pounds fifty?' She's holding out her hand. Eddie is giving her some money. 'And the rest,' she says. Eddie is giving her some more. She's sending him to sit down again. She's looking round the hall. 'Tomos Morris,' she says. 'Is he here? Put up your hand, Tomos Morris.'

I am putting my hand up. I'm putting it up slowly.

'Where's your permission slip?' Mrs Pugh Year Two has a cross face. I am trying to say some words. 'Speak up,' she says with her cross mouth.

'I don't know,' I say.

'What?' Her voice is cross now like her mouth.

'I don't know where my slip is.'

'Don't know?' Mrs Pugh Year Two says with her cross voice. 'Don't know? Did you give it to your mother?'

'Yes.'

'Well, where is it now?'

'I think it's under her bed. In the dark bit.' Some children are laughing. I can hear Wes's scratchy laugh. It's coming from behind me in the hall.

Miss has opened the hall door. She's coming in.

'Well, you can't come without a permission slip,' Mrs Pugh Year Two says. 'That's the law. You'll have to stay in school.'

My eyes are getting prickly. I don't want to stay in school. I want to go to the zoo.

Miss says, 'Has someone forgotten their permission slip?'

'Yes,' Mrs Pugh Year Two says. 'A child in your class.'

'Oh dear.' Miss is looking at the children in the hall. She's looking at all our faces. Some children are pointing to me. Some children are saying my name. 'Oh, there you are, Tomos.' Miss is saying 'shhh shhh' to the children that are saying my name. She's coming over to me.

'Yes, it's Tomos Morris,' Mrs Pugh Year Two says. 'He'll have to give his free packed lunch back, I suppose.'

Miss is holding out her hand. She's holding it out to me. She's helping me to get up. She's putting her arm round my shoulders. She's taking me over to the side of the hall. Mrs Pugh Year Two has told all the children to line up at the door. There is a lot of noise.

'Did you ask your mum to sign the slip?' Miss says. We are standing by the wall. We're standing next to the big dragon. Our class made it out of scrunched up red paper. For Saint David's Day. For *Dydd Gŵyl Dewi*.

'Yes,' I say.

154

'Did she sign it?' Miss is talking quietly. It's hard to hear her. There's a lot of noise in the hall. Mrs Pugh Year Two is shouting. She's very loud.

'I don't know. I don't know if she signed it. I don't know where it is. It might be under her bed. It's very dark under her bed.' I am remembering the stinky smell in the bathroom. 'Or Brick might have used it for toilet paper.'

Miss is biting her lip. She's looking at the dragon on the wall. She's looking at his long red tongue. Seren made the dragon's tongue. I made a bit of his tummy.

'And I haven't got the twelve pounds,' I say. I'm putting my hand in my pocket. My fingers can feel my coin. 'But I've got the fifty pence. Is that enough?'

Miss is squeezing my shoulders with her arm. 'Don't you remember me telling you, Tomos? You don't have to pay the twelve pounds fifty. Not everyone has to pay, so don't worry about that.'

'I want to go to the zoo.' I am saying it quietly. There are tears falling off my chin. I'm wiping them with my sleeve. 'Please can I go to the zoo?'

Miss is squeezing my shoulders again. 'It's all right,' she says. 'I've got a spare permission slip. And I've got a plan.'

She's getting a tissue from her pocket. 'Don't cry anymore.' She's giving me the tissue. 'Wipe your eyes and go and line up with our class.' She's taking me over to the door. She's taking me to Seren. 'Look after Tomos for me, Seren,' Miss says.

'Oh, Mrs Davies.' Seren is making a cross face. 'I'm with Bethany.'

'It's just for a few minutes,' Miss says. 'While I go and do something. Bethany can look after Tomos too.' Bethany is smiling at Miss. Bethany's smiling at me now. Miss is putting her hand on my shoulder. 'Don't worry. I'll sort it out. Put this on.' She's getting something from a chair. It's the blue coat from the lost property box. 'And before I go, I'll have a word with Mrs Pugh.'

I'm standing with Seren and Bethany. I'm putting the coat on. Miss is talking to Mrs Pugh Year Two.

Mrs Pugh Year Two is shaking her head. 'You can't do that. We can't be expected to chase after parents. Mr Griffiths won't like it. And you can't bother him now – he's got the governors in his office. They're talking budgets.'

'I think Mr Griffiths would understand in the circumstances.' Miss is saying it very quietly.

'No.' Mrs Pugh Year Two's face is pink. 'That boy has to stay in school. He's had plenty of time to bring back his slip.' Miss hasn't heard her. She's going through the hall door. She's going fast. 'Mrs Davies!' Mrs Pugh Year Two is shouting it into the corridor. 'Mrs Davies!' She's shaking her head at me. 'Look at the trouble you're causing, child.' She's making a boy hold the door open. She's clapping her hands. She's telling everyone to be quiet and follow her. She's walking out of the hall like a very important person.

I am standing in between Seren and Bethany. We are waiting for it to be our turn to go through the doors. 'Blow your nose,' Seren says. Her face is still a little bit cross. I'm blowing my nose on the tissue Miss gave me. Seren is looking at my hands. 'Where's your packed lunch?'

156

I am looking round. 'There.' I'm running back to where I was sitting. I'm grabbing my brown paper bag from the floor. I'm running back to Seren and Bethany. They are waiting for me. It's nearly our turn to go through the doors. 'Am I going to the zoo?' I say. I'm looking at Seren.

'Maybe,' she says. 'If Miss sorts it out.' She's pointing her finger at me. 'But remember your permission slip next time.'

We are going through the doors. We are following the children out of the hall. We are following them to the bus. We are at the end of the long line of children. We are waiting to get on the bus.

Mrs Pugh Year Two is standing by the steps. 'Stop, Tomos Morris. Don't you get on the bus. You may have to stay in school.' Seren has stopped too. She's telling Bethany to stop. 'Not you,' Mrs Pugh Year Two says. 'You two girls can get on.'

'We're looking after Tomos,' Seren says. 'Mrs Davies told us to.'

'And I am telling you to get on the bus.' Bethany is going up the steps onto the bus. She's looking back at Seren. Seren is not getting on the bus. 'Get on,' Mrs Pugh Year Two says. 'I'll look after Tomos.' She's making her voice sound kind. Her mouth is trying to smile at me. Seren is looking at her like she's not telling the truth. 'Get on, Seren.' Mrs Pugh Year Two's voice is cross again now.

'Stay here and wait for Miss,' Seren says. 'And don't move.' She's shaking her finger at me. 'And don't lose your packed lunch again.' She's going up the steps.

Mrs Pugh Year Two is getting on the bus too. I am the

only one not on the bus. I'm looking for Miss. I can't see her anywhere. I'm looking back up the path to school. I'm looking at the school car park. I'm looking everywhere. There are some people standing by the school gate. They're waving to the bus. There are some people standing across the road too. But I can't see Miss.

Mrs Pugh Year Two is at the top of the steps. She is making all the children listen to her. She's telling them they must not sing on the bus. They must not leave sweet papers on the floor. They must not put their feet on the seat in front. They must not take their seat belts off. And they must not sing on the bus. They must not get lost at the petting farm. They must not take off their waterproof trousers if it's raining. They must not take off their sun hats if it's sunny. They must not be late for the bus when it's time to come home because the bus driver is very busy. And they must not sing on the bus. No one must not spoil Mrs Pugh Year Two's trip. She has spent a lot of time planning it. They must not spoil it for her. And they must NOT sing on the b—

'Sorry to interrupt,' the bus driver says. He doesn't sound sorry. He sounds cross. 'We need to get going. We're already fifteen minutes late.'

Mrs Pugh Year Two has stopped talking. She's looking at the bus driver. 'We're waiting for Mrs Davies, I'm afraid.'

I'm afraid too. I'm afraid Miss won't come back. I am looking and looking and looking. And looking and looking and looking. I want her to come back. I want to go to the zoo.

There. At last. I can see her. She's come round the corner.

She's walking down the road. She's walking very very fast. She's getting nearer and nearer. 'Got it.' Her voice is all blowy. She's waving a piece of paper. She's by the bus now. 'Your mum's signed it. Right, Tomos. Let's get on.'

I'm getting on the bus. I'm getting on fast. She's coming up the steps behind me. I'm turning round. 'Am I going to the zoo?'

'Yes.' Miss's face is pink and she's smiling. 'You are.'

She's giving the slip to Mrs Pugh Year Two. 'Tomos's permission slip, signed by his mum.'

Mrs Pugh Year Two is grabbing it. She's putting it with all the other pieces of paper.

I am remembering something. 'Did Mammy shout at you?' I don't want Mammy to shout at Miss again.

Miss is shaking her head. 'Shhh, shhh, Tomos. She was fine. Don't worry about that.'

Wes is calling me. There's no one sitting next to him. 'Sit here.'

I'm sitting down next to Wes. I'm putting on my seat belt. 'I'm going to the zoo.' I am smiling and smiling and smiling. 'I'm going to the zoo after all.'

'It is not a zoo, Tomos Morris,' Mrs Pugh Year Two says. She is walking down the bus. She's checking that everyone has not taken their seat belts off. 'It's just a petting farm. There won't be lions or tigers or any animals like that.' Eddie has put his feet on the seat in front. She's giving him a row.

'Can we go now?' the bus driver is shouting.

'Yes,' Mrs Pugh Year Two says in her loud voice. She's making Miss sit next to her at the front of the bus. The bus

159

is making a rumbly noise. It's starting to move. The people by the school gate are waving and the people across the road are waving too.

'Do you think there'll be monkeys at the petting farm?' I'm saying it to Wes and I'm looking out of the window. I'm watching the school going away. 'I like monkeys.'

'Yes,' Wes says. 'Lots of monkeys. And they bite.'

I'm holding my packed lunch bag. I'm holding it tight. It's making a crinkly sound. 'They bite?'

'Yes,' Wes says. 'And there'll be rhinoceroses.' He's looking in his backpack. He's taking out a big bag of sweets.

We are going down my road now. Some people are standing by their gates. They're waving to the bus and it's going past our house but Mammy's not by our gate. I'm trying to look through our windows. I'm trying to see Mammy. I want her to see that I'm going to the zoo. I'm looking and looking. But the curtains in her bedroom are still closed.

'And there'll be crocodiles,' Wes says. 'At the petting farm.' He's putting a lot of sweets in his mouth. I can't see Mammy. I can't see her in our house. 'And the crocodiles are huge.' Wes's voice is squeezing through the sweets in his mouth. It sounds all wonky. 'They're as long as this bus.'

Kaylee's mammy is standing by Kaylee's gate. She's waving to the bus and I am waving to Kaylee's mammy. I'm waving and waving and Kaylee is waving too.

Wes is twisting his bag of sweets. He's twisting it round and round and he's putting it back in his backpack. 'And they run after you, the giant crocodiles at the petting farm.'

He's putting his feet up on the seat in front and he's taking the brown paper bag off my lap. He's looking in it. He's poking the sandwiches. 'Yuck.' And the apple. 'Yuck.' He's taking out my chocolate biscuit. 'And when they catch you…' He's looking at my chocolate biscuit. He's taking the wrapper off it '…those giant crocodiles at the petting farm…' He's taking a big bite of my biscuit. He's biting it in two. He's pushing the other bit of my chocolate biscuit into his mouth '…when they catch you…' He's chewing and chewing and chewing and chewing.

He's opening his mouth and he's showing me all the bits of chocolate biscuit. Chocolatey spit is running down his chin '…they eat you,' he says.

* * *

We're at the zoo and everyone has put their backpacks in a special room for bags and I've put my brown paper bag in the room and I've zipped up my coat from the lost property box.

I am with Nadia and Kaylee and Rhys and I'm with Taylor and Eddie too and we are in Miss's group and we are going round the zoo together and a man has given us little paper bags that are white and there are lots of bits in the bags and we must not eat the bits because they are for the goats in the field that we are going into and the goats are running up to us and there are lots of them. They're quite big. Nadia and Eddie are screaming. They're trying to run away. And the goats are chasing them.

The man says, 'Don't worry. Don't worry. They just want their breakfast. They won't hurt you.'

Miss is holding Nadia's hand. She is trying to hold Eddie's hand too but he's still running away. The man is saying we must take the food out of the bags and put it on our hands. We must hold our hands out flat and let the goats eat from our flat hands.

'Careful,' the goat man says. 'They're a bit lively in the morning. And hungry too.'

I'm trying to put my hand into the bag to get some food. A big goat is right next to me. He has bulgy white eyes. The little black bits in his eyes are watching me. He looks very cross. I'm trying to get some food for him. I'm putting my hand into the bag but he is pulling at it. He's pulling with his big yellow teeth. He's making a hole in the bag. All the food is falling out of the hole. He's eating the food off the floor.

All the goats are looking for bits on the floor now. Everyone's bags are empty. 'There we are,' the man says. 'Put the bags in the bin by the gate.'

'Come on,' Miss says. 'I think the goats have enjoyed their breakfast.' We're going to the gate. I'm holding the white paper bag.

'Look!' Nadia says. We're turning round. We're looking where Nadia's pointing. The big goat is running after us. He's running fast. He's running round and round us. He's trying to jump up at me. I'm running round and round too. I'm trying to run away from him.

'Over here, Tomos,' Miss says. She's trying to catch up

with me. The big goat is chasing me. He's going in front of me now. I'm turning round. He's going behind me. He won't leave me alone. I can't get away from him.

'It's all right,' the goat man says. 'He's just being friendly.' The man has gone through the gate. Another group is waiting to feed the goats. The man is giving bags of food to them.

Miss is trying to get to me but the goat won't let her. He's standing in the way. 'Give it to him.' Miss is shouting it over the goat's back.

'What?' I say.

'Give him the bag.'

'This?' I'm holding up the bag. 'We have to put them in the bin.' The goat is jumping up at me. I'm moving the bag away from him.

'Just give it to him,' Miss says.

'Look,' a loud voice is shouting. 'That goat is going to kill Tomos.' I know that voice. It is Wes's voice. I can hear him laughing now. And the goat is jumping up again. He's knocking me over. He's standing on top of me. His feet are hard and pointy. They're hurting my legs. He's pulling at the empty bag. He's trying to pull it out of my hand. He's pulling and pulling.

'Let go,' Miss says. I'm letting go of the bag. The goat is holding it in his yellow teeth. He's looking at me with the black bits in his eyes. And he's pulling the bag into his mouth. He's pulling it in with his long pink tongue. He's looking down at me with his cross eyes. And he's chewing with his big yellow teeth. Miss is pushing the goat. She's pushing him off me. The goat is running away. Miss is grabbing my hand. She's pulling me up. 'It's okay,' she says. 'He's gone now. You're fine.' She's rubbing the dirt off the back of my coat. We're walking to the gate.

'Ha, ha,' Wes says. He's pointing to me. He's with some other children. Bethany's mammy is looking after them all. 'A goat nearly ate you.'

'Shhh, Wes,' Miss says.

'Yes,' Bethany's mammy says. It's very hard to hear her. 'Quiet, Wes.'

Miss is holding my hand. She's finding Eddie and she's holding his hand too. 'Right, are we all here?' She's looking at Nadia and Kaylee and Rhys and Taylor. 'Good.' We're starting to walk away from the field full of goats. Miss is looking back at Bethany's mammy. 'We're going to see the guinea pigs next.' Miss is making her eyebrows go up high. 'I'm hoping that won't be so terrifying.'

* * *

We've seen lots of animals at the zoo. We've seen sheep and baby sheep called lambs in a place called the barn. Some of them were jumping up. Some of them were sleeping in the hay. The lamb man said they like sleeping in the hay when they're little. And they jump a lot when they're bigger. We've seen guinea pigs and we've had a ride on a tractor too. It was a blue tractor. And we've walked round the pond. It was a very big pond. My legs are very tired from walking round it. And we fed the ducks that live on the big big pond.

Miss has told us to sit in the shelter. We're sitting on benches. There are lots and lots of benches and tables too. They are made out of wood. We're having our packed lunches. I'm sitting with Nadia and Kaylee and Rhys and Taylor and Eddie. Wes is sitting on the next table. He's with some children I don't know. I'm eating my ham sandwiches from the brown bag Mrs Jenkins from school gave me. I'm eating the tuna mayo and sweetcorn sandwiches Miss brought too. There's a big box of them. Nadia and Kaylee and Taylor and Rhys and Eddie are having some too. We're all having lots. They're lovely.

'Right,' Miss says. She's putting the lid on the box because it's empty. 'Finish your biscuits. Then we're going to see the deer.'

I'm looking for my chocolate biscuit. I'm looking for it in my paper bag then I remember. 'I haven't got a biscuit,' I say. 'Wes took it.'

Miss looks cross. 'That Wes.' She's getting something out of her bag. It's a box of cakes. They have white icing and a cherry on the top. 'Have one of these.' Miss is letting us all have a cake. They're very nice. We're licking the icing off them.

Wes is coming over to our table. 'Can I have one of those?' He's picking up the box and he's looking at the picture on it. There are no cakes left in it now.

'You've had enough already,' Miss says. 'I hear you've been stealing other people's food.'

'Haven't,' Wes says.

'You took my biscuit,' I say. 'On the bus.'

'I only borrowed it.'

'Go and get it then,' Miss says. 'And give it back.'

'Can't. I ate it.'

'Well, that's not borrowing,' Miss says. 'If you borrow something, you have to be able to give it back.'

'Like our school library books,' Nadia says. 'We have to give those back.'

Miss is nodding. 'Exactly, Nadia. And if we kept them, then that would be stealing.'

'I didn't steal his biscuit,' Wes says. 'I'm borrowing it.'

Miss is letting out a big breath. 'Go back to your own seat, Wes.' She isn't smiling at him.

'Mrs Roly said I could come over.' Wes is pointing over to Bethany's mammy. She's sitting on the bench and her legs are squashed in under the table. Her face is red. She has very big arms. They are red too.

'You mean Mrs Rowlands,' Miss says.

'Yeah, Mrs Roly-Poly,' Wes says.

'Don't be rude, Wes.' Miss looks very cross. 'Or I'll ask Mrs Pugh to move you into her own group.'

'Mrs Pugh won't do that,' Wes says. 'She doesn't want me in her group.' He's throwing down the empty box of cakes.

'Go back to your table, Wes,' Miss says. 'I'm not asking you again.'

Wes is going back to his table. He's looking over his shoulder at us. He's staring at Miss. She's tidying up our table. 'Slag,' he says.

Miss is looking up. 'What did you say?'

Wes is smiling at her. 'Nothing.'

Nadia says, 'He said sla—'

'It's okay, Nadia,' Miss says. 'Let's just ignore him.'

* * *

We are standing in a big line. We're standing outside the shop. We are all mixed up. I was with Eddie and Junior and Rhys. We were in the toilets for boys. But I can't see them now. Miss is with Nadia and Kaylee in the toilets for girls. There's a long line for their toilets. I'm standing next to Wes. Mrs Pugh Year Two is standing by the shop door. We have been at the zoo a long time. It's nearly time to go home.

'You can only go into the shop if you've got money to spend,' Mrs Pugh Year Two is saying. 'You can't go in to cause trouble.' Her eyes are looking at us all. They're looking down the line of us. They've stopped on me. 'You. Tomos Morris.' She's pointing her finger at me. 'Have you got money to spend?' Her eyes are looking and looking at me. 'Well,' she says. 'Have you?' My fingers are in my pocket. They can feel my coin. I'm nodding my head. 'That's all right then. The first five can go in.' She is counting us. Wes is number four. I am number five. 'Three minutes,' she says. 'And don't touch anything you can't afford.'

We're going into the shop. There are lots of things everywhere. There are things hanging down and things piled up. There are lots of toys in boxes. Everything is yellow and red and silver and blue.

'What's wrong, thicko?' Wes is a long way away from me.

He's standing by a big tower of boxes. There are cars in the boxes. I'm still by the door. 'Come on,' he says.

'No shouting,' Mrs Pugh Year Two says. She is shouting it. She's standing by the door and she's watching us. 'And NO TOUCHING ANYTHING YOU CAN'T AFFORD.'

Wes is taking a box off the tower of cars. The tower's wobbling a bit. I'm going over to Wes. I'm looking at the cars too. I'm not touching them. 'See these.' He's pointing to the cars. 'I've got loads of them. More than all these.'

'Have you got a red one?' I say. I'm looking at a red car. It's in a black box. It looks nice. I'm wondering if it's something I can afford.

'I've got loads of red ones. They're crappy.' He's putting the box back on the tower. It's wobbling again. 'Silver ones are best.'

'One minute left,' Mrs Pugh Year Two says. 'Hurry up.'

Wes is going away from the cars. I'm going with him. We've come to some plastic animals. 'Have they got crocodiles?' Wes is pushing his hand into the box of animals. I'm looking at Mrs Pugh Year Two. She's not looking at Wes. She's pointing to someone outside the shop. I'm looking at the animals again. I can see a goat. It's got black bits in its eyes.

'Go to the till now,' Mrs Pugh Year Two says. 'Your time's up.' Wes is grabbing lots of animals. He has a cow and a dog and a sheep and some ducks.

'That's five pounds, please,' the lady at the till says. She's putting Wes's animals into a paper bag. Wes is holding some money out to the lady. The lady's looking at Wes's hand.

'You've got one pound there. You can have one animal for that.' She's tipping the animals out of the paper bag. Wes is picking up a cow. The lady's putting it back in the bag. Wes is giving her his pound.

I'm taking the plastic goat to the till. 'I'll wait for you,' Wes says. He's standing next to me. He's looking at the things by the till. He's touching some of them. I'm looking to see if Mrs Pugh Year Two has seen him. She's looking another way.

'Thanks, Wes.' I'm holding up the goat. The lady's looking at it.

'One pound, please,' she says. She's taking the goat from me. She's putting it in a paper bag.

'I haven't got a pound,' I say. My fingers can feel the coin in my pocket.

The lady is tipping the goat out of the bag. 'How much *have* you got?'

'Fifty pence.'

Wes is laughing. 'Only fifty pence. Thicko.'

The lady's looking at Wes. She's not smiling. 'Well, let's see. What could you have for that?' She's looking at all the things on her table. 'You could have a postcard. They're thirty pence. There's one with a goat on it.' She's holding out a postcard to me.

I'm taking it. 'Thank you,' I say. I'm getting my coin out of my pocket and I'm giving it to the lady.

'Oh goodness.' She's looking at my coin. She's turning it over on her hand. 'I haven't seen one of these for years.'

'Wesley,' Mrs Pugh Year Two is saying. 'Have you paid?'

'Yes,' Wes says.

'Come out of the shop then.' Wes is going out. There's just me in the shop now. And the lady.

She's turning my coin over again. 'It's an old fifty pence. You can't spend these anymore.'

'I haven't got a new one,' I say.

'Where did you get it?' She's still holding my coin.

'The lady next door gave it to me. For Christmas.'

The lady's looking down at her hand. 'Have this back, love. Keep it safe.' She's giving me my coin. 'It could be worth a lot of money one day when you're as old as me.' She's smiling. I'm taking my coin back.

'Tomos Morris, your time's up,' Mrs Pugh Year Two is saying. 'Come out. You've had long enough.' Some more children are coming into the shop. I'm giving the postcard back to the lady.

'Keep it,' the lady says. She's saying it quietly. She's smiling again. 'You can have the postcard on me.'

'Thank you,' I say. 'Thank you very much.' I'm putting my coin back in the pocket in my trousers. I'm smiling at the lady. I'm taking my postcard out of the shop. I'm waiting outside with Wes and Mrs Pugh Year Two. We're waiting for the rest of the children to go into the shop. And for some to come out. I'm looking at my postcard. There's lots of blue sky on it. And a big goat like the goat that chased me. The goat is showing his scary yellow teeth. He's laughing and laughing with his big teeth. He looks like he's laughing at me. And I'm putting the postcard away. I'm putting it away fast. I am putting it away in my coat pocket.

* * *

We are standing in a big line again. It's the line to get on the bus. We've been waiting a long time. I want to sit down because my legs are very tired. But we are not allowed.

Miss has gone to look for the bus driver. Mrs Pugh Year Two is very cross with him. 'He said to be here on the dot of two and here we are. And no sign of him.' She's saying it to Bethany's mammy. 'He has to drop us off and then go and do the secondary school run. He kept saying we couldn't be late or we'd mess up his schedule. And look!' She's waving her arms round. 'Where is he?'

Bethany's mammy is lifting her shoulders. Mrs Pugh Year Two said Bethany's mammy must keep an eye on Wes. But she's not keeping an eye on him. She's just sitting on the grass. Her face is pink and wet. And Wes is standing next to me.

'This is boring,' he says. I'm nodding. My legs are very tired. My eyes are tired too. 'Let's play a game,' he says.

'What game?' I think I am too tired to play a game.

'Chase.'

I'm too tired to play chase. 'We're not allowed to move,' I say.

'Where on earth is the driver?' Mrs Pugh Year Two is saying with her loud voice. 'And where has Mrs Davies got to?' She's looking back down the path. 'Where are they?' She's walking down the path a bit. She's trying to see them.

'Hide and seek,' Wes says. 'Go hide. I'll come and find you.'

'We're not allowed to move,' I say. 'Mrs Pugh Year Two said.'

'She's not even looking. Go on. Quick.' He's pushing me out of the line. 'Go on, thicko. Mrs Pugh won't mind.'

Mrs Pugh Year Two isn't looking at me. I think Wes is right. She won't mind if we play for a bit. I'm running behind the bus. I'm only going to hide for a minute. Wes is running after me. 'That's a rubbish place to hide,' he says. I'm trying to think of a better place.

Seren is putting her head round the side of the bus. 'We're not allowed to move.'

'Shut up,' Wes says to her. He's grabbed a lot of stones from the car park floor. He's throwing them at her.

'Telling Mrs Pugh.' She's gone back round the bus.

'Quick!' Wes says. 'Run and hide!'

'No,' I say. 'We're not allowed.'

'Quick!' He's pushing me.

'We can't.'

He's pushing me again. 'Quick!' He's pushing and pushing me. 'Mrs Pugh will catch us. Run!'

I don't want her to catch us.

We are running. We are running away from the line of children. We can't see them. They're on the other side of the bus. We're running away from Mrs Pugh Year Two.

We have run a long way. We've run past the field of goats. We've run past the ducks and the big big pond. We're at the barn. 'Hide!' Wes says. 'Hide!'

I know a good place to hide. I'm running inside the barn and I'm finding a big pile of hay. I'm lying down on it. I'm pulling the hay all round me and on top of me. I'm inside the big pile of hay.

'Wes?' I'm saying it quietly. I don't want Mrs Pugh Year Two to hear me. Wes is very quiet. I can't hear him at all. 'Wes? When can we come out?' I'm listening and listening but I can't hear Wes. I can hear the sheep and the lambs. I'm listening and listening. And listening and listening. But I can't hear Wes. My legs are very tired. My eyes are tired too. 'Wes? Wes?' I'm listening and listening. And listening and listening. My eyes are closing.

And I can't hear Wes at all.

* * *

I am running. I'm running fast fast fast. I'm running to get away from the crocodile and the monkeys and the goat.

The crocodile is very slow and the monkeys are too. But the goat is running fast. He's chasing me with his big bulgy eyes and his sharp feet. He wants to knock me over. He wants to stand on me again. I'm running away and I'm trying to hide but Mrs Pugh Year Two is stopping me. She's making me stand still. She's saying, 'Stupid kid, Tomos Morris.' She's saying and saying it. And I am trying to say, 'The goat is coming' but she isn't listening. She is just saying, 'Stupid kid, stupid kid.' And her pointy teeth are yellow like the goat's teeth. And her breath is stinky.

The crocodile is catching up. And the monkeys are too. They're running round and round and round and round me. And the goat is laughing and laughing. 'You're going to get eaten,' the goat says. The crocodile is showing me his sharp sharp teeth and the monkeys are showing me their teeth too. And the goat is laughing and laughing and laughing.

Mrs Pugh Year Two tells the goat to be quiet. She tells the crocodile to go away. And the monkeys too. They're all running away. They're all hiding from Mrs Pugh Year Two. She is smiling at me. She's smiling with her pointy teeth and her stinky breath. And she's growing. She's growing as big as the BFG in my library book. She's huge. And she's smiling and smiling at me. She says, 'Would you like a biscuit?' She is holding one. It's like the ones Miss gave me to eat in the holidays. But it is a giant biscuit. Mrs Pugh Year Two is picking me up. She's putting me on the biscuit. I am trying to eat it but Mrs Pugh Year Two is shaking me too much. She's opening and opening her mouth. I'm moving up and up. I'm moving towards her mouth and she's going to swallow the biscuit. She's going to swallow me too.

'Well, well,' a kind voice says. 'You were very comfy there.'

I'm trying to open my eyes. It's very hard to open them. They are stuck shut. I'm still moving up and up but I don't think I'm on a biscuit. I don't think I'm going into Mrs Pugh Year Two's mouth.

Someone is holding me. 'Dat?' I say. I am trying hard to open my eyes. I want to see Dat. I haven't seen him for a long long time. He used to hold me like this sometimes. He used to carry me to bed when I was very very sleepy.

'You've caused a bit of a fuss,' the voice says. I am making my eyes open because I want to see Dat. But it's not him carrying me. It's someone else with a kind face. It's the lamb man. 'Over here,' he says. 'He's fine.'

I can hear someone running. 'Oh thank goodness,' a voice says. It's Miss's voice. She's grabbing hold of me. She's taking me from the lamb man. She's squeezing me very tight.

'Fast asleep.' The lamb man is smiling. 'In the hay.'

'Like little Lord Jesus,' I say. My voice is very quiet. 'Away in a manger.'

The lamb man is laughing and laughing. I'm laughing now too but Miss is crying. 'Oh thank goodness.' She's saying it over and over and she's squeezing and squeezing me.

The lamb man is running off. 'I'd better tell the others,' he says. 'So they can stop searching the lake.'

* * *

We are nearly back at school and we've all been good. We have nearly all been good. Miss is bringing a plastic tub round. It's a tub with lots of sweets in. The sweets are tiny bars of chocolate. Miss is showing me the tub because it's my turn to choose a chocolate.

'Mammy likes these.' I'm taking a chocolate. 'She has big bars of these. She keeps them on top of the cupboard in the kitchen.'

'Well, enjoy it, Tomos,' Miss says.

'I'm not going to eat it. I'm keeping it for Mammy. It's her favourite.'

'Oh.' Miss is smiling. 'That's kind of you.' She's showing

175

the tub to Kaylee. I'm putting the chocolate safe. I'm putting it in the pocket in my coat.

The bus is stopping at school. There are lots of people standing at the gate. Mrs Pugh Year Two is talking to them now. 'I'm terribly sorry we're so late,' Mrs Pugh Year Two is saying. 'I'm afraid there was a…an unavoidable delay.' The bus driver is shaking his head. He's looking cross.

All the children are getting off the bus. I've stopped crying. But I don't want to walk past Mrs Pugh Year Two. She might shout at me again. Her breath is very stinky when she shouts. Her teeth are very pointy. And I don't want to start crying again.

Miss is putting her hand on my shoulder. 'Okay now, Tomos?' I'm nodding. 'Zip up your coat.' I'm zipping up my coat. 'Wear it home,' Miss says, 'because it's started raining. But don't let your mum see it. Give it to Kaylee's mum when you get to your gate.' She's smiling at me but her eyes are sad. 'Ask her to look after it for you 'til tomorrow.'

'Okay. Goodbye, Miss.' My voice is still a bit jumpy.

'Goodbye, Tomos.' Her voice is still a bit jumpy too. And her eyes are red. Mrs Pugh Year Two is looking another way. I'm getting off the bus fast. Kaylee and her mammy are waiting for me. I'm showing them my postcard of the goat.

'That's nice,' Kaylee's mammy says. 'Put it away now, though, so it don't get wet.' I'm putting it in the pocket in my coat with the chocolate I'm saving for Mammy. 'And put your hood up.' I'm putting my hood up. We're walking home. We're walking home fast because of the rain and my legs are very tired. I'm yawning. I'm yawning lots and lots and my yawns are all bumpy and jumpy.

We are nearly at the corner of our road.

'Oi!' It's a lady. She's shouting at us from across the road. There are a lot of other ladies with her. And lots of children. 'That's my Joey's coat.' She's crossing the road and she's marching over to us. All the other ladies are crossing the road too. All the children are crossing with them. There's a long line of them. 'You've nicked my Joey's coat.' The lady's saying it to me. She's a very big lady. She's looking down at me. 'It's got that hole there.' She's poking my shoulder. She's doing it hard. 'That's where I burnt it with my fag.'

The ladies are all round me in a circle. It's hard to breathe because of the flowery smell. And the cigarette smell. The ladies are all looking at me. The children are too. They're looking at my coat. And they're looking at the burnt bit. They're all nodding. 'Yeah,' they're saying. 'That's Joey's coat.'

'Yeah,' says a boy. He is quite small. 'That's my coat.'

The big lady is grabbing the coat Miss gave me from the lost property box. She's pulling the zip down. 'Give it back.'

'Miss gave it to me.' I'm trying to make my words loud. But they have come out tiny.

Kaylee's mammy is pushing into the circle. Kaylee is holding her hand. Kaylee's mammy is putting her arm round me. She's pushing herself in front of the lady. 'Leave him alone. It's his coat.'

'It's not,' I say. But my words are too small. It's raining very hard now. The lady has grabbed me again. She's pulled the zip right down. She's pulling the coat off one of my arms. She's pulling it off the other one now.

'Leave him alone,' Kaylee's mammy is saying again. 'I'll report you to the Head.' Kaylee is crying. She's holding onto her mammy's leg. Her hood has come down. Her hair is very wet.

Joey's mammy has got the coat off me. The rain is going on my jumper. 'Report me,' she says. 'And I'll say your kid stole my son's coat.' She's pointing to me.

'That's not her kid,' one of the ladies says. 'That's Rhiannon Morris's boy. You know, that slag that lives round the corner. The one that's going with Nick Brickland.'

'Oh my God,' Joey's mammy says. 'That loser Brick. That drug dealing piece of sh…' She's poking my shoulder again. 'He's a good enough match for your mother. She's always been trouble. And now you're stealing coats. Like mother, like son.' She's walking back across the road. She's taking the coat with her. All the other ladies are marching after her. The children are marching with them. They're splashing through the puddles.

'It was in the lost property box.' I am trying to say it loud. I want the lady to hear me. The rain is making my hair very wet. The water is running down my nose. 'I didn't steal it.' I'm trying my best to say it loud but the rain is very splashy. Kaylee's mammy is lifting the side of her coat. She's putting it over my head. She's holding my hand. She's pulling me along. We are rushing home. We're rushing as fast as we can.

I'm looking over my shoulder. I'm looking at the ladies. They are a long way away now. I'm remembering Mrs Pugh

Year Two. I'm remembering her shouting at me outside the barn. I'm remembering her shouting at Miss. I'm remembering Miss shouting back. I'm remembering Miss crying. And me crying too. I'm crying again now.

'I didn't steal it!' I'm shouting. My words sound funny. They're all jumpy. I'm shouting and shouting. 'I didn't steal it. I didn't steal it. I DIDN'T STEAL IT!'

They can't hear me shouting. They've gone round the corner. I'm putting my hand in my pocket. My pocket in my trousers. My fifty pence is in there. And then I remember my goat postcard. The one the lady in the shop gave me. And the tiny chocolate bar. The one I'm saving for Mammy. They are in my other pocket. The pocket in my coat. In Joey's coat. In the coat Miss gave me.

In the coat the lady has taken.

* * *

We are writing letters to the zoo. We must call it The Petting Farm. I like writing letters.

I'm writing quite a long letter. I'm copying some of the words Miss has put on the board. I'm saying *Dear Mr Petting Farm, How are you? I am well. Thank you for letting us feed your goats. Your lamb man is very nice. Love from Tomos xxx P.S. I like your hay.*

I am writing another letter. My other letter says *Dear Mr Bus Driver, How are you? I am well. Sorry I made you late for the big children. Love from Tomos xxx P.S. I hope the big children did not mind.*

Miss is helping me with my spelling. I am standing by her desk. 'I like your P.S.s.' Miss is looking at me. She's pushing her brown hair behind her ear.

'Thank you,' I say. 'A P.S. is an important thing that you forgot to put after *Dear* and before *Love from*. Nanno told me.'

'Well done for remembering,' Miss says. 'Perhaps you should write a letter to Mrs Pugh too.'

My hand is very tired. I have been writing letters for a long time. I say, 'Can I draw a picture for her instead?'

'That's a lovely idea,' Miss says and she gives me a big bit of paper.

* * *

It's playtime. Mrs Pugh Year Two is on guard. She's standing by the wall. She's seeing no one is spitting or climbing over the fence or poking each other in the eye.

I am holding my picture. It's a picture of yellow flowers. I have rubbed out the barn and all the hay. And the lambs like Miss said. I am going to stand close to Mrs Pugh Year Two.

She's seen me. 'Where's your coat, Tomos Morris?'

'Do you mean the one from the lost property box?' I am trying not to look at her. She's a bit scary when I look at her. 'The lady took that coat. It was Joey's.'

'I mean your own coat,' she says.

I'm thinking. 'It's in Nanno and Dat's house. In the cupboard under the stairs.'

'Well, it's no good there,' she says. 'Remember it tomorrow.'

I am remembering it now. It's green with yellow bits and it's snuggly. I'm trying to remember to remember it tomorrow as well.

I'm still standing close to Mrs Pugh Year Two. She's looking at me again. 'What do you want?' I am holding out my picture. 'Is that for me?' She's taken my picture. She's looking at it. I'm hoping she can't see the lambs. And the barn and the hay I've rubbed out. She says, 'Is this to say sorry?' I am nodding. I'm looking at my shoes. 'Well, thank you, I suppose.' She's making sniffy noises. 'But NEVER try to spoil my school trip again.'

'I didn't try to spoil it,' I say.

'Yes you did. And even though you were asleep in the hay, Tomos Morris, you were not like our Lord Jesus. You were not like our Lord Jesus at all.' She's waving her finger at me. '*He* would never have run off and got lost.'

I am thinking about a story Dat read to me. From his book of Bible stories. I'm remembering a story about when Jesus was a big boy. He went to a church and his mammy and daddy couldn't find him. 'What about when Jesus—'

'Don't try to be clever with me,' Mrs Pugh Year Two says. Her face is very cross now. Her cheeks are very red. She's waving her finger next to my face. She's poking it at my nose. 'Don't try and drag *Him* into this. Our Lord would never have ruined my trip.'

'Sorry.' I'm looking at my shoes again. 'It was just an accident.'

181

'Just an accident?' she says. 'Just an accident to run off and fall asleep in a barn? Just an accident to make the bus late back and cause all the parents to worry that we'd crashed into a ditch and were lying maimed and bleeding in the middle of nowhere? JUST AN ACCIDENT?'

'Yes. I was tired.'

'Don't lie to me. You did your best to spoil it.'

'I'm not telling a lie.' I'm trying not to shout it but my words are getting loud. 'Nanno always says not to tell lies and I'm not telling a lie.'

'YES, YOU ARE.'

'NO, I'M NOT.'

Mrs Pugh Year Two's face is very red. 'DON'T YOU SHOUT AT ME.' She is putting out her hand. She's grabbing my jumper.

Eddie is running up to us. His face is red too. 'Miss! Miss! Malky Morgan is eating worms in the vegetable patch.'

'Oh,' Mrs Pugh Year Two says. 'Not again.' She's letting go of my jumper. She's pointing her finger at me. 'Stay right where you are.' She is walking away like a soldier. Like a busy round soldier. She's walking all the way to the Look What We're Growing corner. She's going to find Malky. I am standing by the wall. I'm staying right where I am. And I'm looking through Wes's class window.

Wes is inside. He's writing. He's writing very slowly. I'm knocking the window. He's looking up and he's waving to me. I am waving back. He's sticking out his tongue and he's making a funny face. I am making a funny face. Wes is waving to me again. He's waving with his fingers. He's

182

dancing and waving with his fingers. I'm dancing and waving with my fingers too.

Some children have come to see me dancing. Wes is moving his bottom now. I'm moving my bottom too. I'm moving it like Wes. I'm moving it in and out and in and out. I'm dancing with my bottom and waving with my fingers. I am waving my long finger on one hand. And I'm waving my long finger on my other hand. I am waving them up to the sky like Wes. I'm laughing and dancing and moving my bottom in and out and in and out and waving with my fingers.

Lots of children are watching me now. Some of them are laughing. Some of them are clapping.

'Tomos Morris,' Mrs Pugh Year Two says. 'Stop that at once!' She is with Malky Morgan. He has a dirty mouth. I've stopped dancing. 'How dare you behave like that on the playground. Your shouting was bad enough. Go with Malky to Mr Griffiths' office,' she says. 'And make sure you tell him why I sent you, you horrible child.'

* * *

We are in Sir's room. Malky and me.

'Now, boys,' Sir says, 'why are you here?'

'Mrs Pugh sent me,' Malky says.

'Right, Malky. Been eating worms again I see.'

'Yes, Sir.'

'Oh dear, oh dear. What will we do with you, Malky?'

Malky's looking down at the floor. 'I don't know, sir.'

183

Sir is shaking his head. 'Neither do I.' He's holding his chin. 'Neither do I.'

Sir's looking at me now. 'And what about you?' He has big glasses and big eyes and no hair. 'Did Mrs Pugh send you too?'

'Yes, Sir,' I say.

'What have you done, Tomos?'

I am thinking.

'Well?'

'I think it was the hay,' I say.

'The hay?'

'The hay I rubbed out. On the picture I drew for her. And the barn and the lambs.'

Sir is looking at me with his big eyes. He's knocking his pen on the table. He's looking and looking at me. 'Oh, the barn and the lambs! You mean the trip to the petting farm.' He's shaking his head. 'No, Tomos, we talked about that the other day. Mrs Pugh has said that's all forgotten now. It must be something else.'

I am thinking. 'It could be my coat.'

'What about your coat?'

'It's under the stairs in Nanno and Dat's house. And I had another one, but the lady took it.'

'The lady took it?' Sir says.

'Yes, Joey's mammy took it off me when I was walking home from school.'

'Did she now?' Sir is writing something down. 'That family…' He's shaking his head. 'I'll have a word with Joey's mum about that and I'll make sure you get your coat back.'

'It wasn't my coat. It was Joey's. Miss found it in the lost property box.'

'Oh,' Sir says. He's crossing something out. 'Well, if it's not about your coat, why do you think Mrs Pugh sent you here?'

I am thinking.

Malky says, 'It's what he was doing on the playground.'

'What were you doing, Tomos?' Sir says.

'I don't know, Sir.'

'You must have been doing something Mrs Pugh didn't like. She wouldn't have sent you here otherwise.'

I am thinking. 'It might be the shouting.'

'Right,' Sir says. 'What were you shouting?'

'That I don't tell lies.' I am remembering something else. 'Or it might be the dancing.'

Malky is nodding. 'It was the dancing.'

'What dancing?' Sir says.

'With my fingers,' I say. 'And my bottom.'

'Really?' Sir's eyebrows have gone up very high on his forehead.

'I can show you,' I say. 'If you want me to.'

'Go ahead,' Sir says. I am showing him. 'Yes.' Sir is nodding his head. 'I think you might be right, Tomos.' He's nodding and nodding. 'I think it might have been the dancing.'

* * *

185

I am up in my bed. I'm waiting for Mammy to come home. I'm waiting and waiting. I'm waiting for her to put my ladder back. So I can go to the toilet. And I'm thinking about a letter I would write to Nanno. A letter I would write if I had some paper. And a pencil. I'm saying *Dear Nanno, How are you? I am well. I have been litter picking all week. I have been doing it instead of having playtime. I have been doing it because Sir told me to. Because Mrs Pugh Year Two didn't like my dancing. I have been doing it with Malky but we are not allowed to go near the vegetable patch because Malky eats worms. I like litter picking. I get to use the pinchy thing. Wes wants to litter pick too because he wants to use the pinchy thing. He took it off me on the first day and he tried to pinch some girls with it. And Miss caught him and gave him a row and now he's not allowed to take my pinchy thing. And he's not allowed to come near me when I am litter picking. And he's not allowed to talk to me. It's very nice litter picking. I think you would like it too. Do you have to do litter picking in Heaven? Love, Tomos xxx P.S. I wish I had one of your lovely dinners. They are yum yum yummy. Mammy doesn't make dinners like your dinners. Sometimes she makes chips and sometimes she makes fish fingers with them and sometimes she makes beans but most of the time I have blue packets of crisps for dinner and I don't like the blue packets very much.*

* * *

I am in class and I'm helping Miss with her sandwiches. All the other children have gone home but Kaylee hasn't. She's watching telly with me. She's eating a chocolate biscuit. It's the one from Miss's packed lunch. I have shared it with her.

Miss is talking to Kaylee's mammy. 'Oh, your poor mum, Karen. How long do you think you'll be looking after her?'

'I told her we'll stay for all of the Easter holidays,' Kaylee's mammy says. 'Until school starts again.'

'That's good,' Miss says. 'It'll give her a chance to get sorted.'

'Yeah,' Kaylee's mammy says. 'Not that she's grateful. She says it's not long enough. The thing is, I'm a bit worried cos…' She's looking over at Kaylee and me. 'I won't be able to keep an eye on the house.' Her voice has gone very quiet.

'I'm going away as well,' Miss says. Her voice is very quiet too. It's hard to hear her. 'Colin says we need a holiday. He's booked us two weeks in the Lake District. I really don't want to go, but he says I'm stressed.' Miss is laughing. Her laugh sounds very sad. 'I'm even more stressed at the thought of going away and not being able to check on…' She's looking at me and Kaylee.

I'm smiling at Miss. She's smiling back at me. 'You two okay over there?' She's saying it loud.

'Yes, thank you.' It's hard to talk with my mouth full. Kaylee and me are watching a funny programme. It has a blue dog in it.

'I'm going to stay at Granny's,' Kaylee says. She's shouting it to Miss and she's jumping on the cushions.

'Well, isn't that lovely?' Miss says. 'Enjoy the programme now, while your mum and I have a chat.'

Kaylee's mammy says, 'I know I'm not allowed to ask,

really.' She's saying it very quietly. 'But did Mr Griffiths have a word with social services?'

'Yes.' Miss is very quiet too. 'They said they'd checked on him recently and he was doing okay.'

'Maybe they're right then. Maybe his mother's coping.'

Miss is shaking her head. I can see her from the side of my eye. 'The thing is, if I hadn't fed him, and bought him a new school uniform and kept washing his old one, he wouldn't have been looked after at all. I'm afraid I'm doing more harm than good.' She's biting her lip.

'What else can you do? You can't let him starve. You can't let him stink of wee all the time.'

I'm giving Kaylee one of the sandwiches now. We're still watching the funny programme and I'm watching Miss a bit too. She's shaking her head. 'I should just let social services deal with it, like Colin says. But it'd break my heart if something happened to him.'

'Yeah, I know what you mean.'

'And what really worries me, Karen, is – who goes to that house? What goes on there? My mother didn't look after me properly. She didn't always feed me or wash my clothes.' Miss is blowing out a big breath. 'But it was just me and her. No one else came round. There weren't any other alcoholics in the house. There weren't any…' Her voice is very very quiet now. 'Drugs. I'm worried about what he sees.'

'Has he said anything 'bout what goes on? Has he said anything 'bout…' Kaylee's mammy's voice is very very quiet now too. 'Her boyfriend or his friends?'

'No. He doesn't mention them. He talks mostly about…'

188

It's very hard to hear Miss. I'm listening and listening and listening. I think she just said, 'Nannette and Dafydd'. I am trying to listen very very hard now. I want to hear what Miss is saying about Nanno and Dat.

Miss says, 'He doesn't have any bruises or anything. I check when he gets changed into the clean clothes I bring him.' She's putting her hand over her mouth. I can see her from the side of my eye. 'Oh, Karen. It's really unprofessional of me to talk like this. Please don't repeat it to anyone else.'

'I won't.' Kaylee's mammy is rubbing Miss's arm. 'God's honour.'

Miss is getting a tissue from the box. And I am waiting and waiting for her to say something about Nanno and Dat. 'I can't talk to Colin about it.' She is very very quiet. 'And I don't want to land Ree in trouble by going to the Head every two minutes. But I feel like I can talk to you, because you know Tomos. And you know Ree, too.'

The blue dog is taking a man for a walk. The man is chasing a cat. But I'm not really watching him. I'm watching Miss with the side of my eye. Because she has said my name and Mammy's name. And I'm listening hard to Miss.

'Granny used to have a cat.' Kaylee's saying it to me. She's got a lot of sandwich in her mouth. 'It got squashed on the road.'

'Look, you're making sure he's fed and you're checking he's not getting knocked about,' Kaylee's mammy says. 'What else can you do?'

Miss is shaking her head again. 'But the Easter holiday's

worrying me. Two whole weeks without school. You know what he looked like after Christmas.'

I'm listening and listening. I'm wondering what Miss is talking about. And I'm waiting for her to say Nanno and Dat's names again. I'm waiting for her to say Mammy's name. And my name.

Kaylee's mammy's biting her lip. 'I know. He was so skinny. But then if social services have been round… God, Lowri, I don't know what to say.'

'I'll try and persuade Colin that it would be best to stay home. He won't like it, though. He's determined I shouldn't get involved.' Miss is biting her lip. 'I'm beginning to think he's right.'

There's another programme on telly now. 'I like this,' Kaylee says. 'It's got a spaceship in it and aliens.' She's jumping up and down on the cushions again. And she's singing the song. The one on the telly.

'I wish I hadn't taken the job now,' Miss says. She is very very quiet. I'm listening hard. 'I knew he was in this school. I shouldn't have put myself in this situation.'

'At least you can help him,' Kaylee's mammy says, 'because you're his teacher.'

'But I can't, that's the problem. I can't help him. Not enough, anyway.' She's getting another tissue from the box on her desk. She's wiping her eyes. Kaylee's mammy is rubbing Miss's arm again.

I'm looking at the funny people on the programme. And I'm trying to listen to Miss. I am wondering if she's going to say Ree again. Or Nannette or Dafydd. Or Tomos. It's hard to listen because Kaylee's still singing. I want to hear what Miss says. And I want Miss to stop crying.

She's throwing the tissues in the bin. 'I've got to pull myself together.' She's getting more tissues and she's blowing her nose. She's standing up straight. 'I better let you go. You must have lots to do before you go away.'

'Yeah, I've got washing to pick up. It costs loads to use the laundrette, but it's been too wet to dry our stuff on the line.'

'You'll be away for the whole two weeks then, Karen.'

Kaylee's mammy's nodding. 'I don't know if she'll be okay on her own after that, but Kaylee needs to get back to school. My mother'll complain though. She'll want me to stay. She don't think school's important.'

'A broken hip,' Miss says. 'That must be painful.'

Kaylee's mammy is making a blowy sound with her mouth. 'It's her own fault. Shouldn't drink so much.' She's looking at Miss. 'You know what it's like. You try your best to make them change…'

The aliens are dancing on telly. Kaylee's standing up. She's dancing too. Miss is shaking her head. 'All you can do is try to help, but it's hard.' She's putting her hand on Kaylee's mammy's arm. 'They have to want to change.' Miss is smiling a bit now. It's nice to see her smiling again. 'You know, Kaylee's lucky to have you as her mum. You'll never do to her what your mother did to you.' She's shaking her head again. 'And what my mother did to me. You're taking responsibility. You're being Kaylee's parent, instead of Kaylee having to be yours. You're doing your best for her.'

Kaylee's mammy is rubbing her cheeks. Miss is giving her

a hug. 'Well, I'm not looking forward to staying in my mother's house for two weeks,' Kaylee's mammy says. 'And I've said if she starts on the vodka, we're coming straight home. I don't want Kaylee seeing her like that.'

'No, you're right. But I'm sure she'll behave herself. She'll be grateful to have you there. She's so far away from you now. Manchester, isn't it?'

'Yeah,' Kaylee's mammy says. 'Takes ages to get there on the coach but the train costs way too much.'

'Oh well. I hope it goes okay for you. See you after the holidays.'

'And I hope you enjoy yourself,' Kaylee's mammy says, 'if you do go to the Lake District. It's supposed to be nice there.'

'Oh, it is,' Miss says. 'It's beautiful. But I really don't want to go. We can't even afford it. And with all the worry…' She's shaking her head.

She's looking over at us now. She's calling Kaylee. 'Oh, Miss,' Kaylee says. She's stopped dancing. 'This is my favourite programme.'

'No arguing,' her mammy says. 'We've got to go. I've got loads to do before we go to Granny's.' Kaylee's going to her mammy. She's still saying she wants to watch the programme. 'You've got the DVD of this at home anyway,' her mammy says. She's waving to me. I'm waving back. 'Look after yourself, Tomos.'

'See you after the holidays,' Kaylee says. She's waving too. I am trying to answer them. I'm trying but my mouth is full of sandwich. I'm waving and waving instead. They're going out of the classroom.

Miss is rubbing her face. She looks very tired. She looks very sad too. 'Did you enjoy those tuna sandwiches, Tomos?' I'm nodding. 'Good. Eat everything else in that lunch box too, and then we'll see about some packets of biscuits, like the ones I gave you for half term. Do you remember? There was one for each day.'

I'm nodding again. I'm swallowing the bits of sandwich. 'The biscuits were nice,' I say. 'Shall I put them up my jumper, like I did last time?'

'Yes,' Miss says. She's smiling a bit but her eyes look very very sad. 'I think you better had.'

Easter Holidays

It's the school holidays. I've eaten two of the biscuits Miss gave me. I'm eating one every night like Miss said. And I'm thinking about the biscuits now. I am thinking about eating one later. When I'm in bed. And my tummy is making rumbly noises.

I'm on the settee next to Mammy. Brick is on the other side of her. We're watching people shouting on *EastEnders* and I'm driving my truck up the back of the settee and all the little bits of wallpaper are falling out of the tippy bit. I'm picking them up and I'm putting them back in and I'm driving my truck on the arm of the settee and over my legs and onto Mammy's legs.

Brick is drinking from a tin. Mammy's trying to take it from him. 'You've 'ad loads already,' he says. He's pulling the tin back. Some of the yellow stuff inside has spilt out. It's gone on Mammy's pyjamas and on my truck. Mammy's shouting at Brick. Her words are all slippy slidey.

There's a lot of banging on the front door. I'm jumping off the settee. I'm running to hide. I'm running behind the big black chair. I'm taking my truck.

'Saint said he might come over,' Brick says. He's going to the door. I can see him through the gap behind the chair.

I'm hoping and hoping and hoping it's Saint knocking on the door because Saint might give Mammy money for the shop again. And she might get bacon and bread and make sandwiches and she might make one for me this time.

Brick is opening the door a bit and I'm watching him with my one eye and I'm hoping and hoping that Saint is knocking the door.

Brick is saying 'What th…'

Someone is pushing the door from outside. It's not Saint. It's the man with spiky hair. He's pushing the door open. He's grabbing Brick's shoulders. He's pushing him backwards. He's pushing him all the way back into the front room. He's shouting at Brick. He's shouting the word money a lot. He's pushing Brick up against the wall.

The man with the web tattoo is coming in now. He's closing the front door. He's coming into the front room. 'You're always late with your payments, Brick,' he says. He's very loud. 'But now you're taking the proverbial.' He's looking at Mammy. He's looking at her sitting on the settee. I'm watching him with one of my eyes. He's smiling at Mammy. His web tattoo is stretching. 'Glad you're in, Ree.' He's going to the settee. He's kicking all the tins with his boot. They're rolling on the carpet. 'I was hoping you'd be here.'

He's pulling Mammy up from the settee. Her legs are wobbly. She's trying to say something to him. Her words don't sound right. She's trying to hit him. She's trying and trying. He's grabbing her arms. He's calling Mammy a lot of rude names. He's pushing her. He's pushing her against the wall by the window. He says, 'You always had a lot of fight in you, Ree.' He's squashing her against the wall. He's squeezing her face with his hand. 'You were a pretty kid. Always dressed so cute. Remember that mini skirt your mother used to make you wear?' He's laughing. 'Your looks have gone now though.' Mammy's trying to kick him. She's trying and trying. But he's moving away from her feet.

'You're getting a bit old for me and you look wasted, but you'll do for tonight.' He's pulling at her clothes. He's pushing down her pyjama bottoms. He's pushed them to her knees. He's lifting one of his big boots. He's pushing her pyjamas down with his boot. They are round her feet now. He's squashing and squashing her against the wall.

Mammy's trying to hit him. She's trying and trying. But he's holding her too tight. 'Not with my boy 'ere,' she says. Her words have stopped being slidey. They are not slidey at all.

'What, you got standards, Ree?' the man says. 'Not like your mother. She never used to care who watched, so long as she got her fix afterwards.'

Mammy is spitting at the man. There's spit on his web tattoo. He's rubbing his face. 'Bitch.' He's hitting Mammy's cheek. He's hitting it hard.

I am running out from behind the big chair. I'm running across the front room. I am running to Mammy. 'Leave her alone.' I'm holding onto Mammy's leg.

Mammy is looking down at me. Her cheek is very red. She looks cross. 'Go to bed,' she says. 'Now.'

The man with the web tattoo is looking down at me too. He's showing me his teeth. Some of them are brown. One of them is gold. He's holding Mammy's neck with a big hand. He's moving the other hand fast. He's reaching out with it. He's grabbing my tee shirt. He's twisting it. He's lifting me up. 'Stupid brat.' My tee shirt is very tight under my arms and round my neck. It's hurting me. He's pushing me away from him. He's letting go of me. I'm bouncing onto the carpet. I'm sliding. The carpet is rubbing my side. It's hurting a lot.

I have stopped by the man with spiky hair. I've stopped by his feet. He's holding Brick. He's holding him against the wall by the door. I'm looking up at his hands. One hand is holding Brick's neck. The other hand is holding a big knife. It's shiny and curvy. He's pushing the knife under Brick's chin.

My tee shirt is rolled up round my neck. I'm turning over. My side is stinging because of the carpet. I'm saying 'Nine-nine-nine-emergency.' I am saying it very quietly. 'Nine-nine-nine-emergency. Nine-nine-nine-emergency.' It's what Dat told me. 'If there's an accident,' he said, 'or if there's an emergency, call nine-nine-nine on the phone.' We haven't got a phone. Only Mammy's little one. And I don't know where that is. And Dat's phone is a long way away.

The man with the web tattoo is pulling Mammy. He's pulling her away from the wall.

'Go to your room, Tomos,' she says. 'Now.'

He's pushing her to the settee. Mammy's pyjama bottoms have come off her feet. They're on the floor. He's pushing her over the arm of the settee. He's squashing her face into the cushions.

'Go,' she says. 'Go.' Her voice sounds funny because of the settee. 'Go to your room, Tomos.' But I can't go to my room. The man with spiky hair is in the way. He's by the door. The door to the hall.

I'm going back behind the big chair instead. I'm going on my knees and on my hands. I'm going as fast as I can. And I'm not peeping out.

Mammy is saying a lot of rude words.

'You always had a foul mouth,' the man says. He sounds like he's been running. 'Keep it up, Ree. Dirtier the better.' Mammy is quiet now. I am waiting and waiting for the man to stop making the noises. I'm waiting and waiting for the noises to stop. I'm waiting and waiting with my hands over my ears. I'm waiting and waiting and waiting and waiting.

The noises have stopped. The man with the web tattoo is letting out a big breath. 'I'd say it was like old times, Ree. But I liked it better when you were young.'

I am peeping out. I'm peeping out a tiny bit. The man is doing up his trousers. Mammy is pushing herself up from the settee. She's trying to hit the man. He's moving away from her. Mammy is bending down. She's grabbing her boot. It's next to the settee. She's getting something out of the pocket.

The man is very fast. He's kicking Mammy's hand. He's kicking it hard. Something is flying into the air. He's grabbing Mammy's hair. He's twisting it. He's pulling her away from the settee. He's grabbing her neck again. He's holding her up to the wall. 'Think you can pull a knife on me, do you, Ree?' He's pushing his face up to her face. 'Do you?' He's calling Mammy a lot of rude names again. He's grabbing her under her chin. He's lifting her up by her neck. He's sliding her up the wall. Her legs are kicking. They're kicking and kicking against the wall.

I'm peeping out. I'm peeping from behind the chair. I'm peeping out a tiny bit.

'Please,' Mammy says. She's not shouting now. Her voice

is tiny tiny. 'Please.' Her legs are kicking and kicking. And kicking and kicking.

Now they have stopped.

The man is taking his hand away. Mammy's falling onto the floor. She's staying very still.

'Mammy!' I'm running out from behind the chair. I'm running to Mammy. The man is pulling back his boot. He's pulling it back and he's going to kick Mammy. 'No!' I say. 'No!' I am lying on her. I'm lying on Mammy.

'Stupid brat,' the man says.

His boot is by my head. He's saying a lot of rude words. He's saying them to me. And he's tapping his boot on my head. Tap tap tap. But he's not kicking me hard. He's not kicking Mammy. He's going away. He's going away from us now. He's looking at his friend with spiky hair. He's still holding Brick's neck. 'I want my money,' the man with the web tattoo says. He's saying it to Brick. He's saying it in his loud voice. 'You've got a week.'

The man with spiky hair is letting go of Brick. He's taking the knife away. The knife pushing on Brick's neck. He's shaking it near Brick's face instead. 'See you next Monday,' he says. His voice is very quiet.

They are going to the front door. I can hear it opening. The man with the web tattoo is shouting, 'Been nice seeing you.' He's making it sound like he's our friend. The men are going out. They're closing the front door. They're closing it with a bang.

It's very quiet in the front room. I can hear a car engine starting out on the road. I can see Brick standing by the wall.

There's a little bit of blood under his chin. He's rubbing his head. His hands are very shaky.

I'm still cwtching Mammy. 'Are you all right?' She's not moving. I'm trying to see her face. Her hair's hiding it. 'Mammy?' I'm rubbing her arm. I'm shaking it a bit. I'm putting my face by her face. 'Mammy?'

She's not moving.

'Mammy?' I'm shaking her a bit more. 'Wake up, Mammy. Please.' I'm shaking and shaking her. 'Mammy, Mammy!'

She's making a noise. A very quiet noise. She's trying to say something. I can't hear her. I'm putting my head by her mouth. 'What are you saying, Mammy?'

She's saying it again. I still can't hear her. I'm moving her hair. I'm moving it away from her mouth. I am trying to be careful. I don't want to hurt her. 'What did you say?'

'You should,' she says. Her voice is very quiet. 'Have gone.' She's taking a big breath. 'To bed.'

'Sorry, Mammy. The man was in the way. He was by the door.'

'Go…' her voice is still very quiet, '… away.'

I've stopped cwtching Mammy. I'm going away from her. I'm picking up her pyjama bottoms. I'm trying to make them not inside out. It's quite hard. Brick is walking round and round the front room. He's still rubbing his head. He's saying a lot of rude words. The pyjama bottoms are nearly right. I'm giving them to Mammy. She's trying to sit up now. I'm helping her. I want to tell her about my side. I want to tell her that it is all scratched because of the carpet. And

203

because of the man. But she's not looking at me. She's putting her head on her knees. She's making herself tiny tiny.

Brick is saying. 'We'll 'ave to go to Glasgow. Do the job for Saint. I'll call 'im, tell 'im we'll do it.'

Mammy's looking up. She's shaking her head. Her hair is all messy. There are big black lines down her cheeks. They're running down from her eyes. She's rubbing them with her hand. She's making black splodges. She's making them all over her face. She's trying to stand up. She's trying to say something. But her voice is very small. She's falling over. I'm running to help her. She's sitting down again now.

'We've got to go to Glasgow,' Brick says.

'No,' Mammy says. Her voice is tiny.

'You 'eard what they said.' Brick is shouting it. He's rubbing his neck. 'They'll be back. We got to get the money somehow.'

I'm helping Mammy put her pyjama bottoms on. I'm putting them over her feet. I'm pushing them up to her knees. She's pulling them up by herself now.

'We 'ave to do it.' Brick's still shouting. 'We 'ave to go tonight.' He's pushing me out of the way. He's pulling Mammy up. He's pulling her up hard. She's trying to hit him but he's too fast. He's caught her hand. He's hit her face with his other hand. He has hit it hard. Mammy's looking at Brick. Her face is very wet. It's very red too. There are lots of black splodges on her cheeks. She looks sad. Brick's moving his hand back. He's going to hit her again.

'No!' I'm trying to grab Brick's hand. I'm jumping up high. 'Don't!'

He's hit Mammy's face again. He's turning round now. He's hitting my face too. He's hitting it very hard. I can feel my cheek stinging. And the side of my eye.

Mammy's looking at me. 'Go to.' It's very hard for her to talk. 'Your room.' She has a big red mark on her cheek. And her eyes are very sad.

I'm going away. I'm going out into the hall. And I'm rubbing and rubbing my cheek. I'm looking back into the front room. Mammy is sitting down on the settee. She's pulling up her knees. She's putting her arms round them. She's making herself tiny tiny again.

Brick is grabbing Mammy's arm. He's pulling her off the settee. He's calling her a lot of rude names. 'We're goin' to Glasgow tonight. Ge' dressed.' He's pushing her to the door. He's saying more rude things to her.

Mammy's coming out into the hall. Her nose is runny. Her face is red. She's looking at me. Her eyes look very sad. I don't want to make her sad anymore. I say, 'I'm going to bed now.' I'm starting to go up the stairs.

She's grabbing my hand. She's sitting down on the stairs. And she's holding my hand tight. 'Too late,' she says.

I say, 'Too late to go to bed?'

Brick is still shouting rude words. He's still walking round and round the front room. Mammy's looking up at me. She's shaking her head. Her cheeks are very wet. 'Too late.' It's hard to hear her. 'To put right.' Her voice is tiny tiny tiny. It doesn't sound like her voice at all. 'When I,' she says. She's taking a big breath. 'Look at you.' There are tears running and running down her cheeks. 'I see.'

205

She's stopped. She's not saying anything. She's just squeezing and squeezing my hand. 'What, Mammy?' I say. 'What do you see?'

She's taking another big breath. 'Luke,' she says.

'Luke? I don't know Luke.'

She's looking at me. Her face is still very sad. I think it might be because she's seeing Luke. Instead of me. 'He went,' she says. Her voice is very very quiet. 'Everyone leaves.' She's letting my hand go. She's putting her head on her knees. She's crying and crying.

I want to say, 'It's okay.' I want to say, 'Don't cry, Mammy.' But I don't want to make Mammy more sad. I'm going up the stairs. I'm going slow slow. I'm going to my bedroom. I'm closing my door. Brick is still shouting. He's shouting and shouting. Lots and lots of rude words. 'We gotta go. Ge' dressed,' I can hear him shouting. I can hear him through my door. 'And 'ave a bath first, slag. You stink of Fly.'

* * *

I am up in my high sleeper bed. I'm trying to be warm. I have pulled the jumpers and the towels and the trousers round me. I've put Mammy's pink tee shirt under my cheek. The cheek Brick hurt. I like the way the tee shirt smells. It smells of Mammy when she smells nice. It smells like flowers and Nanno. I've put Mammy's white tee shirt on my side. The side the carpet hurt. And I am trying to think about nice things. I'm trying to get to sleep. I'm trying to forget all the shouting. And the men. And Mammy crying. And the knife under Brick's chin. And Brick hurting my cheek. But it's very hard to forget.

If I had some paper I could write a letter to Nanno. I could say *Dear Nanno, How are you? I am well but it is hard to sleep because some nasty men came and they hurt Mammy and Brick and now Mammy and Brick have gone away in Brick's car and they took Mammy's quilt and pillows because they will need to sleep in the car and Mammy said they will see me in a few days and I held onto her leg because I didn't want her to go but she shook it and shook it and she pulled my arms away from her and she said I am not allowed to go outside when she's not here. I'm not allowed to go out of the house until she comes back and she didn't take away my ladder so I can go to the toilet if I want to but I don't want to go to the toilet I just want Mammy to come home and I want her to come home now. Please Nanno make Mammy come home now. Love, Tomos P.S. Can you find Cwtchy for me because if I had Cwtchy I won't be afraid and I like my truck and my fifty pence and your letter but I can't cwtch them like I can cwtch Cwtchy and please can you tell Dat that I need him to come here and get me. And tell him to come here and get me now. Please please Nanno can you tell him to come here and get me now?*

* * *

I'm looking in the kitchen. I'm looking for something to eat. There's a tin in the cupboard under the worktop. A tin of baked beans. I like baked beans. Mammy makes them on toast for my tea sometimes. And Nanno makes them with egg and chips for tea on Saturdays. I'd like to have some baked beans now. I'm getting the tin opener from the drawer. I'm putting it on top of the tin. I'm making the turny bit go round and round. Like Nanno does and like Mammy does. The tin isn't opening. I'm trying and trying. I'm turning and turning the handle. But the tin won't open. I'm banging and banging the tin opener on the tin. Bang bang bang. I'm banging the tin on the worktop. There are lots of dents in the tin now. But it still won't open. I'm throwing it back in the cupboard.

I'm opening another cupboard. I'm putting my hand in. My fingers have found a puddle. I'm shaking my hand. It smells prickly. There's a bottle in the cupboard. It's tipped over on its side. It's a bottle of vinegar. There's a puddle of vinegar on the shelf. Mammy likes vinegar on her chips. But I don't like vinegar. I'm closing the cupboard door.

And I'm looking for something else to eat. There's nothing left in the cupboards under the worktops now. Only the tin with the dents and the bottle of vinegar. I'm looking in the box Father Christmas brought. The box he left outside. With my Santa Sack on it. The box is on the floor in the kitchen. There's nothing in it now. Just a jar of brown jam. I'm trying to get the lid off. I'm trying and trying. It's very hard to get off. I'm making myself very strong. Very very strong. I am the strongest boy in the world. But the lid won't come off.

I'm knocking it. I'm knocking it with the tin opener. Bang bang bang. But the lid isn't coming off. I'm knocking the jar on the worktop. I'm knocking and knocking the lid. And knocking and knocking it. There's a crack. The glass has broken. The lid has come off. I'm smelling the jam. It's making my nose prickly. It doesn't smell like strawberries. It doesn't smell like the jam in Nanno and Dat's cupboard. I'm putting my finger in the jar. I'm putting my finger in my mouth now. The jam tastes horrible. I don't want to eat it. But I've eaten all the biscuits Miss gave me. She told me to just eat one biscuit. One biscuit every day. But I've eaten lots of them. And now there's nothing to eat. Only two packets of crisps. And they're pink ones. They're Mammy's.

I'm pushing my finger into the brown jam again. I'm putting my finger in my mouth. The jam is making my nose scrunch up. There's a sharp bit in my mouth. I'm trying to get it out. It's moving round and round. It's sticking into my tongue. I'm pulling it out with my fingers. I think it's a bit of the jar.

I'm looking in the cupboard. The one under the sink. There's a plastic bowl in there. It's like the bowl Nanno and Dat use to do the washing up. I'm getting it out. It's like the step-up stool I use in Nanno and Dat's house. When I wash my hands. It's like the step-up stool if I turn it upside down. It's good for making me taller. It's good for helping me reach the taps. I'm turning it upside down and I'm standing on it. I'm putting my hand into the brown water in the sink. I'm finding a mug. I'm finding one fast fast. I'm tipping out the dirty water and I'm turning on the tap. I'm putting lots of water in the mug and I'm drinking fast fast. I'm trying to make the taste go away. The horrible taste of the jam. I'm trying and trying but the taste is stuck in my mouth. It's making my eyes want to cry. I'm filling up the mug again. I'm drinking and drinking it. And my tummy is rumbly. It's hurting too. Because the water is sloshing in it. Sloshing and sloshing. Sloshing and sloshing. I can feel it in my tummy. Slosh slosh slosh.

And I can still taste the horrible jam.

* * *

I am up in my high sleeper bed. I'm very cold. I have pulled the clothes all round me. I've tucked them round my toes. I've tucked them round my legs. I've pulled Mammy's pink tee shirt right up under my chin. I'm trying to be warm. But my arms won't let me. They are very cold. They're covered in little lumps. Nanno calls them goose bumps. I am covered in goose bumps. And my teeth are jumpy.

I have eaten some more of the jam. The jam that tastes horrible. I have eaten it with a spoon. The jam had hard lumps in it. And bits of the jar. I had to take them out of my mouth. The jam tasted like the vinegar Mammy puts on her chips. But my tummy isn't too rumbly now.

I am trying to look at my magazine. It's too dark to find good words. I'm tipping the page to the window. There's a bit of yellow light outside. It's helping me see the pictures in my magazine. I can see them a bit in the yellow light. And I'm thinking about going out. I'm thinking and thinking about it. Mammy said I'm not allowed to go outside when she's not here. But she's been gone a long time. A very long time. I think she might be lost. I think I need to call nine-

nine-nine-emergency. But we haven't got a phone. I think I need to find one.

I am going down my ladder. I'm going down the stairs. I'm going out of the front door. I am not allowed to go outside when Mammy's not home. But I am only going to go out a tiny bit.

I am squeezing through the hole in the hedge. I'm squeezing through to get to the lady next door's garden. It's quite hard to squeeze through the hedge. The leaves smell funny. The twigs are scratchy. Pointy things are hurting my feet. But I'm not stopping to rub my toes. I'm pushing and pushing through the hedge.

I'm in the lady next door's garden now. I think I'm allowed to go to her garden. Going next door is not really going outside. I'm walking up the lady next door's path. It's very dark. I can hear her telly. It's very loud. I can hear people clapping. I'm knocking on her door. I'm waiting. I'm knocking again. I'm making my knocks hard this time. The knocks are hurting my hands. I'm waiting. I'm knocking again very very hard.

I can see a light in the hall. 'All right, all right,' the lady says. I can hear her through the door. 'What's so urgent at this time of night?' The door is opening slowly.

'Hello,' I say. The door has stopped opening. There's a little chain stopping it. I can see a bit of the lady. She's holding onto a stick. I can see a bit of her blue climbing frame. It's at the bottom of her stairs. It's nice and warm in her house. I can feel the warm coming out. I can smell a lovely smell. It smells like the dinners Nanno makes.

'Hello,' I say again.

'No, thank you,' the lady says.

'No, thank you what?'

'No, thank you to whatever you're selling.'

'I'm not selling anything.'

'Do you want sponsoring then?'

'I don't think so,' I say.

'Well, no thank you anyway.' She's starting to close the door.

'Do you know where Mammy is, please?' I am saying it fast. I don't want her to close the door.

'Your mother?' She's stopped closing the door now. 'You're the little boy from next door, aren't you?' She's smiling at me. 'The one with nice manners. I didn't recognise you. I haven't got the right specs on, see.'

I say, 'Have you seen my mammy? I don't know where she's gone.'

'She's out shopping, I expect. They never close these days. Twenty-four hour shopping, that's what they call it. She'll be home when she's finished.' She's starting to close the door again.

'I don't think she's gone shopping,' I say. 'She's been gone a very long time. There were seven packets of crisps in the big bag and I've had one packet every day. And now there are only two pink packets left. Can you ring nine-nine-nine-emergency, please? Can you tell them she got lost?'

'Oh *diawl*, there's no need for that.' She's smiling at me again. 'She'll be back with her shopping soon, you'll see.'

'She hasn't gone shopping,' I say. 'Can you ring on your

phone, please?' I can see her phone in the hall. It's like Dat's phone. 'Please.'

She's smiling and nodding. 'Wait a minute. I'll close the door, but don't you go away. I'll be back soon.'

I'm listening through the door. I'm trying to hear her ringing nine-nine-nine-emergency. I can only hear her telly. I'm waiting a long time.

The door is opening. The little chain has gone now. 'Here.' She's holding something in her hand. 'Too sour for me. But you'll enjoy it cut in half with sugar on top. I told my Moira not to bring them. I prefer bananas.'

'Did you ring? Are they going to look for Mammy?'

'No more nonsense about that now.' She's still holding her hand out to me. 'Go on, take it,' she says. 'It's a lovely orange.'

I'm remembering the orange I tried at Nanno and Dat's house. I'm remembering the way it felt in my mouth. I'm remembering the horrible taste. I am starting to say, 'I don't like…'

'I know you don't like to,' she says. 'You're too polite. I keep telling Moira. That's what our Jason needs – manners, like the little boy next door. Go on, take it.' I'm taking it. I'm taking the orange. 'Enjoy it, *bach*. Now, time you were in bed. Goodbye.' She's closing the door. She's shutting it tight.

I'm knocking the door. I'm knocking again and again. And again and again. She's not coming back. I can hear her telly. It's very loud. I am taking my orange back through the hedge. I'm going back through the leaves. And the scratchy branches.

213

And I am wondering about going to Kaylee's house. It's down the road. I can see it from my bedroom. But I haven't seen a light in the window for a long time. I think they've gone to see Kaylee's granny. Kaylee told Miss when we were in class. When we were watching the programme about the blue dog. And Miss was talking about Mammy and Nanno and Dat. And me.

I'm wondering and wondering about going to Kaylee's house. I don't think I'm allowed to go there. It's across the road. And it's six front doors down. I think across the road and six front doors down is going outside.

I'm going back into our house. I'm taking my orange into the kitchen. I'm putting it on the worktop. With the dirty cups and the dirty plates. And all the old takeaway tubs. I'm putting my orange down. And I have remembered something.

I forgot to say 'thank you'.

* * *

I am back in my high sleeper bed. It's dark. There's a bit of light from the road. I'm holding my tippy truck. And my fifty pence. And Nanno's letter. And I am very cold. I've picked up all the clothes from Mammy's floor. And I've put them on my bed. I've made a big big pile of clothes. And I'm trying to be warm under them. But I'm still cold. My hands are shaky. And my arms are shaky. My legs are shaky too.

I'm looking at my library book. It's about a boy called

Danny. I wish it was about a boy called Charlie. But I had to take the book about Charlie back to school. I'm trying to read the words in this book. But it's too dark. And the words are very hard.

I'm looking at the pictures instead. It's not too dark for them. They are sticky pictures. I'm looking at the ones of Danny. And his father. I'm turning the pages. I'm looking for another picture. I've found one with lots of people in it. The people are laughing in the picture. They're laughing and laughing. And laughing and laughing.

They are laughing at me. They're laughing because Mammy hasn't come home. They're laughing because I don't know where she is. They're laughing because I'm very hungry. And cold and scared. They're laughing and laughing. And laughing and laughing. And they are not helping me with the words.

I'm shutting the book. I'm putting it under my truck.

I'm going down my ladder. I'm going to get a magazine. I'm going to look for some good words. I'm going to find turntable and goods wagon. I'm picking up a magazine. It's very dark. It's hard to see in the little bit of light. I'm holding the magazine near my nose. It smells like Dat. It smells like his cosy armchair. I want to be with Dat. I want to be with him now.

'Dat!' I'm shouting. 'I want you to come and get me. I don't want to be here anymore. I need you to come and get me.' I'm listening. I'm listening to hear Dat running up the path. I'm listening and listening. 'Dat! Mammy has gone and I need you. I need you to come now.'

I'm running to the window. I'm banging on the glass. 'Dat!' I am banging and banging. And banging and banging. The glass is very bouncy. 'I need you to come and get me. Why aren't you coming, Dat? Why aren't you coming to get me?'

I'm banging and banging and banging and banging. Dat isn't coming up the path. He isn't coming to get me. There's no one outside. 'Dat, Dat!' I'm banging on the glass and I'm shouting. The inside of my neck is hurting. 'Dat, Dat!'

There's a dog running down the road. It's the black dog with three legs. It's the dog that walks to school with Nadia. The dog has stopped running. It's looking at me banging the window. It's running again now. It's running away. I'm still banging and banging. There's no one outside. Only the lady in her house across the road. She's moving her curtains. She's looking at me through her window. I can see her eyes looking at my eyes.

And now she has gone too.

* * *

It's light outside again. I'm in the front room. I'm peeping out of the window. I'm looking to see Mammy coming home. I've been looking for a long time. I can't see Brick's car. I'm peeping up the road. Now I'm peeping down the road. I can see other cars. But I can't see Brick's blue car anywhere.

Someone is standing by the gate. I can see a bit of their jumper next to the hedge. I'm moving to the side of the window. I'm moving very fast. I don't want them to see me. I'm staying very still.

Someone's knocking on the window. Someone's knocking very hard. Someone's shouting. 'Oi! Oi!' I'm not moving. I'm staying very very still. 'Oi, it's me, thicko!' the voice says. 'Open the door.'

I know that voice. It's Wes's voice! I'm looking through the window. I can see Wes. I'm waving to him. He's waving to me. I'm smiling and smiling. 'Open the door,' he says again.

'I can't.'

'Why not?'

'I'm not allowed.'

'Who says?'

'Mammy.'

'Mammy, Mammy!' He's trying to copy me. He's laughing. 'Thicko. Go ask her if I can come in.'

'I can't. She's not here.'

'Let me in then.'

'I can't.'

'Why not?'

'I'm not allowed.'

Wes is pulling a face. 'Why're you worried if she's not even there?' He's doing a funny dance. I'm laughing. 'Go on,' he says. 'Let me in.'

I'm looking up and down the road. I can't see Brick's car anywhere. I can't see Mammy anywhere. 'Okay,' I say. 'Just for a minute.' I'm going to the front door. I'm turning the little handle. Wes is pushing the door on the other side. He's pushing it open. He's pushing past me. He's running into the front room.

'Urgh,' he says. 'Your house stinks.' He's holding his nose. He's squishing up his face. 'It smells as bad as you. Why're your walls like that?'

'Mammy doesn't like the wallpaper. It's too flowery.'

He's running up to the wall. He's pulling a bit of the wallpaper off. 'Don't do that, Wes,' I say. 'Only Mammy's allowed to do that.'

He hasn't heard me. He's pulling off a bit more. And a bit more. He's throwing the paper all over the carpet. 'This is great,' he says. He's pulling and pulling and pulling. He's looking round the front room now. 'Where's all your stuff?'

'What stuff?'

'Normal stuff, like chairs and pictures and tables?'

'We've got a chair,' I say. I'm pointing to the big black chair. 'And a settee.'

He's looking at the floor. 'Why's your carpet so dirty?' he says. 'Can't your mam clean it?'

He's running into the kitchen. 'What a dump! Haven't you got a bin?' He's pulling his foot back. He's kicking a takeaway tub. It's flying into the air. The orange gooey stuff is falling out of it. 'Uncle Vic would kill Mam if our kitchen was like this.' He's kicking one of Mammy and Brick's empty tins now. It's bouncing round the kitchen floor. It's knocking the other tins and takeaway tubs. 'He'd give her a good slapping.'

He's running up the stairs. I'm running up the stairs too. I'm hoping he won't go into the bathroom. There are a lot of things in the bathroom cupboard. Things you must NOT touch.

The bathroom door is closed. I closed it this morning. He's going past it. He's going into my bedroom and he's stopped. 'What the…?' he says.

He's going to my train table. He's touching the tracks. He's touching the little hedges. The ones Dat and me made. He's touching the little animals in the fields. The fields Dat and me painted with green paint. He's touching the little people Dat and me put near the roads. And the little people we put near the train station. He's touching the barriers at the level crossing. He's pushing down on the ends. He's making them lift. He's letting them drop. He's lifting them up again. And letting them drop again.

'Where did you get this?' He's very quiet now.

'Dat made it for me.'

He's still lifting the barriers. He's still letting them drop. 'What's a dat?'

'My dat.' I'm trying to remember. I'm trying to remember what a dat is. Wes is trying to pick up the animals. And the people. I'm remembering now. I'm remembering what Nanno told me. She said Dat is Mammy's foster daddy and Nanno is Mammy's foster mammy. Nanno and Dat are like my nan and grandad. But not my real nan and grandad. My real nan and grandad went to Heaven. They went a long time ago before I was born. 'Dat is my mammy's foster daddy,' I say.

'Your dat is like your uncle then.'

'I don't think he's my uncle,' I say. 'I haven't got an uncle.'

'I've got loads of uncles. And loads of half-brothers. And millions of cousins.'

'I haven't got any cousins,' I say.

'Why not?' Wes says.

'I don't know.'

He's looking at my table again. 'Why's it like that?' He's pushing his finger into the hole. The hole the rain made when my table was in Brick's car.

'It got wet.' He's trying to pick up the people again now. He's pulling and pulling. I say, 'The people are stuck down.'

'Why?' He's still pulling and pulling.

'They stay still. Just the trains move. And the barriers. Everything else stays still.'

'The trains?' he says. 'Where are the trains?' He's looking round my bedroom.

'They've gone.'

'Gone where? Where are they?' He's looking under the table. He's knocking over my pile of magazines. He's looking under the clothes on my floor. 'These stink,' he says. He's throwing them under my train table. He's climbing up my ladder. He's climbing onto my bed. It's shaking and shaking.

I don't want him to find my truck. Or my coin. I don't want him to find Nanno's letter. I don't want him to talk about Heaven again. 'They're not up there,' I say. I want him to come down.

He's throwing my clothes everywhere. They're falling onto the floor. '*Deee*sgusting! Your bed stinks, stinks, STINKS. And I still can't find the trains. What's this?' He's holding up the jar.

'It's jam.'

He's putting his nose near it. 'Yuck!' He's moving the spoon round and round in it. 'And the glass is all broken.' He's throwing the jar back on my bed. 'Where are your trains?'

'A man's got them,' I say.

'Oh.' He's coming back down my ladder again. He's coming down fast. He didn't find my truck or my coin. Or Nanno's letter. 'Did he steal them?'

'No.' I'm feeling sad again. I'm feeling like I did the first day I went to my new school. And when I came home all my trains were gone. I asked Mammy where they were and she said she'd sold them. Then I cried and she told me to shut up. 'Mammy sold them. To a man called Leper.'

'Leper? Uncle Vic knows him. He tells kids he's got a train track in his shed. Then they go in and they never come out again.' He's hitting the table with the side of his hand. 'Train table's rubbish then,' he says. 'It's rubbish without the trains.' He's hitting the little people now and the little animals.

'Don't do that, Wes. They'll break.' He hasn't heard me. He's hitting the little hedges now. And the little barriers. The little people and the little animals are stuck down. And the little hedges and the little barriers. They are all stuck down with Dat's special glue. They're stuck down tight. 'Please, Wes.' He's not listening. The hedges are bending. They are bending a lot. The barriers are bending too. But they're stuck tight to the table.

He's running downstairs now. He's jumping over the bottom three steps. I'm running downstairs too. I'm jumping over the bottom two steps. 'Come to the park,' he says. He's opening the front door.

'Can't. I'm not allowed.'

'Who says?'

'Mammy.'

'She's not here though, is she?' He's banging and banging the letterbox. 'Where's she gone anyway?'

'I don't know. But she might come back when I'm out.'

'It's only round the corner,' Wes says.

'She might come back.'

'There's loads of kids there.'

'Can't,' I say. 'I'm not allowed.'

'I'm going then.' He's going through the door. He's running down the path. 'See you.' He's shouting it over his shoulder. 'See you, thicko.' He's running up the road.

'Bye.' I'm shouting too. 'Bye, Wes.'

I'm closing the front door. I'm closing it tight. I'm going back to the front room. I'm going to the window. I'm watching Wes running up the road. I'm watching and watching until he's gone.

And I'm looking for Mammy again now. I'm looking for Brick's car. I'm looking for Mammy and Brick. I'm waiting for them to come home. I'm waiting and waiting. And I am peeping through the window. I'm waiting and waiting for Mammy to come home. And waiting and waiting. And waiting and waiting.

I've been waiting a long time.

Someone's running up the path. Someone's running up it fast. It's Wes. He's come back. He's knocking on the window again.

'Oi! Oi!'

'Wes!' I'm smiling and smiling. 'You came back.'

'Open the door,' he says. 'Quick! Open the door NOW.'

* * *

I'm running down the road with Wes and we're running and running to the park and we're going to see Mammy because she's with all the children there and she told Wes I'm allowed to go to the park and she sent Wes to come and get me.

I'm running round the corner on my wobbly wobbly legs and I can see the park and I can see all the children and the big boys sitting on top of the slide and the big girls sitting on top of the climbing frame and I'm looking for Mammy and I'm looking for her yellow hair and I'm looking and running and looking and running.

Wes and me are running through the gate now and we're running into the park and I'm looking for Mammy and I'm looking and looking and Wes is running in front of me. I say, 'Where is she?' It is very hard to talk.

'Wha'cha say?' Wes is stopping. He's turning round.

I'm stopping too. 'Where's Mammy?' I am holding my tummy and I'm looking and looking round the park.

Wes is smiling and he's licking his lips and he's shouting up to the boys sitting on top of the slide. 'Look,' Wes says. 'I brought him.'

The big boys are looking down at us and they're laughing and they're drinking from their tins too.

'Where's Mammy?' I'm saying it to Wes and my eyes are

looking round and round the park because they're looking for Mammy.

'Did you hear that?' Wes is saying it to the big boys. 'He said, "Where's Mammy?" Ha ha!'

The big boys are laughing and they look like they will fall off the slide and they're saying 'Where's Mammy? Where's Mammy?' and they're saying it and laughing.

'Is she still here?' My eyes are looking and looking all round the park.

One of the boys says, 'Yeah, Ree the Slag's here.' He's having a drink from his tin. 'She's round by the bins.'

I'm looking for the bins but I can't see them. I can't see them anywhere. I can't see the bins and I can't see Mammy. 'Where?' I say. 'Where is she?'

The big boys are laughing again. They are very loud. Wes is laughing too. They're making a lot of noise.

'Where?' I say. 'I can't see her.'

The big boys are running down the slide. Some of them are jumping down the ladder. They are standing next to Wes and me. They're very big. They smell like Mammy and Brick's empty tins. One of them's coming close to me. He's bending down. He's putting his face near me. His face has lots of red bumps on it. Some of the bumps have yellow tops. There are bumps all over his cheeks and his chin.

He's taking a big breath in through his nose. 'Urgh!' He's bending away from me. He's holding his nose. 'That's rank.' He's coughing now.

The other boys are laughing at him. Wes is laughing too. Wes is laughing most of all. 'I told you,' Wes says. 'I told you it was disgusting.' He's laughing and laughing. '*Deees*gusting.'

The other boys are bending down to me. They're very close. They're putting their noses next to me. Their noses have got little black dots all over them. And purple lumps. The boys are looking at each other. Their eyes are big. I can see little red lines in them. They're holding their noses now. They're turning away. The air is bursting out of them. It's bursting out through their mouths. The air is bursting out as laughing. They're pointing to me and laughing. They're laughing and laughing.

One of the boys is shouting to the girls. 'Hey, Tallulah. Come and smell this.'

The girls can't hear him. They're shouting back. 'What you saying?'

He's shouting again. 'Come and smell this.'

Two of the girls are getting down from the climbing frame. They're getting down slowly. They're walking over to us. They're tapping their hair. They're tapping their skirts. They're chewing with their mouths open.

'What is it?' one girl says. She's starting to blow a bubble.

'This kid,' the big boy says. 'Smell it.'

The girl's bending towards me. Her bubble is big now. It's getting bigger and bigger.

'Have you seen Mammy?' I say. 'She has yellow hair like you.'

She's moving away from me now. She's moving away from me fast. Her bubble has popped. It's all over her lips and her chin. She's curling her tongue round. She's pulling the popped bubble back into her mouth with her tongue. 'Oh my God.' She's covering her face with her hands. She's holding her nose. 'What is it? What *is* it?'

'Piss,' the big boy says. He's holding his nose too.

She's laughing now. 'Look, look!' She's pointing to my feet. She's still laughing. 'He ain't got no shoes.'

'I forgot to put them on,' I say. 'Have you seen Mammy?' My eyes are getting prickly. 'I want to see Mammy.' I have to find her. I want the children to tell me where she is. I want Wes to tell me where she is. 'Where is she?' I say to Wes. 'Where's she gone?' I'm holding his arm. I'm trying to make him tell me.

'Urgh.' Wes is scratching my hand away. He's shaking his arm. He's shouting, 'He touched me, he touched me.' He's falling onto the ground and he's rolling and rolling. 'I'm going to die. He touched my arm and I'm going to die.' All the children are laughing. The big boy and his friends are laughing. The big girls are laughing too.

'Where's my mammy?' I say. Wes is still rolling and rolling on the ground. The other children are all round us. My eyes are prickly. My nose is prickly too. 'Please, Wes.'

He's sitting up and he's pointing to me. 'He's crying. Look at him. He's crying.'

'Where's she gone, Wes?' My voice is wobbly like my legs. 'I want to see Mammy.'

The other girls have come down from the climbing frame now. Wes is laughing. His mouth is open. His teeth look very sharp. 'He really believed me. He really thinks she's here. He smells *and* he's thick. Thicko!' He's shouting it and pointing to me.

226

The other girls are coming over now. They're all standing round me too. They're looking and looking at me.

'Thicko! Thicko!' Wes is still shouting it.

'Shut up, Wesley,' someone says. It's one of the big girls. It's the one I saw in school. She's the girl that collected Wes. After the Christmas concert. She's looking at him. Her face is very cross. 'If anyone's thick, it's you. Leave the kid alone and pick on someone your own size for a change.'

'Yeah, Rockie,' a big boy says. 'Sort out your little brother.' Everyone's laughing.

The girl called Rockie isn't laughing. 'I wish he wasn't my brother,' she says. 'Horrible kid.'

Wes is getting up. He's sticking out his tongue. He's showing it to Rockie. 'You're the thick one.'

'No, you're thick actually,' she says. 'You're the one who's nearly eight and can't read. You're the one who's still in Year Two when you should have moved up to Year Three ages ago.'

I'm looking at Rockie. 'Where's Mammy?' I say. 'Wes said she's here.'

'She's not,' Rockie says. 'He was lying to you. He's a liar and a bully. Keep away from him.'

Wes is looking at Rockie. His face is very nasty. 'And you're a slag. Uncle Vic says everyone knows you're a slag.'

Rockie's face looks very cross. 'Shut up!' She's running at Wes. He's putting his arms out. He's trying to stop her but she's pushing him. She's pushing him hard. She's pushing him very hard. She's knocked him over. 'Shut up...shut up.' She's hitting him on the floor. She's hitting and hitting him. 'I hate you,' she says. 'I HATE YOU.'

Wes is trying to roll away. He's trying to get away from her. He's trying to knock her hands away. But Rockie is hitting and hitting him again. All the boys are laughing. 'Go for it, Rockie,' one of them says.

I'm turning away from Rockie. I'm turning away from Wes. I'm looking round the park. I'm looking very hard. Rockie's right. Mammy's not here. I know I must go home. Mammy might be there. She won't know where I am. And I'm not allowed to go outside when Mammy isn't home.

I'm running. I'm running out of the park. The stones are hurting my feet. I'm running away from the big boys and I'm running away from the big girls and I'm running away from Wes. I'm running home. I'm running home to Mammy.

I'm running round the corner. And I can see our gate that doesn't close and I can see a car. But it's a long way away and it's outside our house and Mammy might be in it. But it's not a blue car like Brick's car because it's a silver car and there's a lady standing by it. But it isn't a lady with yellow hair because it's a lady with brown hair and she's looking at our house and I can see the side of her face but she's a long way away.

And I'm running as fast as I can and I'm running and running on my wobbly legs and I don't mind the stones hurting my feet because I'm running to our house and I'm running to the lady and I am running and running and running.

And I'm trying to shout. 'Hello!' I'm trying to shout. 'Hello! Hello!' But there's not enough breath in me and my voice can't make a shout.

And the lady's going to the silver car and she hasn't seen me and she cannot hear my shouts because they're too quiet and she's getting into her car and I am running and running and I don't mind the stones and I don't mind them hurting my feet and I am very fast because I am the fastest runner in the world.

But she's started the car and I can't get to her. I can't get to her and I can't stop her. And I can't ask her where Mammy is. I'm not fast enough. I'm not fast enough. She's driving off. She's driving away from me. My legs are not fast enough. They're not fast enough to catch her. They can't catch the lady in the car. The lady with brown hair.

Miss.

* * *

It's very dark. I've been waiting by the window a long time. A long long time. Cars have gone down the road and up the road. But I haven't seen Brick's car. I'm waiting and waiting for Brick's car. The light has come on across the road. And the lights have come on in some houses. I can't see a light in Kaylee's house. I haven't seen a light in Kaylee's house for a long long time. I wish I could put our lights on. I wish I could but the lectric has run out. It ran out a long time ago.

There's someone on next door's path. I can see a tiny bit of them in the dark. A tiny bit that has yellow hair. I can see them going into the house next door. The house that is joined on to our house. The yellow hair was like Mammy's hair. It might be Mammy. She might be next door.

I'm running out of the front door and I'm running down our path and I'm running out of our gate and I'm running along the pavement and I'm running up next door's path. I am very fast. There's a light in the window next to the front door. I'm looking through the window. I can see a chair and a telly but I can't see Mammy. I'm running to the door. It's white like our front door. It's plastic. I'm knocking the door with my hands. I'm knocking and knocking. And knocking and knocking. My knocking is very loud. I'm calling too. I'm calling Mammy. I'm calling and calling.

No one is opening the door.

I'm running to the window again. But I can't see in. The curtains are closed now. They're closed tight. I'm knocking on the window. I'm knocking and knocking. I'm shouting too. I'm shouting for Mammy. I'm running round the side of the house. I'm going to knock on the back door. It might be open. Mammy forgets to lock the back door sometimes. I'm running round the corner. It's very dark. There's a big gate made of wood. It won't open. I'm pushing and pushing it. It's stuck tight. I can't see through it and I can't open it. I'm knocking and knocking.

I'm shouting, 'Mammy, Mammy.' A big drop of rain has splashed on my head. And another one. And another one. 'Mammy, I need you to come home.' I'm making my voice very loud. I'm scratching the inside of my neck. I'm scratching it with the words. 'Mammy, Mammy! Why aren't you coming home? Please come home. Please come home now.' The gate isn't opening. Mammy isn't coming out. I'm running back to the window. I'm knocking on it. The drops of rain are jumping off it. 'Please, Mammy. Open the door. I want you to come home. I don't want to be on my own anymore.'

The curtains are still closed. I'm listening. I can hear some music. It's the music of a programme Mammy likes. It's *EastEnders*. I'm knocking again. I'm knocking very hard. 'Please, Mammy. I'm scared on my own. Please come home.' I can still hear the music but it's very loud now. I'm trying to make my shouting bigger. I'm trying to make it bigger than the music. But the music is too loud.

I am going to the front door again. I'm sitting down on the step. It's very wet. And very dark. I'm waiting for Mammy to come out. I'm waiting and waiting for Mammy to come out.

And waiting.

And waiting.

* * *

I'm inside my box. The box I was a present in. With green shiny paper that is all ripped. I can see Mammy. She's on the settee. I want to go to her but I can't move. I can't move because I'm a present and I'm stuck in the box. I want her to see me. I want her to see I'm stuck. But she isn't looking at me. And I'm calling and calling her but she isn't looking. There's water too. It's running and running down my face. It's filling up the box and I can't get out of it. I can't get away from the water. And Mammy isn't helping me. My face is very wet. My clothes are wet too. And the box is filling up with water.

Someone is tapping me with their foot. I'm waking up. I'm waking up fast. Someone has opened the door. Someone is looking down at me. 'Hey,' the someone says. It's a man. He's tapping me with his foot again. 'Get off my step.' He has yellow hair but it's not long like Mammy's hair. 'Get away home,' he says.

I'm getting up. 'I'm looking for Mammy.' I'm wiping the rain off my face. 'Is she in your house? I want her to come home.'

'She's not here. I don't know your mother. Go home.' He's going to close the door.

I am grabbing it. I'm trying to stop him closing it. I'm trying to stop him with my fingers. 'Please,' I say. 'I saw her coming here. Can you tell her to come home?'

The man is looking at me. He's looking through the gap in the door. He's looking at my feet and my toes. 'Who are you?' he says. He sounds very cross.

'Tomos,' I say. 'I live there.' I'm pointing to our house a bit. And I'm grabbing the door again quick quick.

'You're the kid who makes all the noise,' he says. 'All the shouting and banging. Damn kids. Wherever I go I can't get no peace.' He looks very very cross. He's pushing the door again. 'Move your hands, or your fingers'll get jammed.'

'Please.' I can feel the door squeezing on my fingers. 'Please.'

'Move.'

I'm pulling my fingers away. He's closing the door. He's closing it tight. 'Go away.' He's shouting it through the door. 'Go home. Get off my property.'

232

I'm going down the path. I'm going slowly. I don't think Mammy is in there after all. I don't think I saw her from the window. I think it might have been the man next door. I think it was his yellow hair I saw. I'm going through the man's gate.

There's a van across the road. A white van full of ladies. The lady across the road is getting out of it. She's putting up her umbrella. I'm waving to her. I am waving fast fast. She might have seen Mammy. She might have seen her when she was out in the van with the other ladies. They might all have seen Mammy. I'm waving and waving and the van is driving off.

'Hello!' I say. 'Hello!' I'm waving and waving.

She's not waving back. I think she can't see me because of the dark. She's looking in her bag now. She's getting something out of it. It's her key. I can see a light twinkling on it. She's going up her path. She's going to go into her house. And I want to ask her about Mammy. I'm running to her. I'm running to see the lady across the road. I'm running fast fast fast.

There's a big noise. A screechy noise and a bump and a clattery noise. Something is knocking me. It's a man. A man on a bike. He's falling over. He's falling onto the road. He's nearly making me fall over too. I am jumping out of his way. I'm jumping over the bike. It's on the road. It's fallen over like the man.

'What are you doing?' the man says. He's getting up. He's rubbing his arm. He's rubbing his knees. 'Making me swerve like that. I nearly hit you.' His voice is very loud. 'You ran out in front of me without even looking.'

The lady across the road is turning round. I can see her through the rain. Her eyes are very big. They are looking at my eyes. 'I'm going to see the lady,' I say. 'That lady across the road.' I'm waving to her again. She's still not waving back. I can see her opening her door. I'm running across the rest of the road. I'm running through the puddles. I don't want the lady to go inside her house.

'Well, look where you're going.' The man is shouting it to me. 'You shouldn't be out on your own in the dark. I could have killed you.' I'm looking back at him. He's shaking his head. 'I could have been killed myself.' He's picking up his bike. He's kicking the bike's wheels. He's making them go round and round.

The lady isn't outside her house anymore. I'm running up her path. Her door has a doorbell like Nanno and Dat's. I am trying and trying to make my fingers reach it. I am making myself very tall. But my fingers can't reach it. And I can see the man going away on his bike.

I am banging and banging on the door. 'Please,' I'm shouting. 'Please, have you seen my mammy? She's been gone a very long time and I don't know where she is. Did you see her when you were out in the van? Can you tell her to come home?' I am knocking and knocking on her door. 'Please, please!' She's not opening the door. She's not telling me if she saw Mammy. I am knocking and knocking. 'Please,' I'm shouting. 'Please.'

She's not opening the door. She's very quiet inside her house.

'Please! Please tell me where Mammy is.'

There's a big flash and a cracking noise. It's raining and raining and raining. The rain is running down my hair. And off my nose and off my chin. There's a very very big rumbly noise. It's all round me. I think the lady's house will fall down. I think the whole road will fall down.

I'm running. I'm running down the lady's path. I'm running back across the road. I'm running through the puddles and my toes are finding little stones. They're getting stuck in between them but I'm not stopping. I'm not stopping to get the stones out. I'm running fast fast. I'm running up our path. There's another big flash. It's making everything light light light. I can see into our hall. The floor is all wet and shiny. I forgot to close the door when I ran out to find Mammy. I'm running inside. I'm running fast. And I'm slip slip slipping on the shiny floor. But I'm not falling down. I'm shutting the door. I'm shutting it tight. I'm shutting out the big big rumbly noise. I'm running behind the big black chair. I am curling up small. Small small small. And I am hiding.

* * *

It's very dark. The rumbly noise has gone away. It took a long time to go. I've been hiding behind the big black chair for a long long time.

It's quiet now. I'm coming out on my knees and on my hands. I don't like the dark. I want to make it go away. I'm climbing up onto the big chair. I'm click clicking the switch. The light isn't coming on. The switch has stopped working.

235

I don't like it when the switches stop working. I want to tell Mammy. I want to tell her she needs to put more money on the lectric key. And she needs to buy more food. 'Mammy,' I say. I'm shouting it. 'Mammy, where are you? Where are you?' I'm shaking. I'm very cold. My clothes are wet because of the rain. My hair's wet too. And my tummy is very rumbly.

'I know,' I say. 'I know how to make the lights work again.' I'm running to the settee and I'm pushing my hand down the side. My fingers are looking and looking for the lectric key. They've found it. They're pulling it out quick quick.

I'm running up the stairs. I'm running to get my fifty pence. I'm banging it and banging it on the key. 'See, Mammy,' I say. 'I can put money on the lectric key myself. I can make the lights work again.' I'm banging and banging my fifty pence on the key and I'm running down the stairs and I'm climbing on the big black chair and I'm click clicking the light switch. Clickclick clickclick. But I can't make the light switch work. The light's not coming on.

I'm remembering now. I'm remembering Mammy putting the key in the box in the hall. The box that makes the lights work again. I'm going into the hall. The box is very high up. I'm looking for something to make me big and tall. I'm looking in the front room. My box might make me tall. The box I was a present in. But it's a bit squashed. Mammy squashed it because she put her legs on it. I don't want to make it more squashed. I'm looking for something else. The big black chair will make me tall. I'm pushing it.

236

I'm pushing and pushing it. I'm trying to make it go into the hall. I'm making myself very strong. Very very strong. But it's only moving a tiny bit. A tiny tiny bit. I can't make it go into the hall.

I'm looking for something else. I'm looking in the kitchen. I've found the washing up bowl. The one that is like the step-up stool at Nanno's and Dat's. I'm taking it into the hall and I'm standing on it. I'm stretching and stretching. I'm making my toes and my legs and my arm and my fingers very very long. But I can't put the lectric key in the box. The box is a long long way away.

I'm getting down off the bowl. I'm putting the lectric key back down the side of the settee. And my tummy is still very very rumbly.

I know how to make my tummy better. I'm getting the big bag of crisps. I'm finding it in the dark. I'm getting a pink packet out of it. A packet I was keeping for Mammy. I'm opening it. I'm squashing the crisps into my mouth. I'm squashing and squashing them. My mouth is full of crisps. I'm crunching and crunching them.

'I'm eating your crisps, Mammy.' Bits of crisps are falling out. They're falling out of my mouth. 'I'm going to eat all your crisps,' I'm shouting. 'All the pink packets. I was keeping them for you. Until you came home. But I'm eating them now. See?' I'm opening my mouth. I'm showing Mammy the crisps in my mouth. 'I'm eating them all.'

I'm grabbing the next packet. I'm opening it. I'm squashing all the crisps into my mouth. 'Because I hate you,' I'm shouting. 'I HATE you, Mammy. I hate you and I don't want you to come home.' I'm hurting the inside of my neck. I'm hurting it because my shouting is very loud. And the crisps are scratching it. 'I don't want you to come home ever ever EVER.'

I'm squashing all the crisps into my mouth. 'I'm going to eat your chocolate too,' I say. But I'm not shouting now. I'm very quiet. 'I know where it is. I know where you're hiding it.' I'm throwing the packets. The empty packets of crisps. I'm throwing them onto the floor. 'Your chocolate's hiding on top of the cupboard.'

I'm running into the hall. I'm getting the washing up bowl. I'm taking it to the kitchen and I'm putting it next to the cupboard. I'm making a step. I'm making it with the upside down bowl. I'm going to make myself tall. I want to push my knee on top of the cupboard handle. I'm standing on the bowl. My toes are very cold. They're cold after the puddles. They're still a bit wet too. I'm pushing my knee on top of the cupboard handle. I'm pushing myself up from it. I'm pushing myself up onto the worktop. I'm standing on the worktop. I am trying to put my hand on top of the cupboard. It's a very high cupboard. It's where Mammy hides her chocolate bars.

'See, Mammy? I can do it myself. I can get things. I can get your things.'

I'm standing on the kitchen worktop. I'm standing on my toes. I'm stretching right up. I'm stretching to get the bag of chocolate bars from on top of the cupboard. I'm making my arm as long as I can. I'm making my fingers long too. I can feel the bag with the ends of my fingers. I'm touching the

238

bag. It's making a crinkly sound. I'm touching it but the bag is moving away. I'm touching it again. It's moving away again.

I can't touch it anymore. I'm stretching and stretching but I can't touch the bag. I can't touch it at all. 'Never mind, I know what to do. You'll see, Mammy.'

I'm getting down from the worktop. I'm getting down backwards. My foot is trying to find the bowl on the floor. My toes have found it but the bowl is slipping away. And my chin is bumping the worktop. And my teeth are hurting my tongue.

I'm sitting on the floor. I'm rubbing my chin. My eyes are all prickly and my tummy's rumbly. 'I'm still going to get your chocolate. I can get it myself, Mammy. I'm going to eat it all.' I want to shout it but my voice is tiny. 'I know what I'll do.'

I'm getting up. I'm putting the upside down bowl on the worktop. 'That'll make me taller. You'll see, Mammy. I'll get your chocolate now.' I want to get up on the worktop. I want to climb up again. But I'm not tall enough. Because the bowl is on the worktop. I'm looking for something else. Something else to make me taller. I'm looking round and round the kitchen. I'm looking over the edge of the sink. There are some mugs in there. I can see their handles in the tiny bit of light. The bit of light coming in from the road. The handles are sticking up through the water. I'm trying to catch a handle. It's slipping away from my fingers. The water feels slippy and cold. I'm grabbing a handle fast fast. I'm pulling it out of the sink. A lot of water is falling onto

239

the floor. I'm wiping my hand on my trousers. On my wet trousers. 'You watch me, Mammy. I'm going to get your chocolate. And I'm going to eat it all.'

I'm taking the mug to the worktop. I'm turning it upside down and I'm putting it on the floor. I'm standing on the upside down mug. I'm pushing my knee on top of the cupboard handle again. I'm climbing onto the worktop. I'm standing up. I'm stepping onto the upside down bowl. I'm standing on my toes on the upside down bowl. I'm stretching my feet. And I'm stretching my legs. I'm stretching my body. And my neck. I'm stretching my arms and my fingers too. I'm stretching right up. I want to see on top of the high cupboard.

I can see a corner of the bag of chocolate bars. The light is shining on it a tiny bit. The light outside. I can feel the bag with the ends of my fingers. I'm stretching and stretching. And stretching and stretching.

I have caught it. I've caught the corner of the bag with my fingers. I'm pulling it off the cupboard. I'm pulling it off fast. 'See?' I'm laughing. I'm laughing and laughing. 'See, Mammy? I don't need you. And I'm going to eat all your choc…'

There's a scrapey noise. The bowl is slipping on the worktop. It's slipping fast. And my feet are slipping too. They're slipping with the bowl. I'm trying to grab something. I'm trying to hold on. But my hands can't find anything. And I'm falling. I'm falling back. I'm falling fast fast.

'Dat!' I want him to come and help me. I want him to

catch me with his strong arms. But he's not here. 'Da…' I'm hitting the floor. I'm hitting it hard. I'm hitting it very very hard.

I'm hitting it with my head.

* * *

It's cold. My back is very cold. The back of my head is very cold too. And my arms and my legs. I'm telling my eyes to open. I'm trying to make them listen. But they won't listen. They want to stay shut.

Nanno and Dat are coming. They'll be here soon. Dat will carry me up to bed and Nanno will make me a cup of tea. I'll show Dat my magazine that Brick ripped. And the broken wheels on my truck. And Dat will say, 'Never mind, Tomos, I can mend those.' And Nanno will find my quilt. The one with trains on it. And she'll tuck me up in bed and I'll be warm and cosy. And she'll make me a chicken pie dinner with nice rice pudding for afters and I'll be full up with food and then she'll sing me a song and Dat will read me a story.

I don't want to be cold anymore. I don't want to be on the floor. I want to get up. I want my arms and legs to listen to me. I want them to move. I want them to get up off the floor. But they're not listening. They feel very heavy. They want to stay on the floor. They're heavy and sleepy like my eyes. Heavy and sleepy. Heavy and sleepy.

I'll lie here and wait for Nanno and Dat.

241

There's knocking. Someone is knocking on the door. I'm listening. I'm lying on the kitchen floor and I'm listening. There's the knocking again. I'm trying to open my eyes. I'm trying and trying. They're opening a tiny bit. It's very dark. My eyes are closing.

Knockknockknock.

I'm opening my eyes a tiny bit again. I'm making my head lift up. It's lifting up a bit. It's hurting a lot.

Nanno and Dat have come. They're knocking on the door.

I'm making my arms move. And my legs. My back's hurting. It's hurting when I move my arms and legs. I'm turning over. I'm on my knees and on my hands. I'm going out of the kitchen. I'm going in the dark. I'm trying to go fast but my legs are very slow. I want to let Nanno and Dat in.

The knocking is very loud. There's lots and lots of it. It's not like the lady with the big bag's knocking. Her knocking is knock knockknock. This knocking is knockknockknock knockknocknock. I don't think it's Nanno and Dat. I think they would knock knockknock like the lady with the big bag.

I'm hiding behind the big black chair. It's very dark.

Knockknockknockknockknockknockknock.

I'm peeping round the chair. I'm peeping with one of my eyes. I can't see anyone. It's very dark outside. There's no one at the window. I'm looking hard with my one eye. The knocking's hurting my head. It's hurting the bump on it. It's making the bump knock too. Knockknockknockknock knockknock.

The knocking on the door has stopped. The front room is very quiet now. I can feel the bump on my head. It's still knocking. It's knocking a lot.

There's someone at the window. I can see someone with my one eye. I'm moving my head. I'm trying to move it fast. I'm hiding it behind the big chair. I don't want someone at the window to see me. There's more knocking. It's in my head and on the window. It's very loud. Someone is shouting. Someone's shouting at the window. I'm very quiet. I'm staying very still. I don't want that someone to see me. I'm listening hard.

'Open the door,' a big voice says. 'Open it.'

It's not the lady with the big bag. It isn't her voice shouting at the window. It's a man's voice. I'm staying very still. I am staying very quiet. But the banging in my head is very loud.

'Hey kid, open the door!'

It's Brick. I'm looking round the chair. I can see the shape of him through the window. 'Open the door. Now!'

Brick is back! He's brought Mammy. She's come back at last! I'm running to open the door. I'm running to let her in. I am opening the front door. 'Mammy!'

Brick is pushing the door open. Mammy isn't with him.

'Oh!' I have crashed into Brick. I'm falling back onto the floor. Brick is stepping over me. His big boot is squashing my finger. 'Ow!' My eyes are all prickly.

Brick is running up the stairs. I'm getting up and I'm going out of the front door and I'm looking for Mammy but I can't see her. 'Mammy, Mammy!' I'm shouting it. I'm shouting it to the road but I can't see her anywhere and I'm running down the path and I'm running to Brick's car.

And I can see the lady opposite moving her curtains but I'm not waving to her because I want to get to Brick's car and I want to see Mammy and I'm looking in the car but Mammy's not in it.

I'm running up the path again and I'm running into the house and I'm closing the front door fast and I'm running up the stairs and I'm running after Brick. 'Where's Mammy?' Brick is in Mammy's bedroom but he hasn't heard me because he's pulling up a corner of Mammy's carpet and I am going to stand next to him. 'Where's Mammy?'

He's pulling up a bit of wood now from under the carpet and there's a hole under the wood and he's putting his hand inside the hole.

'I want Mammy.' My finger's hurting a lot. It's the finger Brick's boot stepped on and the bump on my head is banging.

'Shurr up.' Brick's face is cross.

'I want her.' I'm shouting it. 'I want her now.'

'Tha' cow's no use to no one.'

'I want her to come home.'

'Cow.' He's saying lots of rude words. 'She ruined everythin'.'

'I want her to come home now.' I'm hitting Brick. I don't want him to say rude things about Mammy. I am hitting him. And I'm kicking him too.

He's pushing me away. My back has knocked the wall. He's calling Mammy more rude names. 'She's not comin' home. Ge' used to it.' He's looking into the hole again. The hole in the floor. He's getting something out of it. He's getting out the block that has plastic all round it. It's the block Saint gave him. A long time ago.

I'm getting up. I'm kicking Brick again. I'm kicking him as hard as I can. The kicks are hurting my toes. 'She is,' I say. 'She is coming home. I want her now.'

He's grabbing my foot. He's pulling it fast. He's tipping me up and I'm falling onto my back. 'Stupid kid,' he says.

There's a noise outside. Brick is looking out of the window. He's peeping round the curtains. 'Oh no.' He's saying a lot more rude words. I want to look out too. I want to see if it's Mammy outside. I'm trying to get to the window. Brick is pushing me back. 'Ge' to your bed,' he says. His face is very cross. 'Now.'

I am not moving. 'She is coming home. She is.'

Brick is hitting me on my head. He's hitting me very hard. He's making my bump hurt again. 'Ge' to bed.'

'I need the toilet,' I say.

He's grabbing my neck very very tight. He's pushing me back. He's grabbing my neck and pushing me to the landing. I'm trying to get some air. I'm trying to get some into my mouth. But he's squeezing my neck too tight. He's throwing me into my bedroom. 'Ge' to your bed now.' His voice is very scary.

I am running to my bed. I'm running fast. My neck is hurting. My back is hurting. My finger's hurting too. And my head is banging and banging. I'm climbing up my ladder. I'm climbing fast fast. I'm on my bed. I can see through my window. I can see a car next to Brick's car. I can see the lady in the house across the road too. She's moving her curtains.

Brick has come up my ladder a bit. He's giving me something. It's the block he got out of the hole under Mammy's carpet. 'Put this under your pillow.'

'I haven't got a pillow.' It's hard to talk. My neck is hurting inside. It feels like Brick's still squeezing it.

'Put it under your head then. Hide it. Don' say a word if they come in your room.'

I'm putting the block under my head. It's very hard. It's hurting my bump and I need the toilet. Brick's going down my ladder now. I'm pulling the clothes round me. I'm trying to be warm. Brick's stopping by the door. 'Don' move,' he says. 'Preten' you're asleep.' And he's closing the door tight.

There's a loud noise. It's banging on the front door. There's lots of shouting too. 'Hey Brick,' a man is shouting. He's very loud. 'You in there?'

I am staying very still. I'm waiting for Brick to answer the door. I must not get up and answer the door. I must not move. The man is shouting lots of rude words about Brick. Another man is shouting too. The men are calling Brick lots of rude names. They're saying things about his ho. And they are banging and banging on the door.

The shouting has stopped. The banging has stopped. It's very quiet. I'm not moving. I am listening. I've pulled the clothes up over my head. But I'm sticking one ear out. My ear is listening hard. It's listening to the quiet.

There are noises again. The men are still outside. They're not at the front door now. They're round the back. There's another noise. It's a noise like Mammy makes when she's cross with Brick. Or when she's cross with the lady with the big bag. Or with Nanno and Dat. It's the sound of something smashing. Smashing into lots of bits. I think it's the back door. I locked the door with the key. A long time ago. I think the men are smashing the glass in it.

I'm squashing myself on my bed. I am tiny tiny tiny. And I'm trying not to need the toilet. My ear is still listening hard.

The smashing noises have stopped. The door is making a squeak. The one it makes when it's opening. I can hear the tins moving. I can hear them rolling on the kitchen floor. 'Put the light on,' the loud voice says. I can hear the light switch clickclick clickclick. The lights won't come on. They stopped working a long time ago. 'Try in there,' the voice says. I can hear more tins rolling. I can hear more click click click clicks. I can hear more rude words. 'Get your mobile,' the loud voice says. 'Yeah, that's better. Put the TV by the front door. We'll take it on the way out.' I can hear someone moving around. 'Rest of the stuff in here's just trash.'

There are lots of sounds now. There are bumping sounds. There are crashing sounds. There are smashing sounds.

'Let's take a look upstairs.' There are sounds of people coming up the stairs.

I am hiding my ear. I'm hiding it fast. I'm lying very still. I'm not breathing. I'm listening hard. From under the clothes. From under Mammy's tee shirt. From under the jumpers.

247

And the trousers. And the towels. I'm trying to listen hard. But the block under my head is hurting my bump.

They're going into the bathroom. I can hear their shoes on the floor. I can hear them opening the cupboard over the sink. Lots of things are falling out. I can hear the sink catching them. I can hear things falling onto the floor. The men are saying lots of rude words. They're talking about Brick again. And his ho.

The men are on the landing. They're outside my door. I'm staying very still. I'm not breathing at all. I can hear my door handle. I can hear it turning. I can hear my door opening. I can hear the men. I can hear them breathing. I can hear them coming into my room. I can see a blue light. I can see it through the clothes. It's in my room.

'It stinks in here,' the man with the big voice says.

'Gross,' the other man says. His voice is quiet. He's saying a lot of rude words.

I'm not breathing. I'm not moving. I'm staying still. Very very still. I'm watching the blue light. I'm watching it moving.

'Look at this,' the quiet voice says. I can hear knocking on my train table.

'Where're the trains?' the loud voice says. 'They could be worth a bit. That paedo Leper's always after toy trains.'

I can hear the men's feet. They're stamp stamping. I can see the blue light. It's moving round my room. I can hear my train magazines. They're falling over.

'Trains aren't here,' the big voice says. 'The table's no good without them.'

'Nah, no good,' the other voice says.

My bed's starting to shake. It's shaking and bumping. I can hear cracking sounds. They're very loud. I'm staying still. I'm not moving at all. The men are laughing now. They're laughing and laughing.

I can hear another noise. It's not in my bedroom. I'm listening hard. I'm not moving. The men have stopped moving too. 'What was that?' the big voice says.

'Came from the other room.' The blue light is moving. It's moving fast. It's going out of my bedroom. The men are going out to the landing.

I'm trying not to move. I'm trying to stay very still. But my mouth wants to open. I'm taking a big breath. And I am closing my mouth again. I'm closing it fast. And I'm listening again now.

The men are going into Mammy's room. They're making a lot of noise. There's a very big bang. There's a lot of laughing. 'Look at him,' the big voice says. There's more banging. 'Good place to hide.' The man's laughing and laughing. 'Under the bed, like you're a kid.' There's more banging. There are a lot of crashing noises.

'Please, please,' someone says. I think it's Brick. I think it is. But he sounds very small. 'I'll ge' your money.'

'How many chances have I given you?' the man with the loud voice says. There's another big crash.

'I'll get it,' the voice like Brick's voice says. 'Please. Please.'

'You're running out of luck. And I've heard you're doing favours for Saint now. Didn't think you could run off to Glasgow without me knowing, did you Brick?'

'That's wha' I mean,' the voice like Brick's says. 'I can get you your money. Saint'll be payin' me.'

'No, he won't. It went wrong, didn't it?' The man's laughing. He's calling Brick a lot of rude names. 'Amateur. Take an addict with you and it's bound to go wrong. You should have left your whore at home. She's like my friend here – can't resist pulling a knife.'

Brick says, 'I couldn't leave her behind, though, cos—'

'Because you couldn't bear to be away from her.' The man's laughing again.

'No, cos of something Saint's given me,' Brick says. 'Look, you'll 'ave your money. Saint owes me. You'll 'ave all your money when he's paid me.'

The quiet voice is saying something. I'm listening and listening. But I can't hear his words. The block under my head is making my bump bang. Brick told me not to move it. But I want to move the block. It's hard to listen with my bump banging. And I want to listen. I want to listen a lot.

The quiet voice is still talking.

'Yeah,' the man with the big voice says. 'I think we should. If we don't do him, Saint will. And why should he have all the fun?'

There's another sound now. I'm trying hard to hear it. I'm listening and listening. And listening and listening. I think the sound is Brick. I think he's crying. 'No wait,' he says. His voice is very strange. 'I've got some of Saint's stuff. From his last trip to Glasgow. He thought 'ee was being watched, so 'ee gave it to me to keep. That's why I had to take Ree with me. She might 'ave found it in 'er room.'

250

'You're lying. Why would Saint trust you?'

'We go way back,' Brick says. 'He's like my *brawd*.'

'Your what?' the man says.

'Like my brother,' Brick says. His voice is still strange. 'It's worth loads.'

'And he'd trust you with that?' The man's laughing. 'No way. Even Saint's got more sense than that.'

Brick says, 'I can get it for you…'

There's a lot of banging again. 'I told you not to move.'

'Okay, okay.' Brick's voice is tiny now. It's hard to hear. 'I'll tell you where it is, then. Jus' put the knife away.'

'I can't trust you anymore,' the man says. 'You're just a waste of space.'

'No.' Brick's crying and crying. 'Please, please. It's worth ten times what I owe you. It's in the kid's room. In 'is bed. Go get it. Just take it. Take it all.'

My head is banging and banging and banging and banging. I'm trying to listen very hard. But my head is banging too much. The block's making it bang.

'I'll take a look,' the big voice says. 'You stay here, and keep our friend entertained.'

I can hear someone moving. I think I can hear someone on the landing. It's very hard to hear. The banging's too loud. It's too loud in my head. Bang. Bang. Bang. Bang. The block is hurting my head. Brick said not to move it. But I have to move it. It's making my head bang too much.

I'm moving it. I'm moving it fast. I'm pushing it down. Right down to the bottom of my bed. I'm pushing it with my feet. All the way down to the bottom of my bed. It's under the towels. And trousers. And tee shirts. And I'm trying not to make the bed squeak.

I'm pulling my feet up again. I'm pulling them up fast fast.

And now I am very still.

I can hear the man. I can hear his shoes. They're rubbing on the carpet on the landing. I can hear him breathing. My ear can hear the man coming into my room.

I am very quiet up in my bed. I'm very very quiet. I am as quiet as little Lord Jesus. No crying I make. I'm trying not to need the toilet. And I am very small. I'm curled up tiny. I'm curled up round my truck. And I'm holding my fifty pence. And Nanno's letter. I'm holding them tight. I'm right up by the wall. I am tiny tiny. I am under the clothes. I'm squashed into a tiny tiny corner. I'm under the jumpers. And the tee shirts. And the towels. And the trousers. I am nearly not here at all.

There's a blue light in my room again. I can see it through the clothes. I can see the light moving round my room.

I can hear the man's shoes on my ladder. I can feel my bed moving. I am not breathing. And I'm trying to make my heart quiet. It's banging a lot. It's banging in my tummy. And in my neck. And in my head. The bump on my head is banging too. All the banging is very loud. I don't want the man to hear it. I don't want him to find me. I am tiny. I'm so tiny I'm not here. I'm not here at all.

'This stinks,' the man says. His voice is very loud. He's on my ladder. I can see his blue light. It's shining onto my bed. 'Stinks.' He's saying lots of rude words. He's picking up the clothes. He's picking up Mammy's trousers. And her jumpers. He's picking up the towels. And Brick's dirty clothes. The bed's shaking. And squeaking. And shaking. And squeaking.

He's bending over. He's putting his hand on the towels. And on the trousers. And the tee shirts. He's putting his hand on my foot. It's hiding under them. He's pushing down on the clothes. And he's pushing down on my foot too. Because my foot is hiding under them. I can feel something hard pushing my foot. It's hard and flat. It's shining a blue light into the clothes. It's hurting my foot a lot. And he's pushing down very hard. The bed is shaking and shaking. But I'm staying very still. Very very very still. I'm not telling him he's hurting my foot. I'm not making a sound. I am little Lord Jesus. Away in a manger. And I'm not breathing. I'm not breathing at all. And I'm not wetting the bed.

The man's picking up the clothes. He's doing it with one hand. And he's pushing down hard on my foot with his other hand. He's picking up jumpers. And Mammy's trousers. He's picking them up fast. And he's throwing them down again. He's throwing them back down onto the bed. They're landing on top of me. They're making a big pile. Right on top of me. I'm not breathing. I am not breathing. I'm holding my truck and my coin. I'm holding my letter from Nanno. I'm holding them tight. I am little Lord Jesus. No crying I make.

'Ow,' the man says. 'What the...?' He's taking his hand off my foot. My foot is hurting a lot. It's hurting and tickling at the same time. My foot's telling me to wiggle my toes. It's

253

telling me and telling me. But I'm not moving. I'm not wiggling my toes. I'm not listening to my foot. I am staying still. I'm staying very very still. I am little Lord Jesus. I am little Lord Jesus.

He's shining his blue light on something. It's my jar of jam. It's at the bottom of my bed. He's saying a lot of rude words. He's sucking his finger. I can see him a bit. I can see him through Mammy's jumper. It's the man that hurt Mammy. The man with the web tattoo. 'Argh,' he's shouting. He's shouting it like a monster. 'Argh!' He's throwing and throwing the clothes now. The bed's shaking and shaking and he's shouting and shouting.

I don't like the man that hurt Mammy. I'm trying not to see him. I'm trying not to see his tattoo. I'm closing my eyes tight. And I'm tiny tiny tiny. I'm holding my truck. And my coin. And my letter. But I wish I had Cwtchy. I wish I had Dat.

'Yes,' the man says. He's not shouting now. 'Got it.' I'm opening my eyes. I'm opening them a tiny bit. He's holding up the block. The block that Brick gave me. 'Yes,' he says. 'Yes.' He's going back down the ladder. He's going out of my room. I can hear him on the landing. I can hear him going into Mammy's room again. My foot is hurting. The foot he pressed down on. It's hurting and hurting. But I'm not moving. I'm not moving at all.

'Thought some broken glass would stop me finding it, did you, Brick?' He's laughing. 'But surprise, surprise, Saint did trust you, after all. He won't anymore though. Not now you've given me this.'

'I didn' give it,' Brick says. 'You forced me. You 'ad a knife to my neck.'

'And you're going to tell Saint that, are you?' The man's voice is cross. 'You're going to tell him I threatened you and I took his stuff?'

'No, no. I won' tell 'im.' Brick's saying it fast. 'I won' tell Saint it was you, I promise. I swear on my mother's life.'

'See, Brick, this is the trouble with you – one minute you're talking about threats and knives, and the next you're promising not to mention them. You're a problem because you're so stupid. Saint trusts you, but I don't. We'll have to get rid of you.'

I can hear Brick crying. He's saying, 'No, no please.'

'Sorry, Brick. You know how it is.'

'Please, please,' Brick says. 'Please, I'll do anything.'

'Go on, Psycho,' the man says. 'Do it slow. Enjoy.'

I'm not breathing. I am very still. And I'm listening and listening.

There's a horrible noise. It's like crying. And screaming. Crying. And screaming. It's horrible. Horrible. It's changing now. It's changing into a noise like Dat makes. Like he makes after he's brushed his teeth. Nanno calls it gargling. The noise is like Dat gargling. But it's not funny. It's not funny at all. Not like Dat's gargling. I'm keeping my head under the clothes. I'm pulling the clothes tight over my ears. I'm trying to stop the noise. I'm trying to stop it getting into my ears. It's horrible. Horrible. I don't want to hear it. I don't want to hear it anymore. I don't want to hear the horrible noise. Go away. Go away horrible noise. Go away. Go away.

'Finish him with this.' The loud voice is saying it.

There's another noise now. A bumping noise. It's coming from Mammy's bedroom. But my bump is banging and banging. And I'm not listening to the noise in Mammy's room. I'm listening to my bump banging. Bang. Bang. Bang. Bang. Bang. Bang. Bang. I'm not listening to the horrible noises. I'm listening and listening to my bump. Bang. Bang. Bang. Bang.

And I am trying and trying not to wet the bed.

The horrible noises have stopped. I'm moving the clothes. I'm moving them from my ear. It's listening very hard. I can hear the men out on the landing. I can hear them talking again. I'm listening and listening to hear them. The men are saying rude things. They're calling Brick rude names. They are outside my bedroom. I am waiting and waiting for them to go away. I am waiting and waiting.

They are going down the stairs. They're in the front room. I can hear them going out of the door. They're closing it with a bang. I can hear them going down the path. I can hear their car engine. It's like a racing car. It's racing and racing down the road. I'm listening to it going away. I'm listening and listening. And listening and listening.

It's gone.

It's very quiet now. I can't hear Brick. I am still listening and listening. And listening and listening. I have been listening for a very long time. And I need the toilet. 'Brick?' I say. I'm saying it quietly. 'Brick? Can I come down now?' I'm listening and listening. I can't hear anything. 'Brick?' I'm trying to make my voice loud. 'Can I come down now?'

Brick isn't answering. It's very quiet. I'm moving a bit. I'm moving slow slow. I'm creeping out of bed. I'm creeping down my ladder. My ladder's hurting my foot. The foot the man pressed down on. My magazines are all over the carpet. My feet are finding them. I can feel the pages bending. But I am not picking them up. I'm creeping to the bathroom. I'm creeping in the dark. I'm creeping as fast as I can. There are things all over the floor in the bathroom. I can feel them with my toes. In the dark. I'm trying not to step on them. And I'm weeing fast fast. I'm weeing as fast as I can. And I'm trying to make my wee quiet.

I'm going back to the landing. Mammy's door is nearly closed. There's a little gap. A little gap I can see through. I'm looking through it. I'm looking into Mammy's room. The light is shining in from outside. And there's something on the floor.

I'm closing the door tight. And I'm running back to bed. I'm running fast fast fast. My feet are slip sliding on my magazines. And my head is bang bang banging. And my foot is hurting too. I'm climbing up my ladder. I'm pulling the clothes all round. I'm pulling them all over me. I'm grabbing my truck. And my fifty pence. And I'm grabbing Nanno's letter. I wish I had Cwtchy. I wish I had Dat. I'm making myself tiny again. Tiny tiny. And I'm trying to breathe. I'm trying to breathe. And breathe. It's very hard. My foot is hurting. The foot the man pushed down on. And my finger is hurting too. The finger Brick stepped on. And my neck is hurting. Because Brick grabbed it. And the bump on my head is banging. It's banging and banging and banging.

And it's hard to breathe. Very. Very. Hard. And my eyes don't want to stay open. I wish I had Dat. I wish I had Dat. My eyes don't want to stay open at all. And it's very very hard to breathe. I want Dat to come and help me quick quick. Because it's hard to breathe. And I can't make my eyes stay open. And they can't watch for Mammy. They can't watch for her to come home.

They can't watch for her anymore.

Not Remembering

There's a sound. It's a long long way away. Tap tap. Tap tap. I'm listening. But just a bit. Tap tap. Tap tap.

Nanno's in the kitchen. She's making breakfast. She's making a big bowl of porridge. She's putting the kettle on. Then she'll come and say, 'Wake up, Tomos.' And I'll get up. I'll have breakfast at the table. With Nanno and Dat. We'll have porridge and brown sugar. And cups of tea. With lots of milk. And then Dat and me will walk to school.

I can hear another sound. It's a long way away.

'Tomos? Tomos?'

It's Nanno. She's calling me for breakfast.

'Tomos? Tomos?'

Nanno's calling me. She wants me to wake up. She wants me to get ready for school. I'm trying to make myself wake up. I'm trying to say, 'I'll get up in a minute'. I'm trying to make my eyes open. I'm trying to make my voice say some words. I can't make my eyes open. My voice won't talk. My head hurts too much.

I can hear Nanno. She's calling me again. 'Tomos!' she's saying. 'Tomos!' And I'm trying to call back to her. I'm trying to say, 'It's okay. I'll get up in a minute. And Dat and me will walk to school.' But my mouth won't open. And my head hurts.

And I'm remembering. I'm remembering I'm not allowed to see Dat. And I'm remembering Nanno's in Heaven. And I'm remembering there's something in Mammy's room. Something I don't want to remember. And my head is very heavy. It's heavy with all the remembering.

Tap tap. Tap tap.

And my eyes are very tired. They don't want to open. They don't want to wake up at all.

'Tomos. Tomos.'

I am curling up. I'm pulling the tee shirts and towels all round me. I'm making myself very small. I'm trying to make myself warm.

And I'm going back to sleep.

* * *

There's a light. It's in my bedroom. It's the sun. It's shining through my window. My eyes feel funny. They don't like the sun shining in them. My side is hurting. My neck's hurting too. And my head feels funny. I'm touching it. There's a big bump on the back of it. A big big bump. And my hair feels funny all round it. I'm wondering how the bump got there. I'm trying and trying to remember. And I'm sitting up a bit. I need to go to the toilet. I'm sitting up slowly. I don't want to make my bump hurt more. I'm wondering if there's school today. I haven't been to school for a long time. A long long time. I think the school holidays might have finished.

I need to go to the toilet but I'm looking for the boxes first. The boxes of biscuits Miss gave me. They're on my bed. Under the clothes. My hand is trying to find them. My finger hurts when I move it. I'm opening my eyes a little bit more. I'm looking at my finger. It's purple and a bit black. It feels funny. I don't know what hurt it. I'm trying to remember and I'm trying to find the boxes. I've found them now. The biscuits are all gone. Miss said it would be school again when the biscuits are all gone. I'm wriggling to the bottom of my bed and I'm smiling and smiling. I'm looking forward to going back to school and I'm looking forward to seeing Miss. She might have some sandwiches for me and they might be tuna mayo and sweetcorn and my tummy's making a rumbly sound. I'm starting to go down my ladder.

'Ow!' I say. My foot's hurting. It's hurting when I put it on my ladder. I'm looking at it. There's a big black patch on it. Right in the middle of my foot. But I need to get to the toilet fast. I'm making my foot go down my ladder. It's hurting and hurting. My magazine pile has fallen over. My magazines are all over the floor in my bedroom. And all over the landing. I'm wondering and wondering who knocked them over. But I'm not stopping to pick them up. I need to get to the toilet. I need to get there fast. I'm trying to walk to the bathroom now. 'Ow!' I say. I'm hop hopping on my other foot. I need the toilet fast fast. Fast fast fast.

I'm in the bathroom and Mammy's things are in the sink. And all over the floor. The things I must NOT touch. I am trying not to step on them. Mammy must be home. She must have forgotten to put them away again. And she must have knocked my magazines over. I'm weeing fast fast because I want to go and see Mammy because I haven't seen Mammy for a long long time and I'm weeing fast fast fast fast fast and now I'm running across the landing and I'm running on my bad foot and I am slip sliding on my magazines and the bump on my head is banging and I'm running to Mammy's room but her door is closed. She must be asleep. I don't want to wake her up. But I want to see her and I want to see her yellow hair on the pillow and I want to see her before I go to school. Because I haven't seen her for a long long time. I'm opening the door. I'm opening it very quietly. I don't want to wake Mammy.

'Oh!' Mammy isn't there. Her bed is upside down. Upside down on the floor. A bit of it is broken. A bit of one of the legs. The bit of the leg is by the window. There's red stuff on it. There's red stuff on the carpet too. Lots of it. I can see a bit of something else. Something on the floor. Next to the bed. It's got red in its hair. And all down its face. And a big red patch. On its tee shirt. Its mouth's open. Its eyes are open too. And it's looking at me. It's looking. And looking. And looking.

I'm closing Mammy's door. I'm closing it fast. I'm closing it tight tight.

My tummy feels funny. I'm going back to the bathroom. I'm splashing water on my face. The water's going over Mammy's things. And I'm trying not to touch them. I'm rubbing my face. I'm rubbing it dry on my jumper. I'm doing it fast fast. I'm brushing my hair. It's hard to brush it. Mammy's hairbrush keeps getting stuck. And I'm going downstairs. I'm going downstairs fast. It's hard to go downstairs when your foot hurts. And your head is banging. And your tummy feels funny.

Someone has made a big mess downstairs. The mess is all over the front room. The black chair is on its side. The settee is upside down. It's all ripped. The big black chair is ripped too. All ripped and ripped. I can't see the telly anywhere. And my box is squashed flat. Its green paper is all over the floor. The label is ripped too. The label that said, 'To Mammy, Love from Tomos'. I am picking up the bits of label. I'm putting them in my pocket. I'm going to the window. And I am peeping out.

I'm waiting for Kaylee and her mammy. I'm waiting for them to stop at our gate. I'm waiting to walk to school with them. I'm not watching for Mammy anymore. I don't think Mammy's going to come home. I think she must be a long way away. And I'm trying not to remember the thing in her room.

The lady across the road is moving her curtains. I can see her looking at me. I'm not waving to her. I am not going to look at her. She's moving and moving her white curtains. But I'm not looking at her at all. And my neck hurts. And my foot hurts. And my tummy feels funny.

There are people walking up the road and down the road. There are cars too. Some of them are red. Some of them are black. Some of them are silver like Miss's car. Like the car she had when she came here. When I was in the park with Wes. And one of the cars is blue like Brick's car. Like his car parked outside our house. But I don't want to think about Brick. I don't want to think about him at all. And I can't see Kaylee and her mammy. I think I might be too late. I think they might have gone to school. I think they might have gone when I was in bed.

I don't want to miss school. I'm going to go by myself. I'm going to the front door. The telly is in the hall. Someone has put it by the door. I'm going out. I'm closing the door behind me. I know how to get to school. I know the way Kaylee and her mammy and me walk. I'm going down the road. The lady across the road is looking at me. I can see her moving her curtains. I'm not smiling at her. I'm not waving. I'm going fast fast to the corner. It's hard to go fast when your foot hurts. And when your head is banging. But I'm not stopping. I'm going fast fast. I'm going down the next road. Some cars are going past. I'm looking at them. I can see the people inside. Some of them are ladies. Some of them are men. Some of the cars have children in them. One car is silver. But Miss isn't in it.

The stones are hurting my feet. They're getting stuck in between my toes. But I'm not stopping to get them out. I'm running fast fast all the way to school. I'm running past all the cars. The ones that are parked in the road. I'm running fast fast past some ladies. I'm running fast fast past a man. And I'm running fast fast past some children too.

'Hey,' one boy says. 'Where're you going?' He's a big boy from my school. I saw him in Mrs Gregory's class. When I took Sir's pen round the classes with Seren. When we had an important job to do.

'School,' I say. It's hard to talk. It hurts my neck. But I'm not stopping. I'm still running fast fast.

'Why?' He's shouting it. 'What's going on?' I'm not saying anything. I'm running and running. I want to get to school. I want to get there fast.

I've come to the gates. They're shut. There's a big chain to keep them closed. I'm pulling and pulling on the gate. I'm pulling and pulling. But the gates won't open.

The boy's running up. 'School's shut. It's still Easter holidays.' He's looking and looking at me. 'Are you okay?'

I'm thinking about Mammy. I'm thinking about her not coming home. I'm thinking about Brick. I don't like thinking about him. 'I want to see Miss,' I say. My neck is hurting a lot when I talk. I'm rubbing it. And I'm pulling and pulling on the gate.

'No one's there. School doesn't start again 'til next week.'

I'm looking through the gates. I'm looking at school. There are no lights on in the classrooms. There are no children in the playground. There are no cars in the car park. I think the boy's right. No one's there.

My eyes feel prickly. My neck hurts. And my tummy feels funny. My foot is hurting a lot lot. And my head's banging. I want to see Miss. I want her to help me. I want her to get me more biscuits. But Miss isn't here. She's not in school. She's not here to help me after all.

The boy's still looking at me. I think his face is kind. 'Where're your shoes?' He's pointing to my feet. We're looking at the black bit on one of them. 'How did you do that? What happened to you?'

I'm rubbing my foot. The black isn't coming off. I don't know how the black got there. I'm thinking and thinking. I think it might have been Brick. I don't want to think about Brick.

The boy says, 'You've got bruises on your neck too.' I'm touching my neck. It hurts. It hurts a lot when my fingers touch it. I can't remember how I hurt it. The boy's pointing to my head now. 'And there's blood in your hair.'

I don't like the word blood. I don't want blood in my hair. 'Do you know where Miss is?' I say.

'Your teacher? She's at home, I s'pose. Why do you want to see her?'

I'm thinking about the biscuits. I'm thinking about Mammy being gone. I'm thinking about Brick. I don't want to tell the boy about Brick. I don't want to remember about Brick at all.

I'm thinking and thinking. I'm going to run to Kaylee's house. I know the way. I can run to my house first. Then I can cross the road to Kaylee's. And I can count six front doors down. I haven't seen a light in Kaylee's house for a long long time. But I'm going to run there. I'm going to see if Kaylee and her mammy are home.

'Hey!' the boy says. 'Where're you running off to now?'

I'm not saying anything. I'm running and running. I'm running back to the corner. The boy is running with me. We're running fast fast. We're running past the ladies again. And the children. There's a car coming up the road. It's a silver one. Miss has a silver car. I'm looking and looking at the car. A man is driving it. Miss isn't in it. We are still running fast. We're running round the corner. We are running past all the cars. The ones that are parked on the road. There's another car coming. It's a red one. And another. A black one. And another. A white one. And another. It's a silver one. There's a lady driving it. A lady with brown hair. It's Miss! She hasn't seen me. I'm waving and waving. But she can't see me. I'm running to her car. I'm running in between the other cars. The cars that are parked on the road. I'm running to her silver car and I'm running into the road and I'm waving and waving.

'Oi!' The boy's shouting it loud loud. 'Watch out!'

There's a big sound. It's all screechy. And I'm falling on the road. I can see the wheels on Miss's car. They are right next to my head. And I'm falling flat. I'm falling flat flat on the road.

* * *

It's very quiet. Very very quiet.

And now someone is shouting. It's Miss. She's shouting 'Tomos!' She's shouting and shouting. 'Tomos! Tomos!' And now she's screaming. She's screaming and screaming and screaming.

'It's okay, Mrs Davies.' It's the big boy shouting now. 'You didn't hit him.' The big boy's on his knees on the road. He's putting his face next to mine. 'You are all right, aren't you?'

I'm nodding. I'm starting to get up. The boy is helping me.

Miss is running to me. 'Tomos,' she says. She's putting her arms round me. 'Are you really all right?' She's pulling me to her. 'Did I hit you?' I'm shaking my head. I am trying to say something. I'm trying but my neck is hurting too much.

'You just missed him,' the boy says. 'By that much.' He's showing us a little gap in between his fingers.

'Oh, thank goodness.' Miss is crying now.

We are all in the middle of the road. Another car has stopped behind Miss's car. A man has got out of it. 'Everything all right?'

Miss is standing up a bit. She's still got her arms round me. It's nice to have her arms round me. 'Yes, thank you. A near miss, that's all.'

'He was lucky your brakes are good.' The man's pointing to the road. 'Your tyres have made some serious skid marks there.' We're all looking at the black lines on the road. 'Kids are such a pain in the school holidays. Running riot everywhere.'

'It was an accident.' Miss is still squeezing me. I like it when she squeezes me. 'It wasn't his fault.'

The man's going back to his car. We're watching him go away. He's driving round Miss's car now. Some other cars are driving round too. The ladies have come to look at us. They're standing on the pavement. Some children have come too.

'We'd better get out of the way,' Miss says. She's looking at the big boy. 'Were you and Tomos playing together, Will?'

'No, I just saw him running up to school,' the boy who is Will says. 'And he was asking for you.' Miss is hugging me more. 'He didn't have his shoes on and I thought he looked like he was scared or something,' Will says. 'And he's too small to be running around near a road on his own. So I ran back down here with him.'

Miss is smiling and smiling at the boy. 'Thanks for trying to help him, Will. That was very sensible of you. And kind too.' She's still cwtching me. She's smoothing my hair now. 'When term starts again I'll make sure to tell Mrs Gregory how thoughtful you... Oh!' Miss's fingers have found the bump. The one on my head. She's turning me round. 'You've got a cut, Tomos. I did hit you after all.' Miss's eyes are very very big.

I'm trying to shake my head. I'm trying to but Miss is holding it tight.

'No, he had that already,' Will says, 'all that dry blood on the back of his head. He's got a big bruise on his foot too. And bruises on his neck.'

Miss is looking at the bruises on my neck and on my foot. 'Oh!' She's putting her face in my hair. 'Let's get you in the car.' She's looking at the boy again now. 'You get along home, Will. Thanks for all your help. I'll see you in school next week.'

Miss is lifting me up. She's putting me in her car. She's pulling the seatbelt over me. And she's clicking it shut. We're starting to drive off. Will is waving to us. We're waving to him. Miss is waving a bit. I am waving a lot. I can see Miss's face in the mirror. The mirror that's stuck to the roof of her car. Her face is very white. And her eyes look pink.

'Oh, Tomos,' she says. 'What are we going to do with you? Where are we going to go?'

'I don't know.' It's hard to talk. My neck still hurts. And my tummy feels funny.

'I ought to get you checked over because of all those bumps and bruises you've got. I should take you to the hospital.' She's biting her lip. 'But perhaps we could go to my house first. Colin's not there right now.'

'Okay,' I say. It's nice in Miss's car. It's nice being with Miss. My foot is hurting a bit. And my head is banging a bit too. But it's very nice in Miss's car. I'm putting my hand in my pocket. I can feel some things in there. I'm taking them out. It's the bits of sparkly label. There's Ma on one bit and mmy on another. There's Lov on a bit too. I'm remembering something. I'm remembering something I forgot. 'I haven't got my truck,' I say. I haven't got my letter from Nanno. Or my fifty pence piece. But I am not saying that. My neck hurts too much.

'Is it in your house?' Miss says. I'm nodding. I don't want to lose them. I don't want to leave them behind. I don't want to leave them with the thing in Mammy's room. Miss is biting her lip again. I can see her in the little mirror. 'Is your mum home?'

I'm shaking my head. 'She hasn't been home for a long time.' My voice is very quiet. 'And my biscuits are all gone.' I'm rubbing my neck.

Miss's eyes are shiny in the mirror. 'Oh, Tomos. I've been so stupid…' She's getting a tissue out of her pocket. She's wiping her eyes with it. 'I should never have risked it…' She's blowing her nose. 'I came to your house a couple of days ago. After we'd driven back from the Lake District. I knocked on the door. Did you hear me? Were you in?'

I am thinking and thinking. I'm remembering Miss standing outside our house. I'm remembering running up the pavement. I was trying to run fast. I was trying to get to Miss. 'I was in the park,' I say. 'With Wes. I saw you. But you drove off.' I'm rubbing my neck again.

'I'm sorry, Tomos. I didn't see you.' Miss's eyes look sad in the mirror. 'I came back yesterday morning too. I knocked the door again. And I shouted for you through the letter box. Where were you then?'

I'm trying to remember yesterday. I'm trying and trying. I'm remembering tap tapping. Tap tapping on the door. I think that might have been yesterday. And I'm remembering Nanno calling me. She was calling me for breakfast. It might have been Miss's voice. It might have been Miss calling me. 'I think I was in bed,' I say.

Miss is blowing her nose again on the tissue. We're passing lots of houses. And people and children and dogs. I'm looking at them from Miss's car. It's very nice in her car. I like it a lot. 'What about my truck?' I say.

'Oh yes, your truck.' Miss is pushing the tissue into her pocket. 'Time to make a three-point turn,' she says. 'Let's go and get it.'

* * *

Miss is carrying me. She's carrying me up the path. My foot is hurting a lot. It's hard to walk. We've come to the back door. It's open and the glass in it is all broken.

'How did that happen, Tomos?'

'I don't know,' I say. 'Maybe Brick did it.' My tummy hurts when I say Brick.

'Perhaps we'd better not go in if we don't know who did this.' Miss is saying it quietly. 'They could still be in there.'

'I think it happened a long time ago,' I say.

'Did it? Well, we'd still better be careful… Hello?' She's shouting it. 'Hello? Rhiannon?'

We're listening. It's very quiet. 'Mammy's not back,' I say. We're going in to the kitchen. We're going in slowly.

There's glass all over the floor. Miss is looking at the silver trays. They're on the floor and on the worktops. We're going into the front room. Miss is looking at the upside down settee. And the black chair. She's looking at the rips in them. 'Did Brick do this too?' I'm lifting up my shoulders. 'We'd better be quick. Where's your truck?'

'In my bedroom. I'll get it.' I'm wriggling a bit. I want Miss to put me down.

'I'll carry you,' she says. I don't want Miss to go upstairs. I'm wriggling some more. She's holding me tight. 'You haven't got shoes on, Tomos. And there are bits of glass on the carpet.' She's carrying me up the stairs. 'Rhiannon? Rhiannon?'

'She's not here,' I say. 'No one's in.' My voice is tiny.

We're going past the bathroom. I forgot to close the door. Miss is looking in. She's looking at all the things in the sink. And all over the floor. Mammy's things. The things I must NOT touch. 'Good God.' She's saying it very quietly.

I don't like Miss looking in the bathroom. 'This is my room,' I say. I'm pointing to my door. Miss is taking me into my room. 'I need to go up my ladder. My truck's on the bed.' My voice is still very small. I don't like being upstairs. I don't like thinking about what's in Mammy's room.

Miss is pushing me up my ladder. 'Be careful, Tomos.'

I'm climbing on top of my bed. I'm going to get my truck. And Nanno's letter. And my fifty pence. I'm grabbing them fast fast. I want to get downstairs again. I want to go back to Miss's car.

Miss is coming up the ladder a bit. She's looking on my

bed. She's holding up the jar. The jar of horrible jam. 'Victorian chutney. Have you been eating this, Tomos?'

I'm nodding. 'It's jam,' I say. 'A funny kind of jam.'

'Oh, Tomos.' She looks very sad. 'And the jar's broken too.'

'I didn't eat the glass,' I say.

'Thank goodness for that.' She's rubbing her cheeks. 'Right. Let's get you down off this bed. Have you got what you wanted?' I'm showing her my truck and Nanno's letter and my fifty pence. 'Give them to me,' she says, 'so you can hold on.' I'm giving them to Miss. She's putting my coin in her pocket. She's putting Nanno's letter in there too. 'Come down the ladder slowly.' Miss is putting her hand on my back. 'I'm right here. I won't let you fall.'

I'm putting my foot on the ladder. 'Oh!' I'm stopping. I'm rubbing my foot. The ladder has made it hurt again.

Miss is coming up the ladder a bit. She's looking at my foot. 'You've got a nasty bruise there. What happened to it?'

I'm thinking. I'm trying to remember. 'I don't know,' I say. 'I think Brick might have done it.' I don't want to think about Brick. My neck hurts when I think about Brick. And my tummy goes funny too.

Miss is rubbing her cheeks again. She's lifting her head up. 'I'm so sorry I didn't come for you sooner,' she says. Her voice is all wobbly. She's taking the tissue from her pocket. It's very wet. She's wiped her nose a lot with it already. In the car. She's wiping her nose again now. 'Come on. Let's get you down.' She's putting my truck on the floor. She's putting her hands under my arms. 'Don't put too much weight on that foot.' She's helping me down. We're going down the ladder slowly.

'Look!' I'm pointing to my train table. 'Someone's broken it.' Miss is looking at my train table. She's looking at the big crack in the middle of it. 'Dat made it for me, and now it's all broken.' My neck is hurting and hurting. And my eyes are all prickly.

Miss is hugging me. 'It can be mended. Don't worry about it now.' She's picking up my truck.

'Will Dat mend it?' I say. 'Will Dat come here and mend it?' My voice is tiny tiny. And my tummy's hurting.

'We'll see.' She's helping me out onto the landing. My foot is hurting too. It's hard to walk.

'Dat's not allowed to come here,' I say. I want to see Dat. I want to see Dat a lot lot. But I don't want Dat to come here. I don't want him to see what's in Mammy's room.

Miss is squeezing my shoulder. 'Shall I carry you again?' I'm nodding. She's picking me up. She's swinging me onto her hip. I'm holding round her neck. She's holding round my middle. It feels nice. I like her holding me. She's putting my truck in between us. In between her tummy and my tummy.

Miss is looking at Mammy's door. It's still shut tight. 'Do you think your mum's in there?' Her voice is very quiet. She's putting her hand out. Her fingers are nearly on the handle.

'No.' I'm saying it fast. 'Mammy's gone away. I don't know where she is.' The words are making my neck hurt again.

'But we'd better check,' she says. Her hand is right on the handle now.

There's a funny buzzy sound. It's in Miss's pocket. She's pulling her hand back. She's pulling it away from the handle. She's not opening Mammy's door. She's getting her phone out instead. She's getting it from her pocket. 'Text from Colin,' she says. 'He's just arrived at the nursing home. He'll be there with his mum for a few hours.' She's biting her lip. 'We'd better get a move on if I'm going to work out what to do with you.' She's putting her head on my head. 'I should have come sooner.' She's squeezing me tight. My truck is squashing my tummy.

Mammy's door is still closed. Miss isn't going into her room. We're going back past my bedroom. And back past the bathroom. She's carrying me downstairs. 'You're so light.' She's saying it quietly. She's saying it into my hair. I'm holding tight to Miss. I'm looking over her shoulder. I can see Mammy's bedroom door. And I'm trying not to remember. I'm trying not to remember what I saw in there.

Miss is carrying me downstairs slowly. She's holding onto the rail with one hand. She's carrying me past the front room. I'm looking over her shoulder. I'm looking at the upside down settee. And the upside down chair. I'm looking at my squashed box. I'm looking at its ripped paper. We're going past the telly in the hall. And I am trying to forget. I'm trying to forget the thing in Mammy's bedroom.

Miss is carrying me out of the house. 'The door,' I say. My voice is still very small. 'We have to close the front door.'

'Oh yes.' She's nodding. 'I suppose we better had, even though the back door is completely broken.' She's closing the door.

277

'I always close the front door,' I say.

'You're very sensible.' She's carrying me down the path. She's carrying me to her car. She's opening the car door. She's putting me down on the back seat. She's putting my truck down too. She's pulling the seat belt over me.

'Have you still got my fifty pence?' I say. 'And Nanno's letter?'

'Yes. Here you go.' She's taking them out of her pocket.

I'm taking my coin. I'm taking Nanno's letter. 'Thank you.' I'm putting them in my tippy truck. I have remembered something else. 'What about Mammy? She won't know where I am.'

Miss is smoothing my hair. Her mouth is smiling but her eyes look very sad. She's chewing her lip. 'I could leave her a note, I suppose.' She's looking in her bag. She's found a pen and a bit of paper. 'I'll tell her you're with me, and I'll leave her my mobile number.' She's writing something on the paper. 'Won't be a minute.' She's running back up the path. She's putting the bit of paper into the letter box.

She's running back down the path now. She's getting into the front of the car. 'Right. Let's get you away from here.' She's making the car start. I can feel it all rumbly in my tummy. And in my legs and in my head. She's driving down the road. She's driving fast. She's getting me away.

I'm turning round. I'm putting my knees on the seat. I'm looking back at our house.

'Careful, Tomos,' Miss says. 'You need to sit down in the car.'

I'm sitting down again. I'm remembering something. 'I'm not allowed to leave the house,' I say. 'When Mammy's out.'

Miss's eyes are looking at me in the mirror. The little mirror stuck to the roof of the car. 'It's okay.' She's turning round a bit in her seat. She's looking at me. 'You didn't leave, Tomos. I'm taking you.'

We're driving fast. We are driving fast fast. I'm thinking about something. 'Are you stealing me? Like Wes stole my biscuit on the bus to the zoo.'

I can see Miss's eyes again in the mirror. 'No, I'm not stealing you. I'm taking you somewhere safe.'

'You're just borrowing me. Like a library book.'

'Yes. Is that okay?'

'Yes. I don't mind you borrowing me.'

'Good. I'm glad.'

I say, 'It's nice being borrowed like a library book.' I am driving my truck on the seat. I'm driving it onto my legs now.

Miss is looking at my truck in the mirror. 'It's a shame it's lost the wheels.'

'They're not lost,' I say. 'They're on my bed, under the clothes. I forgot them.'

'Oh what a pity,' she says.

We're still going fast. We're going past lots of houses. We're going past people too. Some of the people have shopping bags. Some of the people have pushchairs. Some of the people have dogs. 'It's okay,' I say. 'I'll get the wheels when you take me back.' I'm parking my truck on my lap. 'After you've finished borrowing me.' Some of the people are women. Some of the people are men.

And I'm thinking about what I saw. What I saw in Mammy's room. Next to her upside down bed. It was lying there on the floor. With a big red patch on its tee shirt. And I'm trying not to remember it. I'm trying not to remember it at all. And I don't care about the wheels. The broken wheels from my truck. I don't want Miss to finish borrowing me.

I don't want Miss to take me back.

* * *

We are in Miss's house. It's a nice house. It smells like Nanno and Dat's house. We're in the kitchen. It's a nice kitchen. I'm sitting on a chair next to a table. Miss is in the kitchen too. She's looking in her fridge. I can see her back.

'You shouldn't really eat anything.' She's saying it into the fridge. 'Not if I'm taking you to A&E later.' I can see lots of food in Miss's fridge. My tummy's making noises. The noises are very loud. Miss is looking at me now. She's biting her lip. 'Perhaps some milk,' she says. 'And how about a jam sandwich? Do you like strawberry jam?'

'Yes.' My voice is a bit better. 'I like strawberry jam a lot.' I'm smiling. My tummy is making more noises. 'And I like milk. I used to drink it at Nanno and Dat's.'

'Okay,' Miss says. She's looking in the fridge again. She's getting the milk. She's getting the jam now. It's red jam. It isn't brown. 'I'm sure a couple of slices of bread won't hurt.' She's getting the bread and she's closing the fridge. She's putting the jam on the bread. 'And we might have to wait ages at the hospital.' She's picking up a plate. There's a nice pattern on it. 'And you do look really hungry.' She's putting the milk into a glass. 'Here you go.'

I'm drinking it all.

'Careful,' Miss says. 'Slow down. You might make yourself sick.'

I'm wiping my mouth. The milk is lovely. It is just like the milk at Nanno and Dat's house. 'Thank you,' I say. My voice is much better now.

She's giving me the plate. 'Eat that sandwich slowly.'

'Okay.' I'm taking a bite. The bread tastes lovely. It's soft. The jam is lovely too. It doesn't have hard lumps in it. It has bits of strawberries and it doesn't taste like vinegar. 'Thank you,' I say. A bit of sandwich is falling out of my mouth. It's on the table. I'm picking it up and I'm putting it back in my mouth.

'Remember to eat slowly.' Miss is sitting down on the chair next to my chair. She's looking at me. She's watching me eating my sandwich. I'm trying to eat it slowly. I am trying to chew and chew. But I want to take a big bite. I want to take a very big bite. My tummy is making loud noises. I'm watching Miss watching me.

'Thank you,' I say. 'Thank you for this lovely sandwich.' I'm taking a small bite.

'Oh, Tomos, don't thank me. I've let you down so badly.' She's getting a tissue from a roll on the table. The tissue has pictures of apples and bananas on it. She's wiping her eyes. She's blowing her nose now. She's blowing her nose and closing her eyes. 'I should never have agreed to go on holiday. I knew it was the wrong thing to do. It was Colin's idea. He said I needed a break.' She's shaking her head. 'But I was just worried all the time.' She's blowing her nose again. And closing her eyes.

I am taking a big bite of sandwich. It's a very big bite. Miss didn't see me. She's opening her eyes. My mouth is full of sandwich. I am chewing and chewing.

'I worried all the time about what was happening to you. And I was right to be worried.' She's blowing her nose again. I'm trying to take another big bite. I'm trying but my mouth is still full of sandwich. She's opened her eyes. 'I thought you'd be in danger,' she says. 'And I was right.' I am chewing and chewing. She's getting another tissue from the roll. I'm waiting for her to blow her nose again. 'I'm so sorry, Tomos. I shouldn't have listened to Colin.'

I am waiting. And waiting. She's blowing her nose again and closing her eyes. I'm pushing all the sandwich into my mouth. I'm chewing and chewing and chewing and chewing. She's stopped blowing her nose. Her eyes are open again. She's looking at my plate. 'You finished that fast. You must have been so hungry.'

I'm nodding. 'Is Colin your little boy?' It's hard to talk. There's a lot of sandwich in my mouth. Bits of bread are falling out of it. They're landing on the table.

'Colin?' Miss is picking up the plate.

'Yes, Colin.' I'm licking jam off my fingers. 'You shouldn't have listened to him. Is he your little boy?' I'm getting the bits of bread off the table. I'm putting them in my mouth.

'No, Colin's my husband.' She's picking up the glass that

had the milk in it. 'And I shouldn't be too hard on him. He's just worried about me. He worries about me all the time.' She's putting more milk into the glass. 'And it's lovely to have someone who cares about me. But he doesn't know what it's like. He doesn't know what it's like at all.' She's bringing the glass over to the table. 'He's always had his family. Well, his mum anyway. That's where he is now, seeing his mum.'

'Is Colin the husband that makes your sandwiches?' I'm thinking about tuna mayo and sweetcorn sandwiches. And my tummy's making noises.

'Makes my sandwiches?' She's thinking. I can tell because her eyes are looking one way. And now they're looking the other way. 'Oh, yes. That's right.' She's laughing a bit. 'I told you he makes my packed lunches, didn't I?' She's putting the glass of milk on the table. 'I was bending the truth a bit, but he's a kind man. I shouldn't complain about him.' I'm wondering about the glass of milk. I'm wondering if it's for me. And I'm wondering how Miss bended the truth. She's rubbing her eyes. 'He doesn't know what it's like to be all alone, having to fend for yourself.' Miss isn't drinking the milk. I would like to have some more. My fingers are creeping near the glass. 'Oh, here you are, Tomos.' She's pushing the glass to me. 'But don't drink it all in one go this time.'

I'm picking up the glass. 'I won't,' I say. 'Thank you very much.' I'm drinking a bit of it. It's lovely. I want to drink it all. I want to drink it fast fast fast. But Miss is watching me. I'm drinking another little bit.

'So we came back early,' Miss says. 'From holiday. We

were only in a caravan in the Lake District, but Colin was cross.' She's throwing her tissues in the bin under the sink. 'He still is. And he'll be very cross if he finds out what I've done. So we'd better have a plan.' She's walking round the kitchen. I'm drinking my milk. I am trying to drink it slowly. 'First of all, we need to get you properly checked.' She's coming over to me. She's looking at my head. 'How did you get this cut, Tomos?'

'I don't know,' I say. I've finished all of my milk. 'I think I bumped my head.' I'm wiping my mouth on the back of my hand.

Miss is touching my bump a bit now. 'Were you knocked out, Tomos?' I'm looking and looking at her. I don't know what she means. 'Did you go to sleep after you bumped your head?'

I am thinking. I can't remember. 'I don't think so,' I say.

She's letting out a big breath. 'That's good.' She's looking at my neck now. 'And how did you get those bruises?'

'I don't know,' I say. I think Brick might have hurt my neck. But I don't want to say Brick's name. I'm trying not to remember him. I'm touching my neck. I'm touching where it hurts. And my tummy is making funny noises.

'And your finger?' Miss is holding my hand. Her fingers are soft. 'How did you do that?'

I'm looking at my finger. It's still a funny colour. 'Maybe Brick did it.' It's very hard to say his name. 'I think he did it.' I don't want to think about him. My tummy's making funny noises again.

Miss is sitting down in the chair. She's looking at her

284

phone. 'Your mum hasn't tried to call yet, so I'll take you to the hospital. We need to get you checked over.' She's biting her lip. 'But we'll have to play a game. A game of pretend. Can you do that, Tomos?'

'Like being a plane? I like pretending to be a plane.'

'Sort of. Let's get you cleaned up first. And then we can think about what type of pretend game we're going to play.'

'Okay. I like pretend games. I hope we're pretend planes. Or trains. Dat was good at pretend trains.'

Miss's mouth is smiling but her eyes look sad. 'You miss your dat, don't you?' She's smoothing my hair.

'Yes.' I am thinking about Dat. I'm thinking about him being a train. I'm thinking about him reading me stories. My nose is tickly. My eyes are tickly too. My neck is hurting a lot. I'm rubbing it. 'He didn't come and get me.' It's hard to say the words. My neck is hurting a lot inside. And my tummy is making funny noises. 'When Mammy went away, he didn't come and get me. And I called him and called him. But he didn't come. And I wanted him to come. But he didn't. He didn't come…' My words have gone. My tummy is making a lot of funny noises now.

Miss is putting her arms round me. She's holding me tight. 'He wanted to come,' she says. 'But you know he's not allowed.'

I don't want to cry. I don't want to cry at all. Not wanting to cry is making my neck hurt more. And my tummy hurts too. 'Did I do something?' It hurts when I talk. It hurts me everywhere. 'Did I do something to Dat, to make him not allowed to see me?'

Miss is hugging and hugging me. 'No, Tomos. You didn't do anything. Dat loves you very, very much. It'll be all right.' She's smoothing and smoothing my hair. 'And you're safe now.' She's cwtching me tight. And rocking and rocking me. 'You didn't do anything to Dat and you're safe now. You're safe.'

And then I am sick.

* * *

I like Miss's bathroom. It smells nice. It smells of Miss. She has toilet paper with little flowers on it and it's very soft like Nanno's toilet paper. I'm having a wash in Miss's bath. The water is lovely. It's all bubbly and it isn't cold.

Miss is giving me a flannel. 'I'm sure Nanno taught you how to wash yourself.' She's giving me some soap too.

'Yes,' I say. I am rubbing the soap. I'm rubbing it in the water. I'm rubbing it on the flannel and I'm washing myself. 'Sorry I was sick.' I'm looking at Miss's cardigan. I can see it in the sink. Miss has washed the sick off it.

'Don't worry. I think it's because you ate too fast.' She's looking at the bump on my head. 'I just hope it wasn't because you're concussed.' She's putting her hands over my eyes. She's doing the thing again. The thing she did lots and lots in the kitchen after I was sick. 'Keep your eyes open, Tomos.' She's counting. I'm trying to look at her hands. I can't see them very well. I can only see two pink bits of light. 'Now look at me while I take my hands away.' I'm looking at Miss. She's looking at my eyes. 'I'm sure you're not

286

concussed. You're pupils are reacting fine. When did you bump your head, Tomos? Was it last night?'

I'm thinking. 'I don't know.'

'Was it yesterday? Yesterday was the day I knocked on the door and you were in bed.' I'm shaking my head. I don't think it was yesterday. 'The day before yesterday? That's the day you said you went to the park with Wes.'

I'm trying to remember the day before yesterday. And going to the park with Wes. I don't like remembering that. I say, 'I don't remember bumping my head.'

'How many fingers am I holding up?' She's holding up her fingers again like she did in the kitchen.

'Four,' I say. 'One more than last time.'

'You're fine.' Miss is smiling now. 'You don't seem confused or sleepy at all. We just need to check out your foot and your finger, make sure you haven't got any broken bones.' She's looking at my bump again. 'Do you think it'll be okay if I wash your hair? I'll be able to see the cut on your head then.'

It would be nice to wash my hair. It feels yucky and it's stuck down over my bump. 'Okay,' I say.

'Lie back. I'll get the shampoo.' I'm lying back. The water is stinging a bit on my cut. 'Up you get.' Miss is making a lot of bubbles on my head. The shampoo is stinging a bit now. 'Are you okay, Tomos?' she says. I'm nodding and the bubbles are falling. They're falling into the bath but she's not letting them fall into my eyes. She's wiping them away with the flannel.

'I'm okay.' The stinging is stopping. It's stopping a bit.

'You're very brave.' She's looking at the bruises on my finger. And on my foot and on my back and on my neck. She's looking at my side now. 'These are nasty grazes.'

I say, 'I got them from the carpet.' I'm remembering the man. The one that came to our house and hurt Mammy. I don't want to think about him. I don't want to remember him hurting Mammy anymore. 'They're getting better now.'

Miss is lifting me out of the bath. She's putting a big towel round me. It's warm and soft. 'Right,' she says. 'I've got some clean clothes you can wear. It's a school uniform but it'll have to do.'

'Are we going to school?' I'm rubbing myself with the towel. It's very very soft. It feels lovely.

Miss is shaking her head. 'It's still the school holidays. But it's all I've got, I'm afraid.' She's helping me to get dressed. She's pulling the white top over my head. It smells lovely.

'Are these your little boy's clothes?'

'No, I don't have a little boy, Tomos. These are the clothes you get changed into in school sometimes, remember? I brought them home to wash for the start of term.' She's picking up my dirty tee shirt and my trousers. 'I'll pop these in the washing machine later.'

'Wait!' I'm grabbing my trousers. I'm finding the bits of my label. I'm taking them out of my pocket.

'What have you got there, Tomos?'

I'm showing Miss the bits. 'My sparkly label. It's all ripped now, but I still like it.' I'm putting the bits on the floor. I'm trying to make the words look right again and I'm reading the label to Miss. 'To Mammy, Love from Tomos.'

She's nodding. 'Well done. It's like a jigsaw now, isn't it? And you've put the bits back together again.' She's smiling a bit but her eyes look sad. 'Keep them safe in the pocket of your clean trousers and let's get your socks on.' She's still smiling a bit. 'Then we'd better go to A&E.'

* * *

We are in Miss's car. We're on our way to A&E. We have left my truck in Miss's house. And my fifty pence and Nanno's letter. Miss says they will be safe there. And we have been making a plan.

'So just agree with whatever I say,' Miss says.

'I agree,' I say. I like the word agree. Sometimes Dat says 'This is the best cup of tea ever. Do you agree, Tomos?' Then we clink our mugs together and I say 'I agree, Dat.'

I'm sitting in the back of Miss's car. Miss has done all the buttons up on my white top. The collar is very tight on my neck. It's squashing my bruises a bit.

'I mean, don't say anything,' Miss says.

I'm not saying anything. I'm just shaking my head. Now I'm nodding.

'Keep your chin down and try not to fiddle with your collar. It's covering your bruises. We mustn't let the doctor see them.' I'm trying not to fiddle. I am trying not to fiddle with my collar. 'And now your hair's clean, your bump is completely hidden. And it's only a little cut after all. It doesn't need stitches. And they won't ask you to undress just to have your finger and foot examined, so they won't see the

289

bruises on your back. Or the grazes. Do you remember your new name?' Miss is talking very very fast.

'Yes,' I say. 'It's Henry Lewis.'

'Well done, Tomos.' Miss is smiling at me in the little mirror. 'I mean, Henry.'

'Am I Henry Lewis for always?' I say. I don't want to be Henry Lewis for always. I like being Tomos Morris.

'No, not for always. Just for a little while. Do you think you can do that?'

'Yes. Easy peasy. I like pretending games. I'd like to be a signal man,' I say. 'Or an aeroplane, but I don't mind being a Henry. Have you really got a son called Henry Lewis?'

'No, I haven't got a son, remember? Henry is my nephew.' We're turning into a car park. Miss's car is slowing down. 'And it's best if you stick to your own birthday. It would be too complicated to try and learn Henry's. Do you know your birthday?'

'Yes, Nanno taught me. It's August 28th.'

'Oh yes,' Miss says. 'You're the youngest child in my class. If you were born a few days later, you'd be in Reception with Miss Parsons.'

'I'm glad I'm not in Reception,' I say. I like Miss Parsons. She says, 'Hello, Tomos,' when she sees me in the playground. Or in the hall at dinner time. But I don't want to be in her class. I like being in Miss's class. I like it in Year One. And after Year One it is Year Two. That is Mrs Pugh Year Two's class. I don't want to be in her class. I don't want to be in her class at all. 'Can I always be in your class, Miss? I like it in your class. Can I stay there forever?'

Miss is smiling. 'Well, you're in my class for now. We can think about what happens later another time.' She's stopping the car. 'Here we are.' Miss is getting out. She's coming to open my door. She's looking at her watch. 'Half past five. Colin will be leaving his mum's nursing home at seven o'clock. He'll be really annoyed if I'm not at home when he gets back.' She's still talking very fast. She's biting her lip. 'Let's hope they don't keep us here for hours.' She's picking me up. 'I'll have to carry you because you've only got socks on. I should have remembered to pick up some shoes from your house.' She's puffing a bit. 'But we were in a hurry to get away.'

I'm glad we didn't get shoes. I like Miss carrying me. And my foot hurts when I walk.

We're at the hospital doors. They are opening all by themselves. 'Right. Here we go.' Miss is putting me down. My foot's hurting a bit.

'Hello,' a lady says. She's looking through a hole in the wall. It's a square hole with glass in it. The lady's smiling at Miss. 'Can I help you?'

Miss is smiling at the lady. 'I was hoping to get my son's hand checked.'

The lady is smiling at me now. I'm showing her my finger. The one that's a funny colour. 'Oh! How did you do that?'

'He got it jammed in a cupboard. Didn't you, Henry?' Miss is looking at me. I'm nodding and I'm still keeping my chin down. 'And he's hurt his foot, too,' Miss says. 'My mum rushed to help him when he got his finger caught, and she accidentally stood on his foot.' I'm nodding again. And I'm not fiddling with my collar.

'Oh, what bad luck,' the lady says. 'You have been in the wars. Well, I'll just take some details.' She's still smiling at me. 'Then we'll ask the doctor to look at your hand and your foot. Right then, your name is Henry.' She's tap tapping on something. 'What's the surname?'

'Lewis,' Miss says. I'm nodding. And I'm keeping my chin down.

'Lewis,' the lady says. She's tapping again. 'Date of birth?' She's looking at Miss.

I say, 'August 28th.' And Miss is saying the year.

'And you're his mum,' the lady says. Miss is nodding and I'm nodding. Because I have to agree with Miss. 'Your name?'

'Elaine,' Miss says. 'Elaine Lewis.' I'm nodding again.

'Address?'

'Ten, The Orchards, Basingstoke. We're on holiday in Carmarthen. We're visiting my mother.'

'Postcode?' The lady is still tapping.

Miss is biting her lip. 'RG… nineteen.' She's biting her lip again. 'Sorry, we haven't been at that address long.'

The lady is smiling. 'I'm the same. Can't remember my phone number half the time.'

'RG nineteen two PR,' Miss says fast fast. I'm nodding.

'Good,' the lady says. She's tap tap tapping. 'GP name and surgery address?'

Miss is biting her lip again. 'Oh, I don't know it off the top of my head,' she says. 'We've only just registered with them.'

'That's okay.' The lady's still tap tapping. 'We can get those details later.'

I'm looking at the people sitting down. There's a girl. She's crying. She's sitting on a lady's lap. There's an old man too. He's in a wheely chair.

'Right, then,' the lady says. 'You take a seat and someone will see to Henry as soon as possible.'

'Thank you.' Miss is holding my hand. Her fingers are very shaky. 'Come on, Henry, let's find a seat.'

I am going with Miss and I am keeping my chin down. Miss is keeping her chin down too. She's looking round the room a bit. 'Good,' she says. She's saying it quietly. 'There's nobody here I know.' She's lifting her chin up now. We're going to find a seat. The floor is slippy. My socks are sliding over it. 'Be careful,' Miss says. 'We don't want you hurting yourself again.'

We're sitting down. Miss is putting her arm round me. It's nice to have Miss's arm round me. We are pretending. We're pretending that she is my mammy and I am her little boy. I like pretending. I like pretending to be Henry Lewis.

It's quite noisy. The girl is crying a lot. The old man is shouting. He's shouting to the lady next to him. 'I only bent down to switch on the gas fire.' He's saying it loud. 'And I felt my back go. Big click there was. Couldn't straighten up.' The man is talking a lot. He's talking about ambulances and doctors. He's talking about injections and operations.

'It's noisy in here, isn't it, Henry?' Miss says. I am nodding and I'm keeping my chin down. I'm trying not to fiddle with my collar but it's very tight. Miss is picking up a magazine. It was on the table. Her hand is very shaky. She's showing me the cover. 'Shall we play spot the word, Henry?' Her voice is shaky too. 'Can you see the word "hello"?' It's very easy to find the word hello. I'm pointing to it. 'Well done, Henry.' Her voice is still very shaky.

'I've got a bad back anyway, though,' the old man is saying. He's saying it very loud. 'I'm eighty-two. Arthritis, see.'

The lady next to him is nodding. 'My dad's got a bit of arthritis. He's eighty-six. Had terrible stomach pains this afternoon. Bent double, he was. He's being seen to now.'

Miss is turning the pages. 'What about the word "you"?'

'I'm bent double at the best of times,' the man says. 'I wish they'd hurry up. I've been here hours.' He's very loud.

I'm looking at the big writing. The big writing at the top of the page. I'm pointing to the word you. 'How about "out"?' Miss says. I'm looking again. I'm pointing to it. She's turning the pages. The magazine is shaking. 'What about…'

Some big doors are opening. A man in a blue uniform has come in. 'Mrs Joyce?' he says. 'Relative of Mr Ray Williams?' He's saying it loud. He's looking round the room.

The lady next to the old man is getting up. 'Yes, I'm his daughter.'

'The doctor wants to see you,' the man in the blue uniform says. 'He wants to have a word about your father.' The lady is going with the man and the big doors are closing.

'That doesn't sound good,' the old man says. He's saying it to Miss. He's saying it loud. 'It'll be appendicitis, or gall stones. Could be cancer at that age.'

Miss is smiling a bit at him. She's looking at the magazine now. 'What about…' The man has started talking again. He's telling us he is eighty-two. He's telling us about his back and his gas fire. 'What's wrong with you then?' he says. He's looking at me.

'My son's hurt his finger,' Miss says. 'We thought we'd better get it checked.'

I'm holding up my finger and I'm keeping my chin down. 'Nasty that,' he says. 'Perhaps the doctor will chop it off.' The man is laughing and laughing. He's very loud. I don't like him laughing. I don't like him laughing at me. I don't want the doctor to chop off my finger. My collar feels very tight.

'The doctor won't do that.' Miss is squeezing my shoulder. The man is still laughing. Everyone's looking at him. The girl has stopped crying. She's looking at him laughing. My collar feels very very tight. Miss is squeezing my shoulder again. I'm looking up at her.

The man has stopped laughing now. He's pointing. He's pointing to me. 'What's he done there?' His voice is very very loud. He's still pointing to me. 'What are all those bruises?' Everyone is looking at me now. They are all looking and looking. I am taking my hand away. I'm taking it away fast from my collar. And I'm putting my chin down. But the man is still looking at me.

'Good God,' he says. 'Who tried to strangle him?'

* * *

The old man has gone. A lady in a blue uniform called him. His name was Mr Preece. Mr Frank Preece. And he waved to the lady. And she came and pushed his wheely chair. She pushed it through the big doors.

'It's okay, Tomos,' Miss says. She's saying it very very quietly. 'The nurse didn't see your neck and that woman and her daughter were too far away to see properly. And I'm sure that old man will forget all about it now he's with the nurse and the doctor.' She's smiling at me. 'He'll be telling them about his gas fire and that he's eighty-two.'

I'm smiling too. 'And that his back made a big click.' I'm tucking my chin down tight. 'I didn't mean to fiddle with my collar. It was an accident. I'm sorry.'

'Oh, Tomos.' Miss is saying it very very quietly. She's smoothing my hair. 'You don't have to say sorry. It shouldn't be like this.' She's smoothing and smoothing my hair. 'But I'm afraid I can't think of a better plan.' She's getting her phone out of her bag.

'Did Mammy ring you?'

Miss is looking at her phone. 'No, not yet.'

'I think she's not coming back,' I say. I'm remembering Brick. I'm remembering him saying that. 'I think I made her sad.'

'Oh no, Tomos,' Miss says. 'I'm sure you didn't make her sad. Why do you think that?'

'Because she cried a lot,' I say, 'before she went away.' I'm remembering the horrible night. The night the men came. The night the man with the web tattoo hurt Mammy. 'She told me to go to my room, and I didn't go.'

'Oh, I'm sure that didn't make her sad.' Miss is smoothing my hair.

I'm thinking again. 'Or it might be because of Luke.'

'Luke?' Miss says. She's stopped smoothing my hair. She's turning in her chair. She's looking at me. 'What about Luke?'

I'm remembering Mammy holding my hand on the stairs. I'm trying to remember what she said about Luke. 'Mammy said she sees him instead of me.' I'm remembering the way she looked at me. The way she looked at me when she was holding my hand. 'It makes her sad.'

'Oh,' Miss says.

'I don't know who Luke is,' I say. I'm feeling sleepy. The nurse is calling the girl. Her name is Emma Roberts. She's started to cry again.

'No,' Miss says. 'No, you don't know him.'

I am very sleepy. I'm putting my head on Miss's lap. She's smoothing my hair and I'm very sleepy. I'm very very sleepy.

* * *

I am in a car. A very fast car. I'm watching the houses and the people and the dogs go past. But I can't see them very well. The car is going too fast.

I want to drive the car. I want to make it go fast too. But I'm in the back and it's hard to drive when you're in the back. I'm trying to make my arms long and my legs long. I'm trying to touch the steering wheel with my long arms. But I'm too far away. My fingers can't touch the steering wheel at all.

A man is in the front. He's driving the car. I can see the back of his head. I was hoping Miss was driving the car. I was hoping and hoping. But it isn't Miss's head I can see. And it's not Miss's eyes in the mirror. The eyes in the mirror are brown like my eyes. And they're looking and looking at me.

'Hello,' the man's eyes say. They look friendly. The friendly eyes are smiling at me. There's a web tattoo round one of them.

I can see his mouth now. I can see it in the mirror. His mouth is smiling at me too. 'Hello, Tomos,' his mouth says. It's smiling and smiling and smiling and smiling. And his web tattoo is stretching. And his mouth is full of blood.

Miss's lap has jumped. 'Henry, Henry.' She's rubbing my back. 'The nurse is calling us.' Miss is lifting me up. She's carrying me through the big doors. 'Sorry,' she says. 'He was fast asleep.'

'That's okay,' the lady in the blue uniform says. 'First door on the left. Dr Hirani's waiting for you.' Miss is carrying me through another door.

There's a man sitting on a chair. He's wearing a white coat. 'Hello,' he says. 'What can I do for you?' He's pointing to another chair.

Miss is sitting down. I am on her lap. I'm still sleepy. I'm trying to wake up. I'm trying to wake up fast. I'm pulling up my collar. 'My son jammed his finger,' Miss says. 'I'm worried he's broken it.' She's holding my hand. She's showing the doctor my finger.

'I see.' The doctor's touching my finger. He's moving it one way. Now he's moving it another way. 'Does it hurt?' It is hurting. It's hurting a bit. I'm nodding. And I'm trying to keep my chin down. 'I don't think it's broken,' the doctor says. 'But perhaps we ought to make sure.'

'And he hurt his foot, too.' Miss is pulling off my sock. We're all looking at my foot. We are looking at the big black patch on it.

'How did you do that?'

'Well, his finger was ja—' Miss has stopped because the doctor is holding up his hand.

'I'd like Henry to tell me himself,' he says. He's looking at me sitting on Miss's lap. 'Is that okay, Henry?'

I am nodding a bit. I'm taking a big breath and I'm remembering to keep my chin down. 'My finger was stuck in the cupboard door.' I'm looking at Miss a tiny bit. She's not looking at me. She's looking at the doctor. 'And I cried. Then my gran ran to help me and...' I am taking another big breath. 'She stepped on my foot.' I'm holding my collar and I'm looking at Miss again. She's still looking at the doctor. He's writing things down. She's rubbing my back. 'By accident,' I say.

'Wow, that was unlucky.' The doctor's stopped writing now. He's touching my foot. He's moving it about. It's hurting quite a lot. 'There are lots of small bones in your foot. You might have damaged some of them. I think you'd better have it X-rayed. And your finger too. I'll just get the nurse to take you...' The doctor's going out of the door.

'Was that right?' I'm saying it quietly.

'Perfect.' Miss is saying it into my hair. 'Well done, Henry.' I'm laughing.

The doctor's coming back in. The lady in the blue uniform is with him. 'Follow Nurse. She'll show you the way to X-ray,' the doctor says. Miss is picking me up. We're going through the doors. We are following Nurse.

'Just along there,' she says, 'on the right. Take a seat outside. They'll call you when they're ready. There's no one else waiting, so you shouldn't be long.' We're sitting down again. Miss is putting my sock back on.

A lady's put her head out of a door. 'Henry?' Henry Lewis?'

'I'm Henry Lewis,' I say. I'm smiling at Miss.

'Come on in with your mum, then.' We're going into the lady's big room. My socks are sliding on the floor. 'Your mum can help you put this on.' The lady is holding up something. It has stars on it. It looks like a dress.

'It's just his hand and foot,' Miss says. 'Surely he doesn't need…'

'Everyone has to get changed,' the lady says. She's giving the dress to Miss. 'If you can help him.' The lady's bending down to look at me. My collar feels very tight. 'I'm going to X-ray you.' She's smiling at me. She's smiling and smiling. 'But first you'll have to get undressed.'

* * *

The lady has X-rayed my hand. She has X-rayed my foot. Miss has had to wait outside but she's coming back in now.

'Everything looks okay,' the lady says. She's smiling at us. 'If you just wait here a minute, I'll get the doctor to check the X-rays.'

Miss is helping me take off the dress. She's helping me put on my clothes. We're putting them on quick. Miss is putting my socks in her bag. 'We'll have to hurry, Tomos,' she says. 'She's seen the bruises on your neck.' She's picking me up. She's carrying me out of the room. She's carrying me fast. We are not going the way we came in. We are not going to the doctor's room. We're going past lots of other rooms. Miss is carrying me past a little shop. It has some newspapers outside it. She's carrying me past a big room. It's full of tables. She's carrying me fast fast. There are big doors in front of us. They're opening all by themselves. 'At last,' Miss says. Her voice is tiny. We're going through them. We're going out into the dark. We're going out to the car park. Miss is slow now. 'Just a bit further.' Her voice is tiny tiny. We're by the car. Miss is opening the door. She's putting me on the seat in the back. She's holding on to the door. She's closing her eyes. I can hear her breathing. And breathing. And breathing.

She's opening her eyes. She's looking right at me. 'Okay, Tomos,' she says. 'Time to face Colin.'

* * *

We're back at Miss's house. Miss is carrying me to the front door. She's opening it. We're going in.

'Good grief, Lowri, put him down!' a man says. He's standing in the hall. He's got a red face. 'You're supposed to be careful. Wasn't one miscarriage enough?'

Miss is putting me down. I'm holding onto her hand. I'm

301

standing behind Miss. I am peeping with one eye. I am peeping at the man with the red face. 'Quiet, Colin.' Miss is smoothing my hair. 'You're frightening him. He's been through enough without you terrifying him, too.' She's bending down. She's putting her face next to my face. 'This is Colin.' She's saying it to me. 'He's very nice really.' She's looking at the man with the red face now. 'And this, as you've already guessed, is Tomos. We've just been to have him checked over at A&E.' She's still smoothing my hair.

'Have I stopped being Henry Lewis now?' I'm saying it quietly to Miss. I think she might have forgotten to pretend.

'Henry Lewis?' Colin says. 'What the—' I'm hiding behind Miss's legs again.

'I couldn't use our real names at the hospital,' Miss says. 'I had to think of something else.'

'So you used my nephew's name. You thought that would be okay?' He's rubbing his head. He's making a blowy noise with his mouth.

'I needed an actual name and address,' Miss says. 'A proper postcode. Everything's computerised now. They'd have known if I'd made it up.'

'So you used my sister's address?' He's saying it very loud. 'Lowri, what the hell were you thinking?'

'It'll be all right,' Miss says. 'They won't check.'

'Of course they'll check!' Colin is shouting now. I'm making myself very small behind Miss's legs.

'Well then, I'll explain to the hospital. And to your sister. I'll make it all right, I promise.'

'I can't believe you've done this.' Colin is shaking his head.

He's very very red now. 'We talked about this and we decided you would not interfere.'

'You decided we'd do nothing,' Miss says. 'I didn't agree.'

'We agreed you'd check on him, that's all.'

'I did check. And things were even worse than I thought.'

'So call the police,' Colin says. 'Don't take matters into your own hands. Call social services.'

'I told you, I couldn't do that to Rhiannon. I've got to give her some time. I want to make her see what's at stake.'

Colin's mouth is making a very big blowy noise now. 'You don't owe that girl a thing. Look what she did to Nannette and Dafydd. And you still think she's worth worrying about?'

I am listening hard. I'm hiding behind Miss and I'm listening very hard. I can hear Mammy's name. I can hear the names Nanno and Dat call each other.

'She was just reacting badly to Nannette's illness, that's all,' Miss says. 'She wasn't being malicious, not really. I've tried to explain it to you.'

'So you've got a degree in psychology now, have you?'

'I understand her, Col. I know how she behaved when she was little.'

'Well, you would understand her, wouldn't you?' Colin is nodding his head. 'Because you're just like her, deep down.'

'Oh, Colin,' Miss is holding out a hand to him. 'Don't start that again. Let's not argue. Tomos is here now, so just say hello and be nice to him.' Miss is pulling me a bit from behind her legs.

'You're completely crazy,' he says. 'I should have known

you'd turn out like this. My mother warned me you would.'
He's walking up and down the hall. And he's rubbing his
head again.

'Colin, calm down and just say hello to Tomos. *Please.*'

Colin is stopping. He's taking a big breath. He's looking
at me. 'Hello, Tomos,' he says. He's looking at Miss now. 'Is
that good enough for you?'

'And smile.'

Colin's making another blowy noise. He's looking at me
again. His mouth is smiling. It's smiling a bit. But his eyes
still look cross. 'You see, Tomos,' Miss says. 'Colin *is* friendly
after all.' She's holding my hand. She's pulling me a bit more.
She's pulling me out from behind her legs. 'It's okay. Come
and say hello, too, Tomos.'

I am holding Miss's hand. I'm holding it tight. I'm
holding one of her legs. I'm pushing my face into her
trousers. I'm looking at Colin a bit. I'm looking at him with
one eye. 'Hello.' I am saying it quick. I'm pushing my face
back into Miss's trousers. I'm hiding my face from Colin.

'There,' Miss says. 'The two of you are friends now.'

'Lowri, this is crazy,' he says. 'You can't do this.'

'I am doing it.' Miss is still holding my hand. I'm peeping
a bit at Colin. His face isn't too red now.

'This could spoil everything,' he says. 'It could ruin your
career before you've even got it started.' He's sitting down
on the stairs. He's holding his head. 'It could ruin us too. I
can't handle you doing this.' He's looking down at the
carpet. 'I can't handle it.'

Miss is going to him. She's pulling me behind her. She's

putting her other hand on Colin's shoulder. 'Please understand, Col.' She's kneeling down. She's putting her head next to Colin's. 'I can't abandon him. I know what it's like to be small and terrified. And I was eight years old. He's only five.' She's putting her hand under his chin. 'Please, Col, please understand.' She's lifting his chin up.

I'm peeping from behind Miss. Colin is looking up at her. His face isn't red now. His eyes are pink and they're wet. 'We should have been friends back then,' he says, 'back when we were in primary school. I could have helped you.'

'I know,' Miss says. 'You would have saved me.' She's kissing his forehead. 'You have saved me.' She's kissing his mouth.

I am remembering something. I'm remembering something very nice. Something very very nice about Colin. I'm coming out from behind Miss. I'm coming out a little bit. I'm tapping Colin's knee. He has stopped kissing Miss. He's looking at me now.

'I like your sandwiches,' I say.

* * *

I have been to the toilet. I've washed my hands on a flannel and I'm drying them on Miss's nice towel. I'm putting it back on the rail. I'm jumping up and I'm pulling on the light switch. The light has gone off. I'm picking up my truck and my letter and my fifty pence. And I'm closing the bathroom door after me. I've been watching a programme on telly. It's got a yellow boy in it. I'm going back to watch some more.

I've got some sandwiches too. They're tuna mayo and sweetcorn. Miss made them for me and her sandwiches are nearly as good as Colin's. I'm starting to go down the stairs.

I can hear Miss and Colin talking. They're in the kitchen and the door is closed. I can hear their voices. Colin is cross again. He's shouting very quietly. I am sitting down on the stairs. I'm putting my truck and my letter and my fifty pence down next to me. And I'm listening.

'You've been feeding him and clothing him behind my back. What else? Have you set up his college fund yet?'

'Oh, Col. I had to feed him. You wouldn't want him to starve, would you? We're talking a few pounds here and there.'

'Well, I suppose you'd say it was up to you how you spend *your* money. After all, you're the one earning. I'm the one scrounging off you.'

'That's not the way it is.'

'Our money is *your* money really. You made that plain on holiday. *Your* money paid for the holiday so *you* decided to come home early.'

'Don't be like that, Col.' Miss sounds very tired. 'I said that out of desperation. You know that's not how it is. What's mine is yours. We're a partnership. Equal.'

'Well, it's hard to be equal when one person's doing things behind the other's back.'

'Oh, Colin. You knew I was looking out for him. What did you expect me to do? Watch him starve?'

'I didn't expect you to do this. I thought you'd call social services.'

'We've been through all that.'

'This is the worst thing you could do. Think of your job. You've already overstepped the mark by forging a signature.' Colin's voice sounds very very cross. '*Forging a signature*, Lowri.'

'So he could go on the class trip,' Miss says. 'I couldn't leave him behind just because Rhiannon hadn't signed the slip. I know what it's like, Colin, to be the only child left behind while everyone else goes ice skating…or to the theatre. That was me until I learned how to copy my mother's writing.'

'It's no excuse. It wasn't up to you whether he went or not. It wasn't your decision.'

'He was desperate to go. He'd been looking forward to it for weeks.'

'You could lose your job if the school found out.'

'He's more important than my job.'

'And more important than me? Than us?'

'Now you're being ridiculous.'

'Am I, Lowri? And how will we eat if you lose your job?' Colin says. 'How will we pay the bills? This is madness. He shouldn't be here.'

'I'm not going to lose my job, and anyway you'll find something soon, Col.'

'Oh that's right, turn it round onto me. It's all my fault for being out of work.'

'That's not what I said.'

'You might as well have.'

'Look, I couldn't leave him in his own house,' Miss says.

'The whole place was smashed up. Broken glass all over the floor. There were used syringes in the bathroom.'

'Then you should have called the police.'

'I didn't want to scare him. And I don't want to get Rhiannon into trouble. I want to help her.'

'She doesn't deserve your help.'

Miss says, 'She's nineteen, Colin, she's just a kid herself. And she's like a little sister to me. I can't turn my back on her. I just can't.'

'She's only three years younger than you, Lowri. And you think she's a kid? So what are you?'

'I had to grow up fast,' Miss says. 'Because of my mother.'

'Oh yes, blame your mother. It's always about your mother. Well, it's time Rhiannon grew up now. She had a waster of a mother too.'

I can hear the music starting again. The music of the programme I've been watching. But I'm not moving. I'm staying on the stairs. And I'm listening hard.

'He's not stopping here.'

'You're being unfair, Col.'

'Face it, Lowri. Rhiannon is not the little sister you never had. And Tomos is not the child you lost. You can't change the past by trying to rescue him.'

'That's cruel, Colin.' Miss's voice sounds strange. 'I didn't think you were like that. I know I can't change the past. And I know Tomos isn't the child I lost.'

But I am. I am the child Miss lost. I am the child Miss lost at the zoo. I can hear Miss crying again now like she did when the lamb man found me.

'I know you're selfish,' she says. 'And you can be lazy too. And you try and control everything I do. But I didn't think you were cruel.'

'Lazy?' Colin isn't shouting quietly now. 'You think I'm lazy?'

'And I didn't *lose* a child, Colin,' Miss says. 'I didn't have a miscarriage. You never worked it out, did you?' Her voice is all funny. It's sad and cross too. 'I killed it. I *killed* our baby.' And a door is opening. It's opening fast. Miss is calling, 'Tomos! Tomos!'

And I'm picking up my truck and my letter and my fifty pence. I'm picking them up fast fast. And I'm running down the stairs to her.

* * *

We are in Miss's silver car again. We have been driving round and round in the dark. Round and round and round. Miss has stopped crying now. She's blown her nose a lot of times. There are lots of squishy tissues on the seat next to her.

'Tomos.' She's looking at me in the little mirror stuck to the roof. 'I'm sorry I took you to my house.' Her voice sounds all wobbly.

I say, 'I liked your house. It was nice.'

'I shouldn't have taken you there.'

'Colin was cross with me.'

She's shaking her head. 'No, he wasn't. He was cross with me. And he was right to be cross with me.' She's smiling at me in the mirror. 'He likes you. And most of the time he's very friendly. It didn't sound like it tonight, though.'

'I like him too,' I say. It's nearly true. 'He makes nice sandwiches.'

Miss is smiling a bit. 'The thing is, you can't stay at my house. It wouldn't be right. I hope you're not too disappointed.'

I am trying not to be too disappointed. I'm trying hard. I liked Miss's house. It was warm and it smelt nice. 'I'm not disappointed. Are you taking me back to my house?' I don't want to go back to my house. I don't want to think about Mammy's room. And about what's on the floor. 'Did Mammy ring?' My voice is very small.

'No,' Miss says. 'She hasn't phoned, so she can't have found my note. I'm not taking you back. But I'm going to find the best place to take you. It'll be somewhere safe and warm. You'll be fine there. And you'll have plenty to eat.'

'Is Dat's house the best place to take me?' I'm hoping and hoping it's the best place to take me.

'Well,' Miss says. She's biting her lip a bit. 'You know you're not allowed to see Dat at the moment.'

'I know.' I am hoping and hoping. I'm bouncing up and down a bit.

'But I do need his help. He might know somewhere I can take you.'

'Are we going to see Dat? Are we going now?' The seat in the back of Miss's car is very very bouncy.

'Yes, I need to ask him something. But you can't see him, Tomos, I'm afraid. You'll have to stay in the car.' Her voice is wobbly again. 'Do you think you can do that for me?'

I'm not bouncing now. I'm not bouncing at all. 'I think I can,' I say.

The car is going slowly. We are in a long line of cars. It's stopping at the traffic lights. Miss is turning round to look at me. She's smiling but her eyes look sad. 'Which book did you take home for the holidays, Tomos? Is it another one by Roald Dahl?'

'Ro*wwlll* D*aaa*l.' I am trying to make the name sound right. 'Yes. It's *Danny, the Champion of the World*.' The orange light has come on. It's under the red one on the traffic lights. Miss is starting to move the car.

'Do you like it?' she says.

'I like the pictures but the words are too hard.' We're going fast again. I'm watching the hedges going by and the houses. Sometimes I can see people in the houses. Some of them are watching telly.

'Well, those library books are meant for older children,' Miss says. 'But you read your reading book to me the other week in school, and you knew all the words in that, didn't you?'

'Mmm, I like the words in my reading book,' I say. 'And the pictures of Floppy and Kipper. But I like the pictures in my library book better.' I'm remembering the people in my book laughing at me. I'm remembering them laughing when Mammy didn't come back. 'I like *some* of the pictures,' I say. 'And there's one of the BFG in it. I like that picture a lot.' I'm driving my truck now. I'm driving it on the seat of Miss's car. Nanno's letter is in the tippy bit. And my fifty pence is in the pocket in my trousers. 'I like the BFG. He's a big, friendly giant. Did you really kill a baby?'

Miss has stopped the car all of a sudden. I'm looking for

a dog in the road. Or a cat. I can't see any dogs or cats. Miss is moving the car to the side of the road. I can see her eyes in the mirror. They are very shiny now. 'I've got a story to tell you, Tomos,' she says. Her voice is wobbly. 'Some of the people in the story you already know.'

And then she is turning the key and the car engine stops.

* * *

'Come and sit in the front,' Miss says. She's clicking my seat belt. I'm climbing through the gap in the seats. I'm sitting next to Miss in the front of the car. I've put my truck on my lap. I've put Nanno's letter in my pocket with my fifty pence.

'When I was little my mother was ill,' Miss says. 'She couldn't look after me so I looked after her, before school, after school, weekends and school holidays. It was very hard. It made me sad.'

It's nice in the front of the car. It's nice sitting next to Miss.

'Sometimes people came to our house,' she says. 'But I never let them in.'

'Did you hide?' I say. 'Behind the big chair?'

Miss is smiling at me a bit. Her eyes look sad. 'Yes, Tomos. I used to hide 'til they went away.' She's looking out of the car window now. It's dark outside. 'Then one day, when I was a few years older than you, I was carrying some shopping bags and a lady stopped to help me. I knew the lady a little bit because she lived down the road from my house.' Miss is looking at me. She's smiling. 'She was Nanno,' Miss says. 'Your nanno.'

'Nanno?'

'Yes. And she came all the way home with me. And because she was so friendly and kind I let her come in to our house.' Miss is looking out at the dark again.

'Were you allowed?' I say. 'Were you allowed to let Nanno in?'

'No, I wasn't allowed to let anyone in.'

I'm nodding my head. It's nice sitting next to Miss. 'But she was your friend.'

'Yes. And when she saw the way we lived she made up her mind to help us.' Miss is smiling at me. 'And that's what she did.'

'Did she take you to Nanno and Dat's house?'

'Not straight away. She called a doctor for my mother and she straightened up the kitchen. It was such a relief to hand it all over to someone else.' Miss is letting out a big breath.

'Were they very heavy?' I say.

'What's that, Tomos?'

'The shopping bags,' I say. 'That you handed over.'

Miss is smiling. 'They were,' she says. She's rubbing her cheeks. 'And while we waited for the doctor to come, Nanno made me an omelette.'

'Was it cheese?'

'Yes.' Miss is laughing. 'With tomato ketchup and bread and butter.' I am thinking about Nanno's cheese omelettes. They're lovely. 'And then when my mother had to go into

313

hospital, Nanno and Dat looked after me. And I lived in their house for a while.'

'Were you one of their special children?' I am thinking hard. I'm trying to remember all the photos on Nanno and Dat's piano. There are photos of children with yellow hair and blue eyes like Mammy. And there's a photo of a boy with brown eyes and brown hair like me. I am trying to remember a photo of Miss.

'Yes,' she says. 'I was one of their special children – like you and like your mum. I was quite a big girl when she came to live with us. Your mum was eight and I was eleven.'

I'm looking at Miss. I'm remembering now. I'm remembering the photo of a girl with long brown hair and friendly eyes. 'You're Our Lowri!' I say. 'But your hair's not long anymore. There's a photo of you on the piano. You've got a blue dress on, and there are flowers in your hair.'

'That's me.' She's laughing. 'I loved that flowery hair band. Nanno bought it for me. It was the first pretty thing I ever had.' She's wiping her eyes now.

I am driving my truck a bit. I'm driving it on my lap. I say, 'Did your mammy get better?'

Miss is putting her tissue up her sleeve. 'A bit better. Sometimes she's quite well.'

'Is she still in the hospital?'

'Oh no. She came back from hospital when I was fifteen. And I went home to live with her. But sometimes she had to go back into hospital when she was ill, and then I'd go and stay at Nanno and Dat's house again.' Miss is looking sad. 'She didn't like me seeing Nanno and Dat when I was older. She was sorry, you see, sorry she couldn't look after me when I was little. And instead of thanking them for taking care of me, she was cross with them. I think she was cross with herself, really, but she took it out on them.' Miss is looking out of the window again. 'I used to phone them lots and lots, but I didn't go round there very often… Not after…not after…' She's getting the tissue out from her sleeve again. She's tapping her eyes with it. She's taking a big breath. 'Not after I turned eighteen.' She's rubbing my head. She's making my hair messy and she's smiling again. 'And you were just a baby then. That's why you didn't recognise me when I started teaching you at school.' She's squeezing my arm now. 'But I knew you were Rhiannon's little boy. Nanno used to talk about you all the time before she got ill. And Dat still talks about you lots and lots.'

'I'm not allowed to see Dat.' My eyes are all prickly.

'I know. That must make you feel sad.'

'Yes,' I say. I can feel the sad. It's a big lump in my tummy. 'Were you sad when you couldn't see Nanno and Dat anymore?'

'Yes. I was very sad.'

'Is that why you killed a baby?'

'Oh,' Miss says. 'I was hoping you'd forgotten about that.'

* * *

Miss has found a bar of chocolate in her bag. It's a bit squishy. She's broken off a corner for herself. She says I can have the rest. It's making my fingers chocolatey but it's yummy. Her phone has been ringing a lot. Miss says it's not

Mammy. It's only Colin. She has turned the ringing off. It's warm in Miss's car. It feels nice sitting with her.

'This is cosy,' I say. I can feel the chocolate melting in my mouth.

Miss is laughing. 'That reminds me of Nanno. She always liked saying "this is cosy".'

'Yes. It reminds me of Nanno too.' I'm looking out of the window. The houses outside look nice. There are orange lights in the windows.

Miss is looking out now. There are little orange squares in her eyes. 'Long ago, I had to make a choice. It was a hard choice, Tomos.' Her mouth looks very sad. 'I could choose to have a baby, or I could choose to go to college and learn how to be a teacher.' I am watching the orange squares. They're dancing in Miss's eyes. 'I wanted to be a teacher,' Miss says, 'more than anything else in the world.'

'So you didn't have a baby.' I'm putting some more chocolate in my mouth.

'That's right.' Miss's eyes are very very twinkly. 'It wasn't the right time.' She's taking a big breath. It sounds all bumpy. 'I wanted to make sure I could look after a baby before I had one – I wanted a job and a safe, happy home first. So when Colin said I'd lost a baby,' she's looking at me, 'and I said I'd killed a baby…that was what we meant.'

I am thinking. 'Colin said you lost a child,' I say. 'Not a baby. And you did. You lost me at the zoo.'

Miss is smiling a bit. She's rubbing her hands on her cheeks. 'Yes, I did. You gave me quite a fright.' She's laughing. 'I was so glad when we found you again.'

316

'You cried,' I say. 'You cried when the lamb man found me.' I'm eating the last square of chocolate.

'You're right. I did.'

'I liked the lamb man,' I say, 'at the zoo. He was nice.'

'He was,' Miss says. She's looking at her phone again.

'Did Mammy ring?'

Miss is shaking her head. 'Come on. We'd better get a move on. Climb back through.' I'm climbing through the gap. I'm in the back of the car. Miss is helping me put my seat belt on again. 'Right,' she says, 'off we go.'

I am watching the lights in the houses. They're getting a long way away. 'It wasn't the zoo,' I say. I am trying to still see the lights. They're tiny squares now. I'm licking the last bits of chocolate off my fingers.

'What wasn't the zoo, Tomos?' Miss is looking at me in the mirror. Her eyes look happy again.

'Where you lost me,' I say. 'There weren't any monkeys and there weren't any crocodiles.' The lights are far away now. I'm watching them get smaller and smaller. And smaller and smaller.

'It wasn't the zoo,' I say. My voice is small now too. 'It was the petting farm.'

* * *

Miss has parked the car. She's parked it near Nanno and Dat's house. She's parked it a bit down the road. And I'm feeling happy. It's nice to be near Nanno and Dat's house again. And I'm feeling sad too.

I can see Mrs Newman's house. It has a blue front door and a light over it. Sometimes the light flashes on off on off on off on off. And I can see that light from my bedroom window. My bedroom window in Nanno and Dat's house. And I like that light and I like my bedroom in Nanno and Dat's house and I wish I could see it again. But Miss says I must stay in the car.

It's quite dark. I am waiting in the back of the car. It's near the hedge. There's a little gap in the leaves. I can see Miss through the gap. She's ringing Dat's doorbell.

Dat is opening the door. He looks a bit surprised but now he's smiling at Miss and he's giving her a hug and now he's letting her go and he's looking up the road and I am waving to him through the gap in the hedge. I am waving and waving and waving and waving. But he can't see me.

The window in Miss's car is open a bit. She opened it with a special button. I'm pressing the button. I want to open the window some more. I want to wave to Dat. I'm pressing and pressing the button. But the window won't open any more.

I'm putting my fingers out of the little gap. I'm trying to wave to Dat. But he can't see me. I'm trying to put my truck out now. I want Dat to see my truck. But the gap is too small. He can't see me and he can't see my truck.

He's shaking his head at Miss and I'm putting my ear near the gap in the window and I can hear Dat's voice. It's a friendly voice and I'm thinking about him saying my favourite words. Combination points and pancakes and locomotive and immaterial my dear Watson and Battenberg cake.

'I don't have emergency numbers anymore, Lowri,' Dat is saying. 'Not since we stopped the fostering.'

'Any social services number will do,' Miss says.

Dat is shaking his head. 'I've been clearing everything out ready for the move.' He's rubbing his cheeks now. 'Hold on. I might have one number I can give you.' Dat's going into the house and Miss is waiting on the step. I can see Dat walking round in the front room and I can see the yellow light from the lamp near the telly and I can see a tiny bit of his cosy armchair. It's Dat's favourite chair.

Dat's coming back to the front door and I am waving my fingers at him through the gap in the window and my fingers are waving very very very fast. But he can't see me. He can't see me through the gap in the hedge.

'Try this.' He's giving Miss a bit of paper. Miss is taking out her phone. She's tapping it.

There's someone standing near Miss's car. I'm pulling my fingers in fast. It's a lady. She's wearing a long pink coat. It's nearly down to the pavement. It's got fluffy bits on it. She's pulling it tight round her. She's coming very near the car. And I can see her face now. I can see it in the yellow light. It's Poor Sandra. She lives down the road. I'm moving away from the window. I'm making myself tiny. Tiny tiny tiny on the floor. I am tiny inside the car. It's very dark down on the floor. I don't want Poor Sandra to see me.

She's putting her hand on the window of the car. Her hand is shaking and shaking. She's bending down. She's looking through the gap in the hedge. Her face is near the window now. A smell is coming in. It's a smell like Mammy and Brick's

319

tins. I don't like the smell. I'm holding my breath. And I am making myself tiny tiny tiny. Poor Sandra is watching Dat and Miss. She's watching them through the gap in the hedge.

'No reply,' I can hear Miss's voice saying.

'I don't know what else to suggest,' Dat says. I am peeping a bit. I'm peeping through the window. I want to look at Dat again. I can hear his voice but I can't see him. Poor Sandra's head is in the way.

'Thief!' Poor Sandra shouts. 'Thief!' I've heard Poor Sandra shout that before. I've heard her shout it every morning when me and Dat walk past her house. On the way to school. The school I went to when I lived in Nanno and Dat's house. She's shouting it again and again. She's very loud. I am pretending not to hear her. I'm pretending the way me and Dat always do when we are walking to school.

I can hear someone running. Miss is by the car. She's putting her arm round Poor Sandra. 'Come on, Mam,' Miss says. 'It's too cold to be outside in your dressing gown.'

I am getting up off the floor. I'm standing up in the car. I'm looking at Miss. She's walking down the road with Poor Sandra. Miss is walking with her arm round her. Poor Sandra is very wobbly and she's still shouting. Miss is taking Poor Sandra back to her house down the road.

I'm looking through the gap in the hedge again. I'm trying to see Dat but he has closed the front door. There's a funny feeling in my tummy. I think it's the sad. And I'm waiting for Miss. I'm waiting for her to come back to the car. I can see her now. I can see her running back. She's getting in. 'You okay, Tomos?' Her voice is all jumpy.

I am nodding. I say, 'Can we knock on Dat's door again, please? Can I see him?'

'Not tonight. I'm sorry, Tomos. I know this is hard for you, but you can't see him tonight. Can you put your seat belt back on?'

I am putting my seat belt back on. 'That was Poor Sandra,' I say. 'She puts little black bags through Nanno and Dat's letterbox. They have dog poo in them. I picked one up one day. By mistake.' I'm remembering the squishy bag in my hand. 'It was very smelly.'

'She's a sad lady,' Miss says. 'And she's not very well.'

'I know,' I say. 'Poor Sandra.'

'Yes.' She's shaking her head. 'Poor Sandra.' She's putting her seat belt on. 'What a night.'

'What a night.'

'So much for Plan B,' Miss says. 'There's just Plan C left now.'

Then she turns the key and she drives me away from Nanno and Dat's house.

* * *

We are going to Plan C in the car. I am watching the yellow lights. I have put my head right back. I'm looking out of the back window in an upside down way. The yellow lights are flying through the sky. They are flying like the stars me and Dat saw. The ones we saw from the garden one night. Dat said they were shooting stars. They were tiny. Tiny tiny tiny. Dat said they were a long way away. A long long way away.

My fingers can feel the bits of label in my pocket. I'm getting the bits out. And I'm thinking about the song Nanno taught me. The song about stars. I'm starting to sing it. And I'm holding up the bits of my label. The yellow lights are shining on the sparkly bits. And the sparkly bits are twinkly like stars.

Miss is singing now too. We're singing 'Catch a falling star and put it in your pocket, never let it get away'. Then I sing 'For love may come and tap you on the shoulder some starless night…' Miss has stopped singing. She's looking for something. She has one hand on the steering wheel and one hand in her bag. She's found a tissue and she's wiping her eyes.

'Are you crying again, Miss?'

Her eyes are looking at me. I can see them in the mirror. They look very sad. 'Nanno used to sing that song to me when I was a girl.' She's wiping her eyes again. 'When I couldn't sleep. I'm just being silly.'

'I always make you cry,' I say. I'm putting my bits of label back in my pocket.

Miss is shaking her head. 'No, you don't. It's not you making me cry.' She's smiling at me in the mirror. 'I've got a little surprise to tell you, Tomos.'

Then Miss says she is going to have a baby. She's going to have one now she has learnt to be a teacher. And now that she has a job and a home and a husband. She says going to have a baby makes you cry a lot. 'You can cry when you're happy as well as sad,' she says.

'I know,' I say. And I tell her about when I found Nanno's

322

letter in the train magazine. And about Nanno's P.S. that said *I love you. I love you. I love you.* And about how my eyes were crying but my mouth was smiling.

And then the baby Miss is going to have makes her cry again.

* * *

We are at Plan C. It's the police station.

'Well, well,' the policeman says. 'Lowri.' He has seen us coming through the door. He's smiling at Miss. It's a very big smile. He's holding out his arms. He's hugging Miss. 'Good to see you.' He's still hugging her. 'I didn't know you were back. How are you?' He's letting her go. 'I hope everything's okay.' He's looking at her face. 'We mostly expect trouble in this place.'

'Oh, I'm fine, Phil,' Miss says. She's smiling a bit. 'I'm all right, really.' She's putting her arm round me. I'm holding onto her leg. 'I've been meaning to ring Beth ever since we moved back. It's just been so hectic.'

'So you're living round here again then,' the policeman who is Phil says. 'And Colin?'

'Oh yes. Colin too. We're living in his mother's house for the time being. She's been in a care home for months. She's really poorly, needs round the clock care now. That last stroke she had…'

'Yes, I heard,' Phil says. 'It's such a shame.' He's shaking his head. 'Remember her English classes? God, if we hadn't done the homework…'

'She was terrifying. When Col and I started dating, it took me months to pluck up the courage to go home with him.' Miss and Phil are laughing. 'Colin couldn't understand why.'

'Well, he always was her golden boy. I don't suppose she ever yelled at him the way she yelled at us.'

'No, I don't think he saw her quite the same way we did. She's very frail now and with her being so ill it made sense to come home,' Miss says. 'Colin's still looking for work, but I managed to get a supply post straight away, thankfully.' I am holding tight to Miss's leg. 'Is Beth still teaching?' she says.

Phil's nodding. 'Just gone back after maternity leave.' He's smiling at me now. 'You've been busy in that department too, I see.'

'Oh, no,' Miss says. 'He's not mine. In fact, I need to explain…'

I am smiling up at the policeman. He's smiling down at me. 'What have you got there?' I'm showing him my truck. I'm holding it up for him to see. 'Nice,' he says.

'How is Thomas?' I say.

He's bending his knees. His face is near my face. 'What's that, little fella?'

'How's your son called Thomas?'

He's looking at me. One of his eyebrows is up high. 'Have we met before?'

'Yes. And you asked me my name and I said "Tomos" and you said "My son's called Thomas" and I said "Is he a Tomos or a Thomas?" and you said "Thomas like the tank engine" and I said "I'm a Tomos not a Thomas but I like Thomas the Tank Engine" and I still do.' I'm taking a big breath.

'Wow.' The policeman's smiling at me. 'That was a long sentence.'

Miss says, 'He's overtired.' She's smoothing my hair. 'Should have gone to bed hours ago.'

'Well, tired or not, he's got a good memory.' He's looking at me again. 'Where did I talk to you?'

'In our house,' I say. 'You came round because Mammy was shouting at the lady next door.'

'Okay,' he says. The policeman is still smiling. He's looking at Miss now.

'Bow Street,' she says. 'Rhiannon Morris. Her boyfriend's Nick Brickland.'

The policeman's nodding again. 'Right.' He's rubbing the top of my head. 'Nick Brickland. I know that name.' He's looking at Miss and he's making his eyebrows go high. 'What's the story this time?'

* * *

Miss has been telling Phil about our day. And she's been telling him about the hospital. 'It was pathetic, I know, Phil. I should have just explained things properly.' She's shaking her head. 'I shouldn't have lied about who we were. I shouldn't have rushed off with him.'

Phil is very friendly. He's hugged Miss a lot. 'Well, you caused quite a panic when you ran away. The hospital phoned about an hour ago. Two of my colleagues are over there now.'

'Oh, I'm so sorry, Phil.' Miss is shaking her head. 'It was a stupid thing to do. Stupid.'

'Don't worry,' Phil says. He's rubbing Miss's arm. 'I thought you might be the ones we were looking for when you walked in.' He's nodding at me. 'The school uniform gave it away. I'll text the officers over there, tell them you and Tomos are here.' He's tap tapping on his phone. 'You're both safe, that's the main thing.'

'You know,' Miss says. She's still shaking her head. Her voice is very quiet. I'm trying hard to hear her. 'I went a little crazy for a while. I actually thought I could keep him, just until Rhiannon sorted herself out. I thought I could sneak him into my house and everything would be fine.' She's wiping her eyes now. 'It's the hormones, I suppose. It's being pregnant.' Phil is smiling at Miss. He's smiling a bit and he's rubbing her arm. 'Colin made me see I was being irrational. I just couldn't see it for myself.' She's crying some more. Phil is rubbing her arm again. 'I'm so glad you're on duty tonight, Phil. I've been such a fool.'

'It'll all turn out fine, Lowri,' he says. 'Don't worry.'

He has stopped rubbing her arm. He's looking down at me. 'Okay, big fella, let's see what we can do for you.' He's looking at Miss now. 'Give me all the details then, Low. And I'll give social services a ring.'

* * *

We are waiting for the lady who is going to help me. We're waiting on blue chairs. They're stuck to the floor. We've been waiting a long time. I've parked my truck on the seat next to me. And I am very sleepy. My head is falling down. Miss is putting her arm round my shoulders. It feels nice. I'm putting my head against Miss. She feels soft. She smells like Nanno's soap. The pink one. And we are waiting and waiting.

'Tomos,' Miss says. She's being very quiet. 'Tomos, there's something I want to ask you.' I am moving my head a little bit. I'm looking up at her. I can see underneath her chin. 'I want to ask you about Dat. And I want you to think really hard before you answer me.'

My head is not so heavy now. I'm lifting it up. 'What about Dat?'

Miss is biting her lip. 'I shouldn't ask really.' She's talking very quietly. She's looking round. I am looking round too but there's no one to look at. She's taking her arm away from my shoulders. She's turning in her chair. She's holding my hand and she's looking at me. 'Tomos.' Her eyes are very big. 'Did Dat ever hurt you?'

I am shaking my head. I am shaking it a lot.

'No, Tomos, don't answer yet.' She's squeezing my hand. The one that hasn't got a black finger. 'I want you to think really hard.' She's still looking at me. Her eyes are blue. And there are purple splodges under them.

I am thinking. I am thinking really hard. I'm thinking about Dat. About me and Dat walking to school. We used to chat all the way there and all the way back. Nanno used to call us chatterboxes. I'm thinking about us making train tracks and about us playing with our trains. I used to move them round and Dat used to make the sound effects. I'm thinking about us reading stories. I'm thinking about us reading our train magazines. I can feel the sad. It's a big lump in my tummy. 'I miss Dat,' I say.

'I know you do. That's why I want you to think hard.'

I'm thinking hard. I remember Mammy hurting me sometimes. When she was cross. I remember Brick hurting me. But I don't want to think about Brick. I remember the man hurting me. The man with the web tattoo. He threw me on the carpet. He hurt my side. And he hurt Mammy too. I don't want to think about the man. I don't want to think about him hurting Mammy. I am thinking about Dat again. 'I can't remember.'

Miss says, 'You can't remember if Dat hurt you?'

'No,' I say. 'I can't remember when Dat hurt me.' Miss is still holding my hand. She's holding it very tight. I say, 'Mammy said Dat hit me. I heard her telling the lady with the big bag.'

'Did he hit you?' Her voice is very quiet. 'I want you to think hard.'

'I don't remember him hitting me.'

'Did he hurt you at all?' Miss says. 'Did he hurt you in any way?'

I'm shaking my head. 'No, Dat wouldn't hurt me. I'm his best mate.'

Miss is letting out a big breath. She's putting her head back against the wall. She's putting her arm round my shoulders. I'm putting my head on her again. We're waiting for the lady who's going to help me. We're waiting on the blue chairs. And we are waiting a long long time.

* * *

The big doors are opening. They are making a scrapey noise. My head has jumped up. I'm looking for the lady who is going to help me. Miss is looking for her too.

It's not a lady. It's the policeman who is Thomas's daddy. 'My colleagues are back.' He's stopping in front of our chairs. 'They'll need to talk to you, but it's a bit late tonight. Can you come in tomorrow?' Miss is nodding. I am nodding too. We're looking up at him. 'But there's no need to worry, Low. I've explained everything. It'll be okay.'

Miss is smiling a bit. 'Thank you, Phil.'

'And there's some good news,' Thomas's daddy says. 'The hospital said Tomos's X-rays were fine. Nothing broken.'

Miss is letting out a big breath. 'Thanks, Phil.' Her smile is bigger now. It's very wobbly. She's holding out her hands to him. He's squeezing her fingers.

'I'll be going off duty in a minute,' he says. He's letting go of her hands. 'It's been really good to see you again, even if…' He's looking at me. 'Even if it's not the way…'

'I know,' Miss says. 'Give my love to Beth. Tell her I'll ring soon. And congratulations on the new baby.'

He's smiling. 'Thanks. And the same to you.' He's pointing to Miss's tummy. Miss is smiling too. He's looking at his watch. 'Social services shouldn't be too long now, Low. But you never know with them.' He's smiling a bit. 'Try not to worry. Things will work out in the end.' He's smiling at me now. 'Bye, Tomos.'

'Bye, Thomas's daddy,' I say. He's waving.

'Bye, Phil,' Miss says. He's going through the doors. They're making a scrapey noise again.

'I like Thomas's daddy,' I say. I'm putting my hand into my pocket. I'm getting the bits of my sparkly label out and I'm putting them on Miss's leg. I'm trying to make the bits fit again. 'Has your baby got a daddy?' I'm putting the Ma bit next to the mmy bit. 'The baby you're going to have.'

'Yes,' Miss says. Miss is helping me put the e bit after the Lov bit. 'Colin is my baby's daddy.'

'I haven't got a daddy,' I say. 'Wes says everyone's got a daddy, like in his Uncle Vic's DVDs. But I know I haven't got a daddy. Mammy said.'

Miss is squeezing my shoulder. I like having her arm round me. All the bits of label are nearly right now. It nearly looks all mended. She says, 'Wes has become your sort of friend, hasn't he?'

I'm remembering the park. I don't like remembering about the park. 'I don't think Wes is my friend,' I say. 'I don't think he is anymore.'

Miss is still squeezing my shoulder. 'You don't have to listen to everything Wes says.'

'I know. He's wrong sometimes. He told me Mrs Pugh Year Two wouldn't be cross if we played hide and seek when we were waiting for the bus. But she was. She was very, very cross.' I'm turning round the last bit of label. It's all in the right places now. 'To Mammy, Love from Tomos,' I say. I'm pointing at it on Miss's leg. 'And Wes told me Nanno can't write letters from Heaven, but she can.' Miss is squeezing my shoulder tight. I'm picking up my bits of label. I'm

330

putting them in my pocket again. I'm very sleepy. I'm putting my head back against Miss. I can hear her breaths. I can hear them inside her.

'And he told me I had a daddy,' I say. 'And he's wrong about that too.'

* * *

We are still waiting on the blue chairs. I'm curling up next to Miss. Miss is looking at her phone. We're still waiting for Mammy to ring it. I'm holding my truck. I'm making the tippy bit tip up. I'm making it go back down again. 'I wish I had Cwtchy.' I'm saying it quietly.

'What was that, Tomos?'

'I wish I had Cwtchy. I want to put him in my truck.' I'm showing Miss the tippy bit. 'In here.'

'I'm so sorry, Tomos. Did we leave him behind with the wheels? Was he on your bed too? I was in such a rush to get you away from there…'

I am shaking my head. 'He wasn't on my bed. He's at Nanno and Dat's house. He got lost there.'

'Oh, that's a shame.'

I'm remembering playing with Cwtchy at Nanno and Dat's. Cwtchy and me liked playing hide and seek. Sometimes he got lost but Nanno was good at finding him. I'm remembering something else. 'It was when Nanno was ill. That's when I lost him. Nanno was ill in hospital.' I am remembering Nanno going to hospital. I don't like remembering that. Nanno went to hospital and I went to live with Mammy. And I wasn't allowed to see Dat anymore and I lost Cwtchy. I say, 'I miss Cwtchy. I miss him a lot.' I'm thinking about Nanno too. And Dat. And I'm missing and missing them. Miss is putting her head on top of my head. She's kissing my hair. I'm remembering something else now. I'm remembering the girls in the park. I'm remembering the sound they made when they put their heads near me. 'Am I smelly?' I say.

Miss is lifting her head. She's looking at me. 'Oh Tomos.' She's pulling me onto her lap. She's putting her arms right round me. She's putting her face in my hair and she's taking a big breath. She's breathing in and in and in. I'm waiting for her to say 'Urgh,' like the girls in the park. And like the big boys and like Wes. But I don't think she's going to say 'Urgh.' I don't think she's going to say that at all. 'You smell of shampoo,' Miss says. She's giving me a squeeze. 'You smell wonderful.'

* * *

I am lovely and warm. I am in the lovely warm bath in Miss's house. There are bubbles everywhere. They are on my head and on my arms and right up under my chin. And Miss is stopping the bubbles from going in my eyes. I'm laughing and laughing and she's wiping the bubbles with a soft pink flannel and she's smiling and smiling at me. 'Tomos,' she says and she's wiping my face and she's making my hair feel nice again. 'Tomos, you've got to go now.' And she's putting the big fluffy towel all round me and she's opening the bathroom door. 'Tomos, it's time to go.' And I'm looking out of the bathroom and I can see Mammy's bedroom. The door is open. 'Tomos, Tomos.' And there's something on the floor. 'Tomos. Tomos.' It's eyes are open and there's red…

My head's jumping up. It's jumping up a bit from Miss's shoulder. I'm on Miss's lap and she's rubbing my back. She's saying 'Tomos, you've got to go now. The lady's here for you. Can you open your eyes?'

I am trying to open my eyes. They are very tired. They're opening a tiny bit. I'm trying to see the lady that has come for me. I can see her shoes. They're brown. I can see her trousers and her jacket. I can see her short hair. I can see her face. It's smiley.

'Hello,' her smiley face says. 'Sorry to wake you up, Tomos. I'm Danni, and I'm going to take you somewhere you can sleep for the night.'

I'm looking at Danni. I'm looking at her jacket and her short hair. 'Are you a boy?' I say.

'A boy?'

'Like in *Danny, the Champion of the World*?'

'No, I'm a girl, like…' She's thinking. 'Like me.'

'Okay.' I'm awake now. I'm getting off Miss's lap.

'You will let me know, won't you?' Miss says. 'Where he ends up after tonight.'

'I'll let you know whatever I can.' Danni's tapping her phone. 'I've got your number saved.'

'Oh, I forgot to tell you about his bruises,' Miss says. Her voice is very quiet. 'He has marks on his back and on his neck.' I'm remembering not to fiddle with my collar. But

333

my fingers don't want to listen. 'And there are some on his hand and foot, too. We went to the hospital, but thankfully they said everything looked okay on the X-rays.' Miss has forgotten to say about the bump on my head. I have nearly forgotten it too. It's stopped banging now. It stopped banging a long time ago.

'Well, he'll have a good check-up tomorrow,' Danni says. 'It's better for him to get some sleep tonight.' She's holding out her hand to me. She has blue and green and yellow nails. They are small and sparkly. 'Come on, we've got quite a drive ahead of us.'

I'm holding Danni's hand. 'Okay,' I say. We are starting to go.

'Wait,' Miss says. She's pulling me back. She's hugging me. 'Just a little hug. I don't want to hurt your bruises.' She's putting her face in my hair. She's taking a big breath.

'Do I still smell wonderful?'

Miss is letting me go a bit. 'You do.' Her words sound wobbly. She's holding the tops of my arms. I can see her face now. Her cheeks are wet. 'Look after yourself, Tomos.' She's letting me go. She's smiling a bit. 'You're good at that, aren't you?'

I'm nodding. I'm nodding a bit.

Danni is squeezing my hand. 'We'd better leave. It's really late.' Danni looks nice. Her eyes are smiley but I want to stay with Miss. I want to sit on her lap again and fall asleep. I want to have her arms round me like they were just now. Just now before Danni came. 'Come on then,' Danni says. She's squeezing my arm. 'We've got a long drive, so say bye-bye.'

I'm looking at Miss. 'Bye-bye,' I say.

'Bye, Tomos,' Miss says.

I'm picking up my truck. I'm putting it under my arm. I'm holding it tight. I am keeping it safe. I'm feeling in my pocket. I'm feeling my fifty pence and Nanno's letter. And my sparkly label. They're safe in my pocket. Danni is pulling my hand. She's pulling me towards the doors and I'm going with her. We are nearly there. We are nearly going through the swingy doors. I'm looking back. Miss is sitting down on the blue chair again. She looks very tired. And very sad. I don't like her looking sad.

I have remembered something. I'm pulling my hand. It's slipping out from Danni's hand. I am running back to Miss. 'I remember,' I say. 'I remember.' I'm saying it to Miss. I'm saying it loud. 'About Dat.' Miss is looking at me. Her mouth is opening but she isn't saying anything. 'It's right,' I say. 'It's right. He did hurt me. He did!'

Miss's mouth is like a little circle now. Her face is very white. There are big purple splodges under her eyes. 'He did?' she says. Her words are tiny. 'Dat hurt you?'

'Yes, Mammy was right, he did.' I'm jumping up and down. I'm happy. I'm very very happy. I am very very happy that I've remembered. 'We were in the garden and we were making the patio look nice for Nanno, and Dat moved a big flowerpot and he didn't know my finger was under it – this one…' I'm holding up my pointing finger '… and it got squashed and the nail came off it the next week and Dat said he was very, very sorry.' I'm running out of breath. 'So he did. He did hurt me.' I'm clapping my hands. 'Can I see him again now? Can I see him? Can I go to Dat's tonight? Can I? Can I?'

Miss is putting her hands on my shoulders. Her face isn't white anymore. It's pink. She's letting out a big breath. 'Not tonight.' She's smiling. She's kissing the top of my head. 'Not tonight.'

'But soon,' I say. 'I can see him soon.'

Miss is still smiling at me. She's kissing my head again. 'I hope so. I really do.'

Danni has come back for me. She's holding out her hand again with her sparkly blue and green and yellow nails. I'm holding her hand. We're going back to the swingy doors.

I'm looking over my shoulder. 'Goodbye, Miss,' I say. I am waving and waving to her. 'Goodbye.'

* * *

Danni's car smells like oranges. It smells like the oranges in Nanno's fruit bowl. I don't like oranges. I'm remembering the one the lady next door gave me.

'You could put your head back and go to sleep,' Danni says. She's looking at me in her mirror. It has a smiley face hanging on it.

'I'm not sleepy.' I'm driving my truck on the seat.

'It's very late,' Danni says. 'Or early.'

I say, 'Your car smells like oranges.'

She's pointing to the smiley face. The one on the mirror. 'Air freshener.' She's putting on the radio. There's someone talking on it. 'It's a long drive. You might as well close your eyes.'

336

The orangey smell is making me remember Dat. Sometimes Dat peels an orange. He holds a bit out to me and he says, 'Go on, try it.' And I try a little bit. But I don't like oranges. 'One day you will,' Dat says.

'Are we going to Dat's house?'

Danni's looking at me in the mirror. She's looking at the road and she's looking at me again. There's music on the radio now. 'Not tonight.'

'Sometime soon?'

'Maybe.'

There's a funny sound. It's like the music on the radio but it isn't the music on the radio. Danni says, 'Hi.'

'Hi, Danni,' I say.

Danni's turning off the radio. A voice says, 'It's Sharon.'

'Hello, Sharon,' I say.

Danni says, 'Hi. We're in the car. Can't talk for long, I'm on hands-free.'

Sharon's voice says, 'Sorry I didn't get back to you sooner.'

Danni says, 'It's okay. We're sorted now.'

'It's okay,' I say. 'We're sorted now.'

Danni says, 'I've got Tomos with me. As you can tell, he's wide awake.' She's winking at me in the mirror. The smiley face is twisting round and round. I'm trying to wink back at her. I'm trying to close one eye. But my other eye wants to close too.

'Sounds like you've had a busy night,' Sharon's voice says.

'We have,' I say.

'Four over in West Hill,' Danni says. 'Mum's gone to Malaga.'

Sharon's voice says, 'Known to us?'

Danni says, 'Nope. Neighbour phoned it in.'

'Did you find anywhere for them?'

'It was difficult. No room at Brynmawr. Ameena took them in the end.'

'All four?'

'All four. God love her.'

'God love her,' I say.

'So where's Tomos going?'

'Cardiff. To emergency,' Danni says. 'Jane's.'

I'm sitting up. I am sitting up straight in my seat. 'Will there be fire engines?' I say.

Sharon's voice says, 'She's a trooper, too.'

'Thank God,' Danni says.

I'm bending forward. 'Will there be tanks?'

Sharon's voice says, 'I'll catch up with you tomorrow, then.'

'Okay,' Danni says. 'See you.'

'See you.'

'And ambulances?' I say.

Danni is turning the radio on again. 'Sorry, Tomos. Did you say something?'

'At Emergency Jane's?'

'We'll be there in a little while. We've just joined the motorway,' Danni says. 'Try to sleep.'

'I'm not sleepy,' I say. Danni's driving her car quite fast now. I'm watching the smiley face on Danni's mirror. It is twisting round and round. 'I'd like to go to Emergency Jane's,' I say. 'I like troopers. I'd like to see the fire engines and the ambulances.' I'm parking my truck next to my leg. Danni's singing the song on the radio. She's singing it in a small voice. My voice is quiet too. 'I'd like to see the tanks at Emergency Jane's.' It's very dark outside now. There are no lights. 'I like tanks,' I say. 'I'd like to go to Emergency Jane's.' There are no cars outside. There are no houses outside. Just lots and lots of black road.

My eyes are very tired. They're tired of looking. They're tired of looking at all the black outside. My head is very heavy. I'm putting it on the back of the seat. 'But most of all.' My voice is very quiet now. It's hard for me to hear it. 'Most of all,' I say. 'I'd like to go to Dat's.'

* * *

My head has jumped up. My eyes have bounced open. It's still dark outside. We are still on the black road. We are still going very fast. 'Nine-nine-nine,' I say. 'Nine-nine-nine-emergency.' I can see the back of Danni's head. I can see her eyes in the mirror.

Her eyes are smiling at me. 'What's wrong, Tomos?' She's yawning. Her yawn is making her words funny. 'Were you dreaming?'

'Nine-nine-nine-emergency.' I'm sitting up straight. 'Quick,' I say. 'Quick.' Danni's eyes are looking at me. They're watching me in the mirror. 'Quick.' I'm bouncing. I'm bouncing on my seat. 'Nine-nine-nine-emergency.' I'm very loud.

'Shhh, shhh,' she says. 'It's hard for me to drive when you're shouting.'

'Quick,' I say. 'Quick.' I am still very loud. I'm trying to find the click on my seat belt.

'Whoah!' Danni is loud now too. 'Stop that, Tomos. Don't get out of your—' the click has clicked. The seat belt is slipping off. I'm jumping up. I'm jumping onto my feet. I'm jumping and jumping and my truck has fallen onto the floor. 'Sit down,' Danni says. She is very loud. 'Sit down!'

'Nine-nine-nine-emergency,' I say. I am loud too. 'We need to phone it. Nine-nine-nine-emergency.'

'Sit down!' Danni is very very loud. I can see her eyes in the mirror. They are very very cross. I'm sitting down again. The car's not going fast now. It's going slower and slower. It has stopped. Danni is turning round and she's looking at me. 'Right, tell me, Tomos,' she says. She is quiet again but her eyes are still a bit cross. 'Why do we need to call nine-nine-nine?'

I am taking a big breath. 'Because of Brick.' I'm remembering Brick. I'm remembering something about him. I don't want to remember it. I am closing my eyes. I'm closing them tight. But I can still see it. 'Because of the red.'

'What was red?' Danni's holding my arm. I can feel her fingers. 'Look at me, Tomos.' She's squeezing my arm. 'Look at me.' I'm opening my eyes. I am opening them a tiny bit. 'What red?' Danni eyes are very big. They are looking right at my eyes. They don't look cross anymore.

'The red on Brick,' I say. 'On Brick's tee shirt.'

'On Brick's tee shirt?' She's making her face crinkly. 'I don't understand, Tomos. Is Brick a person?' I don't know what Danni means. I'm lifting up my shoulders. 'Is he a boy?' she says.

340

'He's a man.'

'Where is he? Stay still, Tomos. Where is he?'

I am trying to stay still. 'In Mammy's bedroom.'

Danni says, 'Is Brick your mammy's boyfriend?' I'm nodding. 'He had red on his tee shirt,' she says, 'and he was in your mammy's bedroom?'

I'm trying not to close my eyes. I'm trying not to think about what I saw. 'He's on the floor,' I say. My eyes are closing again. I'm squeezing them tight. I'm remembering seeing him. I'm remembering seeing him through the gap in the door. The door of Mammy's bedroom. 'Brick's on the floor,' I say. 'And his tee shirt's all red.'

I am jumping again. I can't stay still. I'm jumping and jumping and jumping and jumping. I don't want to think about it. I don't want to remember it. I don't want to think about Brick. I am pulling my arm away from Danni. I'm squashing my hands over my eyes. I'm squashing and squashing them. I don't want to remember. I don't want to remember the red. 'And there was a big cut.' I'm squashing my hands over my eyes. I am jumping and jumping and jumping and jumping.

'A big cut where, Tomos?'

She's getting my hands. She's pulling them away from my eyes. She's holding my arms now. I can't jump when she's holding my arms. 'Where's the cut, Tomos?' She's giving my arms a squeeze.

I'm opening my eyes. Danni is looking at me. She's looking and looking at me. A car is zooming past us. It's making Danni's car shake. There are lights on Danni's face.

And in her eyes. They have gone now. It's very dark again. I'm looking at her eyes. They are very very black. 'Where's the cut, Tomos?' Her voice is quiet now. 'Where's the cut?'

My voice is tiny too. Tiny tiny. 'On Brick's neck,' I say.

Miss Again

I am waiting outside the staffroom door because I have come to see Miss. Mrs Wilson told me to come here. She said I could leave after-school choir early and I am waiting outside the staffroom door because Miss has come to see me.

The door is open and I have knocked it, but Miss hasn't heard me. She's right down the other end of the staffroom and she's talking to my new teacher. Her name is Mrs Clarke and she's nice. She has swingy hair. Sometimes Mrs Clarke gets my name wrong like my old social worker used to. But I don't mind too much. Mrs Clarke tries her best to remember that my name is Tomos, not Thomas. And I have a new social worker now. His name is Gavin.

Miss and Mrs Clarke are over by the cups and the kettle and I'm standing in the gap where the door should be and I'm knocking again. And I'm waiting for Miss to see me.

'I heard they went to Scotland,' Mrs Clarke says, 'and left him alone for the whole of the Easter holidays. Getting drugs for some friend of theirs.'

'Well, he was alone for the first week,' Miss says, 'and that was terrible enough.' It's quite hard to hear them talking because the kettle is very noisy. 'The police had been watching the men they were meeting in Glasgow. They'd been under surveillance for weeks.'

The kettle has clicked off. Their voices are much louder now. 'And that's when she was arrested?' Mrs Clarke says. She's pouring water from the kettle into two mugs. 'After she attacked the policeman?'

Miss is nodding. 'Mmm.'

'Pulled a knife.' Mrs Clarke is shaking her head.

I have knocked the door again, but they still haven't seen me. I can see their backs. It's hard to knock the door when it's open, but I'm trying to make my knocks loud.

'Thankfully she only caught his arm,' Miss says.

Mrs Clarke is stirring the mugs. 'But still, it'll be a long sentence when you add assault to it.' She's holding out a mug and Miss is taking it. I'm wondering what kind of long sentences you add salt to. I think they must be sentences about fish and chips, like I eat fish and chips with vinegar and salt, but that isn't a very long sentence really. I'm trying to make it a longer sentence. I'm adding ketchup to it and I'm trying to knock on the door too.

'And I heard she wouldn't say a word when she was arrested,' Mrs Clarke says. 'So they didn't know her name, or where she was from. Or that she had a five-year-old alone back home.' I'm knocking the door again and again, but it keeps moving away from my hand and Miss and Mrs Clarke are not turning round. 'I expect it was handy for her to keep quiet. But the poor boy, all alone in the house. How could she do that to him?'

'They said she went into a kind of shock,' Miss says. 'I remember she barely spoke when she first came to our foster parents. She'd found her mother dead a few days before. Heroin overdose.'

'She doesn't have any other family then?' Mrs Clarke is putting the soggy tea bags into the bin. 'No one looking out for the child while she was in Scotland?'

'Her foster dad and I are the nearest thing to family she's got – apart from her son,' Miss says. 'She was eight when

346

her mother died. The things she saw as a child…' Miss is shaking her head now. 'She can't help the way she is. She just lashes out if she feels trapped.'

'But stabbing a policeman…'

'I know.' Miss is lifting her shoulders. 'Anyway, when we finally found out where she was, we went to visit her in prison. She was putting on an act, being tough. But you could see the scared child in her eyes. It broke our hearts. I asked her to think again about her false accusation. You know…the physical abuse claim against our foster father? She looked right through me.' Mrs Clarke is holding up a carton of milk and she's shaking it a bit. Miss says, 'Just a drop, thanks.'

Mrs Clarke is pouring milk into the mugs. 'You're certain she was making it up then.'

'Absolutely positive,' Miss says. 'She was angry with our foster mum for being ill. And frightened of losing someone again, someone she loved.'

'Strange way to show it,' Mrs Clarke says, 'taking it out on your foster father.'

'Well, yes.' Miss is nodding her head. She's shaking it now. 'It's been very hard on him. He feels people are treating him differently, suspiciously. He's moved from Carmarthen, and he spent all his life there.' Miss is shaking and shaking her head. 'It's very sad.'

I am trying to knock again, but it's hard to knock when the door is open because it keeps moving away from my hand.

'But then last week she rang her old social worker,' Miss says, 'and told her she'd made a mistake.'

'Well, that's something,' Mrs Clarke says.

'She's getting counselling, and help to come off the drugs.' Miss is blowing into her mug. 'If Dafydd and I can support her when she comes out she might be able to manage…'

Dafydd. I know that name.

'That won't be for a while yet, though.'

'No.' Miss is taking a sip of her tea. 'She's got visiting rights as a mother, but she's refused to see him. I think she feels he's better off without her.'

'He's such a lovely child,' Mrs Clarke says.

'Yes,' Miss says, 'he is, isn't he? I hope she'll change her mind soon. I don't want him to forget her. She doesn't deserve that.'

'And the night she was arrested,' Mrs Clarke says, 'her boyfriend got away and drove back home?'

'Mmm.'

Mrs Clarke is shaking her head. 'Practically decapitated they said in the papers. It's too horrible to think about. Have they arrested the person that did it yet?'

'No. The police believe Rhiannon could help, but she's too frightened. She thinks someone might get to her, even in prison. And anyway, Nick Brickland had plenty of enemies.'

I've stopped knocking. I'm listening hard now. I can hear Miss saying names I know. Dafydd. Rhiannon. Brick's real name.

'And the police think that child was probably in the house when it happened.' Mrs Clarke is shaking her head again. 'Terrible. They say children block out difficult memories, don't they?'

'Mmm.'

'And he'd had a blow to his head, hadn't he?'

'A fall. He had a cut.' Miss is touching the back of her hair. 'It didn't seem much at the time. But I wish I'd remembered my first aid training and told them about it at the hospital.' Miss is rubbing her tummy. 'My hormones were all over the place.'

'Well, he seems fine. He's certainly a bright little thing,' Mrs Clarke says. 'He seems so happy most of the time. Chatty. He's always smiling.' She's sipping her tea.

'I'm glad to hear that.'

'What about the neighbours? Did they see anything?'

'No. No one saw a thing.'

'I heard the two main suspects, two local men, have disappeared.'

'Brick's suppliers,' Miss says. 'They've got convictions for violence going way back. Brick had fallen out with them apparently.'

I don't like hearing Brick's name. It makes my tummy feel funny.

Mrs Clarke is nodding. She's sipping her tea again. 'I suppose I shouldn't repeat this.' She's scratching her chin. 'But a friend from Carmarthen told me that one of the suspects is Thomas's father.'

I'm listening. I'm listening hard.

Miss is letting out a big breath. 'Oh, that old rumour. People say it's the drug dealer. The man with a web tattoo on his face.'

I don't like remembering the man with the web tattoo. But I'm listening. I'm listening and listening.

'Well, the gossip is wrong. I know who his father is,' Miss says. 'And he's certainly not a drug dealer. It was a boy who came to stay with Nannette and Dafydd because his mother was very ill.' Miss is putting her mug down. She's tucking her hair behind her ear. 'He and Rhiannon were fourteen, inseparable. Then his mother was offered treatment in Germany because she had family there, and he went with her.' Miss is turning around a bit, but she still hasn't seen me. 'Rhiannon shut down and wouldn't speak to us. She really went off the rails. And then we realised she was pregnant…' She's turning around a bit more and I'm waiting for her to see me. 'Luke was a good boy, a kind person. There's no doubt he's the father. Tomos is the exact image of him.' She's turned all the way around now and I'm waving and waving at her.

She's seen me at last.

'Tomos! How long have you been standing there?' She's rushing over to the door. She's smiling. 'Look at you in your school uniform. Don't you look well? You've grown so much in the last six months.' Her words are falling all over each other. She looks happy. Her cheeks are pink and her tummy is very big. 'How do you like your new school?'

'It's nice,' I say.

Mrs Clarke is coming over to the door. 'He's settled in really well. You've made quite a few friends already, haven't you?'

I'm nodding. I have a friend called Noah and a friend called Matt, and I sit with Beca and Ioan. They're very nice. They never tell me to go away and they never say I smell.

350

'And I'm sure I don't need to tell Mrs Davies what an excellent pupil you are,' Mrs Clarke says. 'So good at sums. And his reading… Well!' Mrs Clarke is calling me with her hand. 'Come into the staffroom, Tomos. You and Mrs Davies can have a proper chat then.'

I am going into the staffroom. I have never been into the staffroom before. I'm standing by the green chairs. Mrs Clarke is going out and she is closing the door behind her. And then it's just Miss and me. We are all alone in the staffroom. Just us two.

* * *

'Oh,' Miss says, 'it's so lovely to see you, Tomos.' Her eyes are a bit watery. 'Come and sit down.' She's tapping one of the green chairs. I'm sitting down and she is sitting down next to me. She's looking at me and smiling and smiling. She's not saying anything. I am smiling and smiling back at her. I'm not saying anything too. She's putting her hand into her bag. 'I've brought you something.' She's showing me a little book. It has a blue shiny cover. Miss is opening it. It has plastic pockets inside and the pockets are full of photographs.

'Nanno!' I say. 'And Dat!'

Miss is smiling. 'Yes.' She's turning the pages of the book. 'And there you are too.' Miss is pointing to a baby in a photograph. The baby's on a lady's lap. The lady is sitting next to Nanno on the bench. In Nanno and Dat's garden. There are lots of other people in the photograph too. There are girls and there are boys.

'Is that me?' I'm pointing to the baby.

'Yes. That's you, Tomos. You're tiny in this photo. Just a few months old.'

I'm looking at the baby. I'm remembering the photographs Nanno and Dat had on the piano. There were lots of baby me.

'And do you know who that is?' Miss says. She's pointing to the lady next to Nanno. The lady with me on her lap.

I'm looking hard at the lady. I say, 'It's you with your long hair!'

'Yes,' Miss says, 'when I was seventeen. And all these other people are the children Nanno and Dat looked after.' She's moving her finger over all the people in the photograph.

'There are lots.'

'Oh yes,' Miss says. 'Lots and lots.'

I have remembered something. 'Is Mammy in the photo too?'

'She wasn't there for that party. That's why you're sitting on my lap.' Miss is smiling. 'Back then Nanno used to call me your "other mother".'

I'm thinking about Nanno. I'm remembering her cwtching me and singing to me and reading me stories. I am trying to remember Miss. I'm trying to remember her from before school. Not this school, my last school when she was my teacher. 'I don't remember you. I don't remember you when you had long hair.'

'No, you were very young when I… When I stopped visiting Nanno and Dat. You were still just a baby. You wouldn't remember me.' Her eyes are very watery. 'But I missed you, Tomos,' she says. She is taking a big breath. 'And then after I decided to be a teacher…'

'… instead of having a baby,' I say.

Miss is looking at me. Her face is very sad. 'Oh you remember that.' She's shaking her head. 'I'm sorry, Tomos. I was so upset in the car that night.' She's taking a tissue from her pocket and she's blowing her nose on it. She's putting it back in her pocket. 'When I decided not to have a baby and to be a teacher instead, it was hard for me to see you.' She's wiping her eyes with the back of her hand.

'Because you had a lot of homework.'

'Yes.' Miss is getting the tissue from her pocket again.

'And because your mammy didn't like Nanno and Dat.'

'Yes, because of that, too.'

'Mrs Clarke gives us a lot of homework,' I say. 'Lots of spellings. I like spellings.'

'Good,' Miss says. It's hard to hear her because of the tissue.

I'm looking at the photograph again. The one of me and Miss and Nanno and the other people. 'I remember it all,' I say.

'All what, Tomos?'

'All the things you told me in the car. On the way to the best place for me. I remember about being a teacher instead of having a baby. And I remember about your mammy calling Nanno and Dat names. And that your mammy went away. And about Nanno's cheese omelettes. And I remember that they are the best cheese omelettes in the world.' I am thinking about the omelettes. 'Not they *are*,' I say, 'they *were* the best cheese omelettes in the world.'

'They were.' Miss is smiling again. 'They were.'

'Nanno's gone to Heaven now,' I say, 'hasn't she?'

'Yes,' Miss says, 'but we can still remember all about her.'

I am touching Nanno's face in the photograph. I'm touching her silver hair and her pink cheeks and I'm thinking of something. 'Is Dat in Heaven too?' I'm saying it fast. I'm saying it with hurt in my tummy. I'm scared because I can't see him in the photograph.

'It's all right, Tomos.' Miss is squeezing my shoulder. 'He's fine.'

'But where is he?' I'm rubbing my finger on the photo.

'You can't see him because he was holding the camera. He was taking the photograph. And this photo was taken years ago when you were a baby.'

'Where's Dat now?' I'm saying it quietly. I'm afraid that he's a long, long way away.

'He's living near Swansea,' Miss says. 'He's got a new house, well…a little bungalow.' She's squeezing my shoulder again. 'And he's fine, I promise you, Tomos. Just like he always was.'

'That's good.' I'm trying to think about Dat in a new house. In a little bungalow. I'm trying and trying. I don't think Swansea is a long way away. And I like the word bungalow.

Miss is turning the pages of the photograph book. 'Mammy!' I'm pointing to a photograph. 'But her hair's pink.'

Miss is laughing. 'Do you think it looks pretty?'

'Yes,' I say.

'I think it looks pretty too.'

'But I like her yellow hair better.' I am touching Mammy's pink hair in the photograph. I'm remembering another thing Miss said in the car on the way to the best place for me. About her mammy going away. 'Do you think my mammy will come back,' I say, 'like your mammy did?'

'Would it be okay if she did?'

I am thinking. I'm thinking about being with Mammy. I'm thinking about cwtching with her on the settee and watching *Murder, She Wrote*. And I'm thinking about Tess and Rob and the way we sing along to the radio in the car. I'm thinking about Tess's big smile when I run out of school and the way she hugs me. I'm thinking about Rob's engine sounds. They are nearly as good as Dat's. He's good at changing the points and moving the signals too. Rob says, 'Move your train out of the station, Mr Engine Driver, please.' And I say, 'Okey-dokey, Mr Signal Man.' I'm thinking about the big shelf in my new bedroom that has seventeen books on it. I'm thinking about Tess reading stories. She sits on the side of my bed. I'm thinking about the way she says, 'Sleep tight, *cariad. Nos da,*' when it's time to go to sleep and she always leaves my door open. 'I can listen out for you in the night,' she says. 'I can hear you when the door is open. In case you need me.'

Sometimes I do need her. Sometimes, when I remember the man hurting Mammy. Or when I remember Brick and the big cut. Or when I remember the night I made myself tiny tiny tiny in my high sleeper bed. Like little Lord Jesus asleep in the hay. When I call for Tess she runs to me. She cwtches me and cwtches me. And I don't feel so scared.

355

I am thinking of Mammy again. And her pretty yellow hair.

'Maybe,' I say.

'Your mammy might come back,' Miss says. 'But not until you're quite a bit older.'

'That's good,' I say. 'It'll be nice to see Mammy.'

* * *

We have been sitting on the green chairs for a long time. We've been sitting and looking at the photographs. I like seeing Nanno and Dat and Miss and Mammy. I like seeing all the other people Nanno and Dat looked after in their house too. Miss has been telling me their names. There are some girls with long hair and some girls with short hair. Their names are Katy, Carrie, Louise and Llinos. And there are boys with long hair and short hair too. Their names are Siôn, Ryland, Robbie and Karl.

Miss is pointing to another boy. 'And that's Luke.'

I'm looking at the photograph. 'Mammy said she sees Luke when she looks at me. A long time ago. Is that the Luke she sees?'

Miss is nodding. 'Yes, that's Luke.'

I am looking and looking at the boy in the photograph. He's smiley and his face is friendly. 'He looks nice.'

'He was nice,' she says. 'I bet he still is.'

'You told Mrs Clarke I'm the exact image of him.'

Miss is biting her lip. 'You heard that, did you?'

I'm nodding. 'Where is he now?'

'I'm not sure,' Miss says, 'but Dat might know.'

I'm still looking at Luke in the photograph. 'I think Mammy sees him when she looks at me because his brown hair is just like my brown hair.' I'm touching his face with my finger. 'And his eyes are like my eyes too.'

'Yes,' Miss says. 'I expect that's what it is.' She's getting another tissue out of her pocket.

I'm moving my finger over all the other children in the photograph now. 'I liked living at Nanno and Dat's house.'

'So did I,' Miss says. We are both smiling. We are smiling lots and lots, and Miss is wiping her eyes on the tissue.

'But I live with Tess and Rob now,' I say, 'and I like that too.'

'Good,' Miss says. 'That's really good.'

'And you live with Colin.'

Miss is biting her lip. 'Well actually, Tomos,' she says, 'I'm not living with…'

Someone is opening the door to the staffroom. Someone is opening it with a bang. It's Mr Jeffries the cleaner. He's coming into the staffroom with his back first and he's pulling his vacuum cleaner.

He's turned around. 'Oh sorry.' He's dropped his hosepipe. 'I didn't know anyone was in here.'

'Don't worry.' Miss is trying to get out of the green chair. She's pushing her big tummy up first. 'We're just about ready to leave anyway.'

'No,' Mr Jeffries is saying. 'Don't you worry. I'll come back in five minutes.' He's picking up his hosepipe again and he's going out of the door.

Miss is standing up now and so am I. 'You can keep that book of photographs,' she says. 'You can look at the photos of Nanno and Dat and your mum.'

'And you, Miss,' I say.

'Yes, you can look at the photos of me too.' She's smiling. 'But you don't need to call me Miss anymore, Tomos. You can call me Lowri now.'

'Lowri,' I say. It sounds nice.

'Or Aunty Lowri, if you like.'

I'm thinking. 'I haven't got an aunty,' I say.

'I know,' Miss says. She's putting her hand on my shoulder. She's biting her lip and her eyes are very twinkly. Her voice is quiet. 'Would you like me to be your aunty? Your Aunty Lowri?'

I'm thinking again. I'd like Miss to be my aunty. I would really like Miss to be my aunty. She would be a very good Aunty Lowri. 'Yes,' I say. 'I'd like it a lot.'

Miss is smiling and smiling. 'Thank you. I'll always look out for you.' She's squeezing my shoulder a bit. 'I love you, Tomos.'

'Do you?' I say. I'm surprised. I know Nanno loves me and I know Dat loves me. And I know Tess and Rob love me. But I didn't know Miss loves me.

'Yes,' she says. 'I do.'

'Can I love you too?' I'm looking at my shoes. One of my laces is nearly undone.

'I would love it if you did,' Miss says.

I'm looking up at her. Her eyes are very, very twinkly now. I'm smiling. 'Good,' I say. 'I will.' Miss is putting her hand on her big tummy. I'm smiling at Miss. Her eyes look all watery. I'm remembering something Miss said in the car. She said that having a baby makes you cry a lot. 'Will you stop crying when you've got your baby?'

Miss is laughing. Lots and lots of tears are running down her cheeks. She's wiping them away with her hand. Her eyes are red but they are very kind. She's smiling at me. 'Maybe, but I'm crying because I'm happy, Tomos. Remember our little chat about that?'

'I remember,' I say. 'When we were in the car. When we were going to the best place for me.'

Miss is smiling. She's hugging me. 'Are you happy now, Tomos? Is it okay living with Tess and Rob?'

'Oh yes,' I say. 'I like it a lot.'

'Good. I'm so glad you're happy there.' She's smiling and smiling at me. 'Oh.' She's putting her hands on her cheeks. 'I nearly forgot.' She's looking in her bag and she's taking something out. She's giving it to me. It's purple and furry.

I'm whispering 'Cwtchy.' I'm hugging and hugging and hugging him. 'Cwtchy, Cwtchy.'

'Dat and I found him under the stairs,' Miss says, 'when we were clearing out the house. He was behind lots of old boxes.'

I'm remembering now. I'm remembering a long, long time ago. 'We were playing hide and seek,' I say. 'And Cwtchy was hiding.'

Miss is bending down. She's holding my hand. She's squeezing it tight. Her face is next to my face. 'Very soon, Tomos, Dat will be able to come and see you.' Her voice is quiet. 'At Tess and Rob's.'

There's a funny feeling in my nose. It's making my eyes feel prickly. 'I can see Dat?' I'm saying it very quietly. I'm saying it through Cwtchy's fur.

'Yes,' Miss says. 'Not today, but soon. Would you like that, Tomos?'

I'm looking at Miss. I am looking and looking at her. And then I'm jumping. I am jumping with both feet at the same time. 'Oh yes, I'd like that. I'd like that a lot, lot, LOT!' I'm hugging Cwtchy. I'm hugging Miss. Miss Aunty Lowri. I'm squeezing her tight. She's squeezing me tight. We are hugging and squeezing and laughing and hugging. 'Oh,' I say. 'What was that?' I'm jumping away from her.

'The baby gave us a kick.' She's laughing and putting her hand on her tummy. 'Your baby cousin is saying hello.'

'My baby cousin?'

'Yes. He'll be your cousin because I'm your Aunty Lowri.'

'My cousin,' I say. I like the sound of the word cousin. I am saying and saying it. I'm looking at Miss again. Her tummy is very, very big. 'You've got your baby already.' I'm pointing to her tummy. 'In there!'

'Yes, I suppose I have.'

'So you don't need to cry anymore.'

She's still laughing. 'Only when I'm happy.'

'Are you happy now?'

'Yes, I am,' she says. She's laughing and laughing. 'I'm very happy. How about you, Tomos? Are you happy?'

I say, 'I'm very happy. I'm very, very happy.'

I'm waving Cwtchy in the air. I am waving him and waving him and I'm thinking about Dat and my baby cousin. And I'm laughing. Miss is laughing – Aunty Lowri is laughing. We are laughing and laughing and laughing and laughing.

Our eyes are crying but our mouths are laughing.

If you have concerns about a child you know, want to learn more about fostering or have been affected by the issues in this book, the following organisations may be of help:

Addaction: for adults and young people and their families: http://www.addaction.org.uk/

Adfam – families, drugs and alcohol: adfam.org.uk

The Fostering Network: Tel. 0141 204 1400; thefosteringnetwork.org.uk

NSPCC Helpline: Tel. 0808 800 5000; help@nspcc.org.uk; https://www.nspcc.org.uk

The Survivors Trust Helpline – supporting survivors of rape & sexual abuse: Tel. 0808 801 0818; thesurvivorstrust.org

ABOUT HONNO

Honno Welsh Women's Press was set up in 1986 by a group of women who felt strongly that women in Wales needed wider opportunities to see their writing in print and to become involved in the publishing process. Our aim is to develop the writing talents of women in Wales, give them new and exciting opportunities to see their work published and often to give them their first 'break' as a writer. Honno is registered as a community co-operative. Any profit that Honno makes is invested in the publishing programme. Women from Wales and around the world have expressed their support for Honno. Each supporter has a vote at the Annual General Meeting. For more information and to buy our publications, please write to Honno at the address below, or visit our website: www.honno.co.uk

Honno, 14 Creative Units, Aberystwyth Arts Centre
Aberystwyth, Ceredigion SY23 3GL

Honno Friends

We are very grateful for the support of the Honno Friends:
Jane Aaron, Annette Ecuyere, Audrey Jones, Gwyneth Tyson Roberts, Beryl Roberts, Jenny Sabine.

For more information on how you can become a Honno Friend, see: http://www.honno.co.uk/friends.php